HER MONSTROUS MATES

IMMORTAL VICES
AND VIRTUES

Claim
Me

USA TODAY BESTSELLING AUTHOR

LEXI C. FOSS

Editing by: Outthink Editing, LLC

Proofreading by: Katie Schmahl & Jean Bachen

Cover Photography: Wander Aguiar

Cover Models: Meg

Cover Design: TrifBookDesign

Interior Cover Photography: Wander Aguiar

Interior Cover Models: Megan, Camden, Forest, Griffin

Interior Design: Manuela Serra

Published by: Ninja Newt Publishing, LLC

Digital Edition

ISBN: 978-1-68530-246-7

Paperback Print Edition

ISBN: 978-1-68530-193-4

Hardback Print Edition

ISBN: 978-1-68530-247-4

To Matt, Laura, Vicki, and Amy, for making this book possible...
And to Baby Luka, please don't ever read Mommy's books <3

CLAIM ME

HER MONSTROUS MATES

IMMORTAL VICES
AND VIRTUES

CLAIM ME

I'm a prisoner. A pet. A being of supreme power on a
leash.
Why?
Because my arranged mate "borrowed" my power and
nearly killed the House of Gold and Garnet's King.

Oh, he knew I was innocent. Just like his successor—*King
Kaspian*—does as well. But that hasn't lessened my
sentence; it's simply made my prison cell a little more
comfortable.

Because instead of bars, I'm stuck in one of the new king's
bedrooms. And he's tasked three immensely handsome
mercenaries to guard me.

Nox, Bane, and Nolan.

Too bad all I want to do is escape—otherwise, I might be
tempted by the buffet of sexy goodness spread out
before me.

Alas, when King Kaspian gives me a task I can't refuse, I

suddenly find myself incapable of thinking about anything or anyone other than the four captors controlling my life.

Because it turns out that breaking a magically forced mate bond can fracture the soul and cause new bonds to form.
Four, to be exact.
With a king and his three mercenary guards.

If any of them reject me, I'll die.
But if they accept me, my death magic might consume us all...

**Claim Me* is a spicy standalone paranormal romance in the Immortal Vices and Virtues universe featuring Fallon and her four "fated" mates.

AN INTRODUCTION
FROM KING KASPIAN

Fifty years ago, a portal opened in Portland, Oregon, causing magic and supernaturals to spill into the streets. It wasn't the first of its kind, but it was the first to be noticed by Earth's mortals. And, well, the world hasn't been the same ever since.

Magic infected the human race, creating a need for a new kind of government structure, one meant to regulate the power of a new era—a supernaturally driven one.

But before the enacted Houses of government could truly take hold, wars ravaged the earth, genocides followed, and those without magic became nearly extinct.

It wasn't until The Great Sacrifice—a devastating bloodbath that ended in ultimate destruction—that the various Houses reached a truce, leaving us with our divisions today. There are eight Houses, all of which serve and protect their various purposes.

Mine is the House of Gold and Garnet. We're mercenaries who love to hunt and revel in the payment of a job well done. Blood and gold are our currency. We're loyal. We're efficient. And we're deadly.

However, we're not the only dangerous land in the world. Every territory has its own risks and rewards.

Except for No Man's Land.

No one wants to live outside of a House territory. In fact, it's considered illegal to many to exist without a House affiliation. But there will always be rogues.

Such as those who created the various Supernatural Syndicates in what used to be New York City. Those crime lords have no interest in rules or regulations. No desire to affiliate with a House. No moral compass to guide their choices. They're deadly. Cruel. And entirely unwelcome in my lands.

Other Houses may choose to negotiate power with them.

I do not.

My mercenaries have charged me with leading, and lead them I shall.

Welcome to the House of Gold and Garnet, where we pay our fealty in *blood*.

THE HOUSES

House of Gold and Garnet
House of Blood and Beryl
House of Air and Amethyst
House of Earth and Emerald
House of Spirit and Sapphire
House of Death and Diamond
House of Fire and Fluorite
House of Sea and Serpentine

No Man's Land
No Man's Circus - Portland, Oregon

Supernatural Syndicates
New York City
Manhattan - The Wards - Shifters
Brooklyn - The Roses - Fae
Staten Island - The Outcast Coven - Witches
Queens - The Divine - Angels & Demons
Bronx - Clan Tepes - Vampires

PROLOGUE

FALLON

Four Years Ago

"Do you, Fallon Doyle, take Nikolas O'Neely to be your forever mate?" Daithi's hazel eyes flash with power as he stares me down, awaiting my acceptance.

Two words.

That's all I need to say.

And then the illegal spell will weave a fated-mate bond around my soul, linking me to the monster before me.

Nikolas O'Neely.

Evil incarnate.

Or I assume he's evil, anyway. He agreed to this madness, after all.

You don't have to do this, my twin sister whispers into my mind. *Please don't do this.*

I swallow, my heart thumping loudly in my ears. It's not

1

enough to drown out my sister's soft tones, her urgency rising with each passing second.

This isn't your punishment to accept, she tells me. *It's mine.*

While that may be true, neither of us has a choice. Nikolas won't accept her, not when he knows what her voice can do.

She killed members of his extended family a decade ago with a few calmly stated words, leaving him orphaned. It wasn't intentional. But that didn't matter. The relationship between the Doyle Clan and the O'Neely Clan shattered that day, ending a century-long alliance.

Today is the day we right the wrongs of that incident.

A day where I agree to have my soul realigned to mate an O'Neely. It'll feel like a fated-mate bond, tying me to him for as long as we both shall live.

While that may seem promising, killing him isn't actually an option. Because it'll rip my soul apart in the process.

Once this is done, we'll be bonded for better or for worse.

And Issy will be safe. That's the bargain—if I do this for my family, my parents will keep Issy hidden from the world.

She's too powerful to be discovered. Too uncontrollable. If the Houses learn of her presence, they'll annihilate her.

Of course, they may do the same to me if I ever let my true abilities be known. I'm more necromancer than witch, and that's not a welcome trait. Especially when some of the Houses are run by undead supernaturals.

Fortunately, I know how to manage and hide my darker talents.

"Miss Doyle," Daithi prompts me, one brown brow inching upward into his matching hairline.

He's a warlock and an O'Neely cousin, making him one of the most influential members of our Outcast Coven. I wasn't surprised to see him standing at the marble stone today, ready to recite an illegal mating spell. He excels in nefarious affairs.

Just like my parents.

Just like *Nikolas*.

My veins ice over at the thought of what all this means.

I shift my focus to the man now, studying his near-black eyes and thick, dark hair. His expression tells me he doesn't appreciate my silence, that each passing second is a tick against me, one that's likely going to end in punishment.

I've heard rumors of his reputation.

Of his penchant for trickery and violence.

The O'Neely Clan Patriarch—the same one who chose this mating match—sent Nikolas to live in Ireland decades ago, planting him within Gold and Garnet territory, where he became a mercenary. From what I understand, the Outcast Coven plans to someday use him and his alliance for corrupt purposes.

Now it will be my task to help him succeed. Commit whatever treasonous acts he requires. Play the role of a dutiful mate.

Make both our families proud.

This won't be a kind courtship or a loving relationship.

This will be hell. One where he's the devil and I'm being castigated for the contrived sins of others.

The sins of my sister, I think, my throat dry. *Only, she didn't mean to hurt anyone, and everyone in this room knows it.*

But that doesn't matter. Because that's not how the games are played in this world full of magic dealers.

"Fallon." My father's voice holds a note of warning in it, his green eyes the same color as my own. Only his irises flare with an unspoken threat, while mine probably reflect resigned acceptance.

Because there is no other option here.

I have to finish this to fix the past. *To protect Issy.*

Clearing my throat, I lift my chin and utter the two words that'll seal my fate for the rest of my days. "I do."

My sister whimpers in my mind, her guilt palpable.

This isn't your fault, I remind her. *This is our parents' doing.*

Not that they have much choice, either.

The Supernatural Syndicates in what's left of New York City is the only place in No Man's Land with any sort of protection. Sure, it's run by criminals, but at least those criminals look out for one another.

Sort of, anyway.

Better than in other areas of this magically corrupt world.

Except I'm about to join a House as Nikolas's mate.

I shiver, uncertain of how this will work. There are eight Houses in the world, all of them strictly governed by the most powerful supernaturals on Earth.

They're selective about whom they accept.

But somehow Nikolas is part of one.

And he'll be taking me "home" as his fated mate.

What if they discover what I can do? I wonder for the thousandth time since I learned of Patrick's choice for my mating.

That choice stares at me now, his eyes flickering with dark flames that threaten to burn me.

"Do you, Nikolas O'Neely, take Fallon Doyle to be your forever mate?" Daithi asks, a sinister lilt underlying his Irish accent.

"I do," Nikolas replies without hesitation.

Magic prickles the air, the scent foul and wrong to my

senses. *Acrid smoke*, I think, nearly gagging as it smothers my nose and creeps into my being.

I'm so sorry, Issy whispers to me, her mental voice a sob that slices at my heart. She's not here to witness this, her presence not welcome anywhere in the city. But she can feel what I'm feeling, hear my thoughts, and nearly see through my own eyes.

We're twins and bonded by birth.

Always.

I would do anything for you, Issy, I murmur back to her. *Even this.*

I jolt as a fiery sensation slithers through my veins, the energy hot and unwelcome and heading straight for my chest. *To my soul.*

Nikolas reaches for my nape, yanking me into him as the spell takes hold, melding our fates together.

His lips take mine, sealing the deal and lighting sparks within me. Not the kind I desire or even enjoy, but flames of furious rebellion.

My spirit is screaming at the wrongness of this mating, my very being trying to fight the dark enchantment.

But I can feel it sinking its anchor into my heart, forcing me to accept and to bow to this change in my destiny. Just as Nikolas's tongue demands submission, taking control and possessing me in a way only a mate can.

It hurts.

It twists my stomach.

It makes me feel physically ill.

Yet there's a lightness at the end, one emboldened by fake promises and a false sense of hope. It's a trick. I can still smell the foulness of it all, but the magic is taking hold now, the power convincing my soul of the rightness.

I can barely hear Issy's cries, her pain a faint thought that whirls with my confusion.

It's then that I hear the chanting, Daithi's voice low and cold.

What is this? I marvel. *What's he doing?*

Issy shouts my name in reply, but I can't seem to reach her. I… I can't connect to her.

What's he saying? It's ancient Gaelic, words I barely hear. *Why do I feel so cold?*

My lips are numb. My tongue frozen.

Nikolas has stopped kissing me. But his hand…

He's still holding my nape.

Securing me.

While he…

While he drinks. I try to jerk backward, alarm racing through my limbs as I suddenly feel his fangs in my throat. *Part vampire, part warlock.* I knew this. But I didn't expect him to bite me.

What the fuck?

And why is Daithi still chanting?

I glance at my father in alarm, noting his reserved expression. "It's for your own good, Fallon," he tells me. "It'll be easier this way."

Easier? I want to ask.

My mother wears a similar look, though her silver eyes glitter with resignation. She reminds me so much of Issy in that moment, her broken features a mask for the fury beneath.

Because Issy often hides behind a glamour of sorrow. But deep down, she's angry at her fate. Furious that she can't voice her own defense. Livid that she's perpetually trapped in our parents' home, unable to see the outside world without risking immediate death.

She's on permanent house arrest. It was that or allow the O'Neelys to kill her. My parents chose to imprison her as a result—a consequence that wouldn't change, not even after today.

One day, I'll free you, I've promised her a thousand times.

Whether it be by playing the part of the perfect mate and earning trust or by breaking all the rules and risking our lives, I'm not sure. But I'm determined to help Issy escape.

Except I can't feel her now, I realize. *I... I can't feel much at all.*

"Fallon," a deep voice says, drawing me back to Daithi. "How do you feel about Nikolas?"

I blink at him. "Nikolas is my mate." The words taste foreign, like someone else spoke them, but they came from my mouth.

"Very good. And what do we do for our mates?"

"Mates support one another. Mates cherish one another. Mates help one another." The mantra rolls off my tongue, causing my insides to churn. *Why do I sound so robotic?*

"Excellent," he praises. "And why do we help our mates?"

"Because that is my duty. That is my place. This is who I am in this world—I am Nikolas's mate." Cold dread blankets my skin with each statement, yet my tone remains exactly the same.

"How long does this last?" Nikolas asks, his voice curious.

"Until you break it," Daithi tells him. "I'll share the details with you privately so that only you can undo the obedience spell."

Nikolas nods while my insides freeze over. *An obedience spell? Forcing me to mate him wasn't enough? Now he adds this?*

"This will be fun," Nikolas says, dark amusement coloring his tone. "An obedient little fuck doll with powerful blood." He glances at Patrick O'Neely, the O'Neely Clan Patriarch. "Thank you for my gift, Uncle."

"Just make sure you use it wisely, Klas," the patriarch replies. "We need you to move up in the Gold and Garnet ranks."

Nikolas dips his chin in acknowledgment. "I will absolutely use her, and often."

My teeth threaten to grind together, except they don't. They just remain placid like the rest of me.

Because I'm spelled to behave.

Neither of my parents says a word or reacts to the exchange regarding *using* me or what the phrase implies.

Instead, my father turns to Patrick to shake his hand. "I'm pleased with our renewed alliance," he says.

"Likewise, old friend," Patrick returns. "Shall we celebrate at O'Mally's Pub?"

The two of them start to walk away, leaving me behind without a second glance.

My mother bows her head and follows, as does Patrick's mate. They're both victims of a fate similar to mine, their matings arranged to powerful male figureheads within the Outcast Coven.

The joining of clans, I think, disgusted by the antiquated practice. *There's a reason these mating spells are illegal.*

"Enjoy," Daithi murmurs, that single word possessing so much sinister intent that I die a little inside.

"Oh, I intend to," Nikolas replies, his palm sliding down my spine to the curve of my ass. "*Thoroughly.*"

Daithi shoots me a salacious glance before refocusing on Nikolas and saying, "Come find me afterward for the reversal instructions. Although, I imagine you won't be using them."

"Very likely not," Nikolas agrees, his palm squeezing my ass to the point of pain.

Yet no part of me outwardly reacts.

I merely take his cruelty as though I feel nothing at all.

However, I very much feel it inside.

Just like I very much experience the influx of fear as he turns his attention to me and says, "I'm going to fuck you until you bleed, and you're going to come every time I tell you to, no matter how much it hurts."

My heart longs to stop beating, but it doesn't.

"Tell me to fuck you," he presses. "Tell me to make it hurt."

"Fuck me, Nikolas. Make it hurt." I flinch inside, furious tears threatening to form. Except they don't. *Because I'm trapped.*

"Klas," he tells me. "Call me Klas." He pulls me even closer, his hand remaining on my ass while the other goes to my throat. "We're mates now, after all. Might as well be a little less formal."

He kisses me and I respond automatically, my body his to command.

It seems only my mind is my own.

But I still can't hear Issy.

I'm a prisoner inside my psyche. Trapped in a nightmare mating.

However, there's something important about nightmares. A key trait I whisper to myself as Klas's palms begin to roam.

Nightmares end.

Which means, one day, I'm going to wake up.

And when I do, Nikolas O'Neely—and everyone else who allowed this to happen to me today—will pay.

FĀLLON

PRESENT DAY

FALLON...

Issy's voice is a whisper, reminiscent of a dream. I long to reply, my heart breaking at the thought of our fractured bond.

All because of *him*.

My enemy.

My mate.

The one who destroyed everything.

He encompassed me in a spell, binding my free will while stealing my magic.

Every bite empowers him more, giving him access to my deadly enchantments.

He makes me teach him how to wield my power, his obedience spell forcing the words from my mouth.

I hate him.

I hate *this*.

Fallon...

I nearly choke at that familiar voice, drugging my

11

thoughts, pulling me toward the past. *I miss you,* I want to tell Issy. *I miss you more than I can properly say.*

Wake up, Fallon, she tells me in response.

I nearly smile. Her mental voice is so stern, so *real,* that I almost obey.

But I don't want to wake up. This nightmare never ends, even when I open my eyes.

Sometimes it's worse.

Like when Klas buries me alive. Drowning me in soil. Ensuring that I can't see the sun again for days and days while he plays with my power.

Oh, Gods, what if I wake up beneath the earth again?

I'll claw at the soil on impulse, incapable of escaping no matter how hard I try.

A punishment.

But for what? I can't remember.

A charm, my mind whispers. *A mystical charm that brings me back, that allows me to override his spell.*

I frown, a memory nagging at my thoughts. One of a goddess. Power. Full of stars.

She broke the obedience curse.

I can picture her perfectly, all that long, dark hair, golden skin, and glowing eyes.

So much power.

A dream or a reality? I struggle to remember.

Fallon. Issy's voice is laced with impatience. *I need you to wake up.*

My brow furrows. *Why does that sound so real?*

Because it is, she snaps back. *Now open your eyes.*

I almost comply. But I don't want to indulge in this trick. It's probably Klas playing with my mind again, luring me to consciousness so he can make me pass out again.

He haunts me at all hours of the day and night, owning my soul, destroying me with each passing breath.

He's in the dungeon, Fallon, Issy says. *He tried and failed to kill the Gold and Garnet King. He was caught. He's no longer in control. You eviscerated him several times. Remember?*

My frown deepens, visions of Klas bleeding into buckets streaming behind my eyes. A fantasy or reality?

They're delivering his sentence today, she continues. *Which is why I need you to wake up. If they kill him...*

It may kill me, I finish her sentence.

We're tied together via an illegal spell. There's no way to know what will happen when he dies.

But does it really matter?

I want him dead. Removed. Gone from my life.

He used my powers to try to create chaos in Gold and Garnet territory. All because he was frustrated by his lack of a promotion within the mercenary ranks.

"I'm tired of being overlooked. It's time for them to see how powerful I really am. Besides, now is a great time with all the dissent brewing from the latest political scandal. It'll be easy to recruit help. Not that I need much."

His rant plays through my mind, reminding me of my mental reply. *Except it's* my *power you're using. Not yours.*

Granted, he had my power on a leash, so I suppose that did make him powerful indeed.

But he doesn't have me on a leash anymore, I realize, my eyes opening. *Because I'm no longer in that nightmare. I'm in a new one.*

A nightmare shrouded in pretend luxuries.

I sit up in the four-poster bed, my surroundings immediately familiar, as I've spent the last thirteen months living in this single space.

It's not the worst prison cell imaginable. I have a balcony that opens to a courtyard below—not that I'm allowed to go explore it. But at least I can step outside for fresh air. That's a few steps above being buried alive for days or weeks on end.

Rubbing my hand over my face, I try to force myself into wakefulness. *Issy?*

Finally, she mutters back at me. *I've been trying to wake you up for over an hour.*

Hmm, I hum back at her, not at all surprised by her comment. The last few years have felt like one long nightmare, only the scenery keeps changing.

I reach over to my nightstand for my water—something I put out last night because I knew I would need it now—and drink the entire cup in a few big gulps.

Most of my "dreams" of late have been about waking up in a grave and inhaling dirt for hours—or days.

That was only one of the ways Klas chose to punish me, but something about it made it the most memorable. And I always woke up from those dreams with a dry throat, as though I were underground again all night.

Slipping out from the silky sheets, I wander over to the en-suite bathroom to refill my water.

Fallon, my sister whispers.

I'm still awake, I reply.

I know. But… but today… She trails off, her uncertainty rolling through my mind as I study myself in the oversized mirror.

My green eyes no longer glow. My blonde hair looks darker now, lacking its former shine. And my skin seems paler somehow. *Like death.*

Appropriate, given my abilities. Or perhaps it's a warning of what's to come.

They're going to execute him, I say to Issy. *Today is just a formality. But I know that's their plan.*

Did one of the phantoms tell you that? she asks, referring to my proverbial prison guards.

They didn't need to tell me anything. It's just what has to be done. Klas tried to kill a reigning monarch. It doesn't matter that

14

the monarch in question is no longer in charge; his successor can't allow the culprit to live.

An image of said successor fills my mind, his dark hair and matching eyes so similar to Klas's. And yet the two men look nothing alike.

Klas is all cruel angles and sharp edges.

While King Kaspian is… soulful. Deep. Undeniably handsome. *And so incredibly off-limits.*

He's only skimmed the surface of my powers. If I allow him to get closer, he'll learn things about me that'll have me sharing a death sentence with Klas.

Which is why I need today to happen.

The sooner Klas is sentenced and executed, the sooner I may be allowed to leave. Unless I die as a result of his death, of course.

I suppose I'll be free either way, though. *Maybe.*

King Kaspian and his guards have monitored me for thirteen very long months now. They've questioned me repeatedly on what I can do, requested brief demonstrations, and drilled me about my past.

I gave them the truth where I could and lied where I needed to.

"I'm an orphan," I told them. "I don't know much about my family history." It was the story Klas gave them after mating me, saying he found me on one of his mercenary missions.

Fortunately, he hasn't spoken the truth about our origins while in captivity.

Likely because he's protecting himself.

If Klas betrays the O'Neely Clan in any way, he'll be punished long into the afterlife.

Bodies can die, but souls are eternal.

And souls can easily be tortured, especially when one has access to death magic. Which my clan obviously does, and thanks to our arranged mating, the Doyle Clan and the O'Neely Clan are very much aligned again.

I finish my third glass of water and sigh. *Has Ayla found anything that can help me counter the mating spell?* I ask Issy.

I already know the answer, but I can't stop myself from voicing it anyway. It's the one thing we've been trying to figure out since Klas's imprisonment.

If I can break the spell, I'll be free. At least from him. The rest... well, that's another situation entirely, as I have no idea what I need to do to convince King Kaspian to release me from his watchful guards.

I could try to run.

But he owns a House of mercenaries. So my chances are not great. Especially when one of those mercenaries is Nolan—an archangel tracker with deadly aim.

I rub at my shoulder, frowning as Issy says, *No. The recent Earth and Emerald trials took a lot out of her, too. She's not been herself lately.*

I nod, understanding that feeling. *I'm glad she's able to visit you; that'll help.*

Only when Father allows it, Issy grumbles. *Sometimes he forgets that she's our cousin.*

He doesn't forget. He just likes control. And controlling who Issy can interact with is one of his favorite activities.

She can't speak to Ayla like she can to me, our twin bond being the reason we can communicate telepathically. But Ayla knows sign language, making her capable of understanding Issy.

It relieves me to know Issy still has someone... in case I don't survive the coming days.

We've been separated before—for three very long years —which was when Ayla and Issy grew closer. That means Issy will go on without me, and Ayla will take over protecting her.

You may not be speaking to me, but I can feel the direction of your thoughts, Fallon Doyle, and I do not approve, Issy snaps. *First of all, I can protect myself with a few choice words. Second of all, you're the one who needs protecting right now. And third of all—*

I wait, my eyebrow arched. *And third of all…?* I prompt, amused by her rant.

Father is here, she whispers back, sending a chill down my spine. He rarely visits Issy, and it's never for anything good.

I feel her apprehension through our bond, her fear causing me to physically shake in front of the mirror.

I don't dare to interrupt her, aware that she needs her full range of mental faculties to deal with our sperm donor.

My fingers curl into fists while I wait, hatred consuming me. Parents are meant to care for and protect their children. But ours never did that. They treated us like property to be traded and discarded.

Or that was my perception, anyway.

Issy is different. She's the family burden in their eyes, a broken princess unworthy of her last name.

I feel her desire to fight, her need to remind our father of her true power. But she doesn't. She's too afraid of what will happen after her explosion.

There's nowhere for her to go. He's the only one ensuring her survival in this harsh world.

My twin falls silent, her emotions seeming to disappear. I have to stop myself from calling her name, knowing she'll reach back out when our father is done doing whatever it is he's doing.

Issy's fine, I tell myself. *I would sense it if she weren't.*

I stare at myself in the mirror again, my pale cheeks suddenly flush with color.

One day, I'll kill him.

Unless I'm dead. Then I'll just haunt him until he dies.

Worrying about my father and Issy is pointless. There's nothing I can do from here.

Hell, there's nothing I've been able to do for a long time now.

But that may change depending on today's verdict. Klas's death is imminent. It's just a question of *when*.

Swallowing, I head to the shower and try to distract myself by preparing for the day. There's nothing I can do to stop what's about to happen. My soul is going to fracture. And my magic… well, I don't know what'll happen there.

Will I spiral out of control? Raise the dead? Show the true extent of my powers?

I really hope not. King Kaspian already fears the abilities he knows about, and those just barely skim the surface of my potential.

I managed to hide most of my talents from Klas over the years, the obedience spell only forcing me to speak the truth when he asked the right questions.

He never bothered to inquire about other spells I could conjure. He simply made a lot of assumptions based on the knowledge he acquired through drinking my blood. And I never attempted to clarify.

I finish washing my hair and soaping off beneath the large showerhead, then I step out of the glass enclosure and select a towel from the heated rack beside it.

As far as cages go, this one certainly has its perks.

I wrap myself up in the fine cotton and grab another one for my hair.

My appearance in the mirror hasn't changed much, my cheeks and eyes still lacking their natural glow. I doubt I'll ever find that again. Klas killed part of my soul when he bound me to him, tainting my very being.

And being here, trapped in this palace while under

frequent observation, isn't doing much to improve the situation.

At least I have an espresso machine, I think, heading toward it in the living area. Like most things in this world, it's magically charged, making it easy to order exactly what I want with a few clicks of a button.

The scent of finely ground coffee beans immediately touches my nose, stirring a dreamy sigh from my lungs. This is probably the one good thing about my captivity.

Well. The eye candy isn't bad either.

Bane.

Nox.

King Kaspian.

Even Archangel Nolan is incredibly good-looking. Although, I want to shoot him in the shoulder like he did to me when we first met.

Sure, he thought I was the one trying to kill his leader at the time, but that didn't keep the bullet from burning like a son of a bitch.

I chew my lip while the mocha starts to form in the cup, my mind drifting to the sexy male guards who frequent my rooms.

Bane and Nox are phantoms, which is a new sect of supernaturals that announced their presence a little over a year ago. They're essentially ghosts who can take corporeal forms.

And what fine corporeal forms they have, I muse. Not that I've seen much of them, but the cut of their clothes tells me they're impressively—

A shock of pain splinters through my mind, the source of it coming from my twin. I grab my head with a gasp, her name leaving my mouth as my legs give out beneath me.

Issy! I shout, my body crashing hard to the ground,

stirring a groan from my throat. Or maybe that's a sound provoked by the agony echoing through my spirit. *Issy!*

She doesn't reply, her anguish spearing through me like a hundred daggers, each one pelting my chest and leaving me breathless on the floor.

I can hear her screaming.

No, wait, that's me, I think groggily, my vision blackening beneath the waves of torment coming from my twin. *What's happening? What's he doing to you?*

Someone says my name, but it's the wrong voice.

It's not Issy's.

It's... it's... it doesn't matter. Only Issy matters.

Tell me what's happening, I try again. *Talk to me!*

Another voice answers, one I don't want to hear, so I don't listen or discern the words.

Issy!

I curl tightly into a ball, tears pouring from my eyes. I can't see. I can barely breathe. All I feel is my sister's *pain.*

I won't! I hear her yell, the fury in those two words dragging across my psyche like sharp claws. *I won't give her that order!*

Who? What are you talking about? I ask her, bewildered and lost. *Issy...*

No! Fallon can't die! she screams, her words not making sense. *Klas's crimes are his own, not hers. Fuck your orders!*

I gasp as another spear goes right through my chest, the sensation reminding me of electric volts, shaking my spirit and demanding submission.

Several more follow, stealing my ability to do anything other than lie on the floor in a complacent ball.

Something warm touches my shoulders. That voice is near my ear. But I'm too focused on Issy, too consumed by her mental exhaustion, to consider anything else.

She's weeping.

Screaming.

Shaking.

Dying.

Something is choking her.

Power.

I try to reach through our bond, to push every ounce of my strength to her, but I feel the moment she snaps, her spirit shattering beneath an explosion of intense energy. She gasps into my mind, her voice a rasp as she says, *The Outcast Coven has spoken.*

I frown at her flat tone, the words unlike anything she's ever said.

If Nikolas O'Neely is subject to death, so is Fallon Doyle, she continues. *Fallon Doyle will honor the Outcast Coven by adhering to our ancient pledge—loyal mates die with their beloved. Or those mates will be punished with fates worse than death.*

NOX

A FEW MINUTES EARLIER

I CHECK my watch for the fifth time, scowling when I see only sixty seconds have passed since my last glance.

Guard duty doesn't suit me. I would much rather be playing in the lab or sparring with Bane. But this assignment is important to King Kaspian, thereby making it important to me.

And I can't say I really mind looking after the pretty charge in the guest suite behind this door. She's a fiery little thing with curves I've thought about more than once over the last year.

Which is why I volunteered to remain on this assignment, even after Kaspian offered me a different option.

I like Fallon. She's cute. Intelligent. *Alluring.*

Of course, she also possesses death magic, marking her as decidedly off-limits to a phantom like me. But what fun is life without a little danger? Besides, it's not like Fallon Doyle has tried anything on me or Bane. The worst she's done is stare for a few beats too long, betraying her curiosity about us.

Bane and I are used to that, though. We're considered new in this world, our powers and abilities as phantoms unknown to the majority of the population. The fact that King Kaspian keeps us both close only incites more interest in our presence here.

I pace outside Fallon's door, counting my steps as the seconds continue to pass.

In twenty-seven—I glance at my watch—nope, make that *twenty-six* minutes, I'll need to knock and request entry into her suite. She'll say yes because she unfortunately has no other choice, and then I'll turn on the broadcast for us to watch.

I swallow, uneasy about what that broadcast will announce.

Kaspian has spent the better part of two months trying to determine how to proceed. Executing Klas will destroy Fallon's spirit.

Alas, Klas's crimes can't be ignored.

He tried to kill the former King of Gold and Garnet. It didn't matter that King Vesperus willingly left this world shortly after it happened; he was still the House King for several decades and a renowned master vampire who was well respected throughout the world.

Allowing Klas to live after attempting to assassinate a monarch—former or not—isn't an option. Least of all because he poses an imminent threat to our current king, Kaspian.

Fallon claimed someone else placed the obedience spell upon her, but she doesn't know the warlock or witch's name.

What if that powerful being returns and ignites the spell again?
What if Klas himself can do it?

The results would be cata—

"Issy!" Fallon screams, her anguish a palpable punch to my chest.

My ghostly form overtakes my body without a second thought, allowing me to cross through the walls into her rooms.

My hand is on one of my vials, ready to throw a stunning potion at whoever is hurting Fallon. But all I find is her crumpled on the floor with her knees to her chest as she cries out in obvious pain.

"Fallon?" I ask as I turn back into my corporeal state.

She doesn't react to my sudden appearance. Nor does she seem to notice me at all.

"Tell me what's happening," she demands. "Talk to me!"

I frown. "What do you mean? I heard you scream and ghosted in here to—"

"Issy!" she screams again, her agony rippling through the air.

I kneel beside her, trying to determine what's happening. She's so tightly curled into a ball that I can't see where she's injured or how. "What does *Issy* mean?" I ask her.

"Who? What are you talking about?" She sounds so bewildered as she speaks. "Issy…"

She's having another episode, I realize, somewhat familiar with these now.

As if to confirm my thought, Fallon begins to convulse.

I reach for her shoulders, trying to keep her on the floor, to ensure she doesn't hurt herself. "Fallon," I say softly against her ear. "You're safe. It's okay. I have you."

Not that I have a damn clue how to help her. Each time, I just talk to her and hold her, and she eventually calms down.

While I don't know the full extent of what Klas did to her, I have gathered that it involved a hell of a lot of abuse.

The first time this happened, I heard her begging him not to drown her again. I found her on her knees on her bed, her eyes wild with tears, with her hands clasped tightly behind her back as though bound with an invisible rope.

It took several minutes for her to realize it wasn't real, that she was awake and no longer dreaming.

Another time, she was choking on invisible dirt while clawing at her sheets like a rabid animal.

And the worst was when I found her screaming in the shower, apologizing over and over again to a figment in her mind.

However, this feels different. Mostly because my presence in the room hasn't snapped her out of this delirious state yet. It usually only takes a few words from me to bring her back. But not this time.

She continues to shake, her arms pebbling with goose bumps as a chill sweeps across her body, causing her core temperature to drop.

I hiss as her skin becomes cold to the touch, her body seeming to die right before my eyes.

"Fallon…" I curl around her, trying to lend her my warmth. But I really have no idea how to help her.

Bane says it's likely linked to post-traumatic stress, but Fallon has refused to talk to anyone about it. She keeps saying she's "fine" after every incident.

I suspect it's because she doesn't want to open up to anyone. Trust is hard to earn, especially after suffering such severe betrayal from a loved one, let alone a fucking *mate*.

If I could kill Klas, I would. A hundred times over. That asshole doesn't deserve to breathe after everything he's done.

The only caveat to ending him is what it'll do to Fallon.

She's an innocent who doesn't deserve this fate.

Yet, there's nothing we can do to help her avoid it.

While Kaspian has approached all of this with a practical mindset, I know the repercussions of Klas's execution are weighing heavily on his mind. He and Fallon may not get along—primarily because she sees him as her captor—but he doesn't blame her for what happened.

Although, he absolutely doesn't trust her power.

Fallon possesses rare magic unlike anything Kaspian has ever seen, which is saying a lot for one as old as he is. He's a master vampire with well over a thousand years of life experience. Not much surprises him these days, but Fallon clearly has.

She's surprised me, too, I think, holding her as she continues to vibrate.

For one, I wasn't expecting to like the witch who cast a deadly sleeping spell over all of Reykjavik. In fact, I originally wanted to murder her.

But everything changed the moment I met her.

Not only did we quickly discern her innocence, but she immediately displayed her fiery side by laying into Nolan for shooting her in the shoulder.

And shortly after that, she gleefully volunteered to eviscerate Klas. *Several times.*

Bane offered her his own blades to help, something that meant a lot more than Fallon would ever know. Knives were as much a part of Bane as his own hands, and to give them to someone else was a show of faith he rarely bestowed upon anyone.

I understood, as I felt very similarly about my toxic vials.

Yet Bane gave Fallon his knives without a hint of hesitation, then stood by while she worked.

Pretty sure he fell in love with her instantly. Not that she noticed, nor is it something he would ever act on.

Fallon is technically a prisoner, under constant observation until Kaspian can decide what to do with her.

And there's the whole problem with her possessing death magic.

Being phantoms means Bane and I are part ghosts, so probably not the best idea to involve ourselves with a necromancer-like witch.

Still, I can't force myself to release her and wait for whatever spell this is to end. She's still ice cold against me, her body shivering almost violently.

Maybe because she's naked, I think, noting her discarded towel on the floor. *Not the best time to notice that.*

I swallow and say her name again, trying to coax her out of her memories. "Klas isn't here. He's in the dungeon."

Although, it wasn't *Klas* she kept saying before, but *Issy*.

Is that a place? A spell? A person?

I've never heard her mention an Issy in conversation, nor do I recognize the term or place.

Her trembles slowly start to subside, her breathing stabilizing.

It takes me a minute to realize she's fallen asleep, her limbs completely limp. "Fallon?" I whisper, my lips still near her ear.

She doesn't respond.

She doesn't even move.

Sighing, I roll her to her back and palm her cheek. It feels icy beneath my hand, her lips holding a touch of blue. *Like death*, I think again, frowning.

This didn't happen during her other episodes.

"Fallon." My voice is louder now, my brows furrowing. "Fallon, wake up."

Nothing.

I resist the urge to shake her, not wanting to risk injuring her in case she's fallen into some sort of catatonic state. I don't know much about these types of post-traumatic situations, but I know better than to force someone out of an emotional episode.

However, I also can't leave her like this.

And I really don't want her to wake up naked on the cold tile floor with me curled around her.

It wouldn't be the first time she resurfaced to find herself in an uneasy situation around me, but that doesn't mean I want her to be even more uncomfortable by waking up on the ground.

I carefully pull my arms and hands away from her, then stand and gently scoop her up against my chest. She's a tiny little thing, her five-foot-one frame dwarfed by my six-foot-two one.

However, her smaller stature merely disguises the strong woman inside. I've seen her fire more than once. Typically directed at Kaspian and Nolan.

She's not a fan of long interrogations. Given that hers has been going on for thirteen months, I'm not surprised.

I settle her into the bed and wrap her chilled form up in a big blanket. Her cheeks are still pale, but her lips are less blue, telling me she's recovering from her episode.

I'll have to let Bane know about the coldness later. He's the one with the psychology background, having chosen to study and teach it at universities before magic showed itself to the world.

Fallon shivers a little in her sleep, drawing my attention to her mouth again.

"Hmm." I return to the living area to grab her towel, then wander into the bathroom to discard it in a basket before plucking a fresh one off the warming rack.

Fallon still hasn't stirred by the time I return, not that I'm all that surprised.

Pulling down the blanket, I lay the warmed cotton over her curves and wrap her back up in the comforter. Hopefully, that'll help heat up her skin.

But just in case it doesn't, I sit on the bed next to her to keep an eye on her.

Stretching my legs over the blankets, I cross my ankles and lean back against the headboard.

Checking my watch, I see that Kaspian will be making his announcement in less than five minutes.

Of course time decides to move faster now, I muse, rolling my eyes. That seems to happen when I'm with Fallon. It's the waiting part that feels long.

"Well, my task was to watch Kaspian's speech with you," I tell her. "It technically counts if it's on while I sit next to you, right?"

She doesn't answer, but a glance at her face confirms her body temperature is returning to normal. Still, I press the back of my fingers to her cheek to check, wanting to be certain, and smile when I feel a kiss of warmth there.

Maybe it was the chilled tiles against her bare skin that made her so cold. Her blondish-brown hair is wet, too. That couldn't have helped the situation.

It's February in Iceland, making it quite cold here. And while magical enchantments—all linked to Iceland's geothermal activity—heat the interior of the palace, the walls and floors can't completely mask the frigid exterior temperatures.

I comb my fingers through her hair and debate grabbing another towel.

Would it be weird to wrap up her hair for her? I wonder, frowning. *Can I even do that with her lying down?*

Her cheeks have a faint pink to them again, her lips

returning to their luscious red shade—something I try very hard not to focus on.

A man could easily lose himself in Fallon's features.

She's beautiful and strong and has the most fuckable mouth…

I clear my throat and pull my hand away, no longer comfortable touching her while she's unconscious.

She's maintained this irresistible pull over me from the moment we met, almost as though we're fated mates. But we're not.

As evidenced by the asshat in the dungeon downstairs.

And about that asshat… I think, shifting focus to my wrist again. *It's time for Kaspian's announcement.*

I pull up a hologram screen from my watch and select an icon that'll connect me to the satellite network. It's sort of like a television, but more advanced and fueled by magic.

Kaspian has all the fun toys, which, thankfully, he shares with his security team.

All of the channels are paused with a note scrolling across the screen regarding Kaspian's impending broadcast. Everyone in Gold and Garnet knows what this is about. I'm guessing a few liaisons from other Houses are tuned in as well.

The attack on King Vesperus last year is widely known. Just as his leaving our world with his new goddess mate is renowned as well.

Kaspian taking over the role of king has been heavily observed, but it's come as a surprise to no one that he's handled the pressure well.

Vesperus groomed him for the position and it shows, especially as Kaspian takes over a podium on the screen. He's wearing a crisp all-black suit, his expression politely bored.

He doesn't immediately speak, instead giving everyone time to settle as he stares down his audience through the camera. His dark eyes are commanding, his presence dominant without coming off as suffocating. It's a natural trait, one that somehow makes him both intimidating and approachable at the same time.

A formidable adversary.

Thankfully, we're on the same side.

Kaspian clears his throat, the subtle sound commanding attention through the speakers. "Members and families of Gold and Garnet, welcome, and thank you for lending me your ears this morning. As most of you know, our Reykjavik base of operations was attacked last year by a deadly sleeping spell that threatened everyone within the city limits."

He pauses for effect, the silence almost threatening.

"The purpose of that attack was to show discontent with King Vesperus's decision to collaborate with and support the newly established House of Death and Diamond. While all of us are aware of the difficulties associated with the territory realignments, violence is never the answer."

I nod, agreeing with him. Primarily because Bane and I were part of that *territory realignment*. Death and Diamond was created to house phantoms, and Vesperus was kind enough to not only agree with the formation of the new House but also reallocate his territories in the United Kingdom and Ireland to Death and Diamond.

As a result, Queen Sabrina's Consort, Kieran, and King Vesperus worked out a partnership to help members of both Houses determine next steps for residence. Several Gold and Garnet members chose to stay and realign their loyalties with Death and Diamond, while others moved to different Gold and Garnet territories.

Meanwhile, Bane and I decided to shift allegiances to Gold and Garnet. Not because we particularly disliked Death and Diamond, but because we preferred the opportunities Gold and Garnet offered us.

"On that topic, I want to take a moment to thank Sovereign Niamh for all of her assistance in the relocations of our beloved Gold and Garnet members and families, as well as her loyalty to her constituents who are choosing to remain and realign themselves with the House of Death and Diamond."

His eyes shift sideways to someone off-screen, presumably Niamh.

"For those of you who have not yet heard, Sovereign Niamh has announced that she will be remaining in Dublin rather than relocating to another Gold and Garnet territory. She will be greatly missed but has my full respect and support for her decision."

The camera shifts to reveal the sea dragoness in question, her turquoise eyes bright against her darker features and skin. She dips her head, sending her black hair cascading forward like water, before righting herself in the chair. "It's been an honor, King Kaspian."

"Indeed it has," he replies. "The House of Death and Diamond is lucky to have you. But know that you will always be welcome back here, should you ever find yourself craving chillier waters."

Her lips curl. "I'm sure I will visit."

"See that you do," he tells her as the camera pans back to show his softening features. That tender look only lasts for a moment before his serious face returns, his gaze once again taking on that regal flair.

The camera pans out to show the room of sovereigns, all of them seated at a round table with Kaspian, demonstrating how he shares power with each of his territory leaders. He doesn't do thrones; neither did Vesperus. They both believe in collaborating rather than dictating.

"I also want to thank the other sovereigns for your continued assistance in offering new homes to our families who are relocating, and for welcoming them into your lands in true Gold and Garnet fashion. Your assistance and cooperation have been noted and are much appreciated."

Several nods ripple around the table as each of the various territory leaders under the Gold and Garnet umbrella accepts Kaspian's words.

"Now, on to more unpleasant matters—we need to discuss the fate of Mercenary Klas. He's been charged by the council with high treason against the House of Gold and Garnet, our former king, and the residents of Reykjavik. Many members lost their homes in his initial attack, and several nearly lost their lives thanks to his deadly sleeping spell."

A soft sound comes from the woman beside me, causing me to glance down at a very awake Fallon. Her intense green eyes are on the screen. I don't ask if she's okay, mostly because I've learned she doesn't like that question.

Instead, I murmur, "Good morning, firefly." It's a nickname I gave her a few months ago—a play on her fiery energy.

She swallows. "Yes. Morning. Good. Just in time to hear what's to become of my future."

FĀLLON

THIS IS the eleventh time I've woken up with Nox in my room.

When it first happened, I screamed and tried to hit him with a bespelled fireball. He ducked, causing the flame to hit the curtains framing the balcony behind him, and that… didn't end well.

Fortunately, I also knew a spell that could reduce the damage, but the curtains were unsalvageable.

Nox helped me replace them without much comment, apologizing instead for scaring me after my *episode*—that's what he and Bane call my nightmares.

I suppose they're not wrong.

Sometimes the *episodes* happen when I'm awake, too. I see something that triggers a memory, and suddenly I lose time. Then I usually wake up in a precarious position with one of them nearby in the room.

A consequence of having an abusive *fated mate* for the last four years, I guess.

Bane has asked me more than once if I want to talk to someone. The answer is always "No." But Nox never pries, choosing instead to offer me comfort where he can without suffocating me with questions or concerns.

Such as now.

I woke up a few minutes ago to find myself snuggled in bed beside him, his focus on his screen and not on me. Rather than react, I studied him for a beat, admiring his square jaw and the dusting of brown hairs there.

He hasn't shaved today, was my first thought.

Followed by, *How did I end up in bed?*

Which led to, *And why am I naked?*

Then the memories of Issy's words and her agony speared through me, nearly rendering me unconscious again.

Until I heard Kaspian's voice.

"Members and families of Gold and Garnet, welcome, and thank you for lending me your ears this morning."

Coldness seeped through my veins, making me mute while I listened to him speak, his English accent familiar after months of enduring his interrogations.

It wasn't until he mentioned *Mercenary Klas* and his *deadly sleeping spell* that I reacted outwardly, my frustration escaping my mouth in a soft snort.

"Do you mean your fated mate?" Nox asks, replying to my comment about it being a not-so-good morning since I'm going to hear about my fate.

"Yes," I lie. Then I think better of it and say, "Actually, no. I mean my fate, since it's directly tied to his." Or, at least, that's how I translate my sister's words.

If Nikolas O'Neely is subject to death, so is Fallon Doyle.

They weren't really *her* words so much as the Outcast Coven's words. But someone—likely our father—forced her to say them to me.

I don't try to reach out to her again, aware that she's no longer conscious. It's something I can sense through our twin bond, our magic and energy linked in ways that can't be explained.

She fought whoever tried to control her mind.

And she failed.

Which suggested it might have been more than our father who coaxed her into relaying that message.

Or maybe it was just him alone.

Our father is powerful, revered, *feared* by many. That's partly why we never stand up to him. But he's also the only one keeping Issy alive and safe.

Although, *safe* is a subjective term.

Is Issy really *safe* if she's kept locked up all the time?

Am I safe here, in this glorified prison cell the Gold and Garnet King refers to as a guest suite?

No, I'm not, I tell myself as Kaspian continues his speech on the screen, detailing the events of the day Klas was caught, and the council's findings.

I half expect Kaspian to mention me—the witch with the deadly power Klas used—but he doesn't. He keeps the focus on "Mercenary Klas" and his many wrongs against Gold and Garnet.

Meanwhile, Nox seems to be entirely focused on me. He hasn't said anything; he's just studying me in that quiet way of his. He does this often after I wake from an *episode*, his presence oddly soothing rather than suffocating.

I like that he doesn't push me.

He simply lets me know he's here.

Although, I suppose that's his job as one of my guards.

He's not here to protect me, but to ensure I don't do anything to hurt others. Which I imagine is his purpose now as well. Kaspian sent him to watch the announcement with me and evaluate my reaction.

Well, I won't be giving you one, I think, my eyes on the broadcast.

There's nothing for me to react to. I know what's coming. And I'm more concerned about what my sister told me.

Fallon Doyle will honor the Outcast Coven by adhering to our ancient pledge—loyal mates die with their beloved. Or those mates will be punished with fates worse than death.

I shiver, her voice running through my head.

The Outcast Coven expects me to take my own life, to die with Klas.

I can think of several *fates* that may await me if I choose not to comply. Most of them don't frighten me, not after surviving four years with my forced mate.

The problem is, they have Issy.

And knowing my father, he'll use that leverage to his advantage to ensure I behave, just like he did for my arranged mating to Klas.

I have to find a way to help Issy escape, I think while Kaspian continues addressing his leadership and his constituents. *But where will she go? She can't go into No Man's Land. No House will accept her. Not even this one...*

Because Kaspian and the others think I'm an orphan without a family.

Even if I tell them the truth, I know they won't allow someone as powerful as Issy to come here. Not to mention all the questions that will follow regarding my own powers and birth and home.

They don't even know Klas's last name.

He's claimed not to have one, and I haven't corrected the lie.

But if they learn his identity as an O'Neely, they'll know immediately that he came from the Outcast Coven, and I highly doubt Kaspian would be pleased with that revelation.

Telling them isn't an option. As Issy's warning stated—there are fates worse than death.

"Now on to the sentencing," Kaspian says, drawing my attention to his handsome features. "The council and I have deliberated endlessly over how to proceed, as there are certain factors we needed to take into consideration."

Me, I translate. *Or I assume I'm one of those* considerations, *anyway.*

"But we've ultimately come to the conclusion that there is no acceptable sentence for Mercenary Klas other than permanent death."

I blink, the statement seeming to float into the air and fizzle around me.

It's not a surprise. It's entirely what I expected.

But now it's accompanied by my own sentence—one bestowed upon me by the very coven that has ruled my entire existence.

I've done everything they've ever demanded of me, even at the expense of my own sanity and health.

I survived hell for them.

I helped Klas even when I didn't want to.

Because they took away my choice. They bound me to him against my will, forcing me to be a good little witch mate and take everything he gave me.

Dying repeatedly.

Only to come back to life each time, thanks to an immortality spell—one Klas cast over me using my own magic.

That was my punishment when I tried to fight him last year. I discovered a foreign piece of magic that helped me focus my mind, to be *me*, and Klas's solution was to bury me underground, making me suffocate on dirt over and over again.

I survived all that madness.

38

And for what?

To be told I have to take my own life and die with the very monster who destroyed my spirit these last few years.

Fuck. That.

There has to be another way. Some avenue I haven't explored. An escape I haven't contemplated.

Yet I've spent my entire life looking for an exit, only to come up short every time.

Because I can't leave Issy behind.

"Fallon?" Nox asks, his Scottish accent gently caressing my name. His isn't very pronounced, but it sometimes comes out when he speaks in lower tones.

"I'm fine," I tell him as Kaspian informs everyone that the sentence will be carried out in three days.

"It will not be a public execution," he adds. "The beheading will be private. However, his remains will burn in the central square—the same one he attacked last year."

The memory of that day threatens my thoughts, my heart icing over at the acts that followed.

That was the first time I fought Klas's hold over me.

And I lost. *Severely.*

Nox closes the screen as Kaspian disappears, his piercing blue eyes on me.

"I'm starting to feel like a science experiment," I mutter. "Every time you come in here, you're staring at me in expectation, as though you think I might do something interesting."

"Well, I did find you naked in the living room this time," he replies, his lips curling up on one side. "So it could be argued that you often do things that are *interesting.*"

I roll my eyes. He's not wrong. He's found me in some bizarre ways—screaming in the shower because I thought the water was ice, clawing at the floor like it was dirt and not cold tile, and huddled in a corner while begging Klas for forgiveness all coming to mind—and this isn't the first time he's seen me naked.

So I'm not really embarrassed.

Just... broken.

Which may be why I have no trouble accepting Kaspian's announcement.

"I'm not going to freak out," I tell Nox. "Klas deserves to die. I'm just not looking forward to experiencing the pain with him."

At least he's prepared me for death-like sensations, I mentally add and nearly snort. *Look at that—Klas did something* good *for a change.*

Sighing, I sit up in the bed while keeping the sheets and towel pressed against my chest. "You can report back to Kaspian that I didn't cast any deadly spells in response to his broadcast."

It should be pretty obvious by now that I'm not going to help Klas. But no one here trusts me. Just as I don't trust them.

There are only two people I can rely on in this world—myself and Issy.

And sometimes Ayla, I decide. *When she's not busy being used by the Outcast Coven for other things—like the Earth and Emerald Chancellor Trials.*

"Who or what is *Issy?*" Nox asks, surprising me not just at the question but also at the abrupt change in conversation.

"What?"

"You were screaming *Issy* when I ghosted in here, and I was just wondering what it means," he says.

"Oh." *Shit.* I can't really answer that without outwardly lying. Although... "Just someone from my past," I hedge, hoping that's enough. "I don't want to talk about it."

He considers me for a long moment, then shrugs. "All right."

Always the easygoing phantom.

It's Bane who usually tries to make me open up. Not directly or in an overbearing way, but with subtle questions meant to coax me into talking. Sometimes I give in, just because it's nice to have someone listen for a change.

However, I don't give him very much.

Typically just enough about what Klas has done to explain my episodes and nothing more.

Except this incident has nothing to do with Klas and everything to do with my twin—who is still unconscious via our link.

I can sense that she's okay and recovering, but not much more.

It gives me a renewed appreciation for how she felt during our three-year mental separation. *So alone…* While I experienced that loneliness as well, Klas kept me otherwise distracted.

"Want some breakfast?" Nox offers, his blue eyes still staring me down. It's slightly unnerving how much he watches me. Not because it makes me uncomfortable, but because it feels as though he can see through me sometimes. Like he can read my mind.

But phantoms are not supposed to have that talent. They can disappear into their ethereal forms at will, making them good at spying on those of us who can't see them outside of their corporeal states. However, this feels different.

Maybe because I'm not used to having someone pay such close attention to me.

"Breakfast sounds good," I tell him, swallowing.

He nods. "The usual?"

"Yes." I don't like heavy foods in the morning, yogurt with fruit being my preference.

"I'll order you a new coffee, too," he says, glancing at the living area.

Right. My espresso drink.

I didn't have a chance to enjoy it because of the death sentence message coming through via the twin bond. Even if I could drink it, I wouldn't. Everything felt tainted. Deadly. *Wrong.*

"No coffee, please." A strange sentence for me to voice, but the thought of it sours my stomach. "Just some yogurt and fruit, or maybe a fruit smoothie."

If I surprise him, he doesn't show it. Instead, he pulls up some screen on his watch and starts typing in an order. "I'll order both. Whatever you don't eat, I'll eat." Then he glances at me. "Any other special requests, firefly?"

"Freedom?" I suggest.

He grins. "We can eat on the balcony."

"Oh, goody," I deadpan. "I can stare at the night sky and pretend I'm not a prisoner in a fancy cage."

"There are worse accommodations," he reminds me as he finishes placing the order.

"I'm aware." And I'm not talking about Klas's cell in the dungeon.

"Your guards are pretty awesome, too," Nox adds.

"Sure, if you consider voyeurs to be awesome."

He chuckles. "I do, actually." With a wink, he slips off the bed. "But I'll give you some privacy while you find your clothes." He starts toward the living area and heads in the direction of the balcony doors rather than the front doors, his words carrying to me over his shoulder. "I'll be waiting for you outside, firefly."

I admire the way his jeans cup his firm ass, then look away.

It doesn't matter how much he flirts or how nice he is to me, I know his real purpose here. Part of me wants to hate him for what he represents—*a prison guard*—but he makes it pretty hard to dislike him.

The least he could do would be to shoot me in the shoulder like Nolan did. At least then I could hold a grudge.

Instead, Nox is kind and takes care of me in his own way.

Bane does as well.

It's too bad I can't stay here and indulge in them a little more. But time is running out.

Three days, to be exact.

Three days until Klas dies.

Three days until I either follow through on the Outcast Coven's suicide order or face the consequences.

Three days to figure out how to escape this fancy prison, save my sister—and hopefully myself, too.

No pressure, I think. *No pressure at all.*

KASPIAN

I SHAKE Khaos's hand at the door. "Thank you for making the trip. I know your grandfather has his hands full with all the new mercenaries in your territory."

Khaos grunts before dropping my hand. "Is that the excuse he gave you?"

"He might have mentioned a mating heat," I hedge, grinning. "I was trying to be polite." Khaos's grandfather is an old friend of mine from well over a millennium ago. If I allowed myself to have favorites, he would be one of them because of his no-nonsense leadership approach.

Which explains how his three grandsons turned out to be some of the fiercest mercenaries in Gold and Garnet territory.

"Polite?" Cara echoes behind me. "You?" She blinks her pale green eyes a few times. "Huh."

I narrow my gaze at my second-in-command. "Are you looking for a sparring match, little fae?"

"Call me *little* again and I will be, yes," she fires back.

My lips twitch as her mate comes up behind her and wraps a protective arm around her shoulder. "Leave

Kaspian alone, Cara. He's had a rough morning," Larus says. He's my other second-in-command, and also a fae. Well, a fae hybrid, anyway.

"He made a speech," she drawls. "That's not hard."

She's not wrong. The hard part is waiting for me in the guest suite beside my room.

"Always trying to cause trouble," Larus laments. "It's a good thing I'm the politically savvy one here. What Cara means to say is 'You did a great job, Kaspian. You're a fine king.'"

Cara and I both snort at the same time. "Suck-up," she says.

"You're not getting out of tonight's call with the new Earth and Emerald Chancellor," I tell him, fully aware of what he actually wants from me. "As the *politically savvy one*, I need you by my side as I extend my warm welcome into the community." Particularly as this *new chancellor* is a former member of the Supernatural Syndicates.

Nikki Ward.

Somehow, the former mafia princess managed to win Earth and Emerald's recent trials for their chancellor position.

I don't know how she pulled it off, let alone how she was even eligible to compete in the first place, but that's neither here nor there. She's my equal now, and I need to extend a professional greeting as a fellow House leader.

Larus's expression falls. "Yes, of course. I'll be there."

Cara smirks and Khaos shakes his head. "I'm not envious of your job, King Kaspian," he says to me. "I'm not sure I could be as accommodating in certain situations."

I know he's referring to accepting a Supernatural Syndicate member into the House leadership ranks—most of us are wary. Although, I've heard from a few allies that

45

Nikki Ward isn't like the usual crime lords from that No Man's Land region.

I just hope those allies are right.

"Oh, Kaspian is *very* accommodating," Cara drawls, her words confirming her desire for a sparring match.

"Stop taunting our king," Larus whispers against her ear. "I need you whole for later."

She shivers visibly. "Kaspian won't break me."

I arch a brow. "In my current mood? I wouldn't be so sure, *little fae.*"

Alas, I have other tasks I need to see to today, including the one in the room beside mine.

I sent Nox up there to keep an eye on our death witch during my announcement. It wasn't that I expected her to react badly; it was more that I didn't know what to anticipate from her. She's entirely unreadable and it's driving me crazy.

She's fine, Nox's report said minutes ago. *She expected this outcome.*

That's all his messages said.

And for whatever reason, it has me grinding my teeth again now.

I want *more*. More information. More of a reaction. More of something so I can set an expectation.

But the fiery little witch won't give me anything. It's as though she's simply accepted her fate and has no argument to the contrary.

Yet that monster mate of hers *destroyed* her. I've seen the aftermath, the way she cringes when a male is too close or when one of us says the wrong thing.

She puts on an impressive front, but deep down, she's shattered. And knowing that makes me want to beat the shit out of Klas.

However, hurting him inevitably hurts her.

Which is why it took me so damn long to sentence the bastard. Killing a fated mate destroys the other half of his soul, which, in this case, will be Fallon's spirit.

From what I can tell, she doesn't deserve that. Alas, there isn't a choice. He has to die. Hence the reason I need to go up and speak with her, to explain the decision, and more or less apologize for what's about to happen to her.

"Unfortunately, I have other items on my agenda today," I tell Cara. "But maybe Khaos will stay for a sparring round." I glance at the hybrid shifter, aware of his unique animalistic heritage. "Don't let the dainty-little-fae act fool you. She has deadly aim." Not as good as mine, but that was my claim to fame back in my mercenary days.

Khaos sizes up the tall female fae in front of him, his nose twitching as he scents her aura. "She's powerful."

"I am," she confirms, taking his measure as well. "But your size and speed would make for an interesting challenge. Can your flight home wait a few hours?"

"It can."

Her expression brightens. "Excellent." She looks at Larus. "You can be our referee."

Larus rolls his silver-blue eyes. He's a few inches taller than Cara, and slightly more muscular, but his powerful aura rivals hers. "If I knew you were craving pain today, I would have given you something else for breakfast this morning, darling."

Cara starts pulling her blonde hair back into a ponytail, her irises gleaming with excitement. "Don't worry, love. You can lick my wounds later." She refocuses on Khaos. "Follow me if you dare, *Duke*." She tosses his official title out there like a taunt, which causes the hybrid shifter to grin.

"I think I'm going to enjoy this, *fae*," he says, following her out the door.

Larus gives me a look on his way out. "If he kicks her ass, I'm skipping tonight's meeting."

"I think it'll be a fair fight," I tell him. "Just don't let them use any weapons."

"His teeth *are* weapons," Larus grumbles.

"True. But you're the referee. Set the rules." It's what he's best at—establishing diplomatic parameters and forming agreements. "Have fun."

With a subtle glare, he turns to follow his troublesome mate, leaving me alone in the council room. I purposely remained behind, wanting to thank Khaos personally for attending, and also to take his measure. We've met a few times in passing, but I'm more familiar with his grandfather, Talino. Not just because of our old friendship, but because of his position.

I typically only deal with my sovereigns. They hire their own dukes within their territories and manage them as they want, only reporting major findings or issues up my way.

But Talino is a little different. He's given his three grandsons more authority than the average duke, marking them as important figureheads within their region.

I suspect Talino wants to retire soon, which would explain him eagerly sending his eldest grandson to today's meeting. Sure, having a mate in heat is a good reason to stay home, but I'm guessing there's a little more to it than that.

It's an item I'll have to follow up on later.

After I deal with the witch in my guest suite.

My shoulders fall as I consider how to approach her, uncertain of what I can even do to improve the situation.

She wants her freedom, which I can't grant. Not when I know how powerful she is and how unstable she's likely about to become.

Keeping her under house arrest is the best I've been able to do thus far. I can't trust her to leave, especially not now.

Fuck, when all the chaos happened last year, we all assumed it was her causing the problems because we thought Klas was dead. We presumed she was reacting to her mate's death by losing control of her powers.

Except the bastard wasn't dead at all. He was using her instead.

And now I have to execute him.

Thus likely causing Fallon to truly become unstable… and essentially bringing us full circle to the events of last year.

Because chances are she's going to lose her shit, which will end in her powers fracturing.

Powers I don't know how to control, I think as I head down the hallway toward the stairs.

I've spent the last year trying to determine the full range of her abilities, but to no avail. She possesses unique magic that I've never seen before, and none of the witches in our territory seem familiar with it.

According to her files, she came from No Man's Land. No known family or relatives. Klas met her on a mission while passing through, fate-bonded her, and brought her home to be his little pet witch.

To abuse.

To take advantage of.

To *hurt*.

My hands tighten into fists as I ascend the stairs to the top floor of the palace.

This used to be Vesperus's home, but I spent the last year remodeling it to make it my own. The Reykjavik palace headquarters is the most secure place for the Gold and Garnet King.

How I wish I could talk to Vesperus now, though. Just wander down to his old rooms and ask for his advice.

Alas, he's no longer of this world. Maybe one day he'll pop back in for a visit, but I doubt it. His mate was too powerful for this universe, making their exit necessary.

She was a goddess from another realm. A being of such extreme power that she could literally control the moon.

At least Fallon can't do that, I think as I reach the last set of stairs. *She can just put an entire city to sleep instead.*

I run my hand down my face, exhausted.

But I can't let Fallon see me this way. I have to be strong. In charge. *A king.*

I pause just outside her room. It's one door away from my own quarters. The dungeons weren't an option for her, as I didn't want her anywhere near her mate. Not because I thought they might work together to escape, but because she didn't deserve to share his fate.

And yet here I am about to force her to do exactly that.

Sighing, I knock twice on the door and wait.

Nox answers with a deferential nod. "She's on the balcony. Want me to stay or...?"

I glance around him toward a set of glass doors and the curvy blonde standing just outside of them. Her eyes are on the sky, her hair blowing subtly in the wind. She's utterly enchanting, her presence an enigma that both intrigues and irritates me.

I can't decide if I want to keep her close or banish her to a remote location where she can't do any harm.

The former is tempting. The latter is probably more practical.

And yet, she's currently living in the room beside mine.

Clearing my throat, I focus on Nox's vibrant blue eyes. "Can you find Bane and Nolan? I want to meet tonight after my discussion with the new Earth and Emerald Chancellor."

Nox dips his chin. "Consider it a date."

Normally, his words would make me grin, but right now I can only manage a slight twist of my lips. While a *date* would be a nice distraction from the days ahead, it will do little to assuage my guilt over the pending situation.

"Do you want me to come back up here to guard her after I talk to them?" Nox asks, his gaze glittering with his real question—*Do you want me to return quickly in case I need to break you and Fallon apart?*

Every conversation I have with the woman seems to end in an argument.

Mostly because she's a disrespectful little brat who won't heed reason.

But today I'll let her win.

It's the least I can do.

"Take your time," I tell him. "This is going to be a long conversation."

He considers me for a moment. "She understands, Kaspian."

"I know she does."

"Then treat her with the respect and intelligence she deserves," he counters. "It'll go a long way."

"When do I not treat her that way?" I demand.

His lips quirk upward. "You two are more alike than you realize."

I frown. "We are not."

He lifts a shoulder. "Whatever you say, Your Highness."

I roll my eyes. "You were on your knees for my cock the other night and refused to call me *king* then, Nox. Don't bother with the false formalities now."

A soft gasp draws my focus to the open doors of the

balcony. Fallon's wide green eyes meet mine, her lips parted in surprise.

Shit. Was the door open the whole time, or did she somehow open it without me hearing her? Given my age and vampiric hearing, the latter would be a feat.

However, everything about this female is impressive. So perhaps she magically removed the glass barrier without me noticing.

"See you in a bit, *my king*," Nox taunts as he disappears into his phantom form, leaving me alone with Fallon.

Way to make it more awkward, I think, chastising myself for giving in to Nox's banter. *Because things were not already awkward enough.*

FALLON

Nox on his knees for Kaspian?

Now there's an image I wouldn't mind taking to my grave.

My thighs clench with the notion of the two men being intimate together. *Why have I never considered that before?*

Because Kaspian is usually too busy grilling me about my powers to let me see this side of him.

He blinks, and the *king* I'm used to appears.

The one with the serious brows.

Sharp cheekbones.

Dark, penetrative eyes.

Regal suit.

Stern expression.

Too-handsome face.

Elegant facade.

Full lips.

Ugh. Does he have to be so damn sexy? I wonder, instantly agitated by his presence. *Couldn't he at least be a troll?*

"Hello, Miss Doyle," he says, his English accent caressing my name with a hint of authority.

"Your Majesty," I deadpan. I can't help it. He walks

into a room and I'm instantly annoyed. Mostly because he's infuriatingly attractive. And dominant. And maybe a tad terrifying.

One slip of the tongue and I'm a dead woman.

That makes it somewhat difficult to have a fluid conversation with the gorgeous king. Especially when he always seems to be on a fact-finding mission with me. Not that I can blame him. But that doesn't mean I *enjoy* his interrogations.

Okay, maybe I do a little bit.

But who wouldn't enjoy being questioned by a sexy master vampire in a perfectly tailored suit?

"How are your accommodations?" he murmurs, his tone overly polite.

"The same as the last time you asked," I reply.

His jaw clenches, revealing a chip in his elegant armor. I've found it increasingly easy to do over the last few months, almost as though my mere voice aggravates him now.

"I assume you saw my announcement?"

I roll my eyes. While he might have gone straight to the point, he's still not being all that direct. "You know I did, *Your Highness*. You sent Nox here to make sure I watched it with him."

Darkness flashes in the Gold and Garnet King's near-black eyes. "*Fallon.*"

"*Kaspian.*"

He growls and shakes his head. "Why are you always like this? I'm simply trying to have a polite conversation, and you're snapping at me."

"I'm not snapping at you. I'm inflecting sarcasm in my replies." I move over to the couch and plop down, my gaze finding his burning eyes. "And there's nothing *polite* about an execution."

He sighs, his fingers clenching at his sides. "I understand that you hate me for this decision, but—"

"I don't hate you," I interject. "And especially not for your decision. It's the right one. Klas deserves death."

"But you don't," he mutters.

My eyebrows lift. "Is that your version of sarcasm?"

He stares at me. "What? No. I mean, you don't deserve what his death will do to you."

I lift a shoulder. "Whatever happens to me is the lesser evil." And maybe nothing will happen at all. Maybe the spell that bound our souls will disintegrate into ash along with Klas's remains.

Or maybe I'll go insane.

And then there's the Outcast Coven's suicide order...

I wince, the reminder of my fate an unwelcome one.

Kaspian takes over the couch opposite me, his athletic frame seeming to melt into the black cushions around him. He says nothing for a long moment, his alluring irises dancing over me with wary interest.

"Do you want to attend his execution?" he asks softly, his gaze still studying me intently.

Do I want to attend Klas's execution? I wonder, frowning. "Yes." I want to see him burn. Suffer. *Die.* Not just for a sense of revenge, but also for peace of mind. *I need to know he's truly gone.*

Kaspian nods as though he can hear my thoughts, or perhaps in response to my confirmation, but something about his expression almost seems understanding. "There will only be a handful of witnesses. The fire afterward will be for the House. But I'll make arrangements to have you at the execution itself."

"Thank you." This might be the first time I'm saying those two words to him and meaning them. Because I'm grateful that he's allowing me this closure, even if it's a moment that will lead to a much darker future.

"For what it's worth, I'm sorry it has to be this way. Punishing you for your mate's sins is... an unfortunate consequence of the situation."

"For what it's worth, I'm not sorry," I counter. "There is no other choice here. Klas is a threat. And by proxy, I suppose I am as well."

He doesn't refute my statement, just continues watching me for a beat before saying, "Is there anything I can do to make you more comfortable here?"

Oh, good, we're back to that question again...

He asks this every time he visits.

And every time I answer the same.

"It's a very fancy cage, my king. I'm content." The saccharine quality of my voice isn't lost on him, as evidenced by the way his jaw subtly ticks in response to my comment.

"I'm not keeping you here as punishment, Fallon."

"No, you're keeping me here for observation," I counter. "Because you don't trust me or my powers."

His eyes flash with impatience. "Perhaps that's because you won't enlighten me on everything you can do."

"I'm skilled in death magic." I utter the words slowly, the sentence one I've voiced a thousand times in his presence. "I can manipulate souls and lure them to the grave." That's only a fraction of what I can actually do, but it's the most dangerous aspect of my abilities.

Necromancer isn't the right term, but it's been tossed around a few times. I can technically animate a corpse and make him or her do my bidding. However, that's not all that exciting. It's akin to turning a dead body into a puppet. And I can't control the walking dead—like vampires or phantoms.

Well, not outright, anyway.

I could cast a spell that would lull them into a deadly sleep where I could torment their souls for as long as I desired, but that's not the same as manipulating someone else's actions.

No matter how many times I explain this to Kaspian and the others, it's not good enough. And I can't exactly demonstrate my skills. It would require putting one of their lives in my deadly hands, and that's not an acceptable risk in their eyes.

Because they don't trust me.

Over a year in confinement and I'm no better off than my first week in Kaspian's custody. It doesn't matter that I assisted in finding Klas after he attacked Vesperus, or that I used one of Bane's blades to eviscerate Klas countless times.

I'm still an outsider.

I have no doubt that if they ever discover my origin, I'll be on the first plane back to New York.

Where the Outcast Coven will kill me for Klas's failures. Or maybe because I helped take him down.

Regardless, New York is the last place I want to go. Unless it's to save Issy.

Which I have no idea how to do.

We'll figure this out, Issy, I whisper to her. *Somehow.*

She doesn't reply, her mind still closed off to mine. I'm not sure what the patriarchs did to her, but it's clearly taking a toll on her mental state.

I'll find a way to make them pay, I add. *Even if I have to do it from the grave.*

"I'm not your enemy, Fallon," Kaspian says quietly. "But I'll become one if you make me one."

I lift my gaze to his, not having realized my focus shifted while thinking of Issy, and shake my head. "I'm not trying to make you my enemy. I just don't know what you want from me. I'm not a threat to you."

Or I don't want to be, anyway.

My powers are unique. They're part of what made me valuable to the Outcast Coven. But the patriarchs didn't trust me to handle my own abilities, which is why I was gifted to Klas. They wanted him to utilize my talents instead.

That worked out really well for you all, didn't it? I think, bitter.

Not that I would ever have used my skills the way Klas did last year. He went on a rampage, his ego wounded by being overlooked time and again for promotions. Then King Vesperus announced that Ireland and the United Kingdom would become part of Death and Diamond territory, and Klas lost his mind.

"He clearly has no respect for anyone here," Klas said while pacing around our home in Ireland. "Including me." He huffed a laugh then, the sound so deranged that even now I can hear it echoing through my mind.

"I'm tired of being overlooked," he added, his fist slamming into the brick walls of our living room. "This is taking too fucking long!"

I shiver, the mental image of his ire a dark memory in my mind.

Everything started to change in that moment. Klas was no longer content with waiting for a promotion or trying to work his way up the mercenary ladder to get closer to the House King. He decided to manufacture his own plan.

With me at the center of it.

My power.

I have no idea what the patriarchs thought of Klas's deviation, but I imagine they weren't pleased. Whatever goal he set out to accomplish in Gold and Garnet territory failed because of his brash decisions. And now we are both paying the price of his impatience.

"You've been hiding things from me since we met," Kaspian says, reminding me of his presence. "Which is why I can't believe you when you say you're not a threat, Fallon. I've experienced your magic. I know what you can do. But there's something you're not saying. And that makes me distrust you."

There are a lot of things I'm not saying, I think. "I don't owe you my secrets, Your Highness."

"Perhaps not. But if you want my trust, then I need your truths."

"Why?" I ask him. "Because my mate's a monster? Because he chose to subdue me with a spell and use my powers to attack your House?" I cant my head to the side. "Have you ever considered that my 'secrets' are irrelevant to your assessment of me and my power?"

They absolutely are not irrelevant, particularly the part about my origin and what little I know about Klas's true purpose for being in Gold and Garnet territory. But the heart of my secrets—the ones involving Issy—have nothing to do with Kaspian.

However, I can't reveal what I know about the patriarchs and Klas without also mentioning Issy.

Hence the reason I say nothing at all.

Kaspian sighs and shakes his head. "The execution is in three days. If you decide you need something before that happens, let Nox or Bane know, and I'll see what I can do." He pushes to his feet, his expression grim. "I'm sorry that I can't do more for you, Fallon. But you've made it clear you don't want me as an ally."

"No," I say as he starts toward the door. "I've made it clear that I won't trust blindly."

LEXI C. FOSS

He pauses, his shoulders going rigid. "I've given you every reason to trust me."

"By what? By not throwing me in the dungeon with Klas?" I ask him. "By keeping me locked up in a fancy room beside yours?"

He faces me again. "Would you prefer the former?"

"You won't put me down there with him because you're afraid he'll be able to tap into my powers again, so don't waste your breath on that threat."

"It wasn't a threat, Fallon. It was a question." The words are spoken through his clenched jaw. "I've made you comfortable in my home, in my own fucking quarters. I've treated you respectfully. I've ensured you have everything you need. What more can I give you to inspire trust?"

"My freedom?" I offer, aware that this conversation is just going to go in a vicious circle like it always does.

He scoffs at that. "Trust works both ways. I can't let you go until I can *trust* your motives and actions."

"And I can't trust you when I'm being treated like a glorified prisoner. So I guess we're at a draw. *Again.*" I've tried giving him small truths, just to pacify him and get him off my back. But nothing I share with him seems to be enough.

Fucking master vampire. Kaspian's too old and experienced to believe my half-truths.

His age and knowledge are also why he doesn't trust me. My powers are ones he's never seen before, and that both intrigues and unnerves him.

So he won't let me go until he's peeled away all my layers.

And I won't let him learn too much.

Issy is mine to protect. I'll never betray her. Not even for my own freedom.

Kaspian rubs a hand over his stubbled jaw, the dark

60

hairs resembling a shadow across his chiseled features. "Let Nox or Bane know if you need anything. They'll contact me if you decide to see reason."

I say nothing as he leaves.

Because there's nothing left to say.

Nothing positive, anyway.

My shoulders fall as the door closes, my gilded cage snapping into place around me with renewed force. Kaspian isn't wrong—he's treated me with respect and kindness. These quarters are certainly more comfortable than my last accommodations with Klas. Hell, they even beat my room back in New York.

But that doesn't change what I am—a prisoner. A ward under watch. A witch no one can trust.

I don't blame Kaspian for his choices. He's the House King. He has to protect his constituents first and foremost, and honestly, that's what makes him a strong leader.

However, that doesn't mean I have to like being caught up in this web of constant interrogation.

Telling him the truth would only lead to further complications, one of which being my immediate deportation back to the Outcast Coven. Or that's how I assume Kaspian would handle the situation, anyway. Neither Klas nor I belong in Gold and Garnet. I'm still not sure how Klas managed to infiltrate the House ranks, but I know it wasn't done legally.

I should be Houseless.

Living in No Man's Land.

Stuck with the Supernatural Syndicates.

Home with my bastard of a father.

Near Issy.

Not here in Reykjavik, in the king's palace.

Fallon? my sister whispers into my mind, her voice instantly grabbing my full attention.

Issy. Oh, thank the stars…

She huffs a little. *No stars here,* she replies, her voice sounding tired. *Just one hell of a headache.*

What did they do?

It doesn't matter, she replies. *And we don't have time to talk about it. We need to discuss what you're going to do.*

I swallow. *I… I don't know.*

Well, I do. Or I have an idea, anyway.

An idea? I repeat. *On how to escape?*

Yes. No. Sort of.

That's helpful, I deadpan.

I'm still waking up, she grates out. *But I think it might work. Just… give me a minute to think.*

I know better than to interrupt her. Issy spends most of her days reading, and she absorbs everything from foreign languages to science books to magical texts. If she has an idea, it's probably from her years of studying ancient spells.

Okay. It's a… resurrection spell… I just need to find the right book.

Resurrection spell? I repeat. *For Klas?*

No. For you. Sort of. It… it mimics death? Hold on. It's in one of these… She trails off, leaving me drumming my nails against my thigh for so long that I'm certain I'll have little indents. *Aha! Here it is. So you'll—*

The door to my rooms opens, causing me to say, *One second,* just as Nox strolls in holding a sundae. His light brown eyebrows waggle at me as he saunters forward, his expression knowing. "I thought you might need one of these after, well, you know."

"After being interrogated again by Kaspian, you mean?" I translate, aware that "interrogate" may be a bit strong for the discussion we just had. Because as far as questioning goes, it was pretty light. Actually, it was basically nonexistent. More of a lecture than anything else.

A game of *I'll trust you when you give me a reason to trust you.*

"Yeah, uh, that," Nox replies, setting the giant ice cream sundae down in front of me. "Two scoops of coffee ice cream on top of a banana and drizzled with fudge. Just the way you like it."

My lips twitch. "Sometimes I feel like we're dating."

He grins. "Well, I have seen you naked. Several times."

"Because you're a voyeur," I taunt him, picking up the dessert.

He collapses into the couch beside me and shrugs. "There's no harm in a little watching."

"It is when you're a ghost who can go through walls and spy on people unknowingly." I glance at him sideways. "Just because you're a voyeur doesn't mean I'm an exhibitionist."

In truth, I have no idea what I am. Klas is my only experience, and, well, he was more of a sadist than anything else.

My mouth curls down at the thought, the ice cream in my hands no longer resembling the temptation of seconds ago.

All because of Klas.

And his dark proclivities.

Memories I long to forget. To override. To ignore.

I swallow, the dish trembling slightly in my hand.

"Fallon?" Nox asks at the same time Issy whispers my name.

I clear my throat. "Sorry. Lost in thought," I tell him. *Nox just brought me a sundae,* I inform Issy.

Coffee ice cream and bananas? she guesses, knowing my favorite flavor combination.

With hot fudge.

I'm telling you, he wants you, Issy replies. *They both do.*

I don't need to ask whom she means by *they*. She's talking about Bane and Nox.

They're my prison guards, Issy. Not my boyfriends.

Uh-huh, she drawls. *Hot phantom bodyguards who want to bang you. Maybe you should let them before the execution. You deserve a little fun.*

I'm still mated to Klas.

Because of dark magic, she points out.

Sex is not what I need right now, I mutter as I force myself to eat a bite of ice cream. If anything, it'll give me an excuse to be quiet for a moment while I talk to Issy. *Tell me about the resurrection spell.*

Right. It'll allow you to fake your own death.

I resist the urge to raise my brows. *How?*

Well, that's going to be the hard part, isn't it? she muses, then clears her throat. *For starters, we're going to need to review some ancient phrases…*

KASPIAN

"She wants to attend the execution." The words taste bitter in my mouth, so I chase them with another sip of my maple-sweetened bourbon.

I'm not surprised by Fallon's decision. But that doesn't mean I like it.

The woman is hiding something. I sense it every time I'm near her. And while she might be right—that her secrets don't apply to our current situation—I want to know everything about her.

How am I supposed to protect my House from her potential threat when I don't know the full extent of her desires? She possesses a power unlike anything I've ever seen or felt. She put an entire city to sleep, for fuck's sake. I can't just give her freedom after that. She may not be the one who actually enacted the spell, but the ability is hers.

And that ability fucking terrifies me.

I take another gulp of alcohol, the burn a welcome sensation in my throat as Bane, Nox, and Nolan all stare me down.

"Say something," I tell them.

"What would ye like us to say?" Bane asks, his Scottish accent somewhat thicker now that he has a few drinks in him. Sometimes I forget his origin, his significant time abroad having smoothed out his lilt in everyday speech. "It's the lass's decision, is it not?"

"But is she making it for the right reasons?" Nox murmurs, his Scottish accent less affected by the liquor. He almost sounds American. Perhaps because he and Bane both spent several decades at the universities there before the supernatural portal opened in the middle of downtown Portland, Oregon.

Bane arches a dark brow, his hair color similar to my own. Only, his hair is shorter than mine, cut closer to the scalp. But we both suffer from a perpetual five o'clock shadow. "What reasons would be considered right?" he inquires, his obsidian gaze on Nox.

"I don't know, mate," Nox mutters. "You're the psychologist. You tell us."

"So yer asking me to psychoanalyze her decision?" Bane's lips twitch. "I don't think it's our place to judge."

Nox folds his thick arms over his chest, causing his dark shirt to stretch across his muscles. "It is if this will hurt her more than help her."

Nolan grunts. "The execution is going to hurt her regardless. That soul bond will shatter, and her sanity will fracture right along with it."

"Forever the optimist," I muse, toasting him with my mostly empty glass.

"You don't keep me around for my optimism," he returns.

He's right, of course, so I simply stand and wander over to refill my drink.

"She'll need to be put down if she loses her sanity," Nolan adds. "I hope you're all prepared for that."

"She doesn't deserve that fate," Nox fires back. "She doesn't deserve any of this bullshit."

"I'm not contesting that, phantom. I'm merely pointing out what we'll need to do if she loses her shit," Nolan says. "She's a liability. Whether her fate is *fair* isn't up for debate."

The archangel warrior is staring down Nox when I turn back around, their stances somewhat aggressive even though they're both sitting.

While I would absolutely enjoy watching the two males spar, now isn't the time.

"Nolan's right," I say, hating that I have to agree with his practical statements. "If she loses her sanity, she'll become an immediate threat to Gold and Garnet. And we can't allow that to happen."

Nox's arms flex, his jaw tight. "Fallon—"

"Rather than prepare for two executions, maybe we can consider ways to prevent Fallon's potential disassociation," Bane interjects, his tone as calm as ever. "We all know how death impacts fated mates, but perhaps there is something we can do to help ground her."

"I'm all ears, Bane." I settle back into my chair, my glass now full again. "What do you have in mind?"

"Well, I think having her attend the execution is a good first step. It allows her some closure. It also means the death won't be sudden or unexpected or even unwelcome, so that may help her cope. And if we can give her something to live for, that could impact the outcome."

"Something to live for," I repeat, frowning as I consider what that may entail. "A purpose, you mean."

"A purpose other than being kept in a room and forever interrogated," Bane translates, his dark eyes meeting mine. "I understand why she can't be allowed true freedom, but keeping her locked up—even in her current accommodations—isn't all that enticing."

"The four of us giving her a purpose to survive isn't going to be enough," Nolan says before I have a chance to reply. "She needs to give herself a purpose and take charge of her own destiny. If she wants to let fate break her soul, there's nothing we can do to stop her."

"I don't think it's that simple," Bane starts.

"No, it really is," Nolan returns as he unfurls from the chair. "Either Fallon is a survivor or she's not. In three days, we'll know the answer." He looks at me. "Is there anything else you wanted to discuss?"

Leave it to Nolan to demand a fast track to the end of the conversation. "Just that I plan for it to be the four of us and Fallon at the actual execution. We'll only publicize the fire."

"You don't want Cara or Larus there?" Nox asks, sounding surprised.

"He doesn't want to risk them being hurt if Fallon implodes," Nolan replies, his gaze on me despite answering Nox's question. "They're the seconds-in-command. You need them alive and well in case shit hits the fan. Right?"

I dip my chin in confirmation of his assessment. "That's not to say I don't value the three of you. I've chosen you to assist me for a reason."

"Protection." Nolan gestures at the phantoms as he says the word. "And you want me there because you know I'll kill her if I have to."

"Yes," I admit, aware that he's likely the only one of us who will be able to execute Fallon if needed.

Normally, I would take on the task myself. However, my mind will barely allow me to think of that consequence, making me concerned that I may hesitate.

While I'll do everything in my power to protect my

House, there's something about Fallon that makes me want to break all my rules. She sets me off with every infuriating conversation, her subtle defiance easily dismantling a millennium of perfected calm.

To say she's capable of getting under my skin is an understatement.

The woman is a conundrum I can't decipher or tame, and she drives me crazy as a result.

Killing her is simply something I don't want to contemplate, even if it's an inevitability. So yes, that's why I need Nolan. He's the practical one. The stoic one. The one capable of carrying out every job handed to him regardless of emotional entanglements.

I may be the mercenary with the best aim in Gold and Garnet, but Nolan is the assassin with a fully focused mind. When he's given a task, he sees it through, even when it hurts.

He nods once, his expression giving nothing away. "Understood. Anything else?"

"No," I admit.

"Good. I need to stretch my wings." The multicolored feathers appear behind him as he speaks, his plumes taking on a goldish hue in the low lighting of my living room. "You know how to reach me if you need me. Otherwise, I'll see you in three days."

He doesn't wait for me to reply, just strolls over to my balcony doors, opens them, and steps outside to disappear into the night.

I run a hand over my face, exhaustion hitting me hard in the chest. Not even my drink can save my mood now.

"You're right about her not deserving this fate." My words are soft and meant for the phantoms, as they've both voiced this thought several times over the last year. "However, I learned long ago that it's impossible to truly divert from our destinies. Sometimes we can run, but we'll never get far. And Klas... he has to die."

Just like Fallon will if her power proves unmanageable after the fated-mate bond is severed.

I shoot the rest of my bourbon into my throat, ignoring the fact that I had far more than a mouthful of it left, and slam the glass down on the end table.

"I don't know how to make her more comfortable, but if you two think of anything, feel free to do whatever is needed." I meet Nox's gaze. "With the exception of taking her out of my quarters."

"What is it you think she's going to do?" Nox asks. "Play in a cemetery?"

"I honestly don't know what she would do if we let her go," I tell him. "Which is precisely the problem. She's hiding something. And until we figure out what that is, she stays."

"There's also the issue of her ties to Klas and the fact her power is what he used to subdue the city," Bane murmurs. "It's not just about what Fallon may do when given freedom; it's about what other House members may do to her, too."

That last point seems to resonate with Nox, his blue eyes sparking with a flare of anger. "I can protect her."

"*We* can protect her," Bane corrects. "*If* she allows it."

Nox scowls and picks up the drink I poured him thirty minutes ago, the liquor mostly untouched. He growls something unintelligible under his breath and downs the contents in one swallow.

"I know you both care about her." *Hell, I do, too, for reasons I don't understand.* Not that I'll admit that out loud. "She's... Well, I don't know how to describe her. Stubborn. A bit of a brat. Fails to comprehend authority."

"Strong. Beautiful. Defiant." Nox tosses the terms at me like arrows directly to the chest.

"She's a survivor," Bane adds, his tone wistful. "The woman has been through hell, yet she still faces every day with a renewed energy about her. She'll carry that same energy with her into the execution. And she'll survive."

"She will," Nox agrees without flinching.

"I hope you're both right," I say, incapable of either agreeing or disagreeing. "Just... try to make her comfortable. Like you've always done, I guess. I don't know what else to do for her."

"You're doing what you can," Bane tells me. "We all are. But I suppose Nolan's right—the only one who can control her fate is Fallon herself. Either she pulls through or she doesn't. Only time will tell."

"Time," I muse, eyeing my empty glass on the table. It feels like a bad omen.

Here I am, nearly two thousand years old, with all the time in the world at my fingertips while Fallon may only have three days. It hardly seems fair.

But that's life—perpetually filled with unjust trials and wavering obstacles. It's how we handle those occurrences that matter most, as they define who we are.

For Fallon's sake, I hope Bane and Nox are right—that she's a true survivor.

One who will pull through the darkness ahead, find light at the end of the tunnel, and thrive.

She deserves better. It doesn't matter that she's harboring secrets or giving me half-truths. I can tell she's a good person beneath her snarky exterior. She's simply distrusting. And given everything she's been through, I can't blame her.

Alas, I can't help her either.

Not in this life, anyway.

Bane slips off the couch and walks over to snag the bourbon. When he returns, he tops off his glass, then refills mine and Nox's, and sets the bottle down. "I think we should toast in her honor."

Seems like a strange thing to do, but I pick up my glass regardless. "Can't hurt anything," I decide aloud.

Nox lifts his drink in the air. "To Fallon."

"She's been through hell," Bane murmurs. "Let's hope Klas's execution frees her soul and allows her to flourish in life."

I nod and add, "To new experiences and second chances."

"Hear, hear," the two phantoms murmur.

Then we clink our glasses.

And drink to the future.

If only this could be enough to save her…

NOLAN

I STAND on Kaspian's balcony, listening to the rest of their conversation and the toasts that follow. I don't have a glass of my own, but I feel my hand rising in the air in solidarity with them.

A pointless gesture.

But it feels right.

To Fallon, I echo as the night breeze ruffles my feathers. *I really hope you're as strong as I think you are.*

My eyes fall closed for a long moment, my heart threatening to bleed.

I've taken countless lives over my very long existence. Most of them deserved their fates. A few didn't. However, my role remains unaltered.

I'm a warrior.

An archangel.

A hunter with deadly aim.

Except for the day I shot Fallon. I was instructed to shoot to kill, yet I hit her shoulder instead. Some part of me couldn't take down the curvy little blonde witch. It was as though my soul took charge of my aim and forced me to falter.

I told her it was on purpose.

It was a lie.

One of the few I've ever told.

The truth was that fate altered my hand and the bullet sailed off course.

Fallon survived.

And some part of me fell into her trap, one I've been trying to escape from since.

She's an enchantress of some sort. A hypnotic genius. *A black widow.*

I'm convinced she has the phantoms under a spell, her death magic clearly a drug for their ghostly halves. But that doesn't explain my obsession with the girl. Nor does it explain Kaspian's innate softness toward her.

He could house her anywhere he wanted to in this palace yet chose to keep her next to his rooms for the last year.

Just as I chose to visit her quietly every night.

Lurking on her balcony like some sort of guardian angel.

Or perhaps I'm simply the angel of death, the one marked to take her to her grave.

If her soul fractures and she unleashes that deadly power, I'll be forced to act. And this time I won't miss. Because our lives will be at stake. Our House. Our *home.*

I won't have a choice.

I'll snuff the vibrant energy from her lively spirit and escort her to the cemetery near the place where I first shot her. And then I'll lay her to rest there for eternity.

Please don't make me do it, sweet canary, I think as I drift over to Fallon's balcony. *Tell fate to fuck off, and take charge of your future.*

I press my palm to the glass door of her rooms.

Be strong. Not for me, but for you.

I release a long breath, my head hanging low. There's nothing any of us can do for her. She needs to face this on her own. And she's already moving in the right direction by wanting to attend the execution.

She'll never know how proud I am of that decision, mostly because I'll never tell her.

She's not mine to cherish or to protect.

She's simply a mark I failed to assassinate. And that perplexes me.

Someday I'll figure her out.

Or perhaps I won't.

Perhaps I'll kill her instead.

Time, I think, musing over the word I heard Kaspian repeat. *Yes, time, indeed, will tell us our fates.*

I lower my hand from the glass.

Good night, little canary, I think at the beauty inside. *Dream of a future. A second chance. Drown yourself in hope. And give yourself a reason to survive.*

"Three days," I whisper as my wings carry me into the night. "In three days, we'll find out if I'm right about you…"

BANE

THREE DAYS LATER

"WHAT IS ALL THIS?"

Fallon's soft voice echoes through the dining area of her room, drawing my attention away from the stove and to the curvy blonde wearing just a towel.

I snuck in while she was in the shower, hoping to surprise her with breakfast.

Only now I'm the one feeling surprised by her half-dressed appearance. It's not like I haven't seen her this way before, but every time feels like a new experience.

The towel isn't even that revealing, the fabric covering her torso and thighs. *She could actually wear that towel as a dress, her short stature making—*

"Bane?" she prompts, cutting off my musings. "What are you doing?"

"Oh." I clear my throat and glance at the table of food before refocusing on the skillet in front of me. "I'm making you an American-style breakfast."

I use the spatula to flip the eggs and sigh in relief to find them perfectly cooked and not overdone. I want this breakfast to be flawless for Fallon. Not because it might be her last—I refuse to even acknowledge that possibility— but because I want to give her a moment of normalcy.

Or at least a moment of peace.

If that's possible, anyway.

"American-style breakfast?" she repeats, wandering over to review the items on the table. "You and Nox usually just do coffee and an egg sandwich."

I lift a shoulder. "Nox told me you didn't eat much last night, so I figured you would need a bigger meal this morning. And I was feeling nostalgic, so I made pancakes and eggs."

"And bacon," she muses, snagging a piece from a plate on the table.

"And bacon," I echo. "Except I made that English-style instead of American-style."

"Mmm, I approve." Her words are followed by a moan as she slides into a chair at the table, apparently completely at ease in her towel.

I try not to notice.

Try and fail.

Because even though the white fabric engulfs her short frame, I know there's nothing but skin beneath it. And a twisted part of me really likes fantasizing about those luscious curves of hers.

It's wrong. She's technically my ward, the one I've been assigned to guard and protect. But the forbidden nature of it all just makes me want her more.

I could write a book about the psychological reasons behind my unhealthy obsession. However, knowing that does nothing to dispel my interest.

There's just something about Fallon Doyle that enchants me, and it's been that way from the first moment I met her.

She's devastatingly broken. And yet, she's utterly perfect at the same time.

An alluring little flame, I marvel, my eyes once again taking in her exquisite beauty. *My forbidden temptation.*

"So what made you feel nostalgic?" she asks before taking another piece of bacon. "Are you missing being a professor?"

I've told her about my history, mostly because I want her to know I'm here if she needs someone to talk to. However, she rarely confides in me, even after suffering one of her many nightmares.

Occasionally, she'll summarize part of the night terrors —which are actually memories of her time with Klas—but she typically dismisses them and moves on.

That's something I've noticed she feels strongly about —moving forward and not backward.

Alas, it's not always healthy to run from the past, which is why her subconscious stirs when she's asleep. I've explained this to her, but I won't push her to talk about it.

Fallon will open up when she's ready to face her history. And when that happens, I'll be here to listen and to help her heal.

"I miss the California sun," I murmur, answering her question about my nostalgia. "This constant state of night is destroying my tan."

She snorts out a laugh. "A ghost who cares about his tan. Now I've heard it all."

I scoop the eggs onto a plate and bring them to the table. "I'm a phantom. And I don't enjoy being *ghostly*."

"Except when spying on people," she corrects me.

"I don't spy on anyone, little flame," I tell her. "You're confusing me with Nox."

Her lips twitch. "You're both voyeurs."

"Only when the situation calls for it, lass. But I'm usually more of an exhibitionist." I wink at her and return to the coffee maker to make her a proper breakfast beverage.

Although Fallon's accent is soft and subtle, she's Irish. Which makes whiskey an appropriate addition to her morning brew.

Her eyes light up when I hand her the mug. "Thank you, exhibitionist Bane." Her expression sparkles with humor. "And for what it's worth, I think your tan is just fine."

I grin at her. "Thank you, little flame. It pleases my ghostly soul to hear you say that."

She giggles, our morning banter doing its daily job of making her smile.

I'm not quite sure when this easy camaraderie began between us, but it was early on. Maybe when I gave her my knives to use on Klas. Regardless, we've always clicked.

Alas, it's never been enough to convince her to truly open up to me. Given her circumstances, I understand. And I'm willing to be patient.

Besides, Fallon deserves to have someone in her court, especially when she's facing Kaspian in verbal sparring matches every other day.

I take the chair opposite her and wait as she fills her plate with food. Once she's done, I start with the pancakes and reach for the bacon just as Nox makes an unwelcome appearance through the wall.

"Speaking of voyeurs," I say, able to see him in his phantom form when Fallon can't.

LEXI C. FOSS

He materializes beside me, his expression beaming. "I thought I smelled bacon in the hallway." He grabs the piece I just put on my plate and takes a bite. "Yesss, so fucking good."

"He's not wrong," Fallon replies, humor dancing in her pretty green eyes.

If she's worried about this afternoon's execution, she's not showing it. She seems as laid-back as ever, taking every moment in stride.

Because she's strong and amazing, I tell myself. *Which is why she's going to survive today.*

Nox grabs a plate and takes over the chair at the head of the table, leaving only one seat open at the other end. Then he steals what's left of the pancakes.

I quickly snag the portion of bacon I want and toss a few extra pieces onto Fallon's plate before Nox can claim them all for himself.

He doesn't notice.

But Fallon does because she gifts me with one of her thankful smiles. I return her grin as I take one of the eggs for myself.

We all eat in comfortable silence, our morning routine falling into place. Sometimes it's just me and Fallon. Sometimes it's Nox and Fallon. And sometimes it's all three of us.

Regardless of the occurrence, it's become a bit of a ritual for us to spend our mornings together in some way. Usually eating or enjoying our coffees in blissful silence.

At least on the days when Fallon doesn't wake from a nightmare, anyway. If she had one last night, it's not evident in her demeanor today.

I study her as she eats, admiring the way her cheeks pinken with pleasure, her enjoyment palpable.

Will she still be like this tomorrow? I wonder. *Or will the fated bonds steal her joy?*

My jaw clenches when I think of the hand she's been dealt in life. It's so fucking wrong. If I could kill Klas for her, I would. But I suspect Kaspian will be doing the honors.

At least I helped her exact some revenge with my blades. Watching her eviscerate Klas was an experience I'll never forget. She took my knives and wielded them with ease, her motions efficient while she remained focused and quiet.

Goddess Nyx needed Klas's blood for some moon ritual that I didn't quite understand. And Fallon agreed to acquire it for her. That was when I offered up my knives, much to Nox's shock. I typically don't allow anyone to play with my sharp toys.

But Fallon is different.

She's... she's something I can't define.

I took to her immediately, almost as though we were fated for one another. Perhaps just as friends. Because we can never be more.

"So where in California did you live? And I assume it was before magic made itself known?"

Fallon's soft tones stir me from my thoughts to find her plate mostly empty.

Good girl, I think, pleased that she ate a full meal. She's going to need her strength today.

"Southern California," Nox tells her. "And yes, before the portal happened." He frowns then and asks, "Why are we talking about California?"

"Because Bane said he misses the California sunshine," Fallon replies. "He feels *pale.*"

Nox smirks. "He's missing his surfboard and the waves more than the sun." His blue eyes glance over at me. "And your tan is looking a little weak. Maybe you need to spend your afternoons outside."

I roll my eyes. I may joke about my tan, but we all know it's fine. My natural skin tone is perpetually sun-kissed despite my Scottish origin. Although, I did darken quite a bit during my surfing days.

"It's too bad there's so much turmoil going on near that side of the world. Otherwise, I'd try to find a way to visit," I admit. "Because Nox is right—I do miss the waves."

"A surfing psychologist," Fallon muses. "Sounds about right."

"Does it?" I ask, arching a brow. "Why's that?"

"I've never actually met a surfer, but from what I understand, they're stereotypically pretty chill. Which I imagine makes for being a good therapist." She sets her now empty coffee mug down. "Would you like me to reward your patience by sharing my feelings about today?"

I can tell she's teasing me by her tone, but I desperately want to reply, *Yes, please do.* However, I hold back and instead say, "Only if you want to, lass."

She's quiet for a moment, her expression thoughtful. "Well, I'm—"

The door opens to her rooms, causing her mouth to snap shut and her posture to stiffen as Nolan and Kaspian enter without knocking.

All her restful energy disappears between a cloud of obvious unease, her green eyes losing their soft appeal and sharpening as she takes in Kaspian's three-piece suit and Nolan's leather jacket.

I swallow a curse, irritated that Fallon was finally about to potentially say something real, only to be interrupted by their abrupt presence.

"Good morning, Miss Doyle," Kaspian greets formally.

"Good morning, Your Majesty," she parrots back at him, her tone heavy with sarcasm.

Nox shakes his head, an amused smile playing over his lips. And I merely sigh.

The tension between Fallon and Kaspian can probably be felt all the way in Scotland. Every time these two go near each other, sparks fly in a dangerous pattern and heated arguments follow.

I had hoped today would be different.

Apparently not.

"We'll be leaving in thirty minutes," Kaspian informs all of us. "The execution is set for twelve hundred hours."

Fallon nods. "Then I should probably change into something more execution-appropriate." She slides her chair against the tile, the wooden legs screeching and echoing through the room. "Excuse me, *Your Highness.*"

She gives the Gold and Garnet King a mock curtsy and leaves the dining area without a backward glance.

Kaspian's jaw ticks in response, his gaze narrowing at her back. "Why is she always like this?" he mutters under his breath.

"Maybe try calling her *Fallon* instead of *Miss Doyle,*" Nox offers. "Or make her food. It works for me and Bane."

Nolan grunts but says nothing else.

I don't bother commenting and instead busy myself with cleaning up the table so Fallon doesn't have to after the execution.

"You could also try a little more small talk before diving into the daily itinerary," Nox adds. "Sort of like how you would handle a woman at the bar—you don't just immediately ask to fuck her, do you?"

"I don't want to fuck Fallon," Kaspian says to him, his tone underlined with a harshness that has me wondering who he's trying to convince here—himself or us.

"Perhaps that's your problem, then." Nox doesn't sound deterred by Kaspian's tone at all, probably because he's used to Kaspian's irritable moods where Fallon is concerned. "You treat her like a responsibility and a burden, Kas, not like a lady you want to seduce. Dating, after all, is the best form of interrogation."

"Is that what you've been doing?" Nolan interjects. "*Dating*?"

"I've been treating her like a person, not a prisoner," Nox tosses back, an uncharacteristic note of steel entering his words. "Perhaps you two should try it."

"And do what? Woo her with desserts and breakfasts? Ask about her feelings?" Nolan scoffs at that. "You two phantoms are drunk on her death magic and losing sight of her purpose."

"Which is what?" Fallon asks, her sharp voice making me wince. "To rot in this gilded cage while you assholes continue to interrogate me about my powers?"

Shit. She's still wearing her towel, which means she likely didn't even make it to her closet before she started eavesdropping on their conversation.

"You know what I can do," she goes on. "You've experienced it for yourselves. What more do you want? A demonstration of what I'll do if my soul breaks this afternoon? Details about my personal life that don't apply at all to this situation? Secrets that are not yours to know?"

While she was initially responding to Nolan, her focus is on Kaspian by the end.

"Has it ever occurred to you that I don't want or need your trust?" she demands.

"You need it if you want your freedom," Kaspian bites back.

Fallon stares at him for a beat before shaking her head and leaving the room, her lack of a rebuttal unlike her.

Usually, these two engage in the same circular argument, both of them escalating until they've repeated their sides fifty different ways.

But Fallon almost appeared too tired to even try, like she was giving up on the entire situation.

Giving up on *him*.

I frown, not liking that approach at all. Her fight is what makes her a survivor. *Is she saving her energy for later today? Or is this another bad omen?*

Kaspian growls something unintelligible under his breath while Nox whistles and shakes his head. "I *know* how good you are at seducing women. Yet somehow Fallon reduces you to a juvenile vampire with no understanding of female emotions. It's amazing, really."

"Because I have no interest in *seducing* her," Kaspian reiterates between his teeth. "Two very different situations."

"Then maybe you need a new approach," Nox drawls as he stands up and carries a stack of dishes over to me at the sink. "Try caring about her feelings a little more and maybe she'll talk to you."

"Because that's working so well for Bane," Nolan points out, making me frown.

"I'm not even involved in this conversation," I tell him. "Leave me out of it."

"You're very much involved, phantom." He glances between me and Bane. "Both of you have tried the soft approach, and it's accomplished nothing. Now we're out of time, the woman is going to implode, and there's not a damn thing we can do about it."

"We don't know that." And I really don't appreciate him losing faith in her so quickly. "She's stronger than you give her credit for, *archangel.*"

He lifts a shoulder. "I guess we'll see."

"We will," Fallon agrees, reappearing again in a pair of jeans and a sweater, her feet bare. "Now, if you all are done talking about me as though I can't hear every damn word you've been saying from the other room, I'd like to go watch my mate die. Please."

FĀLLON

IT'S TIME, I tell Issy as I follow Kaspian into a barely lit room.

The Gold and Garnet dungeon is technically connected to the king's palace via one of the city's many tunnels—all of which were apparently built when Gold and Garnet refashioned Reykjavik as their House headquarters. But it was a good twenty-minute walk, telling me we are at least a mile away from Kaspian's home. Perhaps even farther away since we kept a clipped pace the whole way here.

Nox and Bane enter behind me, their presence nowhere near as soothing as earlier at breakfast. I suppose I have Nolan and Kaspian to thank for that. They reminded me that I can't trust any of these guys, especially not Bane or Nox.

Because they were assigned to me out of an obligation to learn all my secrets. They didn't hang out with me because they liked me; they hung out with me to interrogate me.

Hearing Nox talk about how he and Bane used

kindness as a way to coax me into talking served as the cold wake-up call that I needed.

These men are not my friends. They're my prison guards.

And now they're standing on either side of me, taking up their mantles as Kaspian takes over the center of the room.

There's a stone block situated in the middle, covered in chains. A sword adorned with an ornate gold-and-garnet handle rests nearby, as does an axe with similar markings along the wooden grip.

Which tool will they use? I wonder, aware that they'll need to sever Klas's head from his body. He's a vampire-warlock hybrid; thus there are only a few ways to truly kill him. Beheading is one of them. The fire that'll follow will just ensure the job is complete.

Bane's arm brushes mine, his over-six-foot height dwarfing my five-foot-one frame. It doesn't matter that I put on a pair of three-inch-heeled boots before we left. I'm still nearly a foot shorter than all the men in the room.

Including Klas, I think as Nolan drags him through the door's threshold.

I haven't seen him in months, at least not in person. But his presence has haunted my mind every moment of every day.

His hair is longer than I remember it, the dark strands nearing his jaw. And it looks like he hasn't shaved in months. Maybe because no one trusted him with a razor. I'm not sure.

But his eyes... his eyes are the same twin pools of dangerous ink.

I shiver as his gaze meets mine, the malice dancing in his obsidian depths making my blood run cold. I know that look. It's calculating. Cruel. *Knowing*. It tells me he has a plan. Something he's not saying. A twisted desire he's about to bring to life.

What is it? I wonder, my heart skipping a beat. *What are you planning?* I nearly ask the questions aloud, but I can't seem to find my voice. It's as though his presence has consumed all the air in the room, leaving me with nothing. Suffocating me like all those times he buried me alive.

My fingers curl into my palms, my nails biting into my skin and reminding me that I'm still here. I'm free. At least from him.

But if that's true, why I do suddenly feel so grounded? So... trapped?

Fallon? Issy's voice whispers through my mind, her presence anchoring me in a way no one else can.

Issy, Klas is here. And he... he seems... I don't know. I don't know how to explain it. But I think he's up to something.

He probably knows about the edict, Issy replies. *The patriarchs might have found a way to call upon him or to send him a message.*

Maybe, I hedge, swallowing. *But he doesn't have a mental link to someone like I do.*

That we know of, she points out. *And there are other ways to communicate. Like dreamwalking.*

True. I clench my jaw, recalling the dreadful spells that allow such intrusion into a soul's desired safe space. *But what if there's more to it than that? What if he has a plan like I do?*

I highly doubt you both have the same plan. And besides, even if he tried the same spell, the cremation would destroy it. Your body has to remain intact.

So hopefully they don't throw me onto the fire after him, I say, not for the first time since we concocted this insane idea.

I'm going to fake my death and then hope they send me to the morgue for an autopsy rather than just destroy my remains.

Issy's argument is that my "demise" will be so sudden

that they'll want answers, so they'll send me off for review instead of disposing of me right away. I think she's giving the men a little too much credit. Like they'll care about what caused my death; they'll just be thrilled not to have to worry about my powers anymore.

I can hear you overthinking, Fallon.

Probably because I'm projecting, I mutter back at my twin as I catch Klas's evil stare again.

He blows me a kiss, causing Nox to growl beside me. Bane wraps his arm around my lower back, his muscular hold both soothing and unnerving.

Soothing because it's Bane and we've developed a comfortable friendship over the last year.

Unnerving because that friendship isn't real, yet I'm clinging to it like a lifeline now.

Do you remember the words you need to say? Issy asks.

Yes. I've repeated them in various patterns over the last three days. Although, I haven't said them aloud in the actual spell sequence yet. Because, if I had, I wouldn't be here right now. I'd be in the morgue.

Maybe.

Or burned alive.

Fuck.

Issy repeats my name, fully aware of me freaking out again. But this time I don't reply, because Kaspian is reading Klas's last rights.

I barely hear him.

I barely hear my own mind.

I'm too consumed by the ill intentions pouring off of Klas. *He's up to something,* I think again. *This isn't going to go the way we think it should.*

"Any last words?" Kaspian asks, drawing me from my stupor.

"Yes," Klas replies, his sinister tones seeming to wrap

around my neck like a noose. "I look forward to dancing with your soul in the afterlife, Fallon."

I shudder, not liking the sound of that.

"After all, loyal mates die with their beloved," he adds, his silky tones drowning me in a sea of goose bumps. "Isn't that right, pet?"

Nox snorts. "*Beloved* is a bit of a stretch, isn't it?"

Klas ignores him, his focus entirely on me.

He definitely knows about the edict, I confirm to Issy. *But I think there's more to it. He's implying he'll own my soul for eternity.*

That's impossible.

Is it? I whisper back to her. *Daithi's spell was all black magic. It tied my soul to Klas, maybe even in death.*

Which means our plan won't work at all.

Because I'll follow Klas over to the other side the moment his head is severed from his neck.

My life may be tied to his existence, I continue, my pulse kicking into overdrive. *Issy, I think we misjudged this situation entirely. I—*

Breathe, she demands. *I'm not losing you to that monster again. Just give me a second...*

I don't have a second, I whisper back to her as Nolan knocks Klas's legs out from beneath him and positions the man over the block. *They're about to—*

Stall them, Issy demands.

I... I can't. My lips try to move but I'm rendered speechless by the sight before me. Unraveled by Klas on his knees. Terrified of the axe in Kaspian's hand. Suffocated by the lack of oxygen in the room.

Fallon! Issy snaps. *Pull it together.*

I try. I do. I just... I can barely focus on anything other than the glint of metal. The knowing look in Klas's gaze as he stares me down in anticipation. It's like he's woven a spell around my spirit, forcing one last act of submission out of me despite my desire to rebel.

Something isn't right. He's... he's done something...

Tied me up with a leash.

Bound me to his fate.

I can feel it wrapped around me, the sensation slithering like invisible snakes, hissing and biting at each of my urges to move. To scream. To cry!

Issy starts speaking again, her tone urgent, but I barely hear her. Everything is going dark. Except that metallic edge. The instrument that'll destroy both me and my forced mate.

I part my lips, a plea caught in my throat.

This isn't me. I obey no one. I choose my fate. I'm the master of my own destiny!

I writhe beneath the spell, my soul screaming at the injustice of being tied down.

"Klas, you are hereby excommunicated from the House of Gold and Garnet," Kaspian says, his arms lifting in the air. "And your sentence is death."

Words echo in my mind as I fight the enchantment anchoring me to this wicked soul. *I reject you! I reject this! I am not yours to take into the afterlife!*

Kaspian's arm begins to move.

Downward.

Sharply.

The angle perfect.

And everything seems to still around me.

My mind. My body. Issy's desperate screams. I'm no longer one of this plane, but of another. One I've only ever visited in my dreams.

Death.

A chill whirls along my spine, causing my lungs to freeze.

This is the source of my magic. My enchanted being. My home.

It's where I draw my power. How I connect to the souls of the dead, where I lure the spirits of the living.

I close my eyes and breathe, Klas's spell no longer holding me hostage.

I'm free.

But am I still alive? Is this where he intends to find me? To own me? To claim me for eternity?

No.

I refuse.

He has no right to my soul. Only death can truly claim me, yet all I feel here is empowered. Renewed. *Alive.*

I inhale deeply and open my eyes, unsure of when I closed them, and stare up into a pair of beautiful blue irises.

Not sinister and black like Klas's eyes. But blue and hypnotic. Kind. Adoring. *Mine.*

I frown, that last thought unbidden and unexpected.

Mine?

Where am I?

The death plane has disappeared to reveal the dungeon once more. And I'm surrounded by four men. All of whom I know. All of whom are staring down at me now with looks of wonder and confusion.

And distrust, I realize, my gaze finding Nolan's last. His multicolored irises resemble shadows in this room, his expression dark.

What happened? I nearly ask. But my throat feels dry. Too dry. Like I've been unconscious for hours.

I know I haven't. That's just a side effect of touching the death plane. It literally sucked the vitality from my body, leaving me corpse-like and barely breathing.

"Are you all right, lass?" Bane asks, his soft voice

pulling my attention toward him. "You're as white as a ghost."

I almost smile. But I can't seem to muster up the strength.

Instead, I close my eyes for another long moment.

But when I open them again, the scenery has changed. I'm back in my room. Lying in bed. Exhausted. And watching a fire burn brightly on the television screen.

I blink, confused and alarmed by the shift in time and space. "Wh...?" I try to say, only to cough from the sandpaper sensation lining my throat.

A straw appears then, one I immediately wrap my lips around as I meet Nox's beautiful gaze again. Only, he's not staring at me with compassion or concern this time. He's closed off and unreadable. A guard without emotion.

I take several swallows while I study him, again feeling that strange covetous urge. *Mine.*

But that doesn't make any sense.

Yes, I'm attracted to Nox. I would have to be blind not to notice his good looks, and even then, I'm certain his appeal would be obvious through his personality alone.

However, to call him mine? *Where is that notion coming from?* I stare at him while I drink, taking in his stern expression. He doesn't look mad so much as uncharacteristically serious.

Did something go wrong during the execution? I wonder, my focus shifting to the screen. *Is Klas really dead?*

The straw disappears from my mouth as I finish the glass of water, only for another to take its place. I sip from it without commenting, grateful for the hydration while I watch the flames dance ominously on the screen.

Kaspian is there. Nolan, too. But not Bane.

What happened? I think again.

I go through two more cups of water before I'm finally able to ask that aloud.

When Nox doesn't immediately answer, I glance at him. "Did I do something? With my powers, I mean." *Is that why he's acting so strange?* I visited the death plane, after all. That can't be a good sign.

Except I seem to have freed myself from Klas's grasp. And my soul did not, in fact, join his in the afterlife.

Unless this is a really strange version of hell.

"You died," Nox says flatly. "Or it seemed that way. Until you woke up."

"Oh." I bite my lip. "How long was I out?"

"Only a few minutes. But… you were pale and not breathing." He looks away, his expression hardening. "And then you came back…"

I stare at his profile. "And then…?" I prompt, sensing there's more going on here than a casual date with death's plane.

"And then…" He clears his throat, his gaze finding mine again. "And then fate showed her hand."

My brow furrows. "What?"

"You don't feel it?" he asks, not elaborating on his cryptic fate comment. "The pull?"

"The pull?" I repeat, shaking my head. "No, I…" *Wait…*

I slowly sit up, my body weakened from my soul's momentary departure.

Hold on…

I glance at the screen and then at Nox again. Then back to the screen as puzzle pieces start to fall into place.

Hypnotic blue eyes.
Adoring expressions.
Confusion.
Distrust.

Mine…

My eyes widen. "No…" *Except…* "Shit…" *The mating spell rebounded.* "You and I… we're *mates*?" I squeak out, looking at Nox. *Because of dark magic that had nowhere else to go… so it tied us together.*

Fuck.

Fuck.

Fuck!

"Oh, not just you and me, firefly," Nox drawls, his usual easy candor nonexistent beneath his sarcastic tone. "All four of us."

My eyelashes flutter. "Wait, *what*?"

"Nolan, Kaspian, Bane, and me." He enunciates each name clearly. "We're all your second-chance mates."

My jaw drops. *What?!* "That's impossible." Except it's not. *Because of that fucking spell…*

"It's not unheard of," Nox mutters. "But yeah, it's… not all that ideal either."

"Not ideal?" I repeat, huffing a laugh. "That's an understatement."

Because I just accidentally tied my soul to four men. *With black magic.*

Once they realize what's happened, I'm a dead woman.

So much for freedom, I think, defeated. Even if I wanted to escape, I couldn't.

Because now I'm shackled to four renowned mercenaries.

Running isn't an option and neither is hiding.

What the fuck am I going to do?

Part of me expects Issy to respond, but she doesn't.

Frowning, I try to reach out to her, only to hear nothing in response. Did something else happen when I visited the death plane, or is she in trouble?

I can sense her lingering there, but I can't quite reach her. So either she's unconscious, or something is interfering with our connection.

Maybe the fated bonds to my new mates, I think, groaning.

Seriously, why do you hate me? I want to demand of fate. *What did I do to you?*

Because this is insane. Improbable. Absolutely fucking complicated.

And the way Nox is still looking at me now says he agrees.

I'm guessing the others do as well.

So what happens when one of them tries to reject the mating bond and realizes this is all because of an illegal spell?

They'll blame me. Probably sentence me. And then kill me.

Awesome.

Just. Fucking. Awesome.

NOLAN

FALLON DOYLE IS MY MATE.

No, she's not just *my* mate. She's *our* mate.

I run my hand over my face and palm the back of my neck. *Fuck.*

At least she survived.

Of course, I didn't think *this* was how she would manage it.

Four mates.

All at once.

I would be impressed if it didn't mean I now have to share. That isn't my kink. I prefer having women all to myself, typically whilst tied to the bed and gagged as I test their tolerance for extreme pleasure.

Nox and Bane are never going to let me do that to Fallon, I think, eyeing the latter of the phantoms now as he walks toward me and Kaspian.

"She's awake," Bane says softly as he joins us near the bonfire. "From what I overheard, she doesn't remember much of what happened and she's just as surprised by fate's decision as we are."

"Are you really that shocked?" I ask him. "You and Nox have been obsessed with her from the beginning." Which I still think is because Fallon possesses death magic —something she drove home today by dying and coming back to life.

What even was that? I wonder for the thousandth time. The whole episode stunned the hell out of me. I expected her to fight, not die. Then she came back on a wave of magic that pierced my very soul.

And now we're tied to one another for eternity.

Unless we reject it.

"Am I shocked that all four of us just fate-bonded the same woman?" Bane's tone reveals nothing, as per usual. He rarely ever raises his voice or displays even a hint of annoyance. Actually, he may just be the most relaxed person I've ever met.

Which is what makes him deadly.

He has a penchant for knives and guns, his aim nearly as good as Kaspian's. Add Nox's toxins into the mix— toxins the phantom likes to apply to Bane's weapons—and Bane's a force to be reckoned with.

The fact that he's always calm just adds to his deadly potential.

"Yes, I'm shocked," Bane continues. "I think we all are."

"Let's talk about this in my quarters," Kaspian says quietly as the last of Klas's remains sizzle into ash. He already issued a few public comments regarding the execution, allowing him to leave the scene now without further discussion.

We're in the middle of the village, close to where Klas first attacked Reykjavik last year, making it the perfect place to burn his remains. But that means we have a bit of a walk back to his place.

It's good, though. I need the fresh air. However, it would be more enjoyable if I could spread my wings and fly.

Alas, I choose to walk with Bane and Kaspian.

The latter is wearing sunglasses to help him endure the few hours of sunlight this afternoon. The older the vampire, the more impacted he is by the sun. And Kaspian certainly isn't young.

He probably should have chosen to execute the bonfire at night—it would have been more impressive then, too—but with all the conflicting time zones in Gold and Garnet territories across the globe, a noon execution made the most sense.

And now it was done, leaving him with most of the afternoon and evening to handle this new problem.

Fallon.

Our fated mate.

Hmm.

Kaspian has always enjoyed sharing. Nox and Bane, too. So the three of them may be able to work out some sort of arrangement. But I'm not sure how I'll fit into that picture.

Can Fallon choose? I wonder, frowning. *No. That doesn't seem very likely.*

Unless she doesn't want any of us.

Why am I even thinking about this? The woman died and came back with four *fated-mate bonds. That's not normal.*

There's something else going on here. Something big.

While I'm thankful her soul didn't shatter, I'm not sure what to think of this new development. She's still harboring secrets, ones I suspect are a lot more important than she's let on.

I've read her file. There's nothing there. Just a few vague sentences about how Klas met her on a mission and mated her. That mission isn't even documented. It's cryptic as fuck, and despite putting some of our best trackers on it last year, there wasn't much more information dug up on the topic.

Klas himself had no family. Only friends. And most of those friends died last year after they helped him attack Gold and Garnet headquarters. Vesperus's mate went full-blown goddess, moved the moon, and wreaked havoc on the assholes who tried to take down our House leadership.

Klas was one of the few left alive to answer for his crimes.

The other was Kaspian's former assistant, but he didn't survive for long. Only Klas did. And now he's dead, leaving Fallon as the only one who knows anything about his and her origins.

Is it a coincidence that she mated all four of us after he died?

Is it witchcraft? Some spell? An enchantment?

Or is it real?

How can it possibly be real?

Multiple mates isn't unheard of, but it is rare. And to suddenly find herself fate-bonded to all four of us? That's one hell of a miracle.

But maybe she deserves that miracle, I think as we reach the palace and start heading up to Kaspian's rooms on the top level.

My lips curl down.

What the fuck is wrong with me? Maybe she deserves this miracle? Since when do I even think like that?

This has to be some sort of spell. She's a powerful witch. It's the only thing that makes sense.

Which means we need to reject the bond.

I'm about to say exactly that when we enter Kaspian's rooms, but for whatever reason, the words refuse to leave my mouth. They… they just sort of linger on my tongue. Taunting me. Infuriating me. *Fucking with me.*

"This has to be a spell," I manage to say. "Some sort of trick." *There.* So I didn't say *reject*, but I at least forced the explanation out of my stubborn mouth.

"Maybe," Kaspian says, heading straight for his liquor bar. "But it certainly feels real."

"Because it is." Bane's words are matter of fact, his certainty palpable. "I've felt connected to her from the first day we met. The fated-mate bonds snapping into place just makes sense. It's why I've been so drawn to her, but I couldn't fully connect to her because of Klas's interference. Now that he's dead, she's mine."

The way he explains it makes it sound so simple.

Except it's *not* simple at all.

"You've been drawn to her because she possesses death magic and you're a phantom," I tell him. "That's a natural draw. Kaspian's a vampire. That's also a natural draw. I'm an archangel. I've never been drawn to her, nor am I drawn to her now."

A complete lie.

I've also been inexplicably drawn to the female. Which is why I couldn't kill her last year. But fuck if I'm going to admit that right now.

Bane's dark eyes glitter knowingly, but he doesn't call me on my bullshit. Instead, he shrugs and says, "If you want to reject her, that's fine. I do not share that sentiment."

"You don't want to reject the bond?" Kaspian asks as he pours three drinks.

"No, I don't. And I doubt Nox will want to either. But it's not really up to us. It's up to Fallon. I'll respect whatever she desires." Bane takes a glass. "I'll also respect whatever decision the two of you make. I can only decide for myself, and I'm choosing to go with what feels right."

"None of this feels right," I mutter as Kaspian passes me one of the drinks. "She died and came back, only for the bonds to snap into place. That's not normal."

"No, it's not," Kaspian agrees, his focus falling to the amber liquid in his glass. "I can't accept this bond when I don't trust her. She's hiding something. And this... this all feels a bit too coincidental to me."

I nod. *Coincidental* is definitely the right term.

"If you push her too far, you risk her never trusting you in return," Bane warns.

Kaspian doesn't take his gaze off his drink. "It's a risk I'm willing to take."

Bane studies him intently. "Even if her secrets turn out to be irrelevant to our situation?"

"Yes." Kaspian's attention shifts to me. "We need to go back to the beginning and conduct a thorough search on her background. Our trackers were more focused on Klas than on Fallon the first time around. We need to make her the focus this time and start over."

Bane sighs, making his opinion on that plan known without words. But what the phantom fails to understand is that it doesn't matter what Fallon's secrets are. What matters here is our inability to trust our fated mate. Kaspian and I are on the same page there—neither of us is even sure this is real. And there's no way we can move forward with that kind of doubt hanging over our heads.

"I'll handle the investigation myself," I tell Kaspian.

I don't care if Fallon hates me for digging into her background. It's the price I'm willing to pay to ensure that Kaspian and the others are properly protected.

If she rejects me for it, then she rejects me.

I'll live with that pain.

But at least I'll know if it was all real or not.

"In the meantime, Bane, you and Nox should continue guarding Fallon as you've been doing. Maybe this new bond will help her open up more." Kaspian's tone tells me he doesn't believe this bond will change anything, and I agree with him on that assessment.

Fallon is strong and stubborn. Whatever she's hiding must hold significant value to her, which almost makes me feel bad about what I'm going to have to do.

However, it's a necessary evil. A task I was literally designed to carry out. Just like the potential need to kill her if I find out she's trying to harm anyone in Gold and Garnet, myself included.

I hope it doesn't come to that, for both her sake and mine.

My wings unfurl as I down the contents of my drink, my need to begin this journey itching at my feathers. There'll be no sleeping for me tonight, perhaps not for the foreseeable future. But it'll be worth it if I can prove Fallon's intentions are genuine.

"I'll start in Ireland," I tell Kaspian.

"I'll let Kieran know to expect your presence," he replies.

My lips curl. "If I do my job right, he won't even know I'm there." Sneaking through borders into other House territories has been a penchant of mine since the boundary lines were initially created. "I'll be in touch."

I set the glass down on the bar and head for the balcony.

"Thank you, Nolan," Kaspian murmurs at my back, causing me to pause and arch a brow.

That's new, I think, not looking at him. Rather than point it out, I reply, "Don't thank me until the job is done, Kas."

Then I open the doors and take off into the night.

But rather than head straight for the ocean, I veer toward Fallon's rooms and perch on her balcony railing.

Her doors and her curtains are closed, leaving me to stare at the dark fabric hiding my *mate* from my view.

I'll see you soon, little flame, I think at her. *Be good for Kas and the others while I'm gone...*

BANE

I sneak into Fallon's room in phantom form to find Nox lying on the couch, his gaze on the ceiling.

Drifting past him, I go searching for our mate, only for his soft words to hold me back. "She fell asleep."

The tiny lump beneath the covers of her bed confirms his statement, causing me to go corporeal beside the couch. "Did she eat anything?"

He shakes his head. "Not since breakfast."

"Hmm." That was hours ago. "She needs to eat." I head into her kitchen to prepare a few things that can be easily devoured when she wakes up.

Nox eventually joins me and eyes the deli meat with interest. Rather than wait for him to ask, I make him a sandwich similar to Fallon's and hand it to him before putting one together for myself.

I leave Fallon's on a plate and set it in the fridge, then join Nox at the table.

We eat in silence, our gazes flicking over to the bedroom every few seconds. I'm not sure if it's a result of a protective instinct or the desire to see Fallon move, but I can't seem to stop looking at her.

My mate.

My future.

My Fallon.

Kaspian and Nolan may not trust this development, but I do. It makes too much sense for me to deny it. "She was meant to be ours," I whisper.

The words were for me more than for Nox, but my best friend nods in immediate agreement. "I know."

"Kaspian and Nolan don't feel the same way."

Nox considers that for a moment. "Kaspian's old and set in his ways. He also just became King of Gold and Garnet. He probably sees this as a complication more than a gift, especially since it's Fallon. She won't kneel for him the way other women do, which means he'll actually have to work for her affection."

My lips curl at the prospect. "That'll be fun to watch."

"Unless he fucks it up," Nox points out. "Then we'll have to kick his ass, and I really don't want to deal with a pissed-off master vampire with a royalty complex."

"Or an archangel assassin with a penchant for killing first and asking questions later," I point out, fully aware of Nolan's abilities and reputation.

"Truth." Nox finishes the last bite of his sandwich and takes his plate to the sink before grabbing two bottles of water from Fallon's fridge. He hands me one as he returns, his focus immediately going to the beauty in the other room.

I follow his gaze. "I heard some of what she said when she woke up. She seemed as surprised as us about the fated bonds."

"Definitely surprised. And maybe a bit mortified, too."

I take a sip of the water as I contemplate that

statement. "Do you think she intends to reject fate?"

"Given what her last mate did to her, I wouldn't really blame her if she felt that way," Nox murmurs. "But I'm hoping she'll give us a chance to prove that we're not Klas."

"Me, too." But I'll understand if she can't. While she hasn't told us everything, I know she's been through a lot.

Alas, she seems hell-bent on handling her pain alone rather than trying to confide in anyone else. And something tells me not even fate will change Fallon's mind on that.

I finish my sandwich, and Nox takes my plate for me. We've been a team for so long that our actions are seamless. I usually cook and he cleans. Unless it involves a steak or burger on the grill, then Nox handles it. Not that we have a grill here.

While I like Iceland, there are definitely aspects of living in the United States that I miss. It was my favorite location in the old days, specifically the West Coast. But when the portal opened, we headed back to Scotland where the majority of our kind lived, mostly for safety reasons.

We kept our existence a secret until recently, our inability to be killed something we knew other supernaturals wouldn't like. We're not even sure if phantoms can die of old age or not; no one ever has.

Of course, we all took our own lives initially to become phantoms. So perhaps that's why we stop aging and never die again—we can only perish once.

Nox leaves me at the table to go check on Fallon, his shift into ghostly form guaranteeing he won't wake her with his footsteps. I watch from my seated position, noting the way his expression turns reverent as he reaches her side of the bed.

His fingers flex at his sides as though he's trying not to touch her—a reaction I understand. I've felt that way on countless occasions.

When she doesn't stir, he eventually returns. "I assume our orders are to stay here and guard her?" he guesses after turning corporeal again.

"Essentially, yeah. With the added request to make her open up." Kaspian is desperate to learn everything he can about Fallon, and while I understand his reasoning, I want to be respectful of her privacy, too.

"By pretending to be my friends, right?" Fallon says, her voice soft yet carrying through the room. "Isn't that what you said, Nox?" She rolls over to face us, her tone and expression carefully blank. "No, you mentioned dating. *Seducing* me into talking."

Nox frowns. "I believe I was trying to tell Kaspian to lighten up and stop treating you like a prisoner, firefly."

"You told him to *seduce* information out of me," she deadpans.

Nox pushes away from the table again and saunters toward her. "I was trying to tell him to stop treating you like a prisoner and to remember that you're a person with feelings."

"A person he should *seduce* into giving up my secrets."

"You seem to be quite fond of that term, firefly," he murmurs, his voice lowering an octave. "Shall I try to seduce you now?"

"Like you could," she snaps at him. "You're all just trying to interrogate me in different ways. Bane with his food and kindness. You with your... muscles and... and good looks. Kaspian with his dominance. Nolan... actually, Nolan never questions me. He'd rather shoot me than talk."

"Muscles and good looks," Nox repeats. "I like that."

"And of course that's all you heard."

"When my fated mate is complimenting my appearance? Yeah, that's all I'm going to hear." He goes to kneel by the bed, his elbows landing on the mattress as he carefully gives her space while still being near. It's a purposeful pose—one that shows her he's respecting her boundaries while also literally kneeling for her.

There are very few in this world that Nox will kneel for, making this a meaningful position.

I stand and grab Fallon's plate, as well as a bag of barbecue crisps—a flavor I've noticed is her favorite—and join them in the bedroom. "You need to eat or you'll extinguish your inner flame," I tell her, setting the food on the nightstand. "Consider this my way of *seducing* your senses."

"To make me talk," she mutters.

"I've not once tried to *make you talk*, Fallon. I know better than to force someone to open up when she's not ready to." And I've had several decades of practice when it comes to counseling others. While I don't view Fallon as a patient, I do understand her need for patience.

"So you're just going to ply me with food until I'm ready?" she asks incredulously.

"I'm going to cook for you for the rest of eternity because I want to," I correct her as I kneel beside Nox to be closer to eye level with Fallon. I'm too tall for it to work perfectly; even with her sitting up, I'll still be looking down at her, but it's better than standing over her. "You're our fated mate, sweet flame. And my love language is food."

"It's true," Nox says. "Bane loves to cook, but he only does it for those he likes or cares about. That's why he never offers Nolan any of our leftovers."

I snort. "Nolan wouldn't try to eat any of them even if I did offer."

Nox smirks. "Pretty sure his meal of choice is death."

"It probably is." Or something incredibly unsavory. I've actually never seen the archangel eat. But I've also never paid much attention to his personal choices.

Fallon studies both of us, her green eyes burning with a mixture of accusations and questions. Rather than voice any of them, she slowly sits up and takes the bag of crisps I set on the nightstand.

I do my best to school my expression, not wanting to dissuade her by grinning. But inside, I'm definitely smiling.

I anticipated her needs, and her satisfaction is a reward I'll savor forever.

She pops a crisp into her mouth, chews, and swallows. Then eats another before grabbing a water off her nightstand—one of three bottles that I assume Nox set there while she slept.

We remain silent as she eats, our elbows resting on the bed as though we are her indentured servants. Which I suppose we are. At least to an extent.

She enjoys a few bites of her sandwich, her eyes taking in our kneeling positions with interest.

After a few beats, she sets her plate down, her brow furrowing. "Why are you both doing that?"

"Doing what?" Nox asks, perfectly aware of what she means but infusing his words with flawless innocence.

"Kneeling on the floor," she says, her tone suspicious. "Is this a new way to try to make me talk? By pretending to submit or something?"

"We're not submitting," Nox murmurs. "We're just respecting your boundaries."

"By kneeling on the floor instead of sitting on the bed?" She sounds incredulous. "Since when do you not make yourself at home on my bed, Nox?"

"Since you decided to be mad at me for trying to talk sense into Kaspian," he replies.

"You were on my bed when I woke up earlier," she points out.

"Yes, before I realized you were upset with me." He lowers his chin to the mattress so he's looking up at her. "Now that I know you're angry and why, I'm waiting to be forgiven."

"Typically, one says *sorry* when he wants to be forgiven," she informs him.

He hums in understanding. "I see. Okay, then. I'm sorry Kaspian is an idiot who doesn't know how to talk to you."

She blinks.

Then she breaks out in a laugh that makes my heart soar. *I want to do that,* I think. *I want to make her laugh like that, too.*

But this time it's all Nox, and the way his blue eyes sparkle tells me he's quite pleased with himself for it.

Fallon shakes her head. "That's not what I meant."

"I'm sorry Kaspian needs lessons in how to communicate?" Nox offers, his eyebrows waggling, causing Fallon to giggle again.

"We're sorry our comments implied that we're only kind to you to make you talk," I interject, meaning every word. "That's not what either of us meant."

Although, technically, I didn't say much during the conversation. However, I was looped into it by proxy.

"He's right," Nox adds, some of his mirth dissipating. "I was just trying to tell Kaspian to start treating you like a person. Nolan is the one who mentioned *dating* as an interrogation tactic."

"But you did say *seduce*," she reminds him.

"I did," Nox agrees. "But when I seduce you, it won't be to make you talk; it'll be to make you scream."

Her full lips part at his blatant statement, her cheeks pinkening in response. "I, um, oh." She swallows. "Um." She clears her throat. "Okay."

I try not to smile at her response, but I can't quite hold back the crinkling of my eyes. "Do you know that you sometimes moan when you like a certain food?" I ask her softly.

She blinks, likely startled by the abrupt subject change. "What?"

"You release this gentle sound, one that's barely audible, but I hear it every time." I reach out to tuck one of her blonde strands behind her ear. "That's my only motivation when making you food—that sound." She didn't make it with her crisps this time, but she has before. That's how I knew they were her favorite.

"I…" She clears her throat again. "Thank you?"

This time my smile breaks free. "You're welcome."

Nox unleashes his grin on her as well as he straightens his spine, thus staring down at her again thanks to our size differences.

"This is… getting weird," she says slowly. "Stop kneeling."

"Only if you say you forgive us," Nox tells her.

She rolls her eyes. "Fine. I forgive you."

"Hmm, no. That's not very convincing, firefly. I'm going to need a little more heart."

Her emerald irises glitter as she glares up at Nox. "Excuse me?"

He doesn't reply, just holds her gaze with an expectant expression.

"You know what? If you really want my forgiveness, you'll need to take me out for a day. Somewhere off palace grounds." Her tone suggests a hint of sarcasm, but those green orbs flash with the desperation of her request.

She experienced a subtle taste of freedom today with her walk through the tunnels. And while it probably wasn't the most *freeing* experience, it likely rekindled her need to be allowed to leave these rooms.

"Okay," Nox says.

"Okay?" she repeats.

"Okay," he echoes. "I'll talk to Kaspian."

She snorts. "He'll just say no."

"He will," Nox concedes. "But Bane and I will make him say yes." He glances at me. "Won't we?"

"We will," I agree. Because now Fallon is more than just a guest in the palace—she's our mate. Which means we're entitled to make demands on her behalf.

Both of Fallon's blonde brows shoot upward. "You're really going to try to convince him?"

"Of course. It's what you want." Nox makes it sound simple because it is simple. "Leave it with me and Bane. We'll figure it out. And then we can call it a real date."

"But not one where we're trying to make you talk," I'm quick to add.

"Right. Just a date." Nox focuses on me. "Maybe to the lagoon?"

"The lagoon would be nice." I've only been once and quite enjoyed the thermal spa. "Followed by a picnic?"

Nox nods. "A perfect date."

"With both of you at the same time?" Fallon squeaks out, sounding alarmed. "Wait, does that mean you're both, uh, okay with this?" She gestures between the three of us, causing my lips to curl down.

"Okay with what, exactly?" I ask.

"The, um, multi-bond whatever?"

"Our fated links?" I translate, glancing at Nox before

meeting Fallon's gaze. "Why wouldn't we be okay with being mates?"

"Uh, because I magically linked to four of you?" she suggests.

Magically was a strange word choice, but I ignore it in favor of what she's really saying. "You think we're bothered by you having multiple fated-mate bonds?"

"Well, yeah," she says. "There are four of you and one of me."

"And?" I prompt, arching a brow. "If that's what fate chose, I'm not going to fight it."

"We're used to sharing," Nox adds. "Bane and I have always been a package deal."

I nod. "He's right. We've been together for almost a century. Not romantically, exactly. But as best friends." And we've often enjoyed having a woman between us.

Nox can be a bit more adventurous, though.

Hence his intimate relationship with Kaspian.

I haven't engaged in that bit as much, but I have watched them play a few times.

"Oh." The word rounds Fallon's kissable lips, her cheeks reddening again. "So… a date, then. Outside?"

"Outside," Nox confirms. "But probably not today. We'll need some time to convince Kaspian. Maybe we can watch a movie tonight instead? Your pick?"

Her gaze flicks from his mouth to his eyes before she glances at me and then looks away. "Uh, yeah, a movie sounds good. But, um, I need to shower again first. I still… I still feel like death."

You don't look like death, I think, taking in the blush that's creeping down her neck. *You look very much alive.*

But I know better than to tease her. Especially after everything she's gone through today. "Finish your sandwich, then you can shower," I tell her. "You need the food."

Nox grabs her plate and sets it in her lap, his actions an agreement with my words. "I'll go start you a bath," he murmurs, standing. "You can soak first, then shower."

"I don't need you to do…" She trails off as he disappears into the bathroom, clearly ignoring her weak protest.

"His love language is taking care of others," I inform her quietly. "You'll get used to it, just like you've become accustomed to my meals."

She shakes her head but says nothing and bites into her sandwich.

By the time she's finished, Nox has returned with a fluffy towel hanging over his arm. "I added the salts you like."

She stares at him, one eyebrow inching upward. "How do you know what salts I like?"

He points to himself. "Voyeur, remember?"

"So you have watched me in the bathroom," she accuses, narrowing her gaze.

He shrugs. "Not in the way you think."

"Uh-huh." She slides off the bed and grabs the towel from him.

"I usually avert my eyes," he tells her.

"Sure you do."

"But I won't be averting them anymore," he continues, ignoring her sarcastic reply. "Not now that I know you're mine."

Fallon freezes on her way to the bathroom, and I would give almost anything to see her expression, but she's facing the other way.

After a beat, she resumes walking, clearly out of one-liner comebacks for my brazen best friend.

When the door closes, I look at him. "How many times have you watched her bathe?"

"Not even once," he admits. "But I've found her passed out in there a few times, and one of those times was after a bath. So I noticed the salts."

That sounds more like Nox. He may joke about spying on her, but it's all in good fun because he enjoys teasing. My best friend has always valued consent, and I doubt he would be any different around Fallon.

"So how are we going to convince Kaspian to let us take her to the lagoon?" I ask as I push off of the floor.

"I'm not sure." Nox palms the back of his neck. "I suspect I'll need to do some sensual begging."

"That may not work in his current mood."

"Which is why I suggested a movie for tonight. It'll give me some time to figure out how to approach Kaspian."

I nod. "It'll give us some quiet time with Fallon, too. Maybe help her see what life could be like if she accepts us."

"Yes. Although, I think the last year has provided a pretty good introduction to what that would be like. Except for the whole confinement part."

"True," I agree. "But we'll make it work."

"We will." He smiles. "Because she's ours."

My mouth curves upward to match his expression. "Yes. Yes, she is."

Which means I no longer have to ignore the way she makes me feel.

Because it's no longer forbidden or inappropriate to be attracted to her.

Fate deemed us compatible. Now we just have to convince Fallon to accept fate's path.

Let us worship you, sweet flame. I promise you won't regret it.

FALLON

Issy? I haven't heard from my twin since Klas's execution, and it's making me uneasy. *Are you okay?*

I study my surroundings as I wait for her reply.

Bane and Nox slept on the couch after watching a trilogy with me last night. They both seemed reluctant to leave me alone, reminding me of the times they found me after one of my nightmares.

After waking up this morning, Bane made breakfast and coffee.

Nox cleaned up.

Then they said it was time to talk to Kaspian.

Now I'm staring at the living room, feeling a lot lonelier than I should.

Because I can't hear Issy, I tell myself. *That's why I feel this way. It has nothing to do with my supposed mates or them leaving me in my gilded cage.*

I drag my fingers through my tangled hair, aware that I haven't brushed it yet today. Not that my sleepy appearance seemed to impact Bane or Nox at all. If anything, they both looked at me with open adoration this morning.

Stupid spell, I think, irritated by how it's manipulating me and my "mates."

Bane and Nox don't actually like me. I know that. But experiencing their affection has me wishing these fated links were real.

The way they knelt for me last night… I swallow. *A girl could get used to that treatment really fast.*

Hmm? Issy's groggy voice echoes through my mind. *What treatment…?*

Issy? I sit up straighter on the couch. *Are you okay?*

She hums something unintelligible in response.

I frown. *You don't sound very good.*

She doesn't reply right away, but I can sense her stirring.

Issy. My stomach tightens. *Did something happen?*

Father… She trails off.

What did he do?

No reply.

Issy.

Give me… a minute, she grumbles at me, her snark coming through in those four words.

She hates when I worry about her, but it's kind of hard not to with everything going on.

I stand up and start pacing, my gaze flicking to the clock in the kitchen as I move.

One minute.

Two.

Three.

Five.

My frown deepens with every step. *Something is very wrong.*

Seven.

Ten.

Twelve.

As the clock strikes fifteen minutes, I say her name again.

Damn, she replies. *I bet myself you wouldn't last more than four minutes without talking to me, and you tripled that time expectation.*

I stop walking. *Issy.*

Fallon, she parrots back at me.

You're unbelievable.

I know.

I was worried! I snap at her.

I know, she repeats. *Now tell me about this treatment.*

What?

The treatment you were thinking about so loudly that you woke me up from my spell-induced nap.

Spell-induced nap? I repeat.

Nope. You share your story, then I'll share mine.

I roll my eyes. Issy is just as stubborn as I am, which means she won't bend until I explain myself first.

Fucking mating spell, I grumble to myself.

Fortunately, Issy doesn't hear that part. Mostly because I didn't leave our telepathic link wide open this time. Before, I was waiting for her to reply and essentially thinking aloud. Except I wasn't using my physical voice so much as my mental one, and talking openly to my sister.

Sometimes our connection is complicated.

But we have over two decades of experience perfecting it, which made my *treatment* slipup a rare instance.

I'm waiting, she singsongs.

Yeah, yeah, I mutter at her.

Then I tell her everything that happened, starting with Klas's execution, my visit to the death plane, my inability to carry out the resurrection spell, and my new bespelled bonds, and ending with the reactions from my new phantom "mates."

Huh.

Huh? I repeat. *That's all you've got?*

Well, yeah. It's interesting.

Interesting. I'm starting to feel like an echo chamber. *It's a fucking mess, Issy.*

How so?

If she were standing in front of me, I would have gaped at her. *Because it's not real?* I suggest. *Because it's that black magic spell from Daithi rebounding? I mean, when Klas died, the magic had to go somewhere, and it latched me to all the other souls in the room.*

Issy is silent for a moment. *Maybe.*

What do you mean by "maybe"? I ask, frowning. *What other explanation is there?*

Fate? she offers. *I mean, you've spent the last year with all these guys, and you've told me how attractive they are…*

I scoff at that. *Just because I think they're hot doesn't mean they're destined to be my mates, Issy. And to soul-bond to all four of them? There's no way I'm that lucky. Not to mention that fated bonds are between two souls, not several.*

Typically, she agrees. *But not always. There are multi-fated pairings. Maybe fate decided you'd more than earned your own.*

A humorless laugh escapes me. *Fate's a bitch who would never deal me this good a hand.*

Given all the other hands you've been dealt, it only seems fair for fate to give you a bunch of hot males as playing cards, she argues. *You deserve to be cherished and loved, Fallon. We all do.*

I sigh. *I'm not saying I don't deserve to be loved or cherished, but it seems highly unlikely that this is truly fate. It has to be the spell rebounding.*

There's one way to find out, she says. *You could try rejecting one of them.*

Yes, and when that doesn't work, what then? I press.

If it doesn't work, then you'll know it's the spell.

And so will they, I point out.

True. So maybe it's time you tell them about it and let them know what the Outcast Coven has been doing.

My lashes flutter. *What?*

They're involved now, Fallon. Whether they want to be or not, if the spell has bound you together, they're involved.

I sit back down on the couch, my lungs deflating along the way. *Shit.*

Yeah.

I chew my lip. *I... I don't think I'm ready to tell them yet. I'm not even sure how to begin to explain it, either.*

It doesn't have to be today, Issy points out. *But I would do it soon. If they find out about the spell before you tell them, it's going to paint you in a bad light.*

I know.

So I wouldn't sit on it too long, she stresses. *These guys have known you for a year. And I don't care what you say—those phantoms are smitten.*

You don't even know them, Issy.

I don't need to know them. I know how they make you feel and what they do for you. That's not guard behavior, Fallon. That's worship behavior. They've wanted you for months.

I snort. *All any of these guys want are my secrets.*

Maybe they want your secrets so they can allow themselves to want you, she suggests. *And don't bother arguing with me about it. We've done that on repeat for months. Just... give them a chance. They're not Klas.*

No, they're definitely not Klas, I agree softly, thinking back to how gentle Nox and Bane have been over the last year. Especially last night.

I close my eyes and picture them kneeling again, their eyes intent. My stomach flutters, the image one I'll likely never forget.

They knelt for me, I marvel, the words *for me* and not for Issy. *All because they think we're mates…*

My shoulders fall and I shake my head. I could go in circles for hours on this and not progress forward at all.

What I need is a distraction.

Spell-induced nap, I think, recalling Issy's earlier statement. *What did you mean about your spell-induced nap?* I ask her through our telepathic bond.

Issy blows a raspberry through my mind. *I knew you weren't going to let that go.*

Obviously not. What's going on?

It's… complicated.

I think I know a bit about complicated right now, Issy.

I think I prefer your version of complicated, Fallon, she mutters back. *I… I actually don't really know how to explain it. I think I'm still sleeping right now. Nothing about my room feels right.*

I frown. *What do you mean?*

Well, for starters, my books are blank. So that's not normal, right? And I swear my sheets are a different shade of blue. She sounds frustrated. *Either I'm losing my mind, or the patriarchs put me in some sort of fucked-up com—*

A piercing shriek echoes through my mind, cutting off Issy's words and distorting everything around me.

Issy! I shout, my hands covering my ears in a futile effort to silence the siren. *What the fuck is that?!*

If she replies, I can't hear her.

Fuck. I crumple onto the couch, my knees touching my chest as I curl into a tight ball. *Fuck. Fuck. Fuck!*

My world begins to swim, the air resembling ripples of water that shouldn't exist.

No. Not water. *Mist.*

I shake my head, trying to clear it, but that blaring alarm only rings louder.

My eyes squeeze closed, my body shivering from the torment of blistering sound waves pulsating through my mind.

What's happening? What is that fucking noise?

I feel dizzy.

Unnerved.

Lost.

My hands tremble, my nails digging into my skin, but that resounding screech remains.

Until suddenly it all stops.

And silence unlike any I've ever experienced settles around me in a sea of chilly mist. The icy water droplets kiss my skin, reminding me of death's plane.

Issy? I whisper.

Silence.

Swallowing, I try to peek at my surroundings, hoping with all my heart that I'm still in the living area of Kaspian's guest suite.

But I know before my lashes even begin to lift that I'm not.

I'm at death's door again.

Only this time, I'm not alone.

I'm surrounded by other souls.

The patriarchs, I realize, recognizing their hooded forms. All seven of them are here.

They vowed to drag my spirit into perpetual torment if I denied their edict, and it seems they've carried out that threat.

Because I'm not just lingering in the afterlife—I'm chained to an obsidian death stone.

And the positioning of the patriarchs tells me I'm about to be sentenced.

Fuck.

KASPIAN

A Few Minutes Earlier

These two want to take Fallon on a playdate? *Outside* of the palace? "Absolutely fucking not."

Nox sighs. "Come on, Kas. She's been locked up for over a year. We're asking for one afternoon. A single outing. What's the worst that can happen?"

"I don't know," I reply. "Which is precisely the problem."

"Either you trust us to guard her or you don't," he says, folding his arms. "What's it going to be, mate?"

I stare at him. "You can't be serious. If I didn't trust you to guard her, I wouldn't have given you this post."

"Then let me choose how to guard her," he counters. "Otherwise, I'm really just a fancy babysitter in charge of watching a witch inside an already well-protected estate. That's not very challenging, Your Majesty."

"Sarcasm aside, Nox has a point," Bane interjects. "We're both more than equipped to properly guard her off-site. Especially at somewhere like the lagoon, where we can

125

close it down for an afternoon and make it just the three of us."

"It's not like we're asking to go play in a cemetery," Nox adds. "We just want to take her for a swim."

"Then escort her up to Vesperus's pool on the roof," I suggest. "It's technically out of her room, which is what you're requesting, right?"

Nox gives me a look that says he's disappointed. "That's not going to work, Kas. We promised her a day out of the palace."

"It's not my problem that you made a promise you had no right to voice," I tell him. "Fallon is not allowed off the palace grounds. Period."

Bane places a hand on Nox's chest, pausing whatever the other man was about to say.

"All right," Bane starts. "You want her to talk. You want her secrets. But so far, none of us have been able to acquire her trust."

"I'm aware," I deadpan.

"Well, she's never going to confide in any of us while she's being held captive, and given that she just fate-bonded four of us, I think it's time we start exploring alternatives. All we're asking for is one afternoon. Give us extra guards if you need to. But let us at least try to appease Fallon. Maybe she'll surprise us."

"It's the *surprise* part that I'm worried about," I remind him.

"And I understand that, but none of us can know what she's going to do until she does it," he replies softly. "So why not give her a chance? Perhaps she'll give us one in return. We are fate-bonded to her now, after all."

"We've been trying the same approach for over a year without much success," Nox adds. "We need a new approach, Kas. Let us try this. *Trust* us to guard her. Please."

I run a hand over my face and shake my head. "It's not about my faith in the two of you. It's about the uncertainty of what she can do."

"But we know what she can do," Bane stresses. "We've all felt it. And she hasn't done anything like that since Nyx freed her from Klas's compulsory hold."

"Right. And now he's dead, so we know he can't somehow reignite that spell again." Nox lifts one muscular shoulder in a shrug. "I won't say she's harmless, but I will say that I don't believe she'll intentionally hurt anyone."

"I think even you can agree with Nox's assessment, Kaspian." Bane's dark eyes flash. "She may talk back to you, but she's never once expressed ill will. Hell, she even relayed messages from Slater last year when he accidentally portalled into her room instead of yours."

"Albeit grudgingly," Nox muses. "But she made sure you got the message."

"She's also been polite to all your staff, hasn't truly kicked up a fuss apart from her arguments with you, and has generally respected all your wishes despite disliking her circumstances." Bane's expression isn't quite imploring so much as calculating, yet his tone is simply informative.

"I'll repeat that it's time for an alternative approach," Nox says. "Let us try. Trust us to protect her *and* our House. You know we're loyal to you. You know what we're capable of. All we're asking for is a little faith."

My jaw clenches.

This has nothing to do with faith or trust in Bane and Nox. They proved themselves to me early on, earning themselves a place on my personal staff within weeks of us meeting one another. I quite literally trust them with my life.

How do I make them understand that it's Fallon I'm struggling to—

A scream interrupts my focus, the source of it sending an icy jolt through my veins. *Fallon.*

"What is it?" Nox asks, immediately alert.

A shiny metal blade falls into Bane's palm as he glances around, searching for the threat.

"*Fallon,*" I say, not bothering to elaborate. My vampiric senses are superior to the phantoms', allowing me to hear her shrieks coming from the other room.

Nox and Bane instantly disappear, adopting their ethereal forms. I assume they're taking a shortcut through the wall, which I can't do.

I run to my door instead, rush out into the hallway, and sprint to the quarters beside mine.

The phantoms are already corporeal inside, both of them kneeling by the couch, their hands on a now unconscious Fallon.

She's pale. Ghostly. *Dead.*

Just like after Klas's execution.

"What the fuck is going on?" I demand. "Why does this keep happening?"

Bane's dark eyes hold a note of fear as he looks up at me. "I don't know. This isn't like her other episodes."

"Are we supposed to revive her?" Nox asks, his hands hovering over her as indecision wars in his gaze.

"She's not…" Bane trails off, his head falling to her chest. "She's not dead."

Nox frowns. "But she isn't breathing."

"Her heart isn't beating either," I add, my vampiric ears missing the sound of her alluring pulse.

"I know." Bane's brow is furrowed as he glances at me and then at Nox. "But I can still feel my connection to her. Which means she can't be dead."

Nox considers that for a long moment before saying, "I sense her, too."

My jaw clenches as I realize that I also feel her inside me, her soul tied to mine despite us not finalizing our fated bonds.

Because I haven't rejected her.

Do I even want to reject her? That's a question that's been swirling in my mind since I found myself suddenly bound to her.

A few days ago, I would have said, *Yes, I definitely want to reject her.*

Yet now, I'm not so sure. Mostly because it feels wrong to utter those words aloud. Which is all part of the soul-mate magic—it makes it hard to reject a fated bond for a reason.

I just never thought this sort of thing would impact me.

I've lived a long time without a mate, and I was fine with that.

But Fallon… Fallon's changing everything.

And now she resembles death.

"What do we do?" Nox asks, taking the question right out of my mouth.

"We wait," Bane says. "Just like yesterday."

My teeth grind at that plan. I've always been a patient man, but this female tries my patience at every turn. Even in this. "We'll give her five minutes. Then we're resurrecting her."

"I don't think—"

"She was only out for five minutes yesterday," I interject, cutting off Bane's argument. "So we'll give her five minutes today. Then we're going to revive her."

I refuse to discuss alternatives.

My mate is dead.

That's unacceptable. Not when I haven't even had a

chance to decide how to proceed with this whole bond. Not when I don't know her secrets. Not when I don't know the real her.

If you're truly meant to be mine, then you're going to wake the fuck up and argue with me about it, I think at her, my arms folding across my chest. *So enjoy what's left of your nap, sweetheart. Because we're going to have a long conversation when you wake up.*

FALLON

"FALLON DOYLE, you have been found in breach of edict number three thousand four hundred and seven." The deep male voice belongs to Patrick O'Neely, but I can't see his features beneath his robe.

All seven patriarchs have formed an arch around me.

One of those patriarchs is my father. He reclaimed his position at the council table after securing my mating to Klas.

The other five are all male figureheads in their families, completing the Outcast Coven's leadership circle. Together their power is immense, dwarfing my abilities and those of everyone else in their path.

It doesn't matter that the females of our kind tend to be stronger than the males, because these men have all been blessed with dark arts, thus allowing them a unique brotherhood that surpasses all other magic within our coven.

The matriarchs may serve as figureheads of the Outcast Coven to the outside world, but they're entirely controlled by their male mates.

All because of the hooded men surrounding me now.

I shiver as their presence presses down upon my spirit, forcing me to bow in the death plane.

This is the source of my power. A place I should be able to draw great energy from. Yet I'm shackled to a death stone. I feel so cold. So *alone.*

"*Fallon Doyle will honor the Outcast Coven by adhering to our ancient pledge—loyal mates die with their beloved. Or those mates will be punished with fates worse than death.*" The words are a chant, spoken by all patriarchs at once and creating an eerie reverberation of sound around me.

I swallow, my soul shuddering from the power weighing down upon me. It makes me bow lower, bringing my forehead to the icy rock and driving the sting of death into my spirit.

"You have failed your duty as a mate, Fallon Doyle," Patrick O'Neely continues. "You will be punished."

"You will be punished," the other six patriarchs echo.

"Nikolas O'Neely wanders the afterlife alone, his soul lost as a result of your severed connection. We will pair you once more, draw his spirit to yours, and allow him to administer your punishment for eternity," Patriarch O'Neely says.

My veins ice over, my nonexistent heart seeming to freeze in my chest.

I'm not corporeal here. Not really. But I *feel* corporeal. It's such a bizarre sensation, one that fucks with my mental state.

Am I alive or dead?

I feel alive.

I feel the death stone. I feel the chilly vibrations in the air. I feel the power that thrives here. I feel my pulse racing in an attempt to heat my frigid form. I feel my own breath.

How is that possible? Is it part of my pending damnation? I wonder, my fingers curling into my palms. *I feel that, too—the bite of my nails. Is this normal?*

The patriarchs begin to chant, their words ones of an ancient tongue.

Issy? I whisper, trying to connect to my sister. *Are you there?* She would be able to tell me what's happening, what spell they're calling to them now.

But she's silent.

Severed from my soul.

Tears threaten my eyes, not out of despair, but out of something much stronger. Much angrier. Much more *powerful*.

I'm so fucking tired of being a pawn.

So fucking tired of the way the coven treats me and my sister.

So fucking tired of all this bullshit.

Why is my spirit owed to Klas? I mated him in the real world, fulfilling my familial obligation to protect my sister. It wasn't my fault that Klas went off the rails and tried to take down a House King. Yet I'm the one being perpetually punished for his actions.

Trapped in a gilded tower.

Interrogated for over a year.

Commanded to die alongside him.

Subjected to walk with him in the afterlife.

No. I refuse. I'm done playing nice.

I need to find a way out of here, to fight back, to save Issy. To *run*.

None of this has gone to plan. We were going to fake my death so everyone assumed I left the world to be with Klas, just as I was ordered to do.

And then I was going to help Issy flee. To where, I didn't know. It was a quickly hatched plan that blew up in my face during the execution.

When I mated four new males as a result of a spell...

I frown at the thought.

I... I can still *feel* them—my new mates.

Kaspian. Bane. Nox. Nolan.

Does that mean I'm still alive?

The chanting continues to whirl around me, the patriarchs weaving their spell and drowning me in death magic. It prickles and burns, the sensation reminding me of ice cubes dancing along my skin. But rather than leave a cold kiss behind, the touch feels... *wet.* As though the ice is melting upon contact.

Which has me wondering if I'm truly ethereal here.

How am I melting their magic spell? Is this normal?

If the patriarchs are concerned, they don't show it. Their voices strengthen, their repetitive words coming faster and creating a whirlpool of smoky mist that dances ominously around me.

Except it dissipates as it touches my skin.

Melting. Draining. *Disappearing.*

Only to swirl again.

Harsher now.

Colder.

But I seem to burn hotter in response, my soul rejecting their magic.

What is happening?

Hot air billows in my lungs, spreading more of that delicious warmth to my veins and chasing away the chill of the death plane. Dispelling the enchantment. *Anchoring* me in a plane that shouldn't exist.

Renewed conflict wars around me as the patriarchs' chanting grows harsher, louder, more prominent, all while my spirit fights back.

The death stone rumbles beneath me, the frigid atmosphere pulsing in response to my burning form.

A few of the hoods lift to reveal several sets of red eyes. *Souls of the patriarchs*, I marvel, my throat suddenly thick. Only for another breath to rush out of me.

Pushing. Seering. *Demanding* that I inhale.

Then exhale.

Then inhale again.

My bones start to rattle, my form far more existent in this plane than should be possible. But I suddenly feel very much alive. Vibrant. *Renewed.*

I wonder... I push up against the shackles, their existence one I can feel more than see, and I sense them stretching beneath my motions. *Just a little more...*

Glass shatters around me, the sound startling.

No. Not glass.

Ice.

From the binds.

The death stone crumbles into dust beneath me, then morphs into a strange silvery liquid. I stare down at it in confusion, the glittering substance oddly alluring.

Then it begins to seep into the rocks near my feet, providing me with another burst of vitality.

Another inhale.

Another exhale.

A throbbing pulse.

I close my eyes, reveling in the contentment that sensation brings me. It reminds me of a summer afternoon with the sun beating down on my exposed skin.

A sigh escapes me.

This is peaceful.

This is life.

"Fallon." The deep voice startles me, my limbs immediately freezing.

The patriarchs are trying—

"Fallon," the male repeats.

Solo. One man. Not a series of voices.

My lips curl down.

Patriarch O'Neely?

No. That voice was too... soothing... to be—

"Come on, little flame," the man whispers. "Open your eyes for us."

The brush of knuckles against my cheek accompanies the soft words, the touch chasing away the remnants of the death plane.

I'm warm here.

Safe.

Alive.

But how...?

"Wake up, Miss Doyle," an accented voice demands. "Now."

My brow furrows, my instinct to rebel against that stern tone kicking my heart into overdrive. *Maybe I don't want to wake—*

"Please, firefly," a third male murmurs. "I miss those beautiful green irises of yours."

My defiance melts away, my heart skipping a little at those words.

"Maybe we need something stronger to pull her out of it," the stern one says.

"Or maybe you need to work on your bedside manner," that third voice replies. "Seriously, I don't know how or why you forget all your suave sensibilities when Fallon enters the room, but how about you let me and Bane handle this?"

The stern one grunts.

And the caress of knuckles across my cheek prickles against my senses once more.

All the tension seems to melt from my body, the

residual kiss of death dissipating along with it and leaving me feeling more comfortable than I have in a long time.

If this is the afterlife, I'll take it, I decide. *Or maybe this is a dream.*

Regardless, I'm going to enjoy it.

Because whatever this is won't last long. The patriarchs will call me back for my punishment any second now and—

Fallon! Issy screams into my mind, causing my eyes to fly open.

"Issy," I breathe, sitting upright and nearly colliding with one of the men seated around me. *No, not seated. Kneeling.*

I shake my head, the semantics not mattering.

Issy? I call to her. *What's happening?*

Hide... close... don't let... Her words are garbled, each one coming out in a screech of sound that makes me wince.

"Fallon?" one of the males asks.

"Shh," I hush him, needing to focus. *What's going on, Issy?*

Taking... over... I... I'm sorry... Her words are a breath in my mind, her agony piercing my spirit.

"The patriarchs," I say to myself, lost in a cloud of confusion. "What are you doing to Issy?"

I look around the room, searching for answers, my heart racing so loudly that I can hear it thudding in my ears. A perpetual death march. A ticking time bomb.

The sound of a clock counting down...

I blink, startled.

Where am I? What happened to the death plane?

I'm not sure if I'm speaking aloud or in my mind. I'm not sure of anything at all. But I can *feel* Issy's pain, her mental cries bringing tears to my eyes.

"*Issy…*"

I clutch my chest, her pain piercing my very soul and sending me to my knees.

Because somehow I'm on the floor.

There are hands on me. Hands I don't know. Hands that don't belong to me.

Mates, some part of me recognizes.

But that term sends a shock through me.

It's Klas trying to drag me to the grave… to own me… destroy my soul… torture me for eternity.

"Fallon!" a male snaps, the tone laced with impatience and igniting a scream from my throat.

I don't want to talk to *him*, the one who constantly questions me.

Fuck, I'm confused. Lost. Whirling in a sea of present and past, all while Issy shrieks in my head.

Only to go eerily quiet.

Too quiet.

As though her voice has been snuffed out… *by magic.*

What are they doing to you? I demand.

Punishing her for your sins, Issy replies, her voice dull in my head and very unlike her.

It reminds me of when she issued the edict on the patriarchs' behalf. It's emotionless. And not her at all.

"*Stop,*" I beg. "Stop hurting her!"

You betrayed us all, Fallon Doyle. That cannot go unpunished.

I did nothing wrong, I tell them, trying desperately to focus on my mental voice and not my physical one. *It's not my fault the spell rebounded and tied me to four new mates!*

Silence meets my proclamation, so I try again, worried that I spoke the words aloud and not via my link to Issy.

It's all such a mess, a maze of perpetual confusion.

No one and nothing should be able to touch this

mental link. It's sacred, existing between me and my twin alone.

"What are they doing to you, Issy?" I whisper, tears running down my face. "How are they doing this?"

I feel broken.

Betrayed.

Breached.

This shouldn't be happening. Issy shouldn't be hurting on my behalf. I'm supposed to protect her. Save her. *Free* her.

To whom have you mated, Fallon Doyle? Issy asks in that deadpan voice.

You already know, I say back to her. *You...* I frown. *You're not you.*

Who? she demands, her voice uncharacteristically loud.

I cover my face with my hands, the names spilling through my mind on impulse. *Bane. Nox. Nolan. Kaspian.*

King Kaspian? Issy asks.

Only it's not Issy.

I know it's not Issy.

And yet, I feel compelled to reply, *Yes.*

"Please stop hurting her." My fingers go into my hair, tugging at the strands. "*Please.*"

There are voices murmuring around me, all males, their concern palpable. But I ignore them in favor of the link inside my mind.

I'm waiting for a reply. For her to speak. For *anything*.

It feels as though an eternity passes, my face buried in my knees while I tremble almost violently. Issy's name is a repetitive prayer in my mouth.

I need her to be okay.

I need the patriarchs to leave her alone.

"I need to free her," I say to myself. "Issy..."

How did it come to this? With me a continent away

while she suffers for my supposed sins? It's not fair. It's not—

The council will be in touch, she says suddenly. *Remember your loyalty, Fallon Doyle. Behave and you may be rewarded.*

A quake works its way through me in response, my instinct to sob nearly suffocating every other urge I possess.

My world feels out of balance.

Tilted.

Broken.

A hand grips my nape, squeezing it. "Who's Issy?"

"Issy?" I repeat, confused by the touch accompanied by that deep male voice.

"Yes. Tell us who Issy is," he demands, his accent familiar. His touch is less known, though. However, it's not unwelcome. It's… it's actually quite warm. Anchoring. *Tender.*

"Come on, sweetheart," he murmurs. "Tell us who Issy is."

I swallow, my head starting to shift back and forth in the negative. Something about the request isn't right. "I… I can't say." I'm not supposed to talk about Issy. I don't want to reveal that she's alive. "I have to protect her."

"Why?" he presses, his grasp tightening a little on my nape.

It should feel threatening, but it doesn't. If anything, it soothes me. Makes me feel safe. *Protected.*

"Why do you need to protect Issy, love?" he asks, his English accent caressing the endearment. "Who is she?"

"My…" I blink a little, my vision out of focus. Everything seems so much lighter here. So unexpected. So *lively.*

"Your…?" he prompts softly, his thumb brushing the column of my throat.

My brow crinkles a little bit, my confusion beginning to subside as reality pierces through the fog of my mind.

I'm no longer in the death plane.

I'm... I'm in Gold and Garnet territory.

Lying in... I blink, then squint up into a pair of devastatingly dark eyes. *I'm lying in Kaspian's lap.*

His strong legs cradle my backside, one muscular arm wrapped around my shoulders.

We're on the floor.

And there are two other men staring down at me, too.

Nox and Bane.

They're seated beside Kaspian, all three of them bracing their backs against the couch.

I frown, unsure of how I ended up here. The coffee table has been moved, as have some of the other pieces of furniture, leaving the four of us in the center of the living area with only the sofa.

"Who's Issy?" Kaspian asks again, his gaze burning into mine as I finally refocus on his face.

I stare up at him. "What?"

"Tell us who Issy is," he repeats.

I shake my head, my mind clearing more and more with each passing second. *Issy. Patriarch. Words spoken aloud...*

Fuck.

How much did I say? I wonder. *How much did I reveal?*

I can't remember what I mentally voiced versus physically voiced.

But given the expressions of the three men studying me intently now, I'm guessing I said a lot. Including revealing my sister's name.

They won't know who she is, though, I realize. *They're not from the syndicate world.*

So technically, it can't hurt to admit who she is, right?

Except my Gold and Garnet record states my family is dead. And I haven't refuted that fact.

My lips twist to the side. *Maybe I can say she's dead?* That's what the majority of the syndicate believes already anyway, so it can't hurt.

I'll… I'll say it's a memory.

A bad dream.

A nightmare.

The phantoms are familiar with those. This incident will be no different.

"She's…" I clear my throat, the scratchy quality of my voice suggesting I did a lot more than speak some words out loud—I obviously screamed at some points, too. "Issy… she's my sister."

KASPIAN

"Sister?" I repeat.

"My twin," Fallon clarifies. "Yes."

"What's happening to your twin?" I ask. "How can we help her?"

Fallon's blonde eyelashes flutter as she blinks, surprise seeming to color her features. "Help her?"

"Yes, sweetheart. Tell us who has her so we can help you free her." I'm not quite sure what happened or how, but Fallon's pain was visceral as she spoke about her sister.

She kept saying her name and begging the patriarchs to stop whatever they were doing.

"I need to free her."

"I have to protect her."

Nox and Bane were both at a loss when Fallon started sobbing, their stricken expressions matching her own.

That's when I took charge and pulled her into my lap. She needed someone to ground her, to keep her somewhat lucid and bring her back.

Just like we did when we made her breathe again.

"I…" Fallon trails off, the surprise slowly clearing from her expression. "It was a nightmare. My twin is dead."

I frown at her. "A nightmare?"

She nods, the movement a little too jerky to be believed. "Sometimes I have episodes during the day. I guess I just had one about an old memory."

"Of some sort of *patriarch* hurting your sister?" I deadpan, not buying her lie for a second.

Her cheeks went a little white when I uttered that term —*patriarch*—confirming it's an important one to note.

"Um, yes. Long ago. Before I met Klas."

I narrow my gaze. "You don't actually expect me to believe this bullshit, right?" It's probably the bluntest statement I've ever made to her. But I'm really fucking tired of this game. "Why don't you try giving me the truth now, Fallon? No more lies."

"I'm not lying," she snaps, her curvy form starting to squirm in my lap.

Any other time, I might have enjoyed those movements.

But right now all I want to do is flip her over and smack her disobedient ass.

"You're absolutely lying," I tell her. "That wasn't a fucking nightmare. You looked like death when we came in and had to force you to breathe. Then you screamed and started begging the *patriarchs* to stop hurting your sister."

Fallon flinches with that term again. *Definitely important.*

"He's right," Bane says, his voice much softer than mine. "That wasn't a nightmare, Fallon."

"You were ice cold until we warmed you up," Nox adds.

Fallon scowls and tries to wiggle her way off my legs. I consider pinning her down but think better of it and let her go.

She stumbles to her feet, her stance uneasy, which causes Bane and Nox to immediately jump up with her.

I'm not as keen on coddling her, so I join them all slowly and watch as Fallon begins to pace.

She's obviously trying to think up a new lie, which really fucking pisses me off, but I remain silent and wait for her next attempt.

"I… I went to the death plane," she finally says, her shoulders going rigid. "It's where I draw most of my power from, so I'm familiar with it. But I've never actually visited like that before. At least, not until yesterday… after, well, after the execution."

I lean against the wall, my arms folding across my chest. "Okay." As far as stories go, this one is definitely creative. Maybe it's even true. But it doesn't tell me anything about her sister or the patriarch.

"It's not a corporeal plane, but one linked to the afterlife. So it's my soul that goes, which I guess makes my body cold in the process?"

That's another detail that makes this story somewhat plausible. And it does make sense with her death magic abilities. *But…* "I've never heard of a death plane before." I glance at the phantoms. "Has either of you?"

They both shake their heads.

"Our crossover into being phantoms is unique, to say the least," Bane murmurs. "It's all tied to rituals in Scotland, not a death plane."

"It's not common, nor is it a source of magic that many people can access. I mean, most witches don't even know it exists. Hell, not even many death fae know about it. But it's tied to my family's rites and our specific link with death magic."

That also sounds rather truthful. However, I'm not sure

where she's going with this. "So you visited the death plane yesterday and again today. Why?"

"I don't really know," she says slowly. "Yesterday seemed to be triggered by Klas's death. And today… I just sort of returned for unknown reasons."

I narrow my gaze as her pulse kicks up a notch. *A lie,* I realize. Which suggests that some of what she's said about the death plane may actually be true, but the rest of it is a fabrication—particularly, her explanation of why she visited the death plane today.

"And I saw my sister there," she rushes on to say, her heartbeat singing along at a high-pitch tune that sounds like *lie, lie, lie* to my senses. "Which must have spiraled me into the nightmare when you brought me back." She shrugs as if to say that's it.

My jaw ticks. *Why does this female have to be so fucking infuriating?*

Only minutes ago, I was willing to move heaven and hell to help her sister, all because Fallon's cries resembled deadly arrows to my heart.

And now, all I want to do is throttle the woman in front of me.

If there's one thing I hate in life, it's a liar. Fallon Doyle hasn't exactly lied to me until today. She's omitted a few truths or outright refused to tell me things. But this? This story? It's a blatant fucking lie. And I don't appreciate it. Not after everything I've offered her over the last year.

Shelter.

Food.

Safety.

Fallon's deadly spell last year took down an entire city. While my House knows the truth about that day, there are many constituents who remain uneasy about Fallon's gifts. Which is why I assigned Bane and Nox to guard her. I wanted to ensure her safety in case anyone decided to come after her in some misguided attempt at retribution.

It was never about protecting my House from her, but protecting her from those who may feel wronged by her.

And she thanks me by lying?

Unacceptable.

"I'm going to give you one more chance to tell me the truth, Miss Doyle," I say as I push off the wall and stalk toward her. "I recommend you take that chance seriously."

"Kaspian." Bane tries to slide into my path, but I quickly maneuver around him. Being a master vampire comes with many perks, including increased strength and speed.

Fallon's green eyes widen as I corner her, her feet backpedaling quickly toward the sliding doors of her balcony. They're closed, which stops her from fleeing as her back meets the glass.

I wrap my palm around her throat, my opposite hand going to her hip. "Let's start from the beginning. Where's your sister?"

Her jaw visibly clenches, her emerald irises swirling with barely restrained flames. "Why do you care?"

"Because I want the truth," I growl at her.

"Why?" she demands. "Why do you feel entitled to my secrets, Kaspian? Because you fear my powers? You're worried I may use them to hurt your people? And you assume knowing more about my past, about my sister, will somehow put those fears to rest?"

"I don't fear you, Fallon," I say through my teeth. "But yes, your powers are too intense and overwhelming to be easily accepted. And knowing you're hiding things from me makes it that much harder to trust you with your abilities."

"So you're worried I may combust and put the city to sleep again," she deadpans. "And because *you* are worried,

I have to prove myself to you by giving up my secrets. Even ones that bear no consequence on our situation."

"You just visited a death plane that I know nothing about and essentially died in the process. I would argue that bears relevance to our current predicament," I point out, my hand tightening around her throat. "So stop fucking playing with me and be blunt for once."

"Blunt," she repeats, a humorless laugh following. "Fine. My sister is dead. It's a terrible story that I don't feel like reliving right now. The end."

My eyes narrow. "More lies." And this time I can't just hear it in her pulse; I can feel it against my damn thumb.

"How would you even know?" she demands. "You don't know my truths. So don't tell me what's a lie and what's not."

"I don't need to know your truths to know when you're lying, Fallon. Your pulse tells me everything I need to know."

Her nostrils flare. "Except my secrets."

"Except those," I agree, furious with her.

"They're not yours to know," she says through gritted teeth. "I don't care how entitled you feel toward me and my life; that doesn't mean *I* have to share a damn thing with you. I choose for myself. I decide what I share and what I don't share. And there's not a damn thing you can do about it."

I glare down at her. "Is that how you really feel? That all of this is about *entitlement*?"

"I haven't heard any other reason for why you feel so compelled to know every detail about my life. So yeah. It feels like entitlement to me."

"I'm the Gold and Garnet King. It's my job to protect everyone in this House. Which means knowing every detail of every potential threat so that I can make difficult decisions that safeguard my people. Is that *entitled*, Fallon?"

Her jaw clenches again, those beautiful eyes burning with renewed flames. "My history isn't a threat."

"The flicker in your pulse just now says otherwise," I bite back, causing her eyes to widen. "So that's three times now in the span of thirty minutes that you've lied to me, Miss Doyle. That's unacceptable."

"What's unacceptable is the way you're manhandling me right now, *Mister Antonik*."

"King Kaspian," I correct her. "That's how you should address me at all times, Miss Doyle, but I've been lenient with you. Far too lenient, actually. To the point that I've ensured your comfort at every turn, even when you haven't earned it. That changes now."

Her eyes widen a fraction. "Oh? Is now when you throw me in Klas's old cell? All because you think I'm lying about my sister?"

"I *know* you're lying about your sister, and until I find out why, I don't have much choice. You've disrespected me and my hospitality time and again. Maybe a night in solitary will make you realize how good you've had it here."

"Kaspian," Nox interjects.

But I ignore him.

I'm too pissed off to debate this decision.

I *hate* lying. He knows that. Bane does as well. They both witnessed firsthand how I deal with liars last year, too. Fallon should be thankful that a night in solitary is all I'm threatening her with.

"Wow. Fate really thought you and I would be well matched?" Fallon huffs a humorless laugh. "If I needed proof, I have it now."

"Proof of what?" I demand, ignoring her comment

149

about *fate*. Mostly because it hit me a bit in the chest, the reminder of what we are to each other leaving me uneasy.

Mates.

And I just threatened my mate with solitary.

Because she doesn't find me worthy of the truth.

A growl works its way into my throat, but I don't release it. Instead, I tighten my hold on Fallon, more furious with her than ever before.

We were so close to finally being open with each other, but she chose lies instead of confiding in me.

She's never going to trust me. She's never going to understand how much I value trust—both ways—in a relationship, either.

Because she's impossible.

However, she's right about one thing—fate definitely has this wrong.

We are *not* meant to be mates.

"It doesn't matter," she mutters. "That comment was for me, not for you."

My brow furrows as I try to recall what we were talking about.

Proof, I remember. *Something about proof and fate.*

Whatever. I don't need to know what she meant. Because she doesn't want me to know. She doesn't want me at all. And fuck if I'm going to stand around and beg her to accept me.

"You know what, Fallon?" I say, my grip on her throat weakening. "You can keep your secrets. I'm done trying to figure this out. Done trying to help you. Done protecting you."

Her pupils dilate as she looks at me, her gaze searching.

But she doesn't say anything.

Not that I expect her to. She's made it very clear that no matter what I do or say, she's not going to trust me.

And as a result, I will never trust her.

Which is why I have no choice here.

"I can't remain fate-bonded to someone who so obviously misunderstands me and my motives. Mating is about mutual respect and trust, neither of which exists between us. And you've made it clear those two things are impossible for us to achieve."

Fallon's eyes widen. "Kaspian, wait——"

"Fallon Doyle, I re——"

One minute, I'm uttering one of the hardest sentences I've ever had to say aloud in my very long life.

And in the next instant, I'm silenced by Fallon's plump lips.

I blink several times, startled by her sudden nearness and the way she's clinging to my shoulders.

What the fuck just happened?

Her mouth isn't moving against mine. It's just sort of there, silencing me midsentence and preventing me from finishing the phrase that would sever my ties to her.

When I try to move back, she tightens her grip and digs her nails into my shirt.

I squeeze her throat in response, reminding her that I still have her pressed up against the glass. Trying to claw me isn't going to win her any points here. I have over a foot of height on her, and a hell of a lot of muscle.

Fuck, I'm surprised she could even reach my mouth when her head barely reaches my chin. She must be standing on her toes, hence the need to grip my shoulders for bal——

Her lips move, seizing my attention. It's a subtle twitch, one that feels mysteriously like an invitation.

She's fucking with me. Because there's no way she actually wants me to kiss her.

But after everything we just said to each other? I'm

inclined to do just that and teach her a lesson she'll never forget.

I slide my palm from her throat to the back of her neck and use my thumb along her jaw to angle her head right where I want it.

She shivers in response, her little talon-like nails sinking even deeper into my dress shirt.

I smile against her mouth, teasing her, playing with the lingering moment, making her wait.

And just when I sense her impatience winning her over, I strike.

Fallon wanted to taunt me into a kiss? Then I'll fucking kiss her. More than that, I'll *own* her.

She gasps as my tongue parts her lips, her shock encouraging me to do more, to master her, to make her sorry for ever trying to toy with me.

I tighten my grip on her nape and press myself against her, firmly trapping her between me and the glass behind her. Then I deepen our kiss, my tongue thoroughly exploring her own, laving her with experience and showering her with my dominant preferences.

She responds in kind, her own tongue matching mine stroke for stroke as her arms wind around my neck.

Fuck, she tastes good. Like a decadent wine. Aged to perfection. And set aside just for me.

Her ample breasts are pillowed against my chest, reminding me of her delicious curves. My hand aches against her hip, my desire to explore her causing my fingers to flex involuntarily.

But this isn't meant to be enjoyed. It's supposed to be a lesson. A warning. A... a *something*.

With each brush of her tongue, I fall a little harder, my mind clouding with a hunger unlike any other.

Her blood sings to me in her veins, seducing my inner beast.

I want to bite her. Claim her. *Taste* her.

Who even is this passionate woman? I marvel, our kiss turning violent in nature. *This can't be Fallon. It's impossible. She's too... too irresistible.*

Her teeth skim my tongue, the hint of danger driving me onward as I take her mouth hostage, my tongue mastering every inch of her and ensuring she can feel my unspoken claim.

Mine.

My mate.

My Fallon.

Except...

No. No "except." Only this.

My mind whirls with thoughts, my hunger escalating by the second. I haven't tasted a woman in what feels like years, my preferences of late having been more masculine than feminine.

But Fallon... she reminds me of everything I've been missing. That delicate female touch. The soft skin. *These addictive curves...*

I want to rip off her jeans and sweater and slide into her alluring heat. I can smell her, that beautiful perfume that's all aroused woman.

How will she taste? I wonder. *Sweet? Spicy? A mixture of both?*

I lick her bottom lip, my fangs itching to sink into the plump texture to steal a preview of what's to come.

But then her tongue distracts me once more, followed by a soft moan that has my cock pulsating with need.

Fuck, this is intense, I think, lost to Fallon and the sweet little sounds leaving her mouth. *How could I possibly reject...?*

I frown, the thought slamming through my mind and

causing me to rip my mouth away from the enchantress in my arms.

What the fuck?

I was about to reject her, but then… then she kissed me. Like a seductress.

Only it was more than that.

Because I kissed her back.

Thoroughly.

It was meant to be a lesson. A wicked way of saying goodbye once and for all. *A punishment.*

And looking at her puffy lips, it seems I've accomplished that. Except now… now I can't seem to speak the words I need to say.

She's bewitched me.

Her presence. Her beauty. Her fucking feisty spirit.

I release her and take several steps back, my mind lost in a fog that's all Fallon.

I need a break. Some space. *Something.*

With a shake of my head, I turn around and find two phantoms staring at me with interest.

Well, one looks interested. The other appears deeply aroused, probably because he's been my preferred bed partner of late.

I clear my throat, unsure of what I want to say. None of this went according to plan. Actually, it all went very opposite to the plan.

And now I have no idea how to proceed.

I threatened to put her in solitary, I recall, a strange sort of pang radiating around my heart.

I lost my temper, something that rarely happens. But Fallon seems to bring out the worst in me.

Mostly because I hate that she won't trust me. She constantly wears a wary expression around me, like she expects the worst from me at any second.

And that's precisely what I gave her today.

She very obviously experienced something traumatic, and rather than try to coax her into opening up, I demanded her truths.

Then she put me in my place, calling me entitled and saying she doesn't owe me anything.

I'm not entitled. I'm trying to protect my House *and* her. But now that I've calmed down a little, I can see why she feels that way.

Instead of making it better, I made it much worse.

I nearly rejected her, too.

Fuck.

I palm the back of my neck and blow out a breath. *None of this is working.* We've tried the same thing for over a year, and we've gotten nowhere.

"All right," I say, making an immediate decision. "We'll try it your way."

Nox grins. "Yeah?"

"But it needs to be empty," I continue, ignoring his excitement. "Just the two of you with Fallon. I'll make some calls to arrange it."

I don't stick around to elaborate.

Bane and Nox can handle Fallon for the afternoon.

Meanwhile, I'll call Nolan with an update. Maybe he can find this *Issy* that Fallon insists on lying about.

And perhaps he'll know about these infamous patriarchs. Because I've only ever heard that term used with a certain Supernatural Syndicate and I'm really hoping that syndicate isn't related to Fallon or her sister.

FALLON

I KISSED KASPIAN.

It wasn't intentional. I just reacted. He was about to reject our mating bond, and I knew if he did, the magic connecting us all would be obvious. And the last thing I wanted was more questions.

More accusations.

More *discussion.*

Not when I still didn't know what to do or how to respond to the first round of the inquisition.

Even now, I'm not sure what to do. I'm finally free of the palace grounds, in a remote location where I could technically try to escape, and I'm…

Well, I'm standing in a locker room, wearing a bathing suit instead of trying to run.

I stare at myself in the mirror, conflicted about how to proceed.

Bane and Nox are waiting for me just outside the door, and they're the only ones here. It would be fairly easy to skip out the opposite end of this locker area and try to disappear.

Except I have no idea where I would run to, and I would end up with an entire House of mercenaries chasing me.

I wish you were with me, I think at Issy. *You would know what to do.*

She would probably give me a spell to create a proper escape path. But she's been silent since the patriarchs abused our mental connection.

"What's happening to your twin? How can we help her?"

Kaspian's words play through my mind for the thousandth time.

What would have happened if I'd told him the truth? Would he really help her? I wonder. *Or was he just trying to figure out my most sacred secret?*

I scowl at my reflection.

Trust goes both ways, I think. *How does he expect me to trust him when he doesn't trust me?*

I might have taken our argument a bit too far, but our relationship feels entirely uneven. He's the authority figure, the one in charge, the *king* who can dictate my fate with a few swift words.

And he expects me to tell him everything.

Part of me understands why—he's trying to protect his House, just like he said—but another part of me is hell-bent on rebelling. I shouldn't have to tell anyone anything because I did nothing wrong.

Klas abused me.

He *used* me.

Yet I'm being punished because Klas took my powers and used them as his own. So now I'm the one everyone doesn't trust, purely because they know what I can do.

Which I suppose is somewhat how I feel about Kaspian —I know what he can do, so I don't trust him either.

I narrow my eyes and shake my head. I could talk

157

myself in circles for hours. But what I need to do is face the present.

Nox and Bane were able to free me for an afternoon swim. It's the first time I've truly been outside—aside from my balcony, anyway—in over a year. I can either stand here wallowing in indecision, or I can go out there and have some fun.

I grab a towel from the shelf, slide my feet into a pair of flip-flops, and head toward the door to face my two phantoms.

Neither of them has said much about what happened earlier. Instead, they took it upon themselves to play tour guide on the forty-five-minute drive from Reykjavik to the thermal pool. Then all they did was show me around the facility and hand me a swimsuit—one that Nox apparently procured for me before we left.

I'm grateful to them for not trying to pry. But I'm certain the topic is going to come up again at some point. Maybe by then I'll have a decision in my head on what to say.

A whistle comes from my left as I exit the locker room, the source of it Nox. He's already in the water, but still inside the building.

I glance around, noting that there's a bar to my right, what appears to be a towel area in front of me, and the interior entrance into the lagoon to my left—which is where Nox is waiting.

"Where's Bane?" I ask.

"He's at the outside bar," Nox replies. "Since Kaspian sent everyone home for the afternoon and evening, we're on our own, and Bane doesn't want you to starve."

My lips twitch. "He says his love language is food, but I think he's just obsessed with eating."

"He's certainly obsessed with something all right," Nox

agrees. "Now, are you going to stand there all afternoon, or are you going to join me in the warm water?"

I eye the entry ramp, then walk over to set my towel on the counter in front of me before slipping the sandals off my feet.

It's a little chilly in here, but not too cold. At least not compared to the outside. "The sun will be going down soon," I note as I turn toward Nox. "Will there be lights in the water?"

He nods. "They'll come on soon. It's automated."

My toes meet the edge of the water, sending a bubble of excitement up my limbs. "It's really warm."

"As it should be," Nox murmurs. "The volcanic activity in Iceland is intense. Normally, I prefer the smaller thermal spas. But for your first outing, this one seemed more appropriate."

"First outing?" I repeat as I continue down the ramp toward him.

"Mm-hmm," he hums. "First of many, if I have my way."

"You think Kaspian will allow this again?" I ask, hopeful.

"If you're good, I imagine he'll allow it all the time," he replies, his blue eyes twinkling.

"Define *good*."

He reaches for me as I near him, his hand easily finding my lower back and propelling me into his hard, muscular form. My palms land on his sculpted chest, a soft puff of air escaping me in surprise.

"Not running away was a good start," he murmurs. "Although, I did wonder a bit if I was going to have to chase you down. You were definitely hesitating in there."

I lift an eyebrow. "Were you being a voyeur again?"

He smiles and starts walking me backward toward a

pair of doors in the water. "I think it's safe to assume going forward that I'm going to be a constant voyeur in your life, firefly."

His hands spin me around to face the glass exit, his bare chest meeting my back.

"Push through to go outside," he says against my ear, his proximity and touch making me shiver.

Nox has always been flirtatious, but he's never been this bold with me before. I definitely don't mind the change, even if it's a spell that's bound us together.

Although, he may mind when he finds out, I think, frowning.

But as long as I can break the spell, he'll be free.

I'll… just need to figure that out.

Details, I mutter to myself as I press on the glass.

Chilly air immediately kisses my skin, making me want to duck lower into the warm water. Nox shifts closer, his hot skin a welcome sensation against mine as we move through the glass barrier.

The setting sun casts a golden glitter across the sky-blue water, painting a breathtaking scene that I pause to admire.

Nox doesn't push me forward, just keeps his hands on my hips as I take it all in.

I caught a glimpse of the view when we arrived, but being in the lagoon itself is a whole new experience. There are obsidian-colored rocks framing the exterior, making the water appear even more blue. It's such a unique color, one that appears so much fresher than the dark colors I grew up around in New York City.

"It's beautiful," I breathe, sinking down a little more into the luscious warmth.

"Yes," Nox agrees, his lips still near my ear.

We stay like that for a long moment, his patience a

calming presence that has me leaning back against him in our comfortable silence.

"I'm surprised you're not trying to make me talk," I admit, more relaxed than I've felt in months. "Now would be a good time for the continued inquisition."

He hums a little, his arms encircling my waist in a backward hug. "Maybe. But I know you're not ready to trust us yet. So I'm not going to push you. Let's just have a nice swim and enjoy our evening."

"Trying to seduce me with kindness," I muse.

"Mmm, that's not how I would seduce you," he replies, his fingers trailing across my lower abdomen, just above the top of my bikini bottoms. "My bedroom preferences are not *kind*. *Worshipping*, perhaps. *Dominant*, too. But definitely not *kind*."

He turns me in his arms and starts moving us toward a deeper area of the lagoon—something I only notice because the water rises with each step. His piercing blue eyes hold mine along the way, his irises captivating and radiating a multitude of emotions.

Adoration.

Respect.

Lust.

"You're not upset with me?" I ask, searching his gaze for any hint that he's playing with my emotions.

"I'm disappointed that you're hurting and not letting us help you," he admits. "But no, I'm not upset with you, little firefly. I'm simply frustrated that I can't fix whatever is bothering you."

I swallow. "Even if you knew, you wouldn't be able to fix it." The words leave me before I have a chance to consider the implication behind them. They essentially tell him, *I have a problem, one that even I don't know how to fix.*

Which is more than I've been willing to admit the entire time I've known him.

"Perhaps my resourcefulness would surprise you," he counters.

"Maybe." I continue studying him as we slowly move through the water, my focus on him rather than our surroundings. He could be taking me out to drown, and I wouldn't even realize it until it was too late. But I trust him not to hurt me.

Because he's always taken care of me.

He's always been good to me.

"You're frowning," he says, his forehead crumpling. "Why?"

I try to straighten out my features, not meaning to wear my emotions on my face. However, I... I'm conflicted again.

I've spent all this time holding on to my secrets, afraid to confide in any of my supposed captors, only to suddenly realize that I don't fear Nox at all. And more than that—I trust him to take care of me.

So why am I hiding? Because I'm afraid he'll share my secrets with Kaspian?

No, I *know* he'll share everything with Kaspian because that's his job.

And yet, I find myself wanting to talk to Nox more than anyone else. Maybe even Bane, too.

"What's wrong, firefly?" Nox asks softly, pausing his strides across the lagoon. "What did I say?"

"You didn't say anything." In fact, he has never once pushed me to talk or demanded a single thing from me. He's only ever asked to let him help me or provided comfort when I needed it most.

Nolan accused him of *dating* me for answers.

But Nox simply said he treats me like a person, not a

prisoner. Which is true—he does treat me like I mean more to him than whatever secrets I hold.

Even now, the way he's holding me with care while assessing my expression with his concerned gaze shows he cares.

I just don't understand why.

I would blame the forced mate bonds, but those didn't exist until yesterday. And he's always looked at me this way. The sole difference now is that he's also touching me freely.

"You and Bane accepted the fate bonds immediately." I utter the words quietly, my mind processing what that means. "You didn't even hesitate."

"Of course we didn't." His lips curl a little. "We've both wanted you from the beginning. I thought we made that clear."

They did. Sort of. It's more that my brain didn't accept their statements from before, perhaps because they felt too good to be true.

"You were a forbidden craving we both shared for over a year," he adds. "But neither of us could act on it. Not only were you our ward to protect, but you were also mated to another man." He lifts his shoulder. "Now one obstacle is gone while the other holds that much more meaning to us."

My brow furrows. "Guarding me has more meaning?"

"*Protecting* you has more meaning," he corrects. "Kaspian assigned us to you to *protect* you, Fallon. He was worried that some members of the House might try to exact revenge on you since it was your powers that Klas used to subdue the city. He wanted you *protected*."

My lips open, then close, my words jumbling on my tongue. "That…" *That's not how I understood any of this.* "He doesn't trust my powers."

"He doesn't *understand* your powers," Nox murmurs, his thumb dancing along my lower spine as he holds me in the water. "And he's using that as his primary reason for wanting you to open up. But I've realized there's more to it than just that."

"Because I told you there's more involved." Bane's voice floats to us on the wind, drawing my attention to where he's moving through the water with a drink in his hand.

I glance between both of them. "What do you mean?"

Bane comes up beside us and holds the drink closer to me, the straw poised for my lips. "Try this and tell me if it's good."

That's not an answer to my question, but I do what he asks because pretty much everything Bane makes tastes amazing.

And this drink is no different.

It's a delicious concoction of fruits with a subtle bite of alcohol in its wake. "Mmm, what is that?"

He lifts a shoulder. "A mixture I threw together with some pureed strawberries, pineapple juice, and some sweeter alcohols."

I swallow another mouthful while he talks, a groan vibrating in my chest. "Sooo good," I tell him.

Nox's arms flex around me in response, his body seeming to stiffen. "Fuck, if you sound like that when enjoying a drink, I can't wait to hear what you sound like when you come."

I nearly choke on the liquid in my mouth, his words unexpected and entirely too welcome.

Bane chuckles and takes the straw from my lips, only to press it to Nox's mouth. "Back to Kaspian," he says as Nox tries the drink. "He wants your secrets because he wants to know you. Trust is important to him, but it's so much deeper than that."

"Mm-hmm," Nox agrees. "And this is really good."

"I know," Bane replies, his dark eyes glimmering with approval before meeting my gaze again. "Fallon, we've all been enamored with you in one way or another since we met you. Kaspian isn't an exception. He just displays his fascination in a different way."

"By demanding answers," Nox murmurs. "Like today, you scared him by essentially dying again. Then you came back upset, and he wanted to fix it. Only you won't let him, and that infuriates him."

Bane nods. "He's all about control. However, he can't control a problem he doesn't understand. And he wants to control it—for you."

"No, he wants to protect his House from me," I correct him. "That's his primary objective."

"That's what he tells himself, but that's just one of many reasons." Bane shrugs. "Someday, you'll both see it. But this bond between all of us makes sense. It explains everything."

I twist my lips to the side. "Does it, though? I mean, it could all be… I don't know, a mistake. A fluke. Four fated mates? It's probably a temporary thing brought on by my visiting the death plane. Magic, even." It's as close as I can bring myself to saying the truth—that this is all because of a rebounding spell.

But I'm desperate for it to be a lie.

For this to be real.

For these men to truly be mine.

"You don't think our fated-mate bonds are real?" Bane asks, some of the sparkle leaving his gaze.

"I…" I trail off, trying to figure out how to reply to that

without saying *why* I'm questioning the bonds. "It feels too good to be true?"

He considers me for a beat and nods. "I can understand why you think that after everything you went through with Klas. So let's pretend it's a fluke, as you suggested, just for a second. How did you feel about us before yesterday?"

I blink, startled by his question. It isn't at all how I expected him to address the possibility that this all might be fake. "I... Um..." I swallow, my brow furrowing.

"Okay, how about I answer that question first," he suggests as he places the straw between my lips again. "I've been attracted to you for months, which is what made protecting you so second nature for me. The fate bonds are just a formality, in my opinion. Or a proverbial green light, if you will. Because it means I'm allowed to pursue my interest now."

Nox nods. "That. I agree with all of that. It's just an excuse to be allowed to finally touch you the way I've wanted to from the beginning." He frowns then, his blue irises swirling. "Unless you don't want me to touch you, I mean." His arms loosen. "You're doubting the bonds, so you don't feel the same way?"

I grab his shoulders and push the straw out of my mouth. "No, no, that's not what I mean at all. I just... I'm asking... I don't know what I'm asking. I'm confused and wondering what would be happening if we weren't bonded."

I'm royally fucking this up by overthinking it, I decide.

But I don't want to trick them into anything, either.

Ugh. Why does this have to be so complicated?

Because Daithi O'Neely messed with my soul on Patrick O'Neely's demand.

I nearly scowl.

Fucking patriarch.

Even now, they own me. Control me. Binding my spirit to their will from thousands of miles away.

I hate them. *All* of them. Because this isn't just about Patrick O'Neely and my father. It's about all seven patriarchs and their penchant for commanding every situation.

One of these days, I'll make them pay, I vow. I have no idea how, but I will.

"That's an intense look," Nox murmurs, dragging my focus back to him and Bane. "I hope it's not meant for us."

"It's not," I promise. "I... I started thinking about something unrelated." *Sort of.* I shake my head. "I just..." I pinch my lips to the side. "Actually, you know what? I don't want to think anymore." It's exhausting and overrated, and I'm tired of these mental circles.

"We can help with that," Nox offers, his eyes dancing around the lagoon. "We can swim wherever you want. Just point and we'll venture that way."

"I don't want to swim," I tell him. "I... I want you."

It's a bold statement, one I would never have made mere days ago. But it comes from a place deep within me that needs to feel something other than confusion. Something passionate. Something *warm.*

"I want both of you," I whisper, emboldened by the hungry gleams in Bane's and Nox's eyes. They're both staring at me like I'm the center of their universe, their own personal sun.

Maybe it's all in my head.

Maybe I've lost my damn mind.

But I don't care.

I need this. I need *them.*

"Please," I add, swallowing. "I—"

Nox presses his lips to mine, silencing my plea. It's soft

and tender and so very different from the violence I experienced with Kaspian earlier. But it's absolutely perfect. And it's exactly what I'm craving.

He makes me feel adored. Understood. *Alive.*

"Do you want us here or in a private room?" Nox asks after a beat, the words caressing my mouth. "In the water or on a bed?"

"I..." I don't know. Part of me wants to stay here so my confidence can remain intact. But having our first experience in the water may be too much. While it's romantic and warm, the edges of the lagoon are all surrounded by jagged rocks. *Where will we...?*

"How about we start here," Bane suggests softly, his knuckles running along my arm. "Then we'll move to a room if things progress in that direction."

He probably assumes my hesitation is related to my previous experiences with Klas, but I don't correct him. Instead, I nod.

Because I don't want to make any more decisions. That requires thinking, and I don't want to think.

I just want to *feel.*

To indulge.

To be with these two males who have made their intentions and desires for me clear.

To just exist. Be alive. *Feel wanted.*

Nox presses his lips to mine again. "Okay," he breathes. "We'll start with this..."

NOLAN

Kaspian called three times while I was meeting with some of Klas's old neighbors in Ireland. None of them had anything useful to say. However, their summaries made it quite clear that Klas kept Fallon under close watch.

"We didn't really have a chance to know Fallon; she stayed inside a lot."

"I didn't even realize he was mated until a year ago."

"She wasn't very social."

"The one time I saw her, she kept her head down and didn't acknowledge my presence."

All of their statements caused my stomach to twist, my fury mounting with each passing second. How did not one of these people notice the signs of abuse?

I shake my head after leaving the final neighbor's house and start down the sidewalk before dialing Kaspian's number.

His face appears a second later, his eyes hidden by a pair of shades as he seems to focus on something over his phone.

I frown. "Are you driving?"

"Yeah." He doesn't sound thrilled about it. "Nox and Bane took Fallon to the lagoon. I had it vacated, but now I feel like I need to be there, too."

My eyebrow lifts. "You let her out of the palace?"

His jaw visibly clenches. "Nox and Bane convinced me it was a good idea."

"And now you're not so sure, which is why you're driving out there to check on them," I finish for him.

"Something like that," he mutters. "Anyway, there have been some developments."

"I'm listening."

Kaspian launches into a story from earlier today about how Fallon essentially died again and came back only to fall into some sort of episode where she mentioned her sister, Issy, and something about the "patriarchs."

He continues by telling me about Fallon's lies—or what he interprets as lies—and ends with, "Then I tried to reject her, but she kissed me. And, well, now she's swimming with Nox and Bane."

I stopped walking somewhere around the part when Kaspian said Fallon essentially died again, and I've been gaping at my phone ever since.

"Some developments?" I repeat, using his description of these colossal updates. "And you *kissed* her?"

"Technically, she kissed me. I just... reciprocated." He adjusts his glasses, his focus still on the road and not on his actual phone. Knowing Kaspian, he took one of his favorite sports cars out for a spin and connected his phone to the dash, hence my view of his face.

It's dusk there, but as an older vampire, he's more susceptible to the sunlight, which explains his dark shades. With anyone else, I would assume he was trying to hide his eyes from me, maybe to mask whatever emotion that *kiss* brought on.

"The kiss isn't what I'm worried about," he continues. "It's the lies and her comments about the patriarchs. That's not usual coven speak, which means it could be related to a number of things, but I've only ever heard that term referenced in conversations about a specific witch sect of the Supernatural Syndicates."

The Outcast Coven, I translate, aware of the strange political dynamic within that syndicate. While the matriarchs are considered to be the face of the organization—female witches are usually stronger than male warlocks—there are rumors of a powerful patriarchy operating behind the scenes.

Alas, no one has cared enough to really investigate those claims. Hell, I'm not even sure many have heard about it. I'm only familiar with the rumors because it's my job to know these things.

However, there have been too many other threats to be concerned about, ones that exist within legally formed Houses, not criminally formed sects. Hence the reason no one has bothered to look into the situation.

But we may have cause to do so now, I muse.

"We know Fallon's from No Man's Land, which technically includes that infamous area of New York City," I say, pondering aloud. "Of course, there could be a whole slew of supernatural networks we don't know much about in other areas, ones that use a similar term. But we should research what we know exists first."

"I agree." He glances left and then right as his blinker sounds through the speaker. "And while Fallon claims her sister is dead, I know she's lying. Which means her sister is in some kind of trouble. That also makes me think it's syndicate related."

"So you want me to head to New York City to check it out." It's a logical next step. "I like that plan a hell of a lot more than hanging out here. These neighbors are useless. They didn't even recognize the signs of Fallon's abuse, just assumed she was a recluse."

"A lot of times people turn a blind eye to uncomfortable situations and justify it by saying they're just minding their own business."

I snort. "Yeah, well, if even one of them noticed, Fallon could have been saved years ago."

"She's safe now," Kaspian says. "And she'll be safe going forward, too."

I study his stern features for a beat before musing, "Not worried about that kiss at all, hmm?" Because it seems to me that he's already showing signs of possession.

Actually, I suppose it's been that way from the beginning. Why else would he have insisted on housing her in his personal guest suite? It wasn't just to keep a closer eye on her or because he feared her powers—a part of him wanted her nearby.

A part that's now recognized her as his mate.

"I'm just hoping this theory about the Outcast Coven is wrong," he mutters. "But Klas's report on how he met Fallon is vague at best. And no one thought to really question him since he said they met during one of his missions, so the background isn't noted. Which, in hindsight, seems to have been purposeful."

I nod, agreeing with everything he's saying.

"And being from one of the Supernatural Syndicates would have made her acceptance into Gold and Garnet that much harder," he adds. "Thus mandating Klas's vagueness and making it even more likely that I'm right about her ties to the syndicate world."

"Meaning there's likely a lot more to this story," I say, thinking about all the hazy details surrounding Klas. "His own origin is sketchy, considering every member of his family is supposedly dead. His collaborators last year weren't so much relatives as they were friends, leaving his background just as ambiguous as Fallon's."

None of this is new information to Kaspian, as Klas's records were bare from the beginning. But we originally attributed it to his lack of familial connections. Now it seemed there might be more at play here.

More Fallon isn't saying.

"I'll see what I can find in New York," I conclude. "Do some digging around the Supernatural Syndicates, ask if anyone knows a *Fallon Doyle*."

"I could also ask the new Earth and Emerald Chancellor," Kaspian adds, his tone holding a hint of unease. "Maybe she knows of Fallon?"

"Can you trust her?" I wonder aloud.

"I can't trust anyone in a position of power," he replies. "However, I don't see how she could use this information against me. Maybe she can offer you some assistance while there, too. It may put me slightly in her debt, but it'll be a good way to test her merit for future alliances."

I snort. "I don't need assistance, Kas. I blend in naturally." It's one of my talents—the art of camouflage. My wings retract. My hair and eyes shift colors depending on my surroundings. And my features are generally forgettable. All a win-win as far as espionage is concerned. "I'll check in once I'm in New York."

Kaspian nods. "All right. I should have had a chance to speak with Chancellor Nikki by then, so I'll give you an update as to what she knows, too."

I dip my chin in understanding, not that the Gold and Garnet King can see it. "Brilliant," I tell him. "In the meantime, have fun playing with Fallon. Maybe a few more kisses from you and some orgasms from the phantoms will make our little canary sing, hmm?"

I end the call before he can reply, my suggestion rhetorical and not requiring a response. But it is a fun image to fantasize about—Fallon screaming with pleasure.

Of course, I would deny her the climax several times first. Make her beg a little.

I'm not reverent like the phantoms. Nor do I play sensual games like Kaspian.

I'm direct.

I'm demanding.

And I love making a woman scream in a way she's never screamed before.

When I pull Fallon beneath me, she'll shatter so severely that she'll forget her own name. *That* will be my reward for breaking down her walls and forcing her into a new stratosphere of gratification.

Because Fallon doesn't need her hands held. She needs someone willing to test her boundaries. Push her limits. *Make her talk.*

Whether those words are innocent or not remains to be seen.

Perhaps she's a traitor.

Maybe she's a pawn.

We won't know until she opens up. Or until I dig up the secrets she's trying to bury.

One way or another, the truth will be ours.

Because if New York reveals nothing, I'll be forced to return.

And I'm not afraid to make our sweet little canary bleed.

NOX

I'M ADDICTED to Fallon's lips. So plump and delicious. So soft. So *mine*.

My hands roam her curves, loving the way they fit perfectly into my palms, confirming this female was made for me.

Made for *us*.

Her thighs encircle my waist, her heat pressed right up against my groin, but it's not enough. Our suits are too thick, and the water around us distorts the sensation below.

I want more.

I want *her*.

But I agreed to do this Bane's way—taking it *slow*.

Fallon has suffered so many years of abuse. She deserves to be worshipped. Cherished. *Adored*.

Her pleasure is important, and if she's content to kiss me all night, I'll allow it. I don't care if my balls ache from the lack of friction or if my cock throbs with the need to be inside her; it's her sensations that matter most.

Which is why I've only allowed my hands to wander up her sides and down to her voluptuous ass.

Bane stands behind her, his chest to her back, his lips on her shoulder and then her neck.

I'm fully aware of his movements, our experiences together allowing us to be in tune with each other.

When I stop kissing her, he grabs her nape and turns her head to the side to devour her, and I take over his path on her neck.

She heaves a breath against me, her nails digging into my shoulders as her lower half arches just enough to apply pressure between her thighs.

I grin against her throat. "I wish I could feel how wet you are, firefly. I want to taste you."

She moans against Bane's mouth, her fingers traveling up my nape to thread through my hair. Her opposite hand goes to Bane's neck, her grip tightening on us both. "I need more," she pants. "I... I feel like I'm on fire."

"Because you are, sweet flame," Bane whispers against her mouth. "You're burning for *us*, your intended mates."

She makes a noise, one that trails off on a delectable moan as I press my cock against her sensitive center. "We're burning for you, too, firefly."

"Indeed we are," Bane agrees, his own hips rocking into hers from behind. "Are you ready to move to a room? Or do you want to stay here?"

Her eyelashes flutter as she takes in the darkness around us, the sun having completely disappeared despite the late afternoon hour.

Winter in Iceland makes for some very long nights.

Something I hope we can take advantage of tonight.

"We'll do whatever you want, Fallon," Bane says softly. "We're yours to command."

That's not exactly true, but I'm willing to play along for this first session together. Fallon needs a gentle introduction, one that gives her confidence and understanding of how things will be between us.

We're not like her former mate, something she'll understand with time. Which makes this initial experience extremely important.

Once we garner some more trust, I'll be able to gradually increase the intensity and show her some of my preferences. And all the while, I'll master her expectations along the way.

Because she'll always come first. *My Fallon. My firefly. My mate.*

"The room," she says, arching into me again. "Let's go to the room."

I grin against her neck, my lips hovering right over her thudding pulse. "As you wish, darling firefly." I nip at her tender skin, then lave it with my tongue. "I'll meet you and Bane there with the key."

Kaspian has a suite on-site, one he rarely uses, as he prefers his quarters at the palace. Fortunately, there's a spare key in the reception area.

And as I've stayed here once before, I know exactly where it is.

I brush my lips over Fallon's cheek, then maneuver her into Bane's arms so they can swim back together. She doesn't protest and neither does he, the two of them immediately falling into another kiss that leaves both of them moaning in my wake.

My mouth curves upward in anticipation.

When Fallon told us that she wanted us, my entire plan for the afternoon shifted. I originally intended to show her around the lagoon, maybe give her a mud facial with some of the natural silica found around the edge of the water.

But that all changed the moment she said, "Please."

My dick throbs with the memory of that single word, my desire to hear it again a pulsing need inside my mind.

I want her to beg me to make her come with my tongue. Beg me to fuck her. Then beg me to do it all over again.

And again.

And again.

"Fuck," I mutter, painfully hard as I exit the water inside the main building.

Bane had better not take his sweet time. I need to strip Fallon and worship her with my mouth. Explore her with my hands. Devour her with my tongue.

I grab two fluffy robes from behind the towel counter and lay them out for Fallon and Bane before taking one for myself.

The adjoining hotel area isn't too far a walk, but I shift into my phantom form to go through the walls, eager to ensure everything is ready.

Only, I pause as I reach the reception area, my eyes widening a fraction to see Kaspian leaning against the desk with the key already in his hand.

He can't see me in my ghostly form, but he's clearly expecting me because he's twirling the item around one finger.

"I know you're here, Noxious," he says, using my full name rather than my preferred nickname.

I appear in front of him and arch a brow. "Is this where you lecture me and say I can't fuck Fallon? Because I'm pretty sure that's not your decision to make."

We might play together a lot, but we're not committed to one another.

"No, I was going to give you permission to take my room." He holds out the key. "Although, I suspect you were going to use it anyway."

"I was," I admit, accepting the key. "And we both know you didn't drive all the way here to give us access to your suite." I fold my arms over my chest. "What's really going on? Did Nolan find something?"

Kaspian shakes his head. "Not yet. But he's on his way to New York City to check out a lead."

"What lead?" I ask, my brow creasing. New York City is home to a myriad of Supernatural Syndicates. Surely Fallon isn't related to those.

"Fallon mentioned patriarchs a few times this morning while suffering from her 'episode.'" Kaspian's expression clouds over. "I've only ever heard that term referenced as a rumor, specifically in regard to the Outcast Coven."

My eyebrows lift. "Why didn't you say something earlier?"

"Because it's just a hunch," he replies. "One I really hope I'm wrong about."

Well, that only confuses me more. I can understand being uneasy about a link to a Supernatural Syndicate—they're essentially mafia organizations that deal in dangerous magic and other sinister bullshit—but an association doesn't imply immediate guilt.

"What does it matter if you're right?" I ask him. "We can't help where we're from, Kas. Being born in No Man's Land isn't a crime; it's just an unfortunate fate."

Kaspian's expression darkens even more. "It's a Supernatural Syndicate full of illegal activity. If she's from the Outcast Coven, there may be nefarious activities at play."

"And so you came here to warn us now? Hours later?" I wonder aloud. "You could have saved us all a trip by expressing your concerns earlier, you know, *after* Fallon mentioned the patriarchs." Not that I was complaining about being able to take Fallon out, but this whole conversation just destroyed my evening plans.

Assuming Kaspian is here to make us return, anyway.

But then why offer his room?

"No, I'm not here for that. You asked about Nolan, and I just…" Kaspian trails off and blows out a breath. "Look, I'm just here because I felt like I needed to be closer. I can't really explain why because I don't understand it myself." He winces with the admission, almost as though he feels it makes him appear weak.

"Oh." I grin. *This* is a feeling I very much understand. "You mean you're here because you couldn't stay away from Fallon." *That* was a good reason to interrupt our little date. Much better than casting doubts about Fallon's origin and implying she may be harboring evil intentions associated with her criminal coven back home.

I've spent over a year with Fallon. The female doesn't have a wicked bone in her body.

Just a very naughty tongue, I decide. *One she sharpens whenever Kaspian is around.*

He neither confirms nor denies it, instead saying, "I assume you plan to spend the night here now?"

"If you'll allow it," I hedge.

His dark irises roam over my robe, a calculating gleam entering his eyes. "Are you going to make it worth my while?"

"Are you craving a show?" I counter. "Because Bane and I are about to create a masterpiece, and I know how much you like to watch."

"I do," he murmurs. "What are the chances Fallon will allow me the pleasure of observing?"

"We can ask her." Although, I'm not sure that'll go along with Bane's slow introduction plan.

"Hmm, no," Kaspian says, either noting my

uncertainty or realizing the hesitation on his own. "She's not ready for the three of us. More specifically, *me*. But I may need you to stop by after you're done, just to give me a taste of her."

"Stop by where?" I ask.

"I'll take over the room beside my usual suite. It's technically mine as well, just designed for guests."

"Do you prefer we take that one instead?"

"No, my suite is nicer." He smirks as he adds, "And the bed is bigger, too."

"I'm familiar."

"I know."

"And I'll stop by after she's tucked in for the night. You know, to properly thank you and give you that taste you requested."

"Good." His irises swirl with barely restrained hunger. "You'll also detail her orgasms for me."

"Like you won't be listening through the wall," I drawl.

"Hearing isn't the same as seeing. I want descriptions."

"You'll have them, Your Highness."

He nods, seemingly appeased. "Then go please our mate."

My arms fall to my sides, then I flip his key into the air and catch it. "On it."

"Thoroughly, Nox," he says as I begin to turn.

I arch a brow at him. "When have I ever not been thorough, Kas?"

Amusement flirts with his expression. "Just make sure I can hear her screams."

"Oh, you'll be hearing a lot more than that." Which I know will please him.

Fallon may call me the voyeur, but Kaspian is the one who truly enjoys watching. He'll go a whole night without touching, all while observing the sensual escapades around him with barely restrained hunger in his eyes.

It's those mornings after a night of fun that he uses me the most.

I love his particular brand of sexual fun. It's uniquely him.

Hopefully, Fallon enjoys it, too.

But that's an adventure for another day.

She requires a slow introduction first. Then I'll handle Kaspian's needs for her, just to keep his darkness at bay. And eventually we'll graduate to new levels of pleasure as a group.

Maybe I'll even let Kaspian demonstrate his proclivities on me first. Assuming Fallon would like that, anyway.

It'll all be at her pace, everything being her choice.

Because she's our mate.

And her pleasure will always come first.

FALLON

Oh, stars, I'm going to explode and they've barely touched me.

Bane insisted on taking a shower when we reached the room, saying something about the silica in the water and how it'll hurt my hair.

I thought it was an excuse to strip me.

But he left my bikini on and focused on shampooing my hair while Nox soaped up my skin.

Their hands are everywhere and nowhere at the same time.

Touching. Petting. Scrubbing. *Washing.*

It's an erotic torture that has me squirming between them. If they don't remove my swimsuit soon, I'm going to do it for them.

I've never felt so needy before. So bold. So *hungry*.

Bane's lips caress the sensitive spot behind my ear as Nox's palms move up and down my legs. He's on his knees before me while Bane's hot chest burns against my back.

The conundrum is too much.

It's not enough.

It's driving me *mad*.

A moan escapes me as Bane drags his teeth along the tendon of my neck, his hands clasping my hips.

They're seducing me. Drugging me on their presence. *Teasing* every nerve of my body.

Bane's fingers toy with the strings of my bikini bottoms while Nox's touch drifts down to my ankles.

I wait, holding my breath, hoping Bane will tug on the ties and free me from my suit.

But he doesn't.

He just plays with the knot, taunting my senses.

I lean back into his muscular strength, my head tilting so I meet his gaze. "You're torturing me."

"Am I?" he asks, his dark eyes glittering with amusement.

"You both are," I accuse as Nox's mouth touches the inside of my thigh.

It's an electric sensation, one that intensifies as he draws his fingers up my calves to my knees.

I look down into his vibrant blue irises, noting the grin in his sparkling depths.

"Definitely torturing me," I growl as I thread my fingers through his damp hair. "You can't properly wash me while I'm still in this swimsuit."

"Did that sound like an invitation to take it off, Nox?" Bane asks against my ear.

"It certainly sounded like one to me, Bane," Nox replies. "But I think she needs to say it plainly. Demand we strip her. Tell us exactly what she wants."

"Mmm, I agree." Bane's breath is hot against my skin, his words a low murmur that makes my heart race. His Scottish accent is somehow thicker now, *deeper*. I rarely seem to notice it, his lilt only coming to light in certain phrases every now and then.

But I hear it in this shower, in the way he's speaking

against my ear.

It's still subtle.

As is Nox's accent.

But it's so damn alluring. It has me wondering if any of my Irish roots are showing. I, too, sometimes have a lilt. Typically when emotions run high.

As they are right now.

"Tell us what you want, lass," Bane murmurs. "Tell me to untie these little bottoms and I will."

"Then you can tell me where you want my mouth," Nox adds, his words a breath against my thigh. "Tell me how to use my tongue. Let me lick that sweet pussy and taste your exquisite pleasure for myself."

Bane groans. "If you let him do that, I'll need to sample it for myself. But I can start with yer tits, lass. Suckle your nipples. Drive you mad."

"What color do you think they are?" Nox asks, his blue eyes going to the male behind me. "Rosy pink? A dusky brown?"

"Definitely rosy." Bane nuzzles my neck. "Want us to remove your top? See if we're right?"

I'm panting between them, their words igniting a fire inside me that's burning out of control.

I want everything they just said.

Everything and more…

"Strip me," I beg. "This suit… it's too much. Too constricting. Too—"

Bane yanks at the strings of my bikini bottom as Nox grabs the triangle between my thighs, the two of them working in tandem to yank the material from my skin.

My top is next, only Bane handles that on his own. "Rosy," he growls, the vibration scattering goose bumps down my arms.

"Beautiful," Nox says, his gaze reverent as he remains on his knees.

I swallow, suddenly aware of the fact that he's nearly eye level with my sex. Klas always required me to wax, something I've not done in over a year. Now I'm just trimmed.

Should I have waxed? Shaved more? Prepared for this?

Bane nibbles my earlobe. "Stop thinking, sweet flame. Let us worship you."

"You're perfect," Nox echoes. "Now tell us what you want."

I shiver as I meet his gaze once more, his lust shining up at me via twin sapphire pools of *need*.

"Everything," I tell him. "I want everything." *Everything they said. Everything they want to do. Everything that can possibly exist.*

Because I've never felt this way before. So free. So alive. So *safe*.

Klas only ever used me for his own pleasure.

However, Nox and Bane… they're not him. They're asking me what I want. Asking me to tell them what to do. *Kissing me as though I'm worth something to them.*

It might all be the spell. A twisted, dark enchantment. But I can't help indulging in it now.

One day, I'll find a way to free Bane and Nox. It's the least I can do after how good they've been to me.

What if they hate me for giving in to this magically inspired lust? I worry. *Will they forever hold it against me? Or did they mean it when they said they've wanted me from the beginning?*

Maybe it's true. After all, I've been attracted to them, too.

Which is what makes it impossible to turn them down.

Especially when Nox is staring up at me with delicious intentions dancing in his striking blue eyes.

I tighten my grip in his hair, suddenly feeling as though I need to be anchored or I may fall over.

"I think you should sit down, Bane, and pull Fallon into your lap." Nox's silky tone sends a thrilling shiver down my spine.

"Only if the lass agrees to take off my swim trunks first." Bane's mouth is still near my ear, his hot body a brand against all my exposed skin. "Will you turn around and help me, little flame?"

"Yes." I rotate toward him, my eagerness causing Nox to chuckle as he shifts back to let me move.

Bane doesn't match his amusement, his expression instead one of wonder as his gaze tracks over my nude state.

"Nox was wrong." His Scottish brogue is at an all-time high now. "Yer so much more than just beautiful, my lass. Yer perfect. Stunning. The most exquisite creature I've ever laid eyes on."

My cheeks heat from his comments, my eyes falling to his sculpted torso. *Solid muscle. Just like Nox.*

I knew that already after our time in the lagoon.

But that doesn't stop me from ogling Bane again. He calls me perfect, but honestly, both these males redefine the term.

"Are you going to devour him with your eyes or strip him, firefly?" Nox sinks his teeth into the fleshy part of my ass in the next second, making me gasp.

It wasn't a harsh bite, just a nibble, but it was so unexpected that I'm momentarily frozen as his tongue touches the same spot.

Why does that feel good?

He bites me again on my opposite cheek, the motion waking me up in a way I could never have anticipated.

Because I *like* that sensation. It stings a little. But his tongue chases away the burn and leaves a soothing caress behind.

Bane's palm drifts up my arm to my neck, where he wraps it around my nape. "Undress me, little flame." He leans down to brush his mouth against mine. "Undress me and we'll reward you."

I like the sound of that.

I also want to see all of Bane. He's so much taller than I am—they're *all* so much taller—and muscular, too.

I swallow as my fingers go to the front of his swim trunks to loosen the tie there.

Then, gradually, I start pulling them down.

Down.

Down.

Down.

Stars…

He's definitely proportionate to his size. *And very hard.*

I bite my lip as his swimsuit falls to the tiled floor. Nox reaches around me as Bane steps out of the fabric, the two of them working together to leave the phantom naked in front of me.

"Do you want to touch me?" Bane asks, his palm squeezing the back of my neck.

I nod.

"Use your words, firefly," Nox says, his teeth sinking into my fleshy backside again. "Communication is important to us."

"Yes," I hiss as he follows his bite with a second one. Then I moan as he chases the hurt away once more with his tongue.

Bane presses his lips to mine in a gentle kiss. "Touch me, sweet flame. Light me on fire."

I press my palm to his rigid abdomen, my pale hand a

stark contrast to his tan skin, and slowly trail my touch downward.

So muscular and smooth. So warm. So masculine…

He even has those little dimples by his hip bones.

Stars, I want to lick him…

But first, I need to feel him. Explore him. *Know* him.

My fingers dance lower, down to the short, dark hairs framing his impressive girth. *He's so thick*, I think. *Long, too.*

It's a perfect complement to his muscular frame.

I wrap my palm around him, loving the way his hot arousal brands my skin.

He wanted me to burn him, but it's the other way around.

"How does he feel, firefly?" Nox asks, his hands drifting up and down my thighs. "Does his size impress you?"

"Everything about him impresses me," I admit as I stroke him up and down, my gaze meeting Bane's. "You're far more perfect than I am."

His lips curl. "We're perfect together." His grasp tightens on my nape. "The ideal fit." He pulls me into him, causing my breasts to pillow against his chest. "Now it's time for us to reward you, lass. *Thoroughly.*"

Nox hums against my spine, his mouth having moved to my lower back. "Let me see how tight she is first."

"Mmm," Bane hums. "Good to make sure she's prepared." His mouth claims mine before I can ask what he means, but I can guess.

I said I wanted everything.

It seems my phantoms are willing to oblige.

I wrap my arms around Bane's neck as his tongue parts my lips, his kiss seductively tender. It's just like him— patient and understanding, but underlined with experience. He's telling me with his mouth that he knows how to make me feel good, but he'll wait until I'm ready before he truly begins.

I kiss him back, confirming I'm already there. I want him. I want *them*.

Nox's mouth trails along my lower back to my hip and down to my thigh. I shudder from their sensual touches, my body alive with a myriad of sensations.

Bane traces the column of my throat with his thumb while his free hand runs up my side, teasing my flesh and causing my nipples to bead against his firm chest.

More. More. More, I chant in my head.

"Widen your legs," Nox says, his fingers pressing on my inner thighs. "I need access to your sweet cunt."

A bolt of lightning shoots through my being as I comply. No one has ever done this to me before.

I went to my knees countless times for Klas, but he never bowed for me. Never bothered *prepping* me. He expected me to handle that myself.

And I did because I had to. Even when it took several long minutes just to coax my body into reacting.

But that won't be a problem now. I can feel the wetness pooling between my thighs, my inner muscles clenching in anticipation of Nox's intentions.

I'm not even sure what he plans to do. However, it doesn't matter because it's him. It's *them*.

I trust them, I realize, my heart skipping a beat as Bane takes control of our kiss. *I trust them to help me feel good.*

I may even trust them to do more than that.

The realization should unnerve me, but it doesn't. Instead, I just feel… *safe.*

Protected.

Happy.

And I convey that to Bane with my kiss.

But it's Nox who seems to reply, his head sliding

between my thighs to grant his mouth access to my sensitive flesh.

I groan against Bane as Nox's tongue parts my slick folds, his movements knowing and perfect and exploring me in the best way.

Bane continues to caress my side, his other palm a brand against the back of my neck.

It grounds me in the present. Holds me upright. Ensures I'm stable and capable of accepting so much more.

Which is exactly what Nox gives me as his mouth slides up to suckle my clit.

A foreign sound escapes me, accompanied by a violent tremble that nearly buckles my knees.

Never have I experienced such intensity. Such *insanity*.

Another unintelligible noise leaves my mouth, only to be swallowed by Bane.

"Fucking delicious," Nox murmurs, his voice somehow carrying above the showerheads raining down around us. "And so damn wet."

Bane hums against my mouth, his thumb stroking my neck. "Of course she is," he replies, his voice husky. "She's perfect."

"She's ours," Nox says as his touch circles the heart of my core. "Now let's see how many fingers you can take, firefly. You'll need at least three to be ready for Bane."

BANE

MY LITTLE FLAME tastes like temptation incarnate.

The way she writhes against me, the way her arms tighten around me, the way her tongue dances with mine —it's all enough to bring me close to the edge before I'm even inside her.

But I can't pull away or hold back.

She's addictive. A fiery light that draws me in like a moth.

I want her more than I want to breathe.

And I know Nox feels the same way.

Fallon clings to me as he fucks her with his fingers, his actions intentional.

Just like I know his mouth is drawing her closer to the orgasmic edge, inching her into an oblivion that may shatter us all.

But he won't let her come until I'm buried inside her.

Knowing that has me grinning against her eager mouth, my hand roaming along her curves as I hold her to me with my opposite palm around her nape. "Do you like what he's doing to you, lass?" I ask my darling flame. "Is he making you burn?"

"Yes." She shivers. "I like what both of you are doing to me."

My smile grows. "Good answer, sweet flame."

"Good answer indeed," Nox echoes, causing her to jolt. Likely because he spoke the words against her clit. "She's ready."

"Mmm." I nip her bottom lip. "Do you remember what Nox said about sitting on my lap?"

She nods, her green irises swirling with lust as she gazes up at me with a love-drunk expression. "Yes."

"Good lass," I praise her. "I'm going to sit on the shower bench, then I want you to face Nox and slide into my lap."

"And as you do so, Bane is going to slowly guide his cock into your sweet heat," Nox adds. "Then, once you're seated to the hilt, I'm going to devour your pussy while he fucks you."

Fallon's eyelashes flutter, her cheeks blossoming with a beautiful shade of pink. "*Oh.*"

I study her. "Oh, yes? Or oh, no?"

"Yes," she says instantly, that word one I'll never tire of hearing from her beautiful lips.

I kiss her in response, rewarding her honesty with a subtle swipe of my tongue, then I step backward toward the bench along the wall of the shower. It's all made of marble, but it's warm from the steam produced by our prolonged time beneath the hot water.

I sit down while she watches me from beneath hooded eyes, her expression hungry as I give my throbbing shaft a solid stroke. "I'm very ready for you, Fallon."

She visibly shivers, her tongue sneaking out to lick her bottom lip. That seductive little motion inspires an immediate fantasy of her going to her knees and wrapping that fuckable mouth around my cock.

Fuck, this female slays me. I want her more than I've ever wanted anyone in my entire existence. She's so damn *perfect*. Strong and clever. Stunning.

Sensual, too, I marvel as she steps closer and turns to sit on my lap as expected. I grab her hips, helping to guide her ass against my groin.

Her curves are heaven, tempting me to press up against her and claim her as my own.

Sex will solidify our mate bond for life, tying our souls together for eternity. I don't even need to think about what that entails; I accepted this fate the moment her spirit kissed mine.

I kiss her shoulder as Nox inches forward, his gaze briefly meeting mine to check in.

She's ready, his eyes tell me.

I know, I reply, my palms sliding down to her thighs to bring her legs to the outside of mine. Then I part my knees to widen her stance, presenting her pussy to him.

"Gorgeous," he praises, his nose meeting her knee. "You're so fucking gorgeous, firefly." He starts kissing a path along her inner thigh. "Mmm, I want to see you take Bane's cock into your sweet cunt. Can you do that for me, firefly? Can you lift these beautiful hips and help him slide into you?"

Fallon quivers on my lap, her head bobbing. "Yes." She leans forward a little to brace her palms on my legs, her movement granting me better access to the alluring apex between her thighs.

"*Fuck*," I breathe, my dick throbbing at the sight of her eager form shifting into just the right position.

I wrap my arm around her lower abdomen, needing to hold on to her as I slip my other hand between us.

Her legs clench in response as goose bumps pebble down her arms. Nox straightens upward, his height allowing him to be nearly even with a seated Fallon while still on his knees, and leans in to kiss her.

She melts for him, providing the distraction I need to angle myself up into the sanctuary between her legs.

Fallon freezes the moment my head nudges her entrance, but Nox does something with his tongue to coax her back into the moment.

I wait a beat, then gradually push upward into her contracting sheath.

Three fingers might not have been enough, I think, her walls clamping down around me. *Fucking tight…*

Fallon seems to agree, her limbs tensing around me as her nails dig into my legs.

I move slowly, trying to give her time to acclimate.

All while Nox continues to devour her, his palms on her breasts, teasing her, worshipping her, making her feel good.

I release my shaft and reach around her to stroke my thumb against her clit. She bucks in response, taking me deeper into her slick center.

A groan rumbles through my chest, that movement nearly undoing me. It's been so long since I experienced a woman like this, and the fact that it's Fallon—*my mate* —only makes it that much more intense.

I curse against her shoulder, drawing a chuckle from Nox. "That good, huh?" he taunts.

"Fucking amazing," I correct, my arm tightening around her torso.

He draws back to watch me work my cock into her, his gaze hungry. "Fuck, Fallon. You're taking him so beautifully, firefly." He settles between our splayed legs, his focus glued to where our bodies are joining. "I could watch him fuck you all night."

Fallon moans, her body falling back into mine as she grinds down on me, forcing me in to the hilt.

Another expletive falls from my lips as Fallon's moan turns into a needy purr.

Because Nox is now feasting on her pussy like a starving man.

I can feel the stubble of his jaw near where I've joined with Fallon. It's sinfully decadent. Alluring. *Provoking.* His touch combined with the slick heat contracting around me forces me to move. To thrust. To *take.*

Fallon cries out, the sound bliss to my ears, coaxing me into giving her more. To moving faster.

I won't last long. I can't. This is all too much. Too euphoric.

Her head is against my shoulder, her body tight and hot between me and Nox. I grab her chin and tilt her head back so I can devour her with my mouth.

She accepts me completely, her tongue dancing with mine as Nox and I drive her closer to the edge with our joint attentions.

I can feel her pulsing around me, her inner muscles clenching as she nears her peak.

Nox growls against her, the vibration seeming to reverberate through her and into me. It's fucking erotic and forces me to pump into her harder. Faster. More powerfully than before.

Fallon pants against me, her chest rising and falling in anticipation. This angle is so intense, allowing me to feel every inch of her throbbing core as I plunge in and out of her.

"Be a good girl and come for Bane, firefly," Nox murmurs. "He needs to feel you climax around him. It'll force him to come, too. Then I can lick you both clean."

Fallon releases an unintelligible noise as her inner

muscles clamp down around me. "Mmm, you like that image," I say against her mouth. "Would you rather I come down his throat instead of in your pussy, sweet flame?"

She doesn't answer right away, either because she's debating or because she's too caught up in the sensations to speak. But after a few thrusts, she whispers, "Inside me, please."

"That's my preference, too," I tell her before kissing her again.

I know she's on birth control—only because I've helped her get monthly supplies of it—making protection unnecessary. Especially since diseases are not something we need to worry about.

Which means I can unleash inside her.

But not until she detonates.

Because I need to feel her. I need to experience everything with her. I need to *know* her. Well and truly. Intimately. *Forever.*

I draw my teeth along her plump lower lip. "Ignite for me, sweet flame," I beg her. "Ignite for *us.*"

She draws in a sharp breath, her eyelashes fluttering open as I grab both her breasts, my fingers tweaking her nipples. Nox follows suit below, something I sense more than know, his timing almost always in tune with my own.

"Oh," Fallon moans. "Oh, *stars*…"

Her inner walls squeeze me as her entire body goes rigid.

And then she screams, the welcome sound echoing in the marble-and-glass enclosure, and tightens around me like a noose.

"*Fuck,*" I curse, her climax demanding reciprocation, her sheath clenching so severely that I'm left with no choice but to follow her over the edge into oblivion on an explosion I feel to my very soul.

Everything goes dark. Then light. Hot and then cold, only to be hot again as my cum spills inside her, claiming my mate from the inside out.

Mine. Mine. Mine.

"Ours," a deep voice corrects.

I ignore him, too consumed by the sensual goddess on my lap, her body pulsing and driving mine to the brink of divine insanity.

I swear Fallon comes again, her orgasmic pull too intense to be from one climax alone.

But I'm too lost in the sensations to take note, too destroyed by the perfection of the moment to care about anything other than our mutual pleasure.

She's my ideal match. My mate. The other half of my spirit.

I didn't realize how lost I was until finding her.

"No wonder I've wanted you all along. You're flawless," I breathe, my lips against her ear. "I'm going to cherish and worship you for the rest of our lives, little flame."

She shivers against me, her body replete and utterly sated.

Nox is still kneeling between our legs, his eyes holding a wicked gleam to them. "My turn," he says.

I hum in agreement and gently pull Fallon upward to release my cock from her luscious heat. But before I can hand her to him, he presses her back down and bends to lick her clean.

She jolts and moans, her hands going to his hair to pull him away.

But he's relentless, and soon she's writhing again, too caught up in his mouth to care about recovering. His name leaves her mouth, followed by mine, and I kiss her, helping to ground her in the present while Nox works his magic between her thighs.

I'm not surprised at all when he brings her to orgasm again, nor am I shocked to find myself hardening against her once more.

We've only begun our time together. Not just tonight, but for eternity.

"Are you ready for Nox to fuck you, little flame?" I ask her. "Because he has a surprise for you that you haven't seen yet."

Her eyelashes part to reveal twin pools of emerald ecstasy. "Surprise?" she repeats, sounding adorably exhausted.

"Mmm," I hum, my lips finding her ear. "It's a surprise you'll enjoy."

"What kind of surprise?" she asks.

Rather than answer, I take hold of her chin and turn her face toward a standing Nox. He kicked off his swimsuit at some point while kneeling, probably so he could stroke himself as he devoured Fallon.

Fallon blinks, not understanding right away.

Then her gaze goes to Nox's cock.

And the piercings forming a ladder down his shaft.

Her lips part and I nuzzle her neck. "It looks intimidating," I tell her. "But trust me, you'll love it. Nox will make sure of it."

He reaches for her then, and I release her.

"Bedroom?" I guess.

"Bedroom," he echoes, pulling her out of the shower and into a fluffy towel. "Now that Bane has helped me take the edge off, we can truly begin."

NOLAN

PORTALS ARE SO MUCH FASTER than airplanes, I think as I step into a New York City alley. *Much more discreet, too.*

Fortunately, a good friend of mine mated a witch queen. While the two of them might have run off to rule over the witch's world last year, the legacy of my friendship with the witch queen's mate has afforded me a few favors.

Such as access to very hard-to-find portal potion magic.

With a little sprinkle of the liquid, I close the portal in my wake and take in my dimly lit surroundings. When I left Ireland, night was falling. Which means it's afternoon here. But the sun isn't all that bright overhead, thanks to the towering skyscrapers all around me.

Still a shithole, I realize after only a few steps. It's all run-down with a dystopian flair due to decades of criminal activity. There are some nice areas—those owned by the syndicate boss families—but the city has mostly faded into ruin.

Alas, I never cared much for New York City. In its prime, it was too crowded. And the buildings have always suffocated my wings—something that hasn't changed even now.

I have my feathers tucked in, giving me the appearance of a normal man walking down the street. However, I can feel my plumes craving freedom, to take to the sky and escape these too-tall structures around me.

Rolling my shoulders, I ignore the sensation and focus on the vacant street.

The Outcast Coven is headquartered in Staten Island, making that my—

A prickle of warning caresses the back of my neck, causing the hairs to dance along my skin beneath my leather jacket. I continue forward, my pace steady as I evaluate my surroundings, searching for whatever set off my instincts.

There's no one around, no hints of habitation, and yet, I know I'm no longer alone. It's a sudden disturbance, one that has my hands itching to reach for one of my guns.

Behind me, I realize, the subtle hint of magic tickling my senses in the wrong way.

But I don't turn around. Instead, I keep my head high, pretending not to notice. Not until I have a better vantage point.

Getting closer, I think, feeling the magic strengthen at my back. *Ballsy fucker.*

Of course, I'm the visitor here. And this section of New York City is run by witches.

I pause as I reach the next intersection, feigning interest in the signs, all the while aware of the approaching presence.

Five, I start counting. *Four. Three. Two.*

My wings flare outward as I turn, my hand already pulling up my gun and aiming right at an approaching witch's head. Her black eyes widen, her palms flying upward.

But it's not a gesture of surrender.

It's a gesture of aggression, something that becomes clear as a glittering enchantment forms in front of her.

I narrow my gaze. "I wouldn't do that if I were you, witch."

"Do what?" she demands. "Protect myself?"

I arch a brow. "You're the one sneaking up on me." I stare down the barrel of my gun at her. "Tell me why."

Her obsidian hair blows in an invisible wind, her power mounting as the enchantment before her grows. My finger longs to pull the trigger, my intuition telling me this female is a threat. She may look dainty and delicate, but appearances can be deceiving. Fallon is evidence of that.

And so is this female—something the growing energy before her confirms as it pulses in the air.

"Who are you?" Her tone is underlined with command.

A command I ignore. "Someone you don't want to play with," I warn her. "Just move on and leave me be. It'll save your life."

Her lips curl a little. "My life will be just fine, archangel."

Well, that's interesting. Most supernaturals can't guess my origin that quickly. At least not when I've hidden my wings.

"What have you done to Fallon?" she asks in the next breath, her question giving me pause.

"What?"

"Her aura is all over you. Tell me why and I'll consider letting you live." Black flames dance up her arms while she speaks, all the while that energy continues to pulse in front of her.

I stare at her for a long moment as my instincts war.

Then I do something I never thought I would do.

I lower my weapon.

"You know Fallon." Which means I need this witch alive so she can tell me about my mate. "How?"

That black eyebrow of hers somehow lifts higher. "You're not very good at answering questions, are you?"

"I could say the same about you," I toss back. "Tell me how you know my mate."

Now both her brows are in her dark hairline. "*Mate?*" She huffs a laugh. "That's not possible. Nikolas is her mate."

Nikolas? "I'm her second-chance mate," I clarify. "*Nikolas* is dead. The King of Gold and Garnet executed him earlier this week."

Nikolas must be Klas's real name, I marvel, surprised that such a prominent detail was missing from his files. But it seems that was purposefully omitted.

"Second-chance...?" She trails off, some of the fire dying along her arms. "Oh, fuck..." The flames disappear entirely. "When did this happen?"

"When did what happen?"

"The mating," she says through her teeth. "When did you second-chance-mate her?"

I frown, the concern in her voice very unlike the commanding tone from moments ago. "Tell me who she is to you and I'll consider answering."

Because, so far, she hasn't given me much information, yet I've revealed a key detail about my link to Fallon. I also lowered my gun despite that sphere of energy whirling around her.

If she wants more details, she'll need to give me a compelling reason to comply.

The witch must see the resolve in my expression

because she sighs and draws the sphere-like enchantment back into herself. "Fallon is my cousin."

Now it's my turn to arch a brow. "The family resemblance is uncanny," I deadpan, noting her black hair, olive skin, and almond-shaped eyes.

This woman looks nothing like my curvy blonde witch.

She snorts. "We're not related by blood. Her aunt adopted me when I was a child." She folds her slender arms over her chest. "Did the mate bond happen right after the execution?" she asks, drawing us back to the second-chance-mate conversation.

"Yes. After she came back from the death plane," I say, watching her carefully to see if that trip to the *death plane* surprises her. "She mate-bonded all four of us the moment she started breathing again."

"All four...?" The woman's eyes widen. "Oh, that fucking spell..." It sounds like she's talking to herself more than to me, but her words have me instantly alert.

"What spell?"

"The one that mate-bonded her to Nikolas," she mutters, her fingers running through her hair as she starts pacing. "Do the patriarchs know?" she asks, her long legs eating up the sidewalk. "Never mind. Of course they know. Or they will. Who exactly has she mated?"

She stops then and looks at me, black flames appearing on her arms again.

My hand twitches with the need to rise, her threatening expression immediately putting me on the defensive.

Except her gaze goes over my shoulder in the next second as she softly says, "We can't have this conversation here."

I glance over my shoulder to find the street still empty, but the hairs along the back of my neck tell me that either it's a facade or it's about to change.

"This way," the witch says as a doorway magically appears in the wall of a building.

I stare at the enchantment as she approaches it. "Why should I follow you?"

"Because I know how to break the fated-mate spell," she says. "And I'm probably the only one who will tell you the truth around here."

Fated-mate spell. "You're saying it isn't real?"

"I'm saying we don't have time to discuss it here," she replies as she reaches the enchantment. "Either follow me or I'll track you down later. It's what I do."

She disappears through the threshold without a backward glance, leaving me on the sidewalk.

I narrow my gaze. This is likely a trap. But I'm not easily subdued, even if I'm taken to a place where I can't use my wings.

Besides, I came here for answers, and this female clearly knows Fallon. Which means Kaspian's instincts were right—she's from the Outcast Coven.

But I need more information.

Particularly about this supposed spell.

Right. I run my thumb down the handle of my gun and move toward the door. *Let's see where you go.*

I step through the enchantment, fully expecting an ambush.

Only, I find myself on a rooftop at least fifty stories up. My wings automatically unfurl, the height teasing my senses.

"Those are impressive," the witch says from a lounge chair nearby. "They blend in with the air around you, too."

"I camouflage naturally." It's an explanation she didn't earn, but I'm too caught up in the surroundings to care much about revealing such trivial details. "Where are we?"

Because this doesn't look like Staten Island.

"Manhattan," she replies. "On top of an abandoned apartment building."

"I see." Not sure why she chose this location, but I'm very comfortable here. "Tell me about this spell."

"It's a fated-mate spell, one the patriarchs like to use to force bonds between arranged mates."

I stare at her. "That's…"

"Illegal? Black magic? Exceptionally fucked up?" Each suggestion rivals the comments in my mind. "It's a practice that goes back decades. It's how the males control the females in our coven."

I gape at her. "Why would they do that?"

"To siphon our power, of course," she answers in a saccharine voice. "Fallon was given to Patrick O'Neely's nephew, Nikolas. The ritual was performed, and I'm guessing that Nikolas's death shattered the spell, which led to her soul latching onto yours and… You mentioned there are four of you?"

My feathers ruffle in the wind as I try to process what she's telling me.

The mating isn't real.

But it feels real.

"Are you sure it's from a spell?" I demand, ignoring her question.

Her brow furrows. "I mean, I guess it could be fate. But you mentioned four…?"

Yeah, that part makes it a bit more complex. Most souls only have one mate. Fallon having four is incredibly rare.

Which lends credence to the spell theory.

Yet part of me adamantly disagrees with that notion. *Because I'm under some sort of enchantment?* I wonder. *Am I being tricked into these feelings by dark magic?*

If that's the case, why didn't Fallon say something?

"I assume Fallon knows about this spell?" I hedge.

"Oh, yeah," the witch replies. "We all do."

"But you mentioned a way to break it?"

She smiles. "My being here talking to you is proof of that."

I arch a brow. "I'm not following."

"My *arranged mate* would never allow this," she explains. "But he's otherwise indisposed." She cants her head. "The patriarchs want us all to be puppets. I simply returned the favor."

I shake my head. "Your solution is to turn Fallon into a puppet?" *Does that mean I'm technically one right now because of this spell?*

"What? No. Absolutely not." She sits up straight on the old lounge chair and shakes her head. "I'm clearly not explaining this right. Let's start from the beginning."

That would be appreciated, I think.

Except she looks at me in the next second and says, "Actually, no. You need to tell me why you're here first. Then I'll consider telling you more."

Hmm. It's a reasonable request. She's also given me enough proof of her usefulness to make me want to reveal a little more about my intentions here. "Fallon hasn't been all that forthcoming about her past. So the Gold and Garnet King sent me here to see if we could learn more about her origin."

Her brows furrow. "If you're here, then she's been at least a little bit forthcoming."

"She mentioned *patriarchs* earlier today. While that may not be a familiar term to most of the world, King Kaspian and I recognized it. And with Fallon being a witch, it seemed likely to be related."

"Does she know you're here?"

"No."

The female swallows. "Good. That means the patriarchs won't be able to pull it out of her. But I imagine they know the spell rebounded now. Which... is either good or very bad. Especially for... *Shit.*" She pushes off of her lounge and starts pacing, similar to what she did in the street. "This must be why I haven't been allowed to see her."

"See who?" I ask even though the statement seems to have been for the woman before me alone. However, since I'm here listening, I would like to be part of the conversation.

"Issy." She freezes then, her obsidian irises swirling with panic.

"Fallon's sister." I fold my arms over my chest. "She mentioned her when talking about the patriarchs. Then she claimed her sister is dead, but King Kaspian knows she's lying."

The female blinks a few times. "Wait... You've mentioned him a few times. Is he...? Is he one of the mates the spell clung to?"

My jaw ticks as I debate whether or not to share that information.

But it seems I don't have to because the witch shakes her head. "This is bad. Very fucking bad." She resumes pacing. "The patriarchs are going to force Fallon into using him. And they're going to use Issy to make her do it."

I stare at her. "This would be the part where you should start from the beginning." Because I'm going to need as many details as I can gather.

The female pauses once more, her dark gaze finding mine. "How do I know I can trust you?"

"You can trust that I will do anything to protect King Kaspian. And right now, you've told me Fallon's fated-mate bond to both of us is a spell—one I will break, even if it means killing her. Especially since you just implied the patriarchs will try to use her to get to Kaspian. So either you start talking, or I return to Iceland and carry out my duty."

The words are painful to voice, my soul immediately rebuking my threat to kill my supposed mate. But I mean every statement.

It's my duty to guard the Gold and Garnet King. My pledge. And I'll do whatever is necessary to carry that out.

"Or I could kill you," the witch offers.

"You could try," I reply. "Or you could start talking and perhaps we'll come to an agreement that benefits us both. Assuming you care about your *cousin*, I mean."

Her eyes narrow. "Just because we're not related by birth doesn't mean she's not my family. And trust me, I will do whatever I fucking can to protect her. Just like you and your king."

"Then let's have a conversation and see if we can find some mutual ground to stand on." Because it seems to me that our goals may be somewhat aligned.

The witch studies me for a long moment, inky flames dancing in her irises. My fingers flex, preparing to pull out my gun again as my wings tense behind me.

However, after several beats, the enchantress sighs. "My name's Ayla." It's not exactly the story I want, but it seems to be her version of a peace offering.

"Nolan," I return.

She nods. "Well, Nolan. To understand what's happening, we need to go back in time to the night when Ishara accidentally killed several members of the O'Neely Clan."

My eyebrow arches. "Ishara?"

"Ishara Doyle. Issy. Fallon's sister." Ayla sits down again. "Her actions were an accident, but they created a significant rift between the O'Neely Clan and the Doyle Clan. That rift was healed by Fallon's arranged mating to Nikolas O'Neely. But I suspect you know him as *Klas*."

Yes, I guessed that connection earlier in the conversation.

"Most of the Outcast Coven believes Issy is dead. She's not. The Doyle Patriarch keeps her locked up with a sole purpose—to control Fallon." Ayla's eyes flash with barely restrained fury. "I only know this because I'm considered family. And the patriarchs believe I'm a good little witch on a leash."

"I see. And Fallon?"

"Fallon is… complicated." Ayla swallows. "She's powerful. Issy is, too. But their father has been siphoning their death energy since birth and using their twin bond against them." She draws her jean-clad legs up and wraps her arms around her knees, an uneasy expression on her face.

That look alone tells me I'm not going to like what Ayla is about to say.

"Fallon and Issy care more about each other than anything else in the world, and Patriarch Doyle uses that to ensure their obedience—by torturing Issy." She shudders at whatever vision is rolling through her mind. "That's the only reason Fallon mate-bonded Nikolas. She could have fought the patriarchy, but they had Issy."

I'm starting to see the picture in Ayla's mind. Not literally, but one of my own making.

A picture where a father abuses his daughters in the worst way possible while playing with their lives as though they're cards in a poker game.

"Fallon mentioned an obedience spell," I hedge. "One that she couldn't break."

Ayla nodded. "Patriarch O'Neely added that to the

mating to ensure Fallon couldn't break the mate bond. They know she's powerful. They'll do anything and everything they can to maintain dominion over her *and* Issy."

Which explains why Fallon hasn't said anything over the last year despite the obedience spell being broken— she's been worried about her sister's life.

"They're powerful links to the death plane," Ayla continues. "Key sources of power. I'm fairly certain that's the other reason Patriarch Doyle has kept Issy alive—they need her energy to maintain the patriarchy."

"I'm going to need you to detail this *patriarchy* more," I tell her. "Names, structure, key players. Everything you can give me."

"Why?" she asks, a humorless expression on her face that matches the incredulity of her tone. "Because you're actually going to do something about it?"

"I might," I tell her, my wings disappearing into my back.

"A House involving itself in a Supernatural Syndicate affair for altruistic purposes?" she snorts. "Right."

"Weren't you all just invited to participate in the Earth and Emerald Chancellor Trials?" I deadpan.

"That's not the same. The leadership was bought. Or they attempted to buy it, anyway." Her lips twitch as though amused. "Nikki didn't play their game, though. To be fair, neither did I."

I frown. "You participated?"

"I did." She cants her head. "The Outcast Coven *nominated* me. And by *nominated*, I mean *forced* me to participate. Because all the syndicates had to put forth a contestant, and they needed a female from our coven to be the face. Can't risk anyone realizing the patriarchs are the ones holding our puppet strings, right?"

The bitterness in her tone rivals my own irritation over the entire situation.

But she's right. Most Houses wouldn't get involved with these trivial affairs. If a criminal organization wanted to control its members with dark magic, the world leadership would allow it—unless those activities started impacting someone or something important.

Someone like a House King.

"Gold and Garnet's interference won't be altruistic," I tell her, returning to her sarcastic commentary about a House involving itself in syndicate business. "Fallon Doyle is mate-bonded to the Gold and Garnet King by an illegal dark magic spell. That's grounds for interference."

Ayla shivers. "She wouldn't have done it on purpose."

"I never said she did," I reply. *Nor am I confident it's a spell,* I think, still conflicted on that part. "But the fact remains that the Outcast Coven instigated all of this by placing Nikolas and Fallon in Gold and Garnet territory. I'm going to assume they had a reason. I want that reason."

"I don't have it."

"No, but you do have some details I need—like the patriarchs' names and other relevant information. You also mentioned being able to break the fated-mate spell."

She runs her fingers through her dark waves of hair, the edges of which travel all the way down to her slender hips.

Definitely looks nothing like Fallon, I think, suddenly missing my mate's curves. *Fake mate,* I correct myself. *Maybe.*

With a shake of my head, I add, "I need all the details you can give me, Ayla. Including information on how to break the spell." If nothing else, I can use that information to test the veracity of the claim.

Or at the very least, offer it to Fallon.

No one deserves to be trapped in an *arranged mating*.

While she might have hidden these secrets from us, it wasn't for nefarious reasons. She wanted to protect her sister.

Fallon probably assumed we wouldn't help her as well.

Most House leaders dislike the Supernatural Syndicates, and Kaspian is no different. Hell, he commented on it several times during the Earth and Emerald Chancellor Trials. Fallon likely heard a few of those statements, too.

It probably made her feel trapped, like she couldn't voice the truth without risking being sent back.

And given everything Ayla has just revealed, I can only imagine what the patriarchs would do if they got their hands on Fallon again now.

That's not going to happen, I vow. *Real mates or not, Fallon Doyle is under my protection. And I will not be handing her over to these assholes.*

No, I'm going to kill them all instead.

Deliver their heads to her in a coffin.

Then watch her burn their remains.

It's a date, I decide, my gaze settling on Ayla once more. "Start with Patrick O'Neely. Tell me everything you know."

FALLON

OH, stars, I'm about to detonate…

Except Nox pulls his mouth away, leaving me begging beneath him, *needing* more. He's been teasing me for what feels like *forever*, bringing me to the brink with his mouth and hands, only to stop right when I'm on the edge.

"*Nox.*"

"Fallon," he murmurs, his mouth curling into a grin against my clit. "Do you think you're ready for me yet?"

I groan, my lower half writhing in response. "I already said I am."

"Well, I just want to be certain." His blue eyes sparkle with wicked intent. "When I laid you on this bed an hour ago, you said you weren't sure you could take much more."

Yes. I did say that. Mostly because his piercings intimated me. But now… *now* I feel like I'm going to die if he doesn't finally fuck me.

Bane stretches out beside us on the bed, his head resting lazily on one hand as he stares down at me with a smile. "I think he wants you to beg him, sweet flame." He leans down to brush his lips over mine before pressing his mouth to my ear. "Maybe ask if you can taste him. I bet that mouth of yours could easily drive him insane."

Nox's pupils flare in response, confirming Bane's whispered words.

"It would only be fair," I say, my voice breathless.

"Would it?" Nox asks, lifting a little so I can see how wet I've made his mouth and chin. "You want to taste me, firefly?"

"Yes." I very much want to inflict this pleasurable torment on him. While Nox may be the first man who has ever gone down on me, I do know how to use my mouth on a man.

And I'm very eager to demonstrate that knowledge now.

"All right." Nox's gaze tells me he sees this as a challenge, one he intends to win.

But I'm *very* motivated to make him lose.

I press against his shoulder, wanting him to move so we can switch positions. However, he stops me with a palm against my stomach.

"I'll come to you," he says, confusing me as he starts crawling up my body.

I'm about to ask what he means when he reaches for Bane and openly kisses him while hovering over me.

My lips part in surprise, my body somehow heating even more at the sight.

Because *holy stars*, that's hot.

Their tongues duel above me, their embrace turning feral as Bane growls against Nox's mouth.

My thighs clench, igniting an inferno that burns through my veins. I want to see *more*. Experience their passion. Their virility. Their *heat*.

But the kiss ends almost as abruptly as it started, leaving me panting and thirstier than ever.

"Fuck, she tastes amazing," Bane says, his tongue sneaking out to lick his own lips. "I want more of that."

"Me, too," Nox murmurs. "Why do you think I've been indulging myself in her pussy for so long?"

"To delay your gratification."

"An added bonus," Nox replies. "But the primary reason is the one I just shared with you. Feel free to enjoy a snack while I fuck her mouth." His piercing blue irises return to mine, his lips curling into a smile. "Now who's a voyeur?"

"Two hot phantoms making out in front of me?" My voice is raspy, but I push on anyway. "I would be a fool not to watch."

"So you don't mind a little male-on-male action?" he asks, his palm cupping my cheek.

I shake my head. "It's definitely a turn-on."

"Mmm, that's good to know," he murmurs, his nose brushing mine. "Because I suspect you're going to drive us wild and we're going to want to return the favor." He nips at my bottom lip. "Now how about you give me a demonstration with that fine mouth of yours?"

It's a rhetorical question because he's already moving by the time he finishes speaking, his athletic body shifting with ease up my supple form.

A fire lights inside of me as he settles his knees on either side of my head, placing his impressive length near my mouth. He's longer than Bane, but not as thick.

However, the metal piercings decorating his shaft give him a dangerous appeal that has my insides dancing in appreciation.

"Lick me." His head meets my mouth. "Wrap those

gorgeous lips around my cock and show me what you can do."

The flames inside me burn hotter, my desire to do exactly what he says a searing need through my veins.

I want to please him. Learn his preferences. *Taste* him. And most of all, demonstrate my ability to blow his mind.

My gaze holds his as I part my lips around him to sample the precum lingering on his tip. I groan as soon as it hits my tongue, my yearning for him driving me forward to take more. Swallow him. Lave him. *Devour* him.

His metal piercings are soft against my tongue, the bulbous ends tantalizing and unique. *What will he feel like inside me?* I wonder as I take him even deeper, forcing his head to the back of my throat.

"Fuck, Fallon," he breathes, his blue eyes darkening as he stares down at me. "Look at you taking my cock." His palm wraps around my nape before sliding up a little to help angle my head for a deeper thrust. And his opposite hand goes to the headboard to hold himself steady. "You're so fucking perfect."

"So fucking perfect," Bane echoes as he settles between my thighs.

I jolt as his mouth meets my clit, my stomach tightening with renewed yearning. I was so close to coming before, so near the edge of that rapturous cliff, that I'm almost immediately right back there now.

Bane's name vibrates in my mouth, the sound muffled by Nox driving his length farther into my throat.

Having one man between my legs while another is fucking my mouth is so erotic. So intense. So *overwhelming*.

"You want her to come while you're fucking her mouth?" Bane asks against my throbbing arousal. "Or do you want her to come around your cock?"

"Mmm, both very tempting choices," Nox replies, his grasp tightening against my nape. "What do you want, Fallon?" He pulls himself out to the tip. "How do you want to come?"

I shiver, both from the expectant look on his face and from the deep timber of his voice. I can almost hear his Scottish roots. They're just not as prominent as Bane's, but they're still there. Lingering. Caressing. *Teasing.*

He arches a brow. "Would you like me to decide for you, firefly?"

I consider the option and nod. "Yes. I trust you." And I want whatever he wants.

No, that's not true.

I want both options.

But I'm not sure my body will allow it. I've never experienced pleasure like this before, the unending assault on my senses leaving me exhausted and replete and... *needy.*

Oh, stars, maybe I can do both...

I don't know. I don't know my own limits at all.

However, I mean what I said—I trust Nox.

Actually... "I trust both of you."

Bane hums in approval against me, the vibration zinging through my veins and leaving a tingling kiss behind.

I gasp as his lips seal around my sensitive bud, his tongue doing all sorts of wicked things that stoke my flames so much higher. It's as though he's ignited a fuse that counts down with the beat of my heart. I can hear it thudding in my ears. Feel it hammering in my chest. Sense it warming my veins. Preparing me. *Forcing* me closer.

"Good choice," Nox murmurs as he pushes back into my mouth, his eyes holding mine. "Both will do just fine."

I don't remember voicing that aloud.

But maybe I did.

Or maybe they're mind readers.

It doesn't matter because the maelstrom inside me is spinning out of control. I moan Bane's name, then Nox's name, then realize neither is intelligible because my mouth is too occupied to produce proper sound.

Stop thinking, I tell myself. *Just feel. Experience. Embrace them. This. All of this.*

I grab Bane's head, holding him to me while my opposite hand goes to Nox's hip. I never want to let them go.

They're mine.

My phantoms.

My mates.

I fall apart on that last thought, my world shattering as Nox hits the back of my throat with a groan of his own. He says something about how good I am, but I'm too consumed by what Bane is doing to my lower half to focus.

The whole reason I wanted Nox in my mouth was so I could demonstrate my ability to please him. However, I lost sight of that goal the moment Bane started licking me.

It was all too much.

It's still too much.

But I'm too caught up in the moment to deviate course.

It's perfect in its own way, a reprieve from the reality I long to escape.

Nox pulls from my mouth, his tongue replacing his cock in what seems like a span of seconds. Then I feel him nudging against me below.

This is it, I think, my legs encircling his hips. *I finally get to feel—*

He drives into me, causing my inner walls to squeeze

around him, his piercings resembling a ribbed sensation that has my toes curling in response.

It... I'm... I'm so...

"Full," I whisper. "I feel full." *And... and...* "*Oh, stars...*"

My mind fractures as he begins to move, his hips dancing with mine in a way that steals my breath. I've never felt anything like this. Never knew this sort of pleasure could exist.

It's different than it was with Bane.

But both of them are amazing in their own right. Just uniquely their own, providing me with two very special experiences that I will forever cherish.

And hopefully experience again.

And again.

Because they're mine.

I refuse to let them go.

There's a nagging thought in my mind, threatening my utopian state. But I ignore it and focus on Nox.

Oh, and Bane... He's stretched out beside us again, his palm slipping between our bodies and heading down toward the apex between my thighs.

I tremble as he brushes my throbbing center, his touch knowing. Skilled. *Perfect.*

Nox palms my breast, his tongue mastering mine, his hips engaging me in an endless dance.

"Come for us again, sweet flame," Bane says. "Nox needs to feel that beautiful pussy clamp down around him."

I'm already close again, the hour session with Nox's mouth having primed me more than I realized.

Coupled with everything else... it's a wonder I haven't fallen into a permanent state of ecstasy.

"That's it, Fallon," Bane coaxes. "Fuck him back. Ride us both. Find your pleasure and revel in it."

Nox growls, the sound a vibration against my chest that has me panting beneath him. It's so virile in nature, reminding me of their shared kiss and making me wonder what they would be like when they fuck each other.

Rough. Hard. Masculine.

What would it be like to be between them? One in the front? One in the back?

My whole body seizes at the thought, my insides pulsating.

I want that. I want to know. I want so much more.

And I tell Nox that with my tongue.

I reach for Bane, my palm finding his hardness and giving him a stroke, hoping my message is conveyed. He hisses in response, his thumb pressing down on my center, his mouth finding my ear. "You're such a good girl taking Nox's cock like that, Fallon. But I need you to come around him. Give him that gift. Just like you gave me."

I tighten my grasp on his dick, his words propelling me forward.

These two phantoms are going to fuck me into an early grave with all these sexual comments and skilled touches.

"*Now*, Fallon," Bane demands, making my insides convulse in response.

I tense, shocked that I'm already at the edge again.

Nox tweaks my nipple, and it's all I need to go soaring into a climax that blackens my vision. I'm barely aware of the two men growling their approval, their words of praise sailing somewhere along with me in the clouds as my body floats and convulses.

Euphoria burns through my nerve endings.

My limbs quake.

And my vision remains unseeing.

Until suddenly I find myself staring up into a pool of liquid blue irises brimming with pleasure. Nox's groan rumbles over me, his own rapture touching mine and leaving us to shake in orgasmic bliss together.

I can feel his seed inside me, marking me as his own, *claiming* me, just like Bane did.

It all feels so real. So *final*. So unlike anything Klas and I ever did.

Maybe it isn't a spell at all, I marvel. *Maybe this really is fate...*

I kiss Nox, hoping with everything I am that these phantoms truly are mine. Then I kiss Bane with the same vigor, the same desire, and sigh when he returns my fervor with his tongue.

The two men take turns, our embrace growing heavy as exhaustion settles into my bones.

My eyes are closed.

My lips are moving.

My body is still shaking with residual aftershocks.

But I can sense sleep weighing down upon me.

It must win at some point because when I open my eyes again, the phantoms are both lounging in bed beside me with the blankets covering their hips.

They gaze down at me with reverent expressions that make my heart soar. I feel as though I'm existing in a dream.

When they praise me for how well I took them, my heart races. When Bane surprises me with food, my heart swells. And when Nox tells me they intend to devour me again for dessert, my heart nearly stops.

Only to kick into overdrive as both phantoms guide me into a new level of oblivion.

It's so unworldly.

So rapturous.

So unbelievable.

Yet it's all real.

I've lived in a nightmare for most of my existence. But this is a fantasy come to life.

One I indulge in until I can no longer keep my eyes open.

As I drift into sleep, one thought lingers in my mind. *I hope this dream never ends...*

KASPIAN

My DICK THROBS in my hand as I think about Fallon's screams.

Nox and Bane were thorough, fucking her well into the night. Part of me wants to remind Nox that he owes me a visit, but I don't want to take him away from our mate.

Her pleasure is fucking addicting. I can't wait to experience it for myself. To taste her. Slide into her. *Make her mine.*

I picture her on her knees for me now, all that blonde hair tumbling around her as I bend her over the bed and drive into her from behind.

That curvy ass of hers would push back against my groin with each thrust, providing me with delicious friction.

And she would be so damn wet. So tight. So ready for me to fuck her hard and fast.

I groan, her name leaving my lips as I stroke myself harder, her vision stark and real in my mind. Her tits swaying as I pump into her. Those delicious little moans escaping her plump lips.

Mmm, I would fist my fingers in all that hair and pull

her head back to expose her slender neck. It would tease my fangs, make me crave her that much more.

Then her racing pulse would send me over the edge, forcing me to bite her. Taste her. *Claim* her.

Fuck, I can almost taste her now, her heartbeat a steady rhythm in my mind even while she sleeps.

I release my cock to keep myself from exploding, my entire body strung tight with need.

But I want to wait.

I want to savor the torment and let my desire build.

It's addictive. Consuming. So damn exquisite.

I've been doing this for hours, reveling in the activities next door while torturing myself. I was saving it all for Nox, but part of me wants to give it to Fallon.

This craving for her is immense, the fate bond overwhelming my thoughts. However, if I'm honest with myself, I've been attracted to Fallon all along. Especially her disobedient mouth.

She stands up to me when others normally wouldn't. It pisses me off while making me hard at the same time. She's a brat, one I long to tame.

And yet, I wouldn't have her any other way.

I button myself up again and stand up to pace the guest room, my legs eating up the small area in only a few strides.

What I need to do is head outside, but I can't. While I know this area is safe, I feel this intrinsic urge to guard the phantoms and my mate. Almost as though they're all mine to protect.

Running my fingers through my hair, I continue moving and nearly sigh in relief when my phone buzzes. I've taken a few calls tonight for work purposes, but the one I've been waiting for most hasn't happened yet.

However, Nolan's name appears now.

I immediately accept the call.

"Did you end up flying to New York?" I ask without saying hello. "I expected you there hours ago."

"I used a portal potion ten minutes after hanging up with you earlier," he replies as his face appears on a screen before me.

I frown at him. "Why didn't you call me when you arrived?" That's what we agreed upon.

Of course, I wouldn't have had any updates for him then. But it's been almost twelve hours since we last spoke.

"Because Fallon's cousin ambushed me upon arrival," he deadpans.

Someone snorts in the background, and he tilts his camera so I can see the dark-haired female seated across from him.

"Cousin?" I repeat.

"Adopted cousin," he clarifies. "Her birth parents went missing around the Arcadia portal, and Fallon's aunt adopted her."

"I see." I lock my gaze with the female's. "And you managed to ambush my best assassin?"

"He was drenched in Fallon's aura. I felt him arrive and I thought it was her, so I tracked the soul strand and found..." She waves at him. "An archangel dressed in leather."

Now it's Nolan who snorts in the background.

"Do you have a name?" I press, arching a brow.

"I do." She doesn't elaborate.

"Ayla," Nolan answers for her as he turns the camera back around. "She's been very informative."

"Good. Tell me everything."

Nolan sighs and nods. "You're going to want to sit down for this."

An hour later and I'm pacing the room for very different reasons than before.

Nolan and I hung up five minutes ago, his final words being, "I'm going to do some reconnaissance around Staten Island in the early morning with Ayla as my guide."

He plans to document where all seven patriarchs live and take note of their security.

Because Gold and Garnet is about to declare war on the Outcast Coven.

They sent an emissary into *my* territory. An emissary who attacked our former king. And they gave him a witch to borrow deadly powers from.

Via a forced mating spell.

Which shattered upon his death.

And rebounded by joining that witch's soul with four others.

"Fuck," I mutter, running my hand over my face. "*Fuck.*"

Nox and Bane are next door with her right now, completely unaware that they're under a mating spell. While Fallon…

Fallon is fully aware and didn't say a damn word about it.

That's the part that pisses me off the most. The woman bloody knew that her mating spell rebounded, and didn't say anything. She played along instead.

"Because she's protecting her sister," Nolan said, his voice strained. "I don't like that she didn't tell us any of this, but after everything Ayla has shared, I understand why she chose to stay silent."

I'm not nearly as understanding as Nolan. While Fallon certainly hasn't had the easiest life—far from it—she's in

Gold and Garnet territory. And we take fealty to our House *very* seriously.

When I said as much to Nolan, he replied with, "A fair point, but did Fallon ever actually swear fealty to Gold and Garnet?"

My hands curl into fists as I pace, his words playing over and over again in my head.

How has it come to this? I wonder, furious by all of these developments. *How did I end up spellbound to an Outcast Coven witch?*

I can hear said witch moaning next door, telling me the phantoms have just decided to engage in another round. And I *hate* that my body reacts to it. *Hate* that my body reacts to *her*.

Because it isn't real.

She isn't actually mine.

And she's not theirs either.

Something she bloody knows but has chosen not to admit.

It's so damn wrong, telling me she's not nearly as innocent as she pretends to be.

"She was protecting her sister," Nolan argued at one point. "And she's likely very aware of how most House leadership feels about the syndicates. Why would she trust us to help her?"

Because she fake fate-mated us? I think now. However, during the conversation, I remained silent, mostly to keep from saying something I shouldn't.

But maybe I *should* say something.

Maybe I should fucking *yell*.

Another moan reaches my ears, making me growl.

Patience and strategic thinking have always been two of my strengths. However, I can't seem to call upon either ability now.

My heart and soul are too wrapped up in the knowledge that I've been tricked into a bond by *dark magic*.

And she knows about it. She fucking knows.

That's the part I can't forgive. She roped us all into this fucking mess and didn't deem us worthy of knowing the truth.

Hell, she's even *fucking* two of her fake mates now.

"The spell can be broken," Nolan confirmed thirty minutes ago. "Ayla has provided instructions on how to do it. I'll text it to you. Fallon will need to be the one to carry it out."

"And what if she refuses?" I asked. "Can another witch break the spell?"

"Yes," Ayla said. "But I know Fallon. She'll want to break it herself."

I snort again now, just like I did then, disbelieving the notion that Fallon will follow through. This is the woman who kept all these details from us to begin with and has knowingly played along with Nox and Bane's claim.

"Sex won't make it permanent like a fated-mate bond would," Ayla also told me. "And, unlike a fated-mate bond, you can't reject the connection. The only way out is to break the spell. Or when a mate dies."

"Or it'll rebound, apparently," I muttered.

"That's not normal, but Fallon's a strong witch," Ayla replied. "The O'Neelys would have needed to layer the spells on her to make her compliant."

Compliant, I repeat to myself. *Right.*

There is nothing *compliant* about Fallon Doyle. She's a fiery little rebel whose moans make my balls fucking ache.

"*Damn it*," I snap, heading toward the door. "I need this to stop. *Right fucking now.*"

No more playing.

No more thinking.

No time for strategy.

The phantoms are starting to make her scream, and she doesn't deserve it. She doesn't deserve *any* of us. Not after what she's kept from us.

A fake fated-mate spell.

I growl low in my chest, livid with the dark magic for existing. Angry with Fallon for keeping the truth from us.

And furious that it isn't real.

I've lived so long without a connection to anyone. Which is fine. I haven't been eager to find a mate. But to finally experience this link only to have it be due to a spell…

Fuck.

I palm my chest, my breathing coming in pants.

Fuck. This.

Fallon Doyle is going to break me free of this insanity.

Then I'm going to visit her coven and let those patriarchs know that they fucked with the wrong House King.

Magic or not, I have an entire army of mercenaries at my disposal.

Staten Island is going to fucking burn.

And Fallon Doyle…

Well, we'll see, I think, my hand on the doorknob. *All right,* little mate. *Let's see how well you can lie now…*

FALLON

I'M FLYING.

Soaring through the sky.

Lost somewhere in a euphoric cloud of masculinity and grace.

Tongues. Hands. Fingers.

Nox and Bane are everywhere, owning my body, claiming my spirit, and filling me with a hope unlike anything I've ever encountered.

Because it all feels so amazing.

So anchoring.

So *enchanting*.

I've never experienced life in this way, so hot and vibrant and *vivacious*.

I could live here forever, in this moment, and die the happiest woman alive. All because of—

A crack whips through the air, causing all three of us to freeze. Then Nox and Bane immediately jump to their feet in the next moment, their sudden movement leaving me cold and exposed on the bed.

"What the fuck?" Nox demands as a familiar form stalks into the room.

My eyes widen, and I immediately grab the sheets to pull them up over my nude body, my need to hide making me shrink back into the mattress.

Because Kaspian looks… *pissed*. Which shouldn't be new to me—I constantly seem to infuriate him—but there's something different about him now. He appears unrestrained. Livid. *Dangerous.*

I swallow as he continues forward, my legs kicking a little in response to help propel me up the bed until my back hits the headboard.

"Kaspian." Nox steps in between us, momentarily blocking my view of the furious vampire. "What the fuck are you doing?"

"Leave us." Kaspian's demanding tone has Nox's muscles tightening in response, his shoulders going rigid.

"What?"

"*Leave. Us.*" Kaspian sounds every bit like the Gold and Garnet King and nothing like the man I usually talk to.

It has me wanting to disappear from view. *What's happened?* I wonder, my heart suddenly in my throat. *Why is he speaking this way?*

He's radiating fury to a point where I can almost feel the heat of it on my skin.

I try to hide a little more in the blankets, naively hoping it'll act as a barrier.

But it doesn't.

I may not be able to see Kaspian around Nox right now, but his ire is burning so hot that the entire room is filled with it.

"No." Nox's response shocks the hell out of me. As does his protective stance. "No, I'm not going to do that. Not when you're this close to falling into a blood rage."

"Excuse me?" Kaspian somehow sounds even angrier now. "I am your *king*. You will do what I say, when I say it."

"Almost always," Nox concedes. "But not when you're behaving this way around our mate."

Kaspian huffs a laugh. However, it lacks humor. "She's not our fucking mate," he says, his words dousing me in a bucket of ice water. "It's a *fucking spell*."

My lips part. *Oh, no…*

"Isn't that right, *Miss Doyle*?" Kaspian asks, his tone taking on a silky quality that draws goose bumps along my arms. He peeks around Nox, his dark eyes swirling with savage intent. "Care to enlighten them, or shall I?"

A soft squeak leaves my mouth in response, words failing me.

H-how?

How does he know?

What's he going to do?

What…? What will Bane and Nox…? I glance at my phantoms, the two men who just spent the last however many hours making me feel so special, so *cherished*, my heart thundering in my chest. *Is it…? It's not… They're not…*

But it felt *so* real.

Everything was so intense. So beautiful. So… *so much like a dream.*

Kaspian makes a noise in his throat, one that sounds incredibly ridiculing.

A sound I deserve, I think with a wince. "I… I didn't…"

He scoffs again. "Didn't what? Didn't mean to string us all along with this ruse?"

"What are you talking about, Kaspian?" Bane asks carefully, his demeanor as calm as ever. And somehow that seems to break my heart even more.

He's always been so kind to me. So understanding. But after this… after Kaspian tells him the truth…

"The Outcast Coven patriarchs tied Fallon's soul to Klas's—wait, no, *Nikolas O'Neely's*—soul using dark magic. When we executed him, the spell fractured, and Fallon's soul attached itself to four new mates."

Kaspian's sharp-tongued summary shoots ice through my veins.

How does he know all of that?

Nox slowly turns to look at me, his blue eyes assessing. "Is that true, Fallon?"

My heart cracks a little more at the way he asks me that—as though he'll trust my response over his own king's words.

But it's the worry in his expression that slays me. The worry that Kaspian may be right. Bane wears a matching look as he gazes at me, both phantoms waiting for me to confirm their king's claims.

I swallow, my vision blurring as my inner turmoil threatens to break free.

How did I go from enjoying the best night of my life to experiencing the worst moment of my existence?

Because this hurts more than the ceremony that bound me to Klas. Hurts more than all the torture Klas inflicted upon me. Hurts more than the suicide verdict and my unexpected visits to the death plane.

This... this is *hell*.

Having my hope shattered in seconds.

Realizing that all this pleasure will be short-lived.

Because these males are not truly mine. It doesn't matter how much they feel connected to my soul. Everything was the result of a fractured spell.

And now they know.

Now they'll hate me forever.

Leave me with the agony of one beautiful memory, destroyed by my nightmarish reality.

I swallow again and attempt to clear my throat. All three men are staring at me. Bane with open concern. Nox with growing suspicion. Kaspian with pure hatred.

I hurt them by not telling the truth. *But... but...* "I hoped it was real," I admit in a whisper. "I..." It's not an excuse. Not a good one, anyway. "It felt different with you. All of you." Even Kaspian, really. "I never wanted Klas, even with... the magic. It was always forced." My gaze falls. "But not with you."

My shoulders curl down, and I suddenly feel more defeated than ever before.

Admitting how I feel, how desperate I am for this to be truly tied to fate, just leaves me feeling more inferior than ever. *Weak.* Because I know better. I *know* fate would never be this kind to me.

However, a naive, hopeful part of me wanted this so badly to be real.

But it's not.

It's a spell.

And when we break it, these men will never want to look at me again. Never want to *talk* to me again. Touch me. Be with me.

My eyes close as I try to keep my tears at bay.

I need to be strong. I need to face this. Face *them.* It's what I deserve. I should have told them the truth.

But I... I needed to protect... My brow furrows. *Issy.*

I force myself to meet Kaspian's cruel gaze. "How...?" *How do you know all this? Do you know the truth about Issy?* I can't bring myself to ask, my heart breaking even more.

Because if he knows about the Outcast Coven, it's all over anyway. He's going to send me back. Or maybe he'll just kill me.

"I'll break the spell... when I find out how." The words

are a whisper, my eyes falling closed again as pain prickles my insides.

Why did it never feel this way with Klas? Because he was evil? Because I hated him?

Maybe this pain stems from knowing what I could have had in this life. Bane and Nox were—

"I know how to break it," Kaspian says. "Ayla told me."

"A-ayla?" I force my gaze back to his, the coldness in his dark eyes making me shiver. "You talked to Ayla?"

"Who's Ayla?" Bane asks, his voice still exuding calm.

"Fallon's adopted cousin." Kaspian folds his arms across his chest as Nox moves to his side, both men staring down at me with conflicting expressions. Kaspian appears ready to kill me, while Nox... Nox just looks... contemplative. Maybe he's also thinking about killing me, but in more creative ways.

"I see." Bane doesn't join the other two men, instead choosing to sit on the bed beside me. "And she claims this is all a spell, one she told you how to break."

Kaspian glances at him. "Yes. So Fallon is going to break it for us." He refocuses on me, his stern expression holding me captive. "Right fucking now."

My lower lip threatens to quiver, the notion of severing ties to these men making me feel cold all over. But I dip my chin in resignation, aware that I don't have a choice in this matter.

They're not mine to keep. Even if I want them.

"I never meant to hurt anyone," I say, a slight tremble underlying my words. "I... I..."

"You just wanted to protect your sister," Kaspian replies through his teeth. "At the expense of everyone around you."

My fingers curl into my blankets. "I was going to find a

way to break it, to free you all."

"Sure," Kaspian drawls. "I'll believe that after all the other lies you've told."

I wince, his words a direct hit.

Because why would he believe anything I have to say? I didn't confide in him before. And I truly have no intention of confiding in him now. It's not like he'll help me after all of this. So what would be the point?

He's going to make me break these forced bonds, then either sentence me publicly for the spell or ship me back to the Outcast Coven.

Either way, my moment of bliss is done.

Reality has returned.

"Tell me what Ayla said." The words are soft but steady. I'm not going to fight him. Nor am I going to drag this out any longer. "How do I break the spell?"

"Hold on a minute," Bane says, his palm going to my knee, his touch burning me even through the blankets. "What if I don't want her to break the spell?"

Kaspian arches a brow at him. "What?"

"I'm not sure I believe it's a spell," Bane goes on. "Fallon is my mate. I can feel it in my soul. That may be the result of fate-related magic, but it's certainly not *forced*."

"I agree," Nox interjects before Kaspian can speak. "It doesn't feel forced for me either."

"Because you're both enchanted by her magic." Kaspian glares at me. "We all are."

Bane shakes his head. "No. Fallon said herself that it feels different with us. But with Klas, it felt *forced*. She hated him, yet obeyed him because of that obedience enchantment. Once Nyx broke it, she was able to fight him."

"I don't want to fight this at all," Nox adds. "Even hearing what you just said, I... I don't feel angry or betrayed. Just confused. Because it all feels too right to be a spell. Too *natural*."

"Like fate," Bane says.

Nox nods. "Like fate."

Kaspian blows out a breath. "You both just spent several hours fucking her. Of course you feel *connected*. Once the spell is broken, you'll see what I see: a manipulative dark enchantment that's binding us all together *illegally*. And she"—he points at me—"didn't tell us about it."

There's nothing I can say to that, so I don't speak at all.

He won't care that I wanted to protect my sister. Nor will he care that the spell wasn't of my creation. All he sees is the use of dark magic to create a fabricated link.

It doesn't matter that I wished it was real or that it all felt good for a minute.

He's absolutely right to hate me. And once the spell is broken, my two phantoms will join him in that hatred.

"Just tell me how to break it, Your Majesty," I request, done with this conversation. There's nothing left to say here. I'll follow whatever directions Ayla gave him, then I'll await his judgment. It can't be worse than what the Outcast Coven will do to me.

It can't be worse than how I feel right now, either, I decide, my chest aching with the knowledge that I'm about to destroy the only happiness I've ever really known.

But it's the only way.

The phantoms weren't mine to keep. I've known that since the moment I realized we were bonded.

Nothing in this life can ever truly be pleasurable. Not for me, anyway.

I'm a being of death.

Destined to be alone.

Forever and always.

KASPIAN

My EYES narrow at the meek blonde on the bed.

This has to be an act. Some sort of ploy to avoid judgment.

Because this isn't the Fallon I've come to know. This is some submissive form of her that I've never seen before. And I am not pleased with the development at all. Primarily because it makes me feel uneasy, and I don't appreciate that sensation at all.

Not when I know I'm in the right here.

She lied and withheld important information. Information that fucks with not just my life but also the lives of those around me.

A forced mating spell.

One that clearly has my phantoms enthralled because they're staring at *me* with accusations in their eyes. Like I've done something wrong here, not Fallon. All because she's cowering on the bed, waiting for my instructions.

"Just tell me how to break it, Your Majesty."

Her words play through my head. Primarily the last two. It's the first time she's ever addressed me in a formal way without a hint of sarcasm.

And now she won't even look at me.

Her head is bowed toward her knees, her entire demeanor closed off and frightened, like she's anticipating the worst from me.

She's been abused by authority all her life, I think, recalling everything Ayla and Nolan said. *Is she expecting that same abuse now? From me?*

My heart pangs uncomfortably in my chest, that thought stabbing through me with the sharpness of a well-aimed dagger.

Her comments about Klas come filtering back through my head. She called it *forced*, a word Bane used purposely as well, but mainly to say he doesn't feel *forced* to be with her at all. Even Nox said it feels natural to him.

I study her for a long moment, trying to decipher how this bond actually makes me feel. *Beyond* my anger—which isn't bond related so much as betrayal related. I don't appreciate lies, especially when they directly impact me.

And in this case, her lies very much apply to me.

Especially where the mating bond is concerned.

Yet the notion of rejecting her bothers me. Which doesn't make sense. Ayla said rejection wouldn't work to counter the spell. She also said sex wouldn't solidify it, either.

So Bane and Nox having fucked Fallon shouldn't matter. Yet they both clearly feel fate-bonded to her. *Because of the spell, or something else?* I wonder, my gaze narrowing even more. *What if…?*

I frown, not wanting to finish that thought.

However, it whispers through my mind unbidden. *What if this is the real thing?*

The very idea of hurting Fallon in any way bothers me. Observing her now, I have this intrinsic need to fix this and find the fiery female hidden beneath her broken stature.

This isn't my Fallon. She's stronger than this. And yet, I've severely upset her.

I can see it in the way she won't meet my eyes.

It could be guilt. But somehow, I know it's more.

Is that the spell? Or is it something else entirely?

From what Ayla said, the dark magic creates a link that allows the males of the Outcast Coven to access power through their arranged mates. An obedience spell is often cast on top of it to ensure the female can't fight the connection.

There are no romantic ties.

No sexual inclinations.

No *feelings* involved whatsoever.

Because, as Ayla put it, "That would create a conflict for the male mate, and the patriarchy can't allow that. They need their men in charge at all times, not influenced by love or affection."

So why do I care about Fallon's feelings now? Why do I feel like I've destroyed something precious?

My throat works as I stare at her, some of my ire melting away. She didn't tell us the truth because she was protecting her sister. It's an admirable reason, even if I don't appreciate it.

But it's the reason I dislike it that matters most—*I don't like that she doesn't trust me.*

I want to be worthy of Fallon's trust. Worthy of her secrets. Worthy of *her*.

Those feelings have been with me for a while now, which is why she constantly frustrated me. Knowing everything I do now, I'm still frustrated for the same reason.

Because I need her to have faith in me.

I take care of what's mine. I always have. It's one of my

strengths, a core foundation of who I am as a master vampire and leader.

But Fallon has never once had faith in me to do right by her.

She's constantly fought me, hidden away her truths, and disliked me at every turn.

I only now understand why—because I represent an authority figure in her life. And thus far, all those who have been put in charge of her fate have failed her.

And I'm acting no better right now, I tell myself.

Nox and Bane are convinced this is real.

What if they're right?

If they are, then I've royally fucked up my chance at happiness. Because there's no way in hell Fallon will ever accept me.

Unless I fix this, I think, my gaze on her quivering lip.

She's still waiting for me to tell her how to undo the spell, her obedient pose one I craved mere days ago but hate right now.

Because of what it implies.

She's bowing to me as her superior, not because she's my mate or because she respects me. But because she *fears* me.

I don't want her to fear me.

And that has nothing to do with a forced mating spell.

"I need a moment alone with Miss Doyle," I tell Nox and Bane.

Both phantoms stare at me, their expressions indicating unease.

"I'm not at risk of a blood rage," I say, addressing Nox's earlier concern regarding the notorious vampiric urge to fuck, fight, or feed in response to strong emotions—especially anger. "I just need to have a private word."

"If you're going to force Fallon to undo this mating, then we deserve to be here for it," Bane replies.

"You do," I agree. "I simply need to speak with her alone for a minute." I look between the two men and add, "Please."

Nox arches a brow, aware that I don't usually add platitudes unless I feel they're absolutely necessary.

Bane simply stares at me for a beat. Then he gives Fallon's knee a squeeze and slips off the bed to grab a pair of pants from a drawer nearby. They're technically my pants, but I don't say anything to dissuade him. He snags a second pair for Nox and throws them to him.

"We'll be in the hallway." Bane's gaze meets and holds mine. "Don't break our trust."

With that statement, he heads toward the door.

Nox doesn't immediately follow, his attention going to Fallon. "Call us if you need us, firefly. We don't care about the spell. We're still yours."

She blinks, causing one of the tears lingering on her lashes to fall.

But she doesn't reply to him.

Nor does she look up at him.

Which causes him to give me an irritated glare before heading toward the door. "Don't break our trust, Kas," he echoes, making me sigh.

I fucked up by coming in here angry. It's not like me. But hearing everything Ayla and Nolan said set me off, and no amount of pacing calmed me down.

I needed to see Fallon. Question her. *Demand* answers.

But that wasn't what I did at all.

I blindsided her and the phantoms, broke through Fallon's barriers with a few pointed words, and reduced this strong female to a shell of a person by exuding my dominion over her.

Normally, she fights back.

But something about this situation destroyed her.

And I *hate* that I'm the cause.

"Fallon." I can't help the hint of command in my voice. It's mostly to try to seize her attention. "I need you to do something for me."

She gives a small nod. "Yes, Your Majesty."

Fuck, those two words again. They slam right into me in the worst way. I much prefer her sarcastic address over this defeated formality.

"I need you to reject me," I tell her.

Her brow furrows. "What?"

"I want you to reject me," I reiterate.

Her green eyes remind me of liquid emerald as she gazes up at me, her sadness piercing my very soul. "I'm sorry, Your Highness, but I don't understand. Rejection won't break the spell." Her frown deepens. "Is that what Ayla told you?"

"No, she told me rejection won't impact the spell either way."

"Then I still don't understand," she says slowly. "What will the rejection accomplish?"

I sit on the bed near her legs, but I'm careful not to touch her. "Rejecting me will tell us if this is real or not."

Her watery irises study me for a beat. "It's dark magic, not fate," she whispers then, her gaze lowering once more. "I know better now than to wish for anything else."

I catch her chin and gently return her gaze to mine. "It probably is dark magic," I concede. "However, I would like you to reject me anyway. It likely won't do anything, but at least we'll both know."

She swallows. "Doing this implies hope."

"Yes, I suppose it does. But I need to know this isn't real. And I think you do, too."

"This isn't real." Her voice is a little stronger, but the pain in her expression is heart-wrenching.

I *hate* hurting her. But Fallon has to be the one to reject our bond. It's the only way I can be certain of whether this is fate or a spell.

"Prove it," I dare her. "Prove to me that it isn't real. Reject me."

Some of the water in her gaze sizzles as a hint of fire enters her eyes. "Why? So you have more proof for your formal sentencing?"

"Who said anything about a formal sentencing?" I ask, arching a brow.

Her lips part, but no sound comes out for a long moment, like my words somehow shocked her. I can't see why or how. I haven't said anything at all about *sentencing* her for her actions.

"I see," she finally murmurs, clearing her throat. "Okay."

"You see what, exactly?" I wonder aloud, unclear of how we've arrived at this vague point in the conversation.

Rather than answer me, she shakes her head. "I'll do what you want, Your Majesty."

"Fallon—"

"Kaspian Antonik, I reject you."

I gape at her, stunned that she was able to speak the words so clearly and without flinching. So unerringly. So *thoroughly*.

They sail right through me.

Surround me.

Echo in my ears.

Pummel my chest.

"I…" I trail off, unable to voice whatever I intended to say. Because I don't have enough air in my lungs.

It's like she's sucked the literal life out of me,

dismantling my soul, demolishing my reason for being, *slaying my damn heart.*

Her name is a benediction on my tongue, one I can't seem to voice. Everything hurts. Burns. *Rips through my veins.*

Fuck.

My knees feel weak and I'm not even standing.

My vision is blurring.

My world... *is ending.*

It's real.

All of it... is real.

And she just rejected me without so much as blinking.

Because it's what I deserve. I've mistreated her at every turn, trying to force her to open up to me even when she made it clear she wasn't ready. Used my power over her to intimidate her. Forced my way in here to demand an explanation from her while she was in the middle of playing with her true mates.

The mates she didn't reject.

The mates she actually wants.

"Kaspian?" Her voice sends shivers through my body as the fractured pieces of my soul beg her to take it back. To not reject me. To *want* me.

I need to say those words to her. Reject her. Make this even.

But I can't.

Because I don't want to reject my mate.

I... I deserve this—her dislike and rejection. I've approached this all wrong. Approached *her* all wrong.

She needs someone she can rely on. Someone she can openly confide in. Not someone she feels compelled to *obey*.

I drag my palm down my face, my surroundings suddenly out of balance.

Everything feels broken. Wrong. *Devastating.*

I go to stand, only Fallon's hand on my shoulder holds

me back. "*Kaspian.*" There's a bite to her tone that has me looking at her, my heart in shambles at her feet.

She hates me.

As she should.

I suddenly feel weak in her hands—a feeling I don't know that I've ever experienced.

No, not weak, I realize. *Vulnerable.*

"It's…" Her gaze searches mine. "It's real…"

My throat feels tight, so I nod rather than speak.

"I…" She stares at me. "You need to… to reject me back."

I shake my head and force myself to say, "No. You don't deserve my rejection." I palm her cheek. "But I have very much earned yours."

Her eyes widen. "What?"

"I've second-guessed you. Demanded your secrets. Doubted the fated link between us." Each statement feels like an arrow through my heart. "I've treated you as a prisoner, not a mate, Fallon."

"Because I put your city to sleep," she snaps at me, her tone causing my eyebrows to lift in surprise. "I mean, not me exactly, but Klas using *my* power. You have had every right to question me and second-guess me. And I have been keeping secrets. Obviously."

The Fallon I know seems to be coming back to life before me, her despair and sadness disappearing behind an alluring veil of fiery feminine energy.

How blind I've been, I marvel, staring at the beautiful creature pulsating with growing anger. *It's no wonder I interrogated her myself each time. I wanted to talk to her, to know her.*

She's the reason I haven't sought out female company for over a year. I thought it was a result of boredom, or my fascination with the phantoms, but I see the truth now.

It's always been about her.

I would ask Nox and Bane for an update on her well-being each time before we'd end up playing in bed in some capacity. But there was a reason just talking about Fallon made me hungry.

A reason I've been denying for far too long.

She was meant to be mine.

But I've treated her so poorly, so *wrongly*. I should have been cherishing her and making her feel safe. Instead, I chased her away.

I'm a horrible mate.

"I doubted the bonds, too," she says, drawing my focus to her delectable mouth. "I... I hoped they were real. But I didn't think fate would give me this opportunity. And I assumed dark magic tied us together. That's why I was able to reject you so easily—I didn't think it would do anything."

I draw my thumb across her cheekbone, reveling in the soft texture of her skin. "Fate owes you several worthy mates. Especially after everything you've been through."

"I still think magic has something to do with it." She leans into my touch. "This is all too good to be true, Kaspian. Four mates? In what world does that happen?"

"It's not uncommon," I hedge. "But I suppose it's not all that common, either." I glance at the door and then back at her. "At least your mates don't mind sharing."

Well, Nolan might.

But given the way he defended her on our call earlier, I'm fairly certain he's more than accepted the situation.

"I'm sorry I doubted you." I tuck a strand of her golden hair behind her ear. "I'm sorry for a lot of things."

She frowns. "I'm the one who lied and withheld the truth about, well, everything. I also told you that my secrets weren't your secrets to know. But at the very least, I should have told you about the spell."

"That would have required you to explain everything else, too," I point out. Because there's no way I wouldn't have demanded a full explanation.

"Which is exactly what I told myself, but that doesn't make it right. I should have told you the truth."

"And maybe you would have had I given you reason to trust me." I glance at her mouth before locking eyes with her once more. "I demanded your trust without earning it."

"You also put me in a guest suite for the last year, asked me every day what you could do to make me more comfortable, and put off Klas's execution out of worry for my sanity." She sounds frustrated with herself. Maybe even frustrated with me, I'm not sure. "I'm sorry for not trusting you."

"You were protecting your sister, Fallon." I slowly take my palm away from her face. "I understand your fear and hesitation. But I'm not a patriarch."

"I know you're not." The words come out on a huff of air. "You're... you're *Kaspian*." Her legs shift beneath the blankets as she moves closer to me.

I stay quiet, hypnotized by her movements.

Then she goes to her knees, causing the sheets to fall away.

"You're *my* Kaspian," she says, her palms going to either side of my face. "Which is why I need to undo my rejection."

I grab her wrists. "You don't need to undo anything, Fallon. I've earned—"

Her lips brush mine, cutting off my words.

Just like when I attempted to reject her.

I try to say her name, but she silences me with her

tongue. I should push her away, tell her she doesn't need to do this, inform her that I'm okay living with her rejection…

Fuck, I should do a lot of things.

But I can't.

Not when her plump lips are against mine.

Not when she's kneeling before me. *Naked*.

And wet, I think as I inhale deeply, my vampiric senses allowing me to scent her sweet arousal. *Fuck… How do I say no to this?*

Is it even right to refuse her? To refuse *this*?

I told her to reject me. She only complied because I commanded it.

If she wants to undo it, who am I to stop her?

I want her. I've wanted her for months. A year. Perhaps even from the first moment I saw her. *Because she was always meant to be mine.*

That damn spell tied her to Klas illegally.

If it hadn't existed, I would have known Fallon as my mate from the instant I laid eyes on her.

He stole over a year from us…

Then I ruined our first day as mates.

Now I refuse to waste another second.

I release her wrists, my palms instantly wandering her curves to pull her even closer to me. Her thighs part over mine as I guide her into my lap, her body fitting perfectly against my own. Like she belongs there.

Because she does.

Because she's mine.

The words hum through my mind as I whisper them against her tongue. *Mine. You're mine. And I'm yours.*

She wants to undo the rejection.

I want to undo it, too.

But I'll never force her.

Which is why I'll give her control for our first time together and let her take the lead. It's a gift I've never given to anyone in my very long existence. Dominance runs in my blood, my need to be in charge an instinct I've never ignored.

But for her, I'll bow.

For her, I'll concede.

Because Fallon Doyle is the House of Gold and Garnet's future queen.

FALLON

IT'S REAL. *All of this is real.*

Nox and Bane.

Kaspian.

Nolan, too.

I'm so caught up in the euphoria of the realization that all I can think about is healing the bond between me and Kaspian.

He's the reason I know this is real.

I was feeling so lost and dejected, ready to submit to my fate once more, only for him to pull me out of the darkness and back into the light.

All by demanding that I reject him.

And then he wouldn't reciprocate, saying I didn't deserve his rejection.

"But I have very much earned yours."

His words play through my thoughts, his resignation piercing my soul. I have to fix it. I have to fix *us*. It's an intrinsic need I don't fully understand, but I'm done thinking. I'm done living in my mind and second-guessing everything in my life.

This is real, I marvel again. *This is well and truly happening.*

Kaspian's tongue dances with mine, the pace slow and seductive. It's so thorough and quietly provocative, making my thighs clench around his.

He's fully clothed in one of his suits, minus the jacket and tie. His shirtsleeves are rolled to the elbows, and the top button of his dress shirt is undone.

It's casual for Kaspian.

And sexy as sin.

I can feel his arousal through his dress pants. He's been hard since he pulled me into his lap, maybe even before then.

It's a taunt against my sex, encouraging me to grind down onto him. So I do, and I'm rewarded with a growl.

I need him inside me.

That's how we fix this broken bond, how I make him mine once more.

I'm torn between taking this slow and savoring the moment, and rushing to complete us both.

But I'm already on fire for him, amplified by all the teasing Bane and Nox inflicted upon me before Kaspian arrived.

I rock my hips, pressing my heated center against him, and moan when I brush his erection.

"Fuck, do that again, sweetheart." Kaspian groans. "Moan for me again."

He pushes his hardness into me, driving another sound from my chest. I grab his shoulders and arch, my veins igniting with a second wave of blistering intensity.

"I've been listening to you all for hours." The words are a breath against my mouth. "Hearing your moans up close is an entirely different experience, especially with me being the cause of them."

"You were listening?" I ask, my words barely a whisper.

"Yes," he replies, his palms going to my hips as he gyrates up into me once more. "I like to listen, Fallon." His tongue traces the seam of my mouth. "I also like to watch." He kisses me softly. "You know what I would really enjoy?"

I shiver against him and shake my head, unsure of what he'll say.

"To watch them fuck you together." His lips trail across my cheek to my ear. "To watch Nox take your fine ass while Bane slides into your cunt." He nibbles my earlobe. "I would sit in a chair right over there and stroke myself while you please them." His mouth goes to my neck. "But I wouldn't let myself come."

"Y-you wouldn't?" I stammer, my heart beating wildly in my chest. Because the image of all that... it's... it's intimidating in the best way.

Taking Bane and Nox at the same time.

All while Kaspian watches.

Stars...

"No," he murmurs. "I would wait until they finished cleaning you up. Then I would make you messy all over again." He nips my pulse, making me freeze as a jolt of ice chases away the flames circulating in my veins.

Kaspian pauses and pulls back, his gaze searching.

"Fallon?" he prompts.

I swallow, my heart kick-starting in my ribs for an entirely new reason. *Kaspian's a vampire. He's going to want to bite me. Feed from me. Use me.*

"Fallon," he repeats, his palms going to my face. "Talk to me."

His near-black eyes burn into mine, the color reminding me of Klas's irises. Except Kaspian's gaze is different. He looks at me with compassion and concern.

Not malice and dark intent. The wickedness is there, but it's not the same. It's... *it's Kaspian.*

"Sweetheart, talk to me," he says, his thumbs drawing across my cheekbones. "Do you not want me to watch?"

I blink at him. "What?"

"Do you not want me to watch you with Bane and Nox? Does it bother you?"

My lips curl down. "N-no." No, that idea definitely doesn't bother me. If anything, it reignites the flames inside me. "I..."

I clear my throat.

This is Kaspian. I need to tell him the truth. No more secrets.

Besides, he already knows this. I explained how Klas accessed my power. But Kaspian probably doesn't realize how that made me feel. How *fangs* make me feel.

"Klas used my blood to... to absorb my abilities." I'm not sure if that's something all vampires can do or not. But Klas was a vampire-warlock hybrid. His skills were unique to him. "He did that by biting me. Harshly."

"Hmm," Kaspian hums, his dark eyes flashing with an emotion I can't quite define. "So you don't like being bitten as a result."

"I... I don't like being bitten by him," I hedge. "I don't know about anyone else." Because Klas is the only vampire who has ever fed from me.

Kaspian draws his fingers through my hair, pulling the strands away from my face and neck. "Do you want me to take those memories away from you, Fallon? To replace them with what a powerful vampire's fangs can do?"

His gaze goes to my neck before returning to my mouth.

"Or would you rather I didn't ever bite you?" he continues, his expression giving nothing away regarding his preferences. "I'll do whatever you want, love. Just tell me your limits and I'll respect them."

"I…" I trail off, my focus falling to his full lips. "I don't know."

"Then we can address that limit another day," he replies, his mouth brushing mine. "I won't bite you without permission." Another kiss. "I won't do anything to you without permission, Fallon. You're in charge here. You tell me what you want, and I'll give it to you."

I shiver against him, his fingers working magic against my skull as he massages my head and combs through my hair once more.

This male is enchanting.

And hard.

And mine.

Or he will be, anyway. Once we rekindle our bond.

"Kiss me, Kaspian," I whisper.

He does, this time with a demanding swipe of his tongue that makes everything inside me melt. He's a being of control. A master vampire. A *king*.

But he's letting me lead. I can feel it in the way that he doesn't push me along, just holds me to him as he devours my mouth.

It's overwhelming, this euphoric realization that this powerful male is granting me authority over him. He said I was in charge, that he'd give me whatever I wanted.

That can't be easy for him, something that's evidenced in the way his thighs go taut beneath me. He's holding himself back, forcing himself to be patient, when we both know this partially rejected bond has to be killing him.

Because it's real, I marvel again.

I may never get over that fact. May never be able to accept that *this* is my life. *Four mates. One of whom is a king.*

"Kaspian," I moan, arching into him. "I need you."

"We have another limit to discuss," he says, his words causing my eyes to flutter open. I'm not sure when they shut, but likely when he started consuming me with his mouth.

I stare at him, waiting for him to elaborate.

"Do you want Nox and Bane to watch us?" he asks, his head canting a little to the side and indicating the two phantoms lurking just inside the door, their gazes hungry as they take in my position on top of Kaspian.

They're both shirtless, wearing only matching pairs of low-slung black pants.

I lick my lips at the sight of all that masculine grace.

They're mine, I think. *Truly mine.*

"After listening to them play with you all night, I would very much like to make them watch without being allowed to touch," Kaspian continues, his attention on me. "Because it's my turn now, love. And I've been *very* patient. But it's your decision, Fallon. I'll do whatever you desire."

Nox and Bane both study me with the same intensity as Kaspian, all three men waiting for my answer.

Do I want them to watch while Kaspian fucks me?

"Yes," I breathe, my insides pulsating with intensified need. Being surrounded by these men makes me feel alive in a way I've never experienced before. It's so unlike any fantasy I've ever even conceptualized, so amazingly fantastic that I can barely believe it's happening to me.

"Fate owes you several worthy mates. Especially after everything you've been through."

Kaspian's comments play over in my mind, the adoration and earnest way he said those words a kiss to my very soul.

Because he believes I deserve all of this.

Maybe I do, I think, staring at him now. *But I need to cherish it.*

Which is why I need to rekindle this bond and repair what I broke. Kaspian might have demanded that I reject him, but only I can choose to fix it.

And he's ensuring I have that choice not just in accepting our mating, but in how it's done.

"Let them watch," I tell him. "I want them to watch." Because my phantoms make me feel safe. Because I want them involved, too. At least in their own way. They may not be able to touch this time, but Kaspian mentioned other ideas.

Watching them fuck me while he pleasures himself.

Taking me when they're done.

A tremble works its way down my spine. *Yes, yes. I want all of that.*

But first, I want Kaspian.

To feel him in my soul again. To complete this link. To make him truly mine.

He's all power and grace, a sleek vampire wrapped up in expensive clothes. I want to break his elegant exterior, create more chips in that formal mask he constantly wears.

I want to see him lose control.

Because even though he's allowed me to lead, I can tell he's still very much in charge. He's the dominant in this room. He's just giving me the space and time I need to embrace this, the ability to set our pace, to say *no* if I desire to.

I dig my nails into his shoulders and kiss him as my lower half presses into his erection. He growls in response, his hands leaving my hair to go to my hips.

My lips curl against his, loving the way he immediately grabbed me.

But he doesn't dictate my movements; he simply guides me as I move.

I trail my fingers down his shirt, ignoring the buttons

and going straight to his belt below. His lips part beneath mine, his exhale warm and minty as he shudders in response.

My name leaves his mouth, but I don't let him finish, my tongue sliding in to duel with his as I work on his buckle and start threading the leather through the loops.

His belt falls to the floor behind me as I finish pulling it free.

Then I go to the top button of his trousers to pop open the material and lift up so I can start dragging down the zipper.

Kaspian grins, his grip tightening on my hips.

I understand why when I feel his arousal free itself from his pants.

No boxers or briefs. Just all smooth, hard man.

I press my hot flesh against his, wasting no time to feel all that masculine strength right where I want it.

"*Fuck*, Fallon," he says, his grasp turning bruising. "I'm not even inside you yet and I'm addicted to your cunt."

"Wait until you taste her." Nox's voice is deep and so close to my ear that I suspect he's right behind me.

But I can't look away from Kaspian's midnight gaze.

He's staring up at me with such wonder in his depths that I'm drunk on his presence. Lost to the reverence on his face. The pure, unadulterated need radiating off of him.

This is the real Kaspian.

Not the king with the formal mask. But my intended mate.

And seeing him now, I realize I've witnessed glimpses of him before. Glimpses I never truly understood. Moments of heated need while we argued, all of which I mistook for something else entirely.

Because I was oblivious to our connection before.

Dark magic blinded me, made me incapable of seeing my mates for who they really are. But I see them now. I *feel* them.

Even Kaspian.

Despite the rejection, he's still there, lingering near my spirit, begging me to accept him once more. To allow his soul to join with mine.

I want that, I think, shifting in his lap once more. *I want all of them.*

It's impulsive. Maybe even reckless. But I refuse to fight fate. These men were meant to be mine. I understand that now.

And I'm done second-guessing it all.

I reach between us, my fingers wrapping around Kaspian as I angle him upward toward my damp entrance.

His pupils dilate, his intrigue a palpable kiss to my senses.

"I don't reject you, Kaspian Antonik," I tell him as I slide down, welcoming him inside me. "I *accept* you."

He thrusts upward, forcing me to take him to the hilt. "I accept you, too, Fallon Doyle," he says, his hands beginning to roam. "Fuck, do I accept you…"

He palms the back of my neck and slants his mouth over mine, his kiss domineering in the best way.

Then he presses his opposite hand to my lower spine and begins to move.

"Wrap your legs around me," he demands. "I need to be deeper."

I obey, loving the way he's taking charge without truly meaning to. Because this is my Kaspian. The dominant I trust. The male I want to bond with. The vampire I want to call mine.

His tongue slides over mine, easily controlling our kiss as he drives into me below.

It's perfect.

It's him.

It's exactly what I need right now. Right here. *Between us.*

Each thrust brings us closer, our souls rejoicing at our union, as fate permanently ties our destinies together.

Bane and Nox are still very much present, the heat from their bare chests radiating near my back. They're not touching, but they're close.

Watching.

Lurking.

Being true voyeurs while Kaspian takes me to oblivion.

And I love every minute.

I feel like I'm the center of their world. It's outlandish and maybe even a bit arrogant, but I revel in the temporary glow of being worshipped by all three of them.

My men. My mates. My future.

Warmth touches my chest, hope blossoming deep inside.

With them, I can be happy.

I can be whole.

I can be… free.

Kaspian nips my lower lip, his growl drawing me back to him. "I need you to come for me Fallon," he says against my mouth. "I need to feel that beautiful pussy clamp down around me while I claim you. I need to hear you *scream.* Can you do that for me? Can you do that for *us*?"

I shiver, my insides clenching in response.

It's like these men have complete dominion over my body, over how I experience pleasure, over *when* I come. Because just hearing them utter the words drives me that much closer.

"Be a good girl and come for Kaspian, firefly," Nox

whispers right against my ear. "When you're done, I'll lick you both clean."

"And then we'll make you come again." Bane's promise is a soft hum of sound on my opposite side, confirming that both men are hovering right behind me, watching as I repair my fate bond to Kaspian.

I must look so wanton riding Kaspian's cock while he's still fully clothed.

It's an alluring picture in my mind, one that has me slipping my hand between us to fondle my clit.

Somehow it feels right—being naked while Kaspian is not. Like it grants him that much more control over the situation.

I prefer it this way. Because I trust him to lead. To guide. To master us all.

His fangs skim my lip, causing my eyes to flash open. But he doesn't bite. He merely holds my gaze, forcing me to see his desire and hunger in his near-black depths.

Only it's not a hunger for my blood; it's a hunger for *me*.

I shiver in response, that look sending me that much closer to the edge.

"Nox and Bane are stroking themselves behind you," Kaspian informs me softly. "They're wishing they could touch you, just as I did for the last several hours." His lips brush mine with each word. "Give them a show, love. Let them watch you come all over my cock."

Another tremble rocks down my spine, leaving me quivering on top of him.

Because I can hear the two phantoms breathing harder. Faster. More intensely than before.

Just like Kaspian.

They're all panting because of me. Because of *us*.

Stars, this is... this is true bliss...

I arch back, my legs tightening around Kaspian's waist as I try to take even more of him inside me. He's long like Nox but doesn't have the piercings. Instead, he has Bane's girth, making me feel so incredibly full.

And he wants to watch the phantoms take me together.

What if I somehow take all three? One in my mouth... two below...

Oh, but I need Nolan, too.

Although, his loner nature suggests he's probably not into group sessions.

What does Nolan like? I wonder, my hips gyrating faster now. *Will he take me alone?*

I'm not even sure where he is.

I nearly ask, but Kaspian does something below that has me glued to the present, to him, to the phantoms behind me, to this moment in time.

It all feels so *good.*

So right.

So... *stars...*

A quake rolls through me, throwing me into an unexpected oblivion, my body having been so primed from hours of playing that I didn't realize my orgasm had approached the edge until I fell headfirst over it.

Kaspian's name leaves my mouth, followed by my other mates'. I think I even mention Nolan, my mind too consumed by the pleasure to focus. It's all so unbelievable. So *perfect.*

Because I can feel Kaspian again.

Our bond.

This connection.

How did I ever mistake it for the spell? It's so much hotter. So much more intense. *So exquisite.*

Heat gushes between my legs, Kaspian's claim searing

me from the inside out and joining those of my other mates.

I feel so full of them. In my heart. In my soul. *In my body.*

They've all driven me to unexpected heights, teaching me a new way of being. All the while awakening a hope that burns so bright inside me that I can almost feel it singeing away the cold spires of my past.

Only that heat begins to dim as my climax abates, the warmth slowly leaving my being with each passing second.

I sigh, missing that orgasmic glow already.

But Bane and Nox promised more.

They'll reignite my flame in seconds, taking me right back to this rapturous plane.

I open my mouth to beg for their touch, my eyes fluttering in the process. "I…" I trail off, my gaze unfocused and requiring me to blink a few times.

I expect to find Kaspian's handsome features, maybe even witness a satisfied expression or a charming smirk.

But he's not who I find lurking before me.

Instead, I'm surrounded by seven hooded figures.

"Hello, Fallon," Patriarch O'Neely greets me, his voice sending a chill down my spine as his power forces me to bow over a death stone. "It's time to discuss your fate."

NOLAN

Ayla opens a portal door that leads us to another roof, this one in the heart of Staten Island.

I pause after stepping through it, my instincts demanding that I survey the scene.

Clear, I assess after taking in my surroundings. *Just like the last three rooftops.*

It seems that's Ayla's thing—traveling by rooftop portals.

"That's a handy trick," I tell her, gesturing to the door with my chin. "I've never seen anything like it. How far can you go?"

"I can only create a doorway to places I've been," she replies. "And before you ask, no, it can't be replicated with magic. It's a talent that's tied to my spirit, similar to my aura-tracking ability."

I nod, understanding that more now that we've spent the better half of a day together.

Ayla explained that the Outcast Coven witches are different from others of their kind because of their unique ties to the death plane.

"Most witches come from the witches' world. We technically did as well, but our magic has manifested in a different way. A darker way. I guess you could say death magic infected our coven and changed how we perform spells."

"But how?" I asked earlier. "The death plane isn't another world." If it were, I would know about it. Or, at the very least, a portal would exist that would allow others to visit it.

"No. It's linked to our coven's core—our *souls*." She shrugged. "The members of my coven possess death magic. It's rare and feared, which is partly why we're all outcasts."

That much I knew. "Necromancers," I translated. "Or that's the rumor about your coven, anyway. You're all necromancers."

"Necromancy suggests that we can all control the dead." Her black eyes met mine. "I can't. But my powers are rooted in souls, which is a form of death."

"And Fallon can mimic deadly sleep," I added. "As well as disturb the dead." Those are the spells we witnessed last year when Klas took advantage of his forced-mate's powers.

"Fallon can do so much more than just that," Ayla told me. "And Ishara can, too. They just need to break free of the patriarchs' leashes."

I asked her how to break the leash, and she shook her head. "If I knew that, I wouldn't still be here."

She paces around now, her movements catlike as she prowls the roof's edge.

Most wingless beings would fear the five-story drop to the ground. But not Ayla. She's walked the edge like this of every rooftop we've stood upon. Including the one in Manhattan, which was over fifty stories tall.

"That townhouse over there," she says, pointing to the southwest. "That's Patrick O'Neely's family home."

I walk up beside her to take in the *family home* of the Outcast Coven's perceived leader.

From what Ayla said, there are seven patriarchs. But Patrick O'Neely is considered to be the master patriarch.

He's also the one who forced Fallon to mate-bond Klas.

And is likely the one who sent Klas to infiltrate the Gold and Garnet ranks.

Which makes him target number one, with Fallon's father being a close second.

I'm about to ask her to point out the invisible magical security traps surrounding the home—something she's done at our last two locations—when my phone starts to ring.

"It's a good thing Ayla lent me some magic to charge my battery," I say by way of greeting. "After our last call, you nearly drained—"

"She won't wake up," Kaspian interjects, a note of uncharacteristic panic in his voice.

"What?"

"Fallon," he elaborates, his face appearing on the screen. *"She won't wake up."*

I walk away from the edge with Ayla right beside me, both of us focused on the screen populating the space in front of me.

Kaspian pans over to show an unconscious Fallon, her white skin a stark contrast to the obsidian marble floor beneath her.

That's not her room, I think, recognizing Kaspian's penchant for dark colors.

She's naked, is my next unhelpful deduction.

Her lips are blue, is the thought that finally brings me

back to the relevance of this call. "Have you tried reviving her like last time?"

"Yes. For the last twenty minutes." Nox's voice holds the same note of panic as Kaspian's.

Bane is on the floor beside her, his black pants unfastened and his hair a mess of dark waves. He's checking her pulse. Whatever he finds—likely a lack of a heartbeat—has him leaning down to blow into her mouth as Nox takes over chest compressions.

I flinch as I watch, my heart starting to pound against my rib cage.

If she's really dead, I would feel something, right? A severed link? Her departed soul?

"The patriarchs must be doing something to keep you from waking her up this time." There's a clear note of unease in Ayla's voice. "I don't think any of us want to know what that entails."

"I fucking want to know," Kaspian snaps, his angry tone as uncharacteristic of him as his panic. He remained mostly calm during our previous call, almost eerily so. This display of emotion is... *new.*

"If we know what they're doing, we can wake her up," Nox says, his focus on compressing Fallon's sternum. "She's so fucking cold."

"Because they dragged her soul off into the death plane," Ayla mutters. "She's not really dead, but her body..." She twists her lips to the side. "Don't stop trying to revive her. She needs her blood to circulate, or this could have lasting damage."

My jaw ticks. "Lasting damage?"

"Brain damage, among other things." She looks at Patriarch O'Neely's house. "The patriarchs could be there, performing this spell. But I doubt it. They have secret ceremonial spaces for their meetings that I've yet to find."

"You can't track their souls?"

She shakes her head. "Not without them noticing." She folds her arms. "You sensed my approach because my magic touched your aura. It would do the same to them if I tried to hunt them down."

"So you're saying you can only track those who don't mind being tracked?" That's certainly a limit to what's otherwise a neat talent.

"Or someone who isn't as aware of his or her surroundings," she replies. "Fortunately, most people don't pay attention to their instincts. Unfortunately, the patriarchs are paranoid asshats and therefore not most people."

I decide not to ask if I'm classified as a "paranoid asshat" since I noticed her following me earlier and instead focus on what matters. "Is there anyone you could track that may be near their meeting site right now? Like maybe Issy?"

If the patriarchs have Fallon, then maybe they also have—

"What the fuck just happened?" Kaspian snaps, drawing my gaze to the screen, where Bane and Nox are hovering over an empty floor. "Where the fuck did she go?"

Ayla steps toward the screen, her eyes wide and matching my own expression. Then she swings around, her lips parting as she looks to the north.

Kaspian, Nox, and Bane all start talking at once, but Ayla is the one who has my attention.

Because she's gone completely still beside me.

"What do you sense?" I ask her.

"Fallon," she breathes, her black irises flickering with dangerous flames as she jerks her attention toward me. "It's Fallon."

"What about her?" Kaspian demands through the screen before I can say a word. "Where is she?"

Ayla doesn't look at him, her focus still on me. "She's back." She blinks. "Fallon's *back*."

"How is that possible?" I ask.

"I don't know, but I feel her." She swallows, looking to the north again. "And if she's where I think she is, then we're going to need some help."

FALLON

A Few Minutes Earlier

My fate.

That's what the patriarchs want to discuss.

What gives you the right to dictate my fate? I want to demand, my instinct to voice the question an overwhelming urge that almost makes my mouth move.

For over two decades of life, I've done everything these men have told me to do. I've obeyed them. I've bowed to them. I *mated* for them.

And for what? To have them continue to control every aspect of my life? To demand that I *die* because Klas failed them?

Issy's been telling me for years to stand up to the patriarchs, to not let them use her as a reason for my obedience.

I haven't listened because she mattered more than everything else in the world. She was my only connection in life. My only reason for surviving.

But that's all changed now.

I have a renewed purpose, one that I can feel anchoring me in another plane of existence.

My mates.

Their importance doesn't replace Issy's or belittle my connection to my twin. Their presence somehow *strengthens* my bond to my sister. Maybe because my mates are giving me even more reason to survive.

They'll help me save her. It's not something we've discussed. But somehow I know I can rely on them. *They'll give us a new home. A place to be free.*

Knowing that sparks confidence in me now.

Which is why I lift my head away from the death stone to stare down the hooded men around me.

You want to discuss my fate? All right. We can discuss my fate.

They can't hear me, but it doesn't matter. I show them my feelings with my eyes, tell them with a look that I no longer wish to obey.

I'm done.

We are done.

"Perhaps we need to begin this sentencing with an update on your twin sister," Patriarch O'Neely says, a hint of menace underlying his regal tone. "I'm sure you've noticed your inability to communicate with her. Maybe it reminds you of a previous experience?"

My jaw ticks, my eyes narrowing. *The obedience spell.* It cut me off from Issy, making me focus entirely on Klas and his wishes.

Issy? I whisper to her, realizing it's been too long since I last sensed her in my head.

Not since they used her to interrogate me after the last time I left the death plane.

Oh, Issy, what have they been doing to you?

I swear I see one of the patriarchs grin. Or maybe I

just feel it more than see it because their hoods are shrouded in shadows. I can't even identify who is who.

And when one of them speaks, the words echo around me.

I only recognize the voice's owner, not the hood it originates from.

"Your sister has been newly mated," Patriarch O'Neely continues. "Unfortunately, her powers made it difficult for us to perform a proper ceremony, so improvisations had to be made. And, well, she's rather indisposed at the moment."

A few chuckles follow his words while my heart ices over.

Mated? Indisposed?

Fuck.

Issy!

She doesn't reply. And I can't sense her at all.

This is unacceptable. I've done *everything* these assholes demanded of me.

Except the suicide, I realize. *They threatened to punish me. But... but it's Issy who is paying for my disobedience.*

Of course.

Assholes. I curl my fingers into a fist. *You're all a bunch of assholes.*

And they're still *laughing*. Enjoying my torment.

No, not just *my* torment, but Issy's as well.

My innocent sister who's cursed with a deadly voice. Who's lived so much of her life in a room without windows. Whose very existence has been ridiculed and hated by our coven.

Yet they *mated* her to someone.

To whom? I want to demand.

Because whoever it is, I'll incapacitate him. Maybe

even kill him, since apparently Ayla knows how to break the forced-mating bonds.

That would have been useful information to know a few years ago, but something tells me she's only recently learned how to accomplish that. Otherwise, she would have shared those details with Issy.

Did she learn it during the trials? Maybe shortly after? I'm not sure. But I'm going to find out. Then I'll use that knowledge to free my sister.

Because these hooded assholes will not control me or my sister anymore.

I'm done. We *are done.*

The death stone warms beneath me, reminding me of my last visit to this plane. *My mates?* I wonder, feeling their presence all around me. *Are they bringing me back again?*

"*Fallon Doyle,*" the patriarchs say in unison, their voices whipping around me and securing my focus. "*You have failed us. We require recompense.*"

"The recompense will be taken from Ishara Doyle," one of the patriarchs says.

Patriarch McCarthy? I guess, only vaguely familiar with his gravelly tones.

"*Yes,*" the patriarchs confirm as a cluster of voices again. "*Ishara Doyle will suffer for Fallon Doyle's failures.*"

"Unless you would like an alternative fate?" Patriarch O'Neely offers, that silky tone of his filled with sinister intent. "You could save your sister some pain, Fallon. But it'll require your complete devotion to our cause."

I narrow my eyes, this rhetoric growing tiresome.

I've devoted myself to their cause my entire life, and where has it gotten me?

Arrange-mated to a monster.

Grounded by an obedience spell.

Sexually assaulted.

Buried alive on countless occasions.

Used and abused.

Disassociated from my own magic.

Ripped apart from my twin, both mentally and physically.

Again. And again. And again.

The death stone warms even more beneath me, seeming to grow hotter with my mounting ire.

Because this is all bullshit.

I've done everything for these soulless creatures, just to be knocked down at every turn.

And now they've taken my sister from me again? Threaten to make her suffer for my supposed failures?

Fuck. That.

"Klas failed, not me," I tell them, surprised by my ability to speak so fluidly. Maybe they're allowing me to speak. That would explain my ability to move, too. They must not have felt it necessary to chain me this time.

I push away from the death stone, no longer feeling the weight on my shoulders—the power that originally forced me to bow.

I'm free.

It's a realization I prove by standing up. It feels good. Powerful. *Right.*

The deadly magic around me pulsates in agreement, the chilling strands swirling through the air and floating closer to kiss my skin.

"*Fallon Doyle,*" the voices echo sharply. "*You will obey.*"

"I have obeyed," I tell them. "I've *obeyed* you my entire life. I've given up everything. All for Issy's safety. But you started this discussion with an update about her *fate.*"

I step forward as more icy tendrils swim around me, each one seeming to melt the moment it touches my overheated form.

It doesn't hurt. It actually feels quite good. Revitalizing, even. A strange sensation for a death plane, but I don't second-guess it. I *embrace* it.

"I mated Nikolas O'Neely and *obeyed* him for four years. *He* chose to attack the Gold and Garnet King. *He* failed. And you wanted to reward him for that failure with my soul in the afterlife."

I take another step toward the hooded patriarchs.

"I wasn't given a chance to obey." Not that I intended to, but these assholes don't need to know that. "The death plane sucked me in and returned me to new mates. And your response to that was to *mate off my sister?*"

Those last four words reverberate through the air, similar to how the patriarchs sound.

"You cut me off from her. *Again.* Inflicted an obedience spell on her. *Subdued her. And you think to taunt me with that knowledge, to convince me to select an alternative fate?*"

My words are all beginning to echo now, my voice vibrating in a way I've never experienced.

The patriarchs try to say my name again, a jolt of power seeming to pulsate around them.

But it doesn't touch me.

I'm too wrapped up in all the frigid wisps that keep melting against my skin. It's like I've formed a strange sort of shield. Or perhaps I've just *absorbed* one. I'm not sure, but I feel safe. Empowered. *Emboldened.*

"*What improvisations were made?*" I demand. "*How is my sister subdued? Where is she?!*"

Those last three words leave me on a roar as a deadly wind whirls around me.

"*Tell me who you mated her to. Tell me who has my sister!*"

The wind turns into a cyclone of energy and rushes toward the patriarchs, knocking the hoods from their startled faces.

They resemble ghosts here, their souls quivering from the force of my chilly gust.

It's strange that they're ethereal in nature, yet I feel corporeal. A glance at my hands confirms my solid state.

I'm not just a soul here; I'm *me*.

Because this place is the source of my power.

I call upon it now, telling it to give me strength. Because I need to channel it to my twin. Help wake her from her obedience spell. *Save her from her pain.*

The patriarchs start shouting, but I ignore them, too focused on the mounting energy around me.

Siphon through me and find Issy, I tell the deadly magic. *Free her from her confines. Wake her from her slumber. Give her back her voice!*

I close my eyes and command the death plane to do my bidding, the manipulation of power reminding me of the spells I know that can raise the dead.

But I'm not playing with souls or corpses right now. I'm simply calling on the heart of my gifts. This plane is powered by spirits, their collective energy creating a pulse that fuels my existence.

It requires respect. Reverence. *Understanding.* Otherwise, it would be easy to lose myself to the void of power.

Fortunately, I have several anchors that make it easier for me to focus. Help me strive to *survive.*

My mates.

My real *mates.*

I feel their vitality pulling me back into the real world, their presence stabilizing me as I continue to absorb more magic. My soul is hungry for it.

More. More. More.

Go to Issy.

Wake her up.

Make her whole again.

I no longer hear or feel the patriarchs. They're a distant memory in my mind.

This plane has never truly been theirs to own, I think, the mental voice sounding like mine. Except, I'm not sure how I know that information—it's a foreign concept.

But it… it feels like my magic just whispered that into my mind.

How is that even possible? I marvel, my eyes opening. *How is any of this…?*

My thought trails off as I realize my scenery has changed yet again.

Only, I'm not back in Iceland with my mates.

I'm in a dark room. One that feels far too cold.

A freezer, I realize as goose bumps pebble up and down my exposed arms. *I'm naked in a freezer.*

It's pitch black, making it impossible to see.

However, I know I'm not alone in here.

Because I can hear someone else breathing.

It's shallow and accompanied by a strange beep.

What is that? I feel around slowly, searching for a wall or a door or anything I can use to *see.*

Beep. Beep. Beep.

I move closer to the sound.

Beep. Beep. Beep.

The breathing is louder than it should be, almost as though it's being amplified by something.

Beep. Beep. Beep.

What the fuck is going on? I can still feel the vestiges of the death plane whirling around me, the power kissing my spirit and stirring warmth from within.

Beep. Beep. Beep.

I step closer while I dig through my mind for a spell that'll allow light. Maybe even fire.

Because fuck, it's cold in here.

Beep. Beep. Beep.

I murmur a phrase in the ancient tongue, one Issy taught me long ago.

It stirs a glimmer of light, one that floats around the small space before me.

Beep. Beep. Beep.

It's a machine, I confirm, the glittery bulb swimming around it to reveal a pump-like instrument that's pushing air into…

My eyes widen at the horrifying sight unfolding before me. The machine is meant to help someone breathe.

And that someone is… *"Issy."*

KASPIAN

"WE'RE GOING to need a portal spell," I tell Cara, irritated that I can't use one now to teleport back to Reykjavik. Alas, I have to drive. And this is not the time of year to speed.

Fucking snow.

Fucking magic.

Fucking everything.

"I'll pass a message on to Slater via our normal channels, see if he can expedite the request," she replies. "Unless Nolan already has one stashed away somewhere?"

"Not in an easily accessible place," I mutter.

Nolan likes to hide things in elevated places.

The types of places only those with wings can reach. Normally, I would respect that. Right now, I'm annoyed. Because he's in New York alone. With Fallon. And there's nothing I can physically do yet to reach them.

"What else do you need?" Cara asks, all business.

"I need at least six mercenaries, preferably more, who are willing to join us in New York. They need to be experienced. And they need to be well versed in witches and warlocks."

"On it," Cara says. "I'll call Talino, see if his grandsons are interested. Because if Eryx and Tallis are anything like their brother Khaos, you're going to want them on your side."

"He impressed you?" I guess.

"He *bested* me. Twice," she tells me. "He'll be useful to you in New York. Trust me."

"I do," I reply. "Which is why you're going to stay in Iceland to lead while I'm gone."

She blanches. "*Excuse me?*"

"It's your job as second to stay behind and lead in case something happens to me. You *and* Larus have to stay."

She growls. "I had no idea that agreeing to be your second meant being taken out of the field."

"You're only out of the field when I'm in the field," I tell her. "And I have to go to New York. She's my mate, Cara."

I already explained this to her at the beginning of the conversation, much to her surprise. It's not often that happens, as Cara has seen almost as much as I have in this world.

But four mates is certainly impressive.

Especially when one of them is an old master vampire like me.

Cara clears her throat. "Anything else, Kas?"

I consider everything we've discussed and shake my head. "That's all for now. We'll be there in fifteen minutes."

"I'll have updates ready for you when you arrive," she promises, ending the call.

Nox and Bane remain silent in the car, their concern palpable and rivaling my own.

Our mate just teleported to New York.

To a place we can't get to anytime soon.

281

A location where we can't protect her.

The knowledge of it all sits heavily on my heart, making my stomach twist with dread.

My only saving grace right now is the thriving link I feel beating between me and Fallon. *She's still alive.*

But the question is, for how long?

We're coming for you, Fallon Doyle.

And when we get there, we're going to destroy everyone who has ever wronged you.

I vow it.

FALLON

I HAVE no idea how I ended up here. I've never teleported before. But I've also never been to the death plane until this week.

Nor have I ever stood up to the patriarchs.

And what was that with all the power absorption? I wonder. That was certainly new.

I feel so incredibly alive right now, like I'm bursting with energy. Which is strange, given that death magic is usually draining. It typically takes a lot out of me to perform even the smallest of spells.

But somehow I teleported to Issy's side without much effort at all. If anything, it all felt very freeing. Like I just removed a set of invisible chains that have been weighing me down for years.

I roll my shoulders, convinced that everything feels lighter. Easier. More... vivacious.

It's invigorating.

However, the scene before me is anything but.

"Issy..."

I cast another flare of light, sending it to the machine

pumping air into my twin. It's archaic-looking. But it seems to be keeping my sister alive.

There are tubes going into her mouth and down her throat, the image grotesque and making my stomach twist. "What have they done to you?"

It's so wrong.

So *horrible*.

I'm going to destroy all of them, I tell her through our broken bond. *All. Of. Them.*

I place my hand on her chest, right over her heart, and flinch at her frozen frame. She resembles an ice cube.

"How long have you been in here?" I wonder before casting more light spells, causing over a dozen flickers to flutter around the small freezer space.

This spell would have exhausted me mere hours ago, especially having uttered it so many times. But I feel perfectly normal now. Those little lights are fresh from the death plane, the twinkles reminding me of stars. I cast them all around Issy, needing to see what they've done.

She has an intravenous line inserted into her arm, the plastic tubing connected to a half-full bag of saline liquid. Otherwise, apart from the machine and her nearly frozen state, she appears to be mostly untouched.

She's wearing a pair of jeans and a sweater, just like she normally would. Her blonde hair is a little longer than the last time I saw it. And she's lost weight over the last few years, too. Although, she's always been more slender than me. I'm the curvy one. She's the taller, thinner one.

"All right," I say to her, my gaze narrowing. "How am I going to wake you up?"

Issy is the spell master, the one who has read all the ancient death-magic texts. I've learned a lot from her over the years, but this is a moment where our connection would be most beneficial because she would be the one with the answers right about now.

However, that's clearly not going to work.

I twist my lips to the side, my hand still over her heart. *Can I somehow push the energy into her?* I wonder. I absorbed it for her. Or that was my intention. *So maybe... maybe I can... shove it into her...?*

My brow furrows as I attempt to push some of the power into her chest.

Nothing happens.

You know, I really need you to magically wake up, I tell her through our shattered connection. *Because I could use your advice here.*

Of course, she doesn't reply.

My jaw ticks. "It's not like you to give up this easily," I say conversationally. "You're usually in my head, demanding that I fight. So how about you do the same?"

It's a taunt, one my sister would normally rise to, but there's nothing normal about this situation at all.

The lights in the freezer start to dim, causing me to create more.

They flutter around as I pace the freezer.

I only pause once to try to open the door. I'm not at all surprised to find it locked. *A problem for after I wake up Issy,* I decide.

They have her in some sort of magically induced coma, no doubt to keep her quiet.

And she's mated now, too.

"Did your *mate* put you to sleep?" I ponder aloud. Because that's definitely something Klas would have done. A freezer isn't all that different from being buried alive.

Nyx pulled me out of a gravesite when she found me last year. Then she used her goddess magic on me to break the obedience spell.

I don't have that kind of power.

But I do have a lot of excess energy, I think, sensing the chilly essence of the death plane crawling over my skin. It's all about souls, the power rooted in spiritual energy.

And Issy is lingering at death's door, I realize. The machine is literally keeping her alive, her heart likely having slowed to a dangerous rate.

I check her pulse to confirm, my jaw tightening.

This is fucking cruel.

The patriarchs lack humanity, their goal to control everything and everyone around them regardless of the cost. This is no different.

They used Issy to control me, and the second they felt it no longer worked, they put her in this frigid coma.

I *hate* them. They've held dominion over me for too long.

But not anymore.

I have a new loyalty now—a loyalty to myself. *And to my mates.*

Stars, they must be so confused right now. I wish we were telepathically bonded like my sister and me, but we're not.

However, I can feel them in my chest, our bonds pulsating with life.

And power, I realize, frowning. *Is that related to the death plane or something else entirely?*

I can sense their souls, at least the three I've officially mated myself to. Only Nolan is missing, yet his essence is lingering near my own, almost as though his spirit is circling mine.

It's a strange feeling to sense my soul bonds in this way, but it's also second nature. Because souls are the literal root of my power.

So where's your soul? I think at Issy, my gaze narrowing. *Where did the patriarchs put you?*

I walk back over to the metal table she's lying on and place both my hands on her torso, near her heart.

Where are you? I demand, my eyes falling closed. *You can't be far…*

The death plane appears around me once more, but it's different now. It's… less cold. And there are no hooded figures this time. No death stone to bow over. Just an expanse of eerie landscape, the array of rocky tombstones reminding me of a graveyard.

More wisps of power linger in the air, resembling a frosty fog hovering near the ground.

I wander through the cemetery, noting the names along each of the graves.

Many of them are ones I recognize from the past—former witches who have all died.

A few, however, depict live witches. *Future gravesites?* I wonder. *Do I have one?*

From what Issy has told me, our souls add to the magic in this plane. Both when we're alive and when we're dead. Perhaps that's the link?

I wander through the morbid courtyard, reading each name as I pass. The gravestones are all in pristine condition, the surfaces smooth and appearing freshly engraved.

It's almost eerie how perfectly spaced each one is, too. How picture-perfect the entire scene is… until it's not.

There's a noticeable deviation ahead. A cracked surface. One that draws me forward with interest.

Amala, the tombstone reads, the last name indecipherable due to the cracked marble.

My brow furrows.

I've never met Amala, but I'm familiar with the exiled witch. The patriarchs made an example of her shortly before my forced mating to Klas. Apparently, she refused to follow their orders. But rather than kill her, they banished her.

And cracked her stone? I wonder, frowning. *Why?*

I continue searching, this time looking for Issy's name and for more fractures in the perfect facade. It's all instinctual. I need to find Issy's soul, and something pulled me here. My power, maybe. Or perhaps even her.

Where are you?

My bare feet whisper over the cool ground, the icy tendrils of power whispering around me with each step.

I'm still absorbing the energy, almost as though my spirit is starved and needs every bit of vitality that I can take. It's that or my soul needs the death magic to survive this plane. But being here feels too natural for it to be a threat to me. If anything, the kiss of death invigorates me.

Mist curls around my fingertips as I walk, the cold fog gliding up my bare arms and swirling around my neck.

I embrace it as I move, my gaze scanning for Issy's name and not finding it anywhere. *Does she not have a tombstone?*

No. She has to have one.

Her soul is here somewhere.

I can feel it. She's my other half. My twin.

Where are you? I repeat, my eyes narrowing at the vast graveyard. *Which site is yours?*

Minutes seem to pass in a blur as I search for Issy. Those minutes may turn into hours. I'm not sure. Time is strange here.

I can feel my mates tugging on my heart, their constant pull a reminder that I'm still alive. Still *theirs*.

I palm my chest, my corporeal form making me wonder if my body is truly here with my soul. It's strange.

This isn't a realm or another world so much as a state of existence. A place only a soul should be able to go. Yet somehow I'm walking around.

Do the patriarchs ever do this?

The few times I've been here now, they've been hooded and stationary. Completely unmoving. Just creepy voices that echo.

I picture their ethereal states from earlier, my lips curling down. They actually appeared ghostly, like apparitions being projected into this plane.

Because they can't actually exist here? I wonder. None of the tombstones bear the names of warlocks. Only witches. *Are males not allowed to be here?*

If that's the case, then how is the patriarchy accessing the magic here? *By siphoning it off of their mates? Like Klas did to me?*

I shiver, the realization slapping me across the face.

That's exactly what they're doing.

So how am I free? How have I broken…?

My thoughts trail off as another damaged headstone comes into view. I walk quickly toward it, curious to learn the identity associated with the grave, and gasp when I read, *Fallon*. The crack through my last name makes it illegible.

Very unlike the headstone beside mine.

Issy Doyle.

I study it for a long moment, comparing my gravesite to Issy's.

Why is mine fractured while hers is intact?

I run my fingers along the jagged marble, then trace the smooth contours of Issy's gravesite.

She's here. I can sense her beneath the surface. Not buried in the ground necessarily. Just… *trapped.*

I frown. *How do I set you free?*

I glance at my grave again, then down at my solid form. *Is this related? Did I break free of my grave?*

How symbolic that would be. Over a year ago, a goddess freed me from the ground and shattered my obedience spell. Is that what damaged my headstone? Or is this a more recent development?

I don't have time to debate it.

I need to break Issy's headstone and see if it frees her.

The only question is, how?

I circle our graves and try to think of a spell that might fracture the stone. *But I didn't cast a spell to break my own gravestone.*

Although, Nyx might have when she destroyed the obedience curse.

I kneel on my gravesite.

Did Nyx do this? Or did I?

Because I doubt Nyx broke Amala's stone. Amala was exiled well before Goddess Nyx's arrival.

So Amala probably broke her own gravestone. *And maybe that's why the patriarchs really exiled her.*

She rebelled.

And so did I…

I glance at the misty ribbons circling my hands and melting against my skin. This started when I decided I was done adhering to the patriarchs' wishes. It's like I broke free of their hold and started absorbing power to replenish my empty reserves.

I originally wanted to siphon it into Issy. But that's not what happened. My soul has been inhaling magic and bolstering my inner power.

That's why the repeated flickering spells were so easy. Why I was able to travel back here.

I couldn't push the energy into Issy's physical form, but maybe…

Maybe I can shove it into her grave.

Not necessarily into the ground—which appears to be made of solid rock—but into her *stone.*

It's… it's like the death stone I kept bowing over. Only it's ice cold. Although, I suppose mine was like that initially as well, but then it started to warm beneath me.

When I started to fight back, I realize. *Does that mean I need Issy to fight back? To break her own stone? Or do I have the power to free her?*

There's really only one way to find out.

I kneel in front of her name and rest my palms on the hard surface. Then I close my eyes and call every ounce of my rebellious need to the surface.

I think of my years of torment. Every sacrifice. Every false promise from the patriarchy. Their oppression. The way they used my twin as collateral. My mating to Klas. That damn obedience spell. The things my *mate* made me do. The feeling of being cut off from Issy.

Her vegetative state in that freezer…

I did *everything* I was supposed to do to protect her. And it wasn't enough. But I understand now that nothing would ever have been enough for the patriarchs. They want absolute control over every aspect of our lives.

And I refuse to give them that.

I refuse to give them another drop of my *anything.*

This power is *my* birthright. Not theirs. *My* plane. Not theirs. *My* life. Not theirs.

Energy hums around me, creating a chilly breeze that caresses my warm skin. It grounds me. Makes me feel whole. And reminds me that I'm not alone.

My mates are here, I marvel. *Not physically. Not even spiritually. But within me. Holding me together. Protecting me from everything else.*

It's a bizarre sensation that anchors me in the moment

and provides me with the focus I need to thrust this abundance of power into Issy's tombstone.

There's yelling in the distance. Masculine voices. *Chants.* But I ignore them, my attention on Issy. On my *mates.* They're doing something to protect me, my ties to them seeming to have dismantled my association with the patriarchs.

Is that how I fought back? I wonder. *Did they help me sever some sort of tie I didn't know existed?*

I force more power into the stone, my eyes falling closed as ominous echoes circle around me.

The words are of the ancient tongue, the male tones reminiscent of the patriarchy.

They're trying to stop me.

But they can't.

This is *my* plane now.

My power. My world. *My right.*

I scream as a burst of vitality rushes out of me, followed by a deafening crack.

It's not enough, I tell myself. *More. More. More.*

I repeat the action, this one even more painful, but needed. *So very needed.*

Again.

Another sharp pulse leaves my spirit, followed by a thunderous rumble. The masculine chanting sounds urgent now. I ignore them and push everything I can into the gravestone.

My chest aches from the effort, my throat raw from my screams, my limbs weak from the power I've just expelled.

But I still do one more.

One more expulsion.

Then everything goes quiet. The chants. My breathing. The sound of grating rocks.

Nothing.

I sigh, my arms falling to my sides.

Issy? I whisper, my mental voice tired. *Issy, are you there?*

The silence that follows has my hands clenching into fists.

Issy.

I wait a beat.

Issy!

This felt too right to be wrong. *If she's not here, then where is she?* I open my eyes, my focus on her fractured gravestone.

My efforts worked.

So why isn't Issy answering me?

I swallow and slowly sit back, my body exhausted from everything I've just done. But the cold fog is already surrounding me once more, the chilly kiss of power a welcome embrace against my clammy skin.

Maybe I need to try again. My mental voice is as tired as I feel. *Maybe I just needed a little...*

The thought trails off as I take in the full scene before me.

Wait...

I blink at the desecrated graveyard. I didn't crack just Issy's headstone, but... but *all* the headstones around me. Maybe even more.

Every single one within eyesight is split along the witch's last name.

Oh, stars...

I stand up on shaky legs and move forward.

It's all of them, I marvel. *I... I destroyed all of them.*

I continue walking, passing dozens of splintered stones.

What does this mean? Did I go about this the wrong way?

Probably, a voice replies, sounding tired. *Depends on what you did, though.*

I freeze. *Issy?*

Mmm, she hums.

I spin around, searching for her. *Where are you?*

Not sure. It's... it's cold...

My eyes widen. *The freezer.*

How do I get back there? I spin around like I'll find a door. A ridiculous proposition.

No. I need to focus like last time and demand to see Issy.

If only it could be that simple, I mutter to myself as I close my eyes. *But nothing is ever that simple.*

Still, I try. I focus on wanting to find Issy, telling my soul to go to her, and wait to see if I feel any magic helping me along.

When I don't, I sigh and open my eyes again, fully expecting to see the graveyard. But I don't. I'm shrouded in darkness once more.

I instantly cast a flicker of light and see Issy on the metal table. *You're still unconscious.*

I am? She sounds confused. *I'm in my room.*

No, you're in a freezer. I'm looking right at you.

She's quiet for a long moment. *I knew something was wrong when my books kept showing me blank pages.*

What?

Nothing. It's not important. But I need you to help me wake up.

What do you think I've been trying to do here? I ask her. *Tell me how to wake you up.*

You really should have read more books when we were younger, she replies, as snarky as ever. *They're very useful.*

Why do I need spell books when I have an omniscient sister?

I'm not omniscient, just well read.

I start to reply, when the sound of metal clanking outside the door makes me freeze. *Someone's coming.*

What?

They're unlocking the door. Issy, I... I need—

Repeat after me, she says, a series of ancient words following.

I immediately utter them out loud and follow her instructions, all the while ignoring the sounds at the door. Fortunately, it seems they have a lot of locks to undo.

The last word leaves my lips just as the lights are turned on in full, momentarily blinding me.

"I thought I might find you in here." Daithi O'Neely's voice slithers around me like a dangerous snake, his power venomous and eager to bite.

He's on me before I can reply, a spell slipping from his lips that steals the literal air from my lungs.

"You've been a very bad little witch, Fallon Doyle," he says against my ear. "I'm going to enjoy watching what they do to you."

My mouth moves without sound, my body suddenly feeling incredibly weak.

Weaker than in the death plane after my explosion of power.

Weak… like I'm not getting enough oxygen to properly breathe.

Because I'm not, I realize. *My lungs aren't working at all.*

Whatever he just did has caused my body to shut down.

He's made me resemble death.

I begin to convulse.

Which makes him smile broadly.

"Don't worry," he murmurs. "You'll wake up in a few minutes. Then you'll get to experience this all over again until I lift the spell. Maybe a few days like this will help you relearn some manners, hmm?"

My fingers long to flex, to move up to my throat, to demand that I breathe.

But I don't move at all.

He's turned me into some sort of frozen corpse.

I'm still standing. However, I can't feel the ground. I can't feel anything other than the burning in my chest that begs me to inhale.

Only I don't.

Black spots begin to dance through my blurring vision.

This is worse than being buried alive...

"At least my mate understands obedience," he continues, his focus going to Issy. "She's such a pretty little frozen doll, isn't she?" He starts toward her. "I've been given permission to warm her up a little this week." He glances back at me. "You know, to have a little fun."

My stomach twists at the insinuation in his words. *You will not touch her,* I want to snarl at him. But I can barely see him now.

He's chuckling about something, maybe my torment, or the thought of what he wants to do to my sister. Either way, he's a monster.

Just like the patriarchs.

When I wake up, I think, my vision going fully dark, *I'm going to—*

Wind whips through the air, reminding me of the death plane. Only it's a different sensation. A different sort of power.

Daithi growls in response to it. "*You.*"

"*Me,*" a familiar voice says.

Ayla? I can barely think her name, the world around me disappearing.

Issy screams something in my mind.

Then a jolt of power hits me dead center, and my body goes flying backward into the air.

I blink awake, confused by the sharp pain encompassing my being and relieved by my sudden ability to breathe again. I cough and choke and grasp at nothing as I go sailing through time and space.

What is happening to me? My vision is slowly coming back to me. *Why does it feel like I'm falling?*

My legs and arms come alive at the same moment, my limbs flailing around me as I try to grasp at something to hold on to.

Fallon! my sister screams.

I try to look for her, but all I see is glass. And a night sky.

What…?

I blink again.

And then I shriek as I realize the *glass* is a wall of windows. On a building. A very *tall* building. That I appear to be flying alongside of.

Not flying. Falling.

I glance down to see the ground rapidly approaching.

Oh, shit!

My arms and legs pinwheel as I try to lock onto the death plane again, needing to teleport, to do something. But there isn't enough time!

Focus, I tell myself. *Focus and—*

I slam into a hard object, the impact making my head loll. *Is this it? Did I just hit the ground?*

A fall from that height should kill me.

The hint of minty aftershave tickles my nose as the sound of beating wings touches my ears.

Am I dead?

Because I swear I'm being held by an angel.

"I've got you, Fallon," a deep voice says. "I'll always catch you when you fall."

NOLAN

"WHERE IS SHE?" Kaspian demands as he steps through the portal. "Where's Fallon?"

I shake my head. "Ayla still hasn't been able to reconnect to her aura." And it's been hours since she could last sense her.

"It's like she just disappeared," Ayla said when it first happened. "I don't understand. She was here and now she's gone."

We were standing on a rooftop, observing one of the O'Neely residences, when she initially lost the connection. Not a home owned by the main patriarch, but by someone high up in his family clan. *Daithi O'Neely*, Ayla called him.

"She was in there, though," Ayla added. "I'm certain of it. But she's... she's not there now."

"What about Issy?" I asked.

Ayla just shook her head. "No. I haven't been able to track Issy for the last few days. I'm not sure what they've done to her, but her aura is... untraceable."

I fully intended to break in and grab Fallon, but I paused when Ayla lost her aura. We needed to keep the element of surprise. And my barging into an O'Neely home would ruin all of that.

"It's only worth showing our hand if we know Fallon is in there," I told Kaspian earlier after bringing him up to date on what we found here. "But Ayla can't sense her anymore. I don't want to alert them to my presence unless I know I can save Fallon."

Kaspian agreed with my plan, telling me he would be here soon with reinforcements.

I now watch with an arched brow as all those reinforcements step through the portal.

"I'm surprised Cara and Larus didn't demand to join," I comment as I fold my arms over my chest.

"They're my seconds. If something happens to me, I need them in Iceland to act as King and Queen of Gold and Garnet," he replies.

"I'm sure they loved that speech," I drawl.

Nox snorts as he joins us. "Cara said she didn't agree to be his second just to be put in time-out when something *fun* happens."

Bane twirls one of his blades, his dark eyes flashing with dangerous intent. "How are we doing this?" he asks, cutting straight to the point as the portal closes behind the last of the mercenaries.

We're back in Manhattan again, playing on the rooftop of the abandoned building Ayla seems to favor. I learned why when I met Amala—the witch who taught Ayla how to break the forced-mate-bond magic. Apparently, the exiled witch cast a deterrence spell around the upper floors and roof of this building, making it an area that most supernaturals avoid.

"I have to live somewhere," Amala explained with a shrug. "And I certainly don't want to live in Staten Island."

She stands beside Ayla now, her purple hair blowing in the breeze from being so high up in the sky. Like Ayla, she seems undisturbed by the fifty-plus-story drop off the side.

It's a sentiment the mercenaries Kaspian brought with him don't seem to share.

Well, the gryffin-god hybrid seems at ease. The others, not so much.

Meanwhile, Nox and Bane seem fine. And Kaspian just seems impatient.

It's a feeling I understand.

I've been standing around for hours, waiting for Ayla to pick up on Fallon's aura again, while also hoping she somehow made it back to Iceland.

Alas, no one knows where she is.

And something is brewing in Staten Island. Ayla said she could feel the power rippling through her coven, leaving her uneasy.

Even Amala could sense it, despite being exiled.

"The patriarchs are doing something," Ayla told me, her hands rubbing up and down her arms as though she felt cold. "I don't know what it is, but I can feel it. Something big is coming."

Which is why we need to work quickly.

Ayla pulls up a map of Staten Island—one she casts in the air using magic. We've already mocked it up in color to show the various patriarch homes. I point at each one to say the clan name and also show where Fallon's aura was last felt.

"Who is this Daithi O'Neely?" Kaspian interjects. "Why would he have Fallon?"

"He specializes in obedience spells," Ayla replies. "As to

why he would have Fallon, I'm not sure. But something drew her aura to his home."

"And we're certain she's not still there?" Kaspian inquires, the question one that's been asked a few times now, not just by him but by Nox, Bane, and me. Because all of us are eager to track down our mate.

"Her aura isn't in his home," Ayla tells him. "The only links to her aura that I'm sensing right now belong to the four of you."

Kaspian studies her for a beat and nods before looking at me. "Continue."

"Ayla and Amala think the patriarchs may be holding Fallon captive in the death plane," I explain. "She suspects Issy is there, too."

"As well as dozens of other witches," Amala mutters, her green eyes flashing. "The patriarchs use our souls to bolster their own magic. They're like fucking leeches. And they do it all through the death plane."

I nod. "So the theory holds merit. Which is why I agree with Ayla's recommendation for how to proceed—we need to take out the patriarchs. If we do that, we sever their magical hold, and that should allow Fallon to come back to us."

"Or trap her there indefinitely," Bane says, his brow furrowing. He looks at Ayla. "We were able to pull her back when we had her body before. But earlier, she didn't respond to us at all. And without her body now, we can't even try to replicate what worked the one time."

"I think they did something to counter your ability to revive her this time." Ayla doesn't sound entirely confident, but it's a theory I agreed with when she mentioned it to me before. "If we disable the patriarchs, it should disable that spell."

"But we still don't know where her body is," Bane points out.

"It may be in Daithi's house." Ayla lifts a shoulder. "I just know her aura—her *soul*—isn't there. But it's possible we'll find her body."

Nox's eyebrows lift. "If that's true, then it has probably suffered catastrophic damage since we weren't there to keep it alive. You're the one who said to keep doing compressions…"

Ayla shakes her head. "If the patriarchs have her body, they're keeping it alive. They wouldn't want her to deteriorate too quickly; otherwise, they would lose their ability to use her."

"She's right," Amala agrees. "They need Fallon intact. She's too young and too powerful for them to allow her to rot."

I know all this already because we had a similar argument shortly after Fallon's soul disappeared. While I didn't want to blow my cover prematurely, I also wasn't going to just let Fallon's body start to decompose.

But Ayla and Amala convinced me this was the right path.

"So we need to take out the patriarchs," I say, bringing us back to the plan. "We don't know where they are, just where they live. And Ayla thinks they may have some secret meeting locations in the city, too. But I think we should start by taking down their homes and declaring open war on their clans."

Kaspian nods. "I've already spoken to a few other House allies on the topic. They're aware the Outcast Coven attacked us first. Not that it truly matters—this is still No Man's Land and fair game—but I wanted them all informed."

"Chancellor Ward knows as well?" I guess.

"She does," Kaspian confirms. "She's neither supportive nor unsupportive. She's neutral."

Given that she recently escaped this hellhole, I'm not surprised. She probably wants nothing to do with Supernatural Syndicate issues.

"All right, so I assume we want to hit each house at the same time, take full advantage of catching them off guard?" Nox proposes.

"Yes. That's the general idea." I glance around at the group. Kaspian brought eight mercenaries with him, all of them more than qualified for this mission. "There are fourteen of us, so we'll go in pairs." I look at the phantoms. "I suggest you two split up. If all four of us head to different locations, we have a better chance of finding Fallon."

Nox and Bane dip their chins in acknowledgment.

"I'll partner with Khaos," Kaspian says.

The shifter-god hybrid arches a brow. "You sure?"

"You bested Cara in a fight. *Twice.* I'm sure." Kaspian starts divvying up the group and pairs me with one of Khaos's brothers. I haven't spent much time with the three hybrids from Talino's territory in Finland, but I'm familiar with their impressive mercenary records. So I agree to the pairing.

"All right, we—"

Kaspian's words are cut off by Ayla's gasp, her knees suddenly buckling as she begins to collapse. Amala catches her, only for her own legs to give out on her, sending both females to the ground.

I dart forward at the same time Bane and Nox do, but all three of us come up against an invisible barrier of sorts. One that's ice cold and prickles goose bumps all over my skin.

"What the fuck is that?" Nox demands.

I shake my head.

Bane simply frowns. "It…" He doesn't finish his statement, his brow furrowing as he prods at the air around him.

Kaspian wears an expression that matches Bane's. "It smells like Fallon."

"What?" My nostrils flare on impulse. "All I smell is New York City."

Two of the shifter mercenaries snort at my comment but otherwise stay quiet.

However, Bane and Kaspian seem to be entranced by whatever they're sensing around the witches. Nox joins in on their fascination in the next beat, his head canting to the side. "It feels like her."

"It does," Bane replies. "But I don't understand why."

My heart pangs a little in my chest, my lack of a true connection to our mate making me feel inferior in this moment. I haven't had a chance to bond with Fallon like I've wanted to. She probably doesn't even know I want to accept our fated links.

Ayla gasps again, her body shooting upright into a seated position as Amala swiftly follows, the two women sharing alarmed gazes. "Did that…?" Ayla trails off.

"Yes," Amala confirms.

"*All* of them?" Ayla stresses.

Amala nods, her face a little white. "That's what it feels like, yes."

"All of what?" Kaspian asks. "What just happened?"

"Fallon just happened." Ayla pushes up off the ground, her limbs noticeably shaky. "I don't know how she did it. But she… she just set us all free."

My forehead crinkles. "Free?"

"From the patriarchs' hold," Ayla explains, her focus on something off to the side. I try to follow her stare, but all I see is more rooftop. "She just *shattered* their control over every woman in the Outcast Coven."

My eyebrows shoot upward. "*What?* How?" She already said she doesn't know how, but the questions are automatic. Because that... *that's incredibly impressive.*

"What are you doing?" Kaspian asks, his gaze narrowing as Ayla begins weaving a spell in the air.

"Going after Fallon," Ayla replies. "She's back."

My wings flare out of me on impulse. "*Where?*"

"Same place," Ayla says.

I start toward the ledge, prepared to fly to Daithi O'Neely's home in Staten Island.

But Ayla stops me by adding, "I'm creating a portal that'll go right to her."

"You know exactly where she is?"

Ayla nods. "Yes. And it's a place I've been before."

"Why didn't you do that earlier?" I demand. When she sensed Fallon then, she couldn't get us closer than the rooftops.

"Because I wasn't positive of her location." She glances at me. "And I wasn't sure I could break through Daithi's protection barriers."

My eyebrow arches. "But you feel more confident now?"

She nods. "I do. Because I'm *free.*"

Amala chuckles, drawing my focus to her and causing my brow to lift even higher.

"All hell is about to break loose in Outcast Coven territory," she muses. "Hell hath no fury like a woman scorned and all that. Only it's *women*, not *woman*."

"I don't understand what's happening," Khaos says, his words seeming to be for one of his brothers.

"The patriarchy has kept the women of our coven on magical leashes for years, forcing us to mate whomever they choose, all in the name of giving the males power and dominion over us," Ayla explains. "They've been using *our* magical birthrights to empower themselves."

"How?" Khaos asks. "If your birthrights make you the more powerful of the duo, how have they managed to subdue you?"

"By taking control of the most powerful members of the coven at birth," Amala replies. "Powerful members like Fallon and Ishara Doyle."

"When you're raised in a world that calls you weak, tells you that it's your place to obey, convinces you that your only worth in life is as a marriage commodity to a superior male, you believe them," Ayla adds. "But it seems something helped Fallon wake up."

"*Someones,*" Amala corrects, her green eyes dancing over Nox, Bane, Kaspian, and then me. "Her links to you have provided her with new perspective. She just may not realize that's the cause."

"Her desire to save her sister would also have been a motivating factor," Ayla murmurs, her eyes falling closed. "I'm almost done."

This portal seems to be taking her a lot longer than the others. I'm guessing it's related to the *protection barriers* she mentioned.

"When I open this door, there will be no going back. They'll know I'm involved. But something tells me that I will be the least of their concerns," Ayla says, a smile in her voice. "Once the others realize they're free…"

"Blood will be shed," Amala finishes for her. "Fucking finally."

"Ready?" Ayla asks after a beat, her gaze roaming around the rooftop. "It'll open to a small freezer area, but I don't know what's waiting for us beyond. I just know both Issy and Fallon are there."

I stare at her. "Wait, you can sense Issy again?"

She nods. "Whatever Fallon did to free us all freed Issy, too. They're together."

"In a small freezer," Kaspian growls. "Did I hear that right?"

Ayla clears her throat. "You did. It's… it's one of Daithi's favorite torments."

My eyes narrow, but it's Nox who says, "This *Daithi* needs to die."

Bane twirls a pair of knives in his hands as I pull out one of my guns. "He does," we say at the same time.

"Open the portal," I add. "We're very ready."

The mercenaries behind me all make noises of agreement, the sounds of weapons being armed littering the air.

Let the war begin.

Ayla pauses for a moment, her shoulders squaring. Then she nods and mutters a few words in a language I've never heard before.

A second later, the door opens to reveal a scene that has my blood running hot and then cold.

Fallon's naked.

Her face is turning blue.

And the male inside is *chuckling.* Although, that chuckle dies swiftly when he sees Ayla's portal creation.

"*You*," he growls.

"*Me*," she returns, black fire dancing down her arms.

I assume this brown-haired male is Daithi and quickly take aim at his head. But he blocks my bullet with a spell, his hazel eyes glittering with power.

Ayla tries to hit him with a fiery sphere. He sends it to the side, then does something that lifts Fallon from the ground, causing me to freeze.

There's a maniacal gleam in his gaze that shoots ice through my veins. *This male is not sane.*

Power bursts from his fingertips—power that goes right into Fallon as he throws her through the portal door with a force that has time stilling around me.

"Fallon!" Kaspian yells as her body sails across the roof, the spell taking her right over the edge.

My wings flare out around me as I take off after her, my heart racing in my chest.

She's moving with such incredible speed... *Too fast. She's flying too fast!*

I dive off the roof after her, determined to catch her. To *save* her.

This can't be happening.

A fall from this height will kill her instantly. There will be no recovering from it.

We haven't even mated yet! I want to shout at her. *Don't you dare die on me, Fallon!*

I can hear Nox and Bane yelling from above, as well as the sounds of fighting.

But my focus is solely on Fallon.

Faster, I tell my wings. *We need to go faster!*

The air whips by my face as I push myself to my limits while ignoring the approaching ground below.

Fallon's arms and legs start pinwheeling as she realizes what's happening, the motion seeming to dispel some of the enchantment encircling her.

It's as though she's slowing herself down.

Impossible, I think. But somehow, she's decelerating. *Magic?*

Whatever it is, I'm thankful for it. Because it gives me the edge I need to swoop beneath her.

And catch her in my arms.

She jolts against me, her head falling back against my

shoulder. I beat my wings upward, saving us both from an impact with the ground.

And sigh as she stills against me.

"I've got you, Fallon," I tell her, my lips near her ear. Then I bury my face in her hair as I vow, "I'll always catch you when you fall."

FĀLLON

FALLON! Issy screams in my head. *Fallon!*

Issy? I whisper back, dazed by everything that just happened. One minute, I was suffocating to death.

And the next…

I blink. *I'm flying. With an angel.*

Oh, thank the stars, Issy breathed. *I tried to give him time to catch you. By countering Daithi's impact spell. But I was worried… I was worried it wasn't fast enough.*

I frown at the concern in my sister's voice.

He used *me to hurt you,* she continues. *He* froze *me under an obedience spell.* Infiltrated *our mental connection to let the patriarchs talk to you through me.* Mated *me against my will.*

She sounds furious now.

He. Will. Die. Those three words resemble bullets in my mind.

Wait, Issy—

No. No waiting. He. Will. Die!

But we don't know how the forced bond—

A catastrophic *boom* echoes through the air, jolting me upright in my angel's arms. I look around, startled and confused, only to find Nolan staring down at me as we hover in the sky.

"Are you all right?" he asks, his voice softer than I've ever heard it.

My eyelashes flutter, my heart pounding in my chest.

Am I all right?

"I'm alive," I tell him, my brow furrowing a little. "And no one shot me this time." The quip comes naturally to me. Mostly because it's what I always comment on when Nolan comes around.

His lips twitch. "The day is still young, sweet canary."

I narrow my gaze a little, another taunt tickling my tongue. But a second magical explosion has my focus shifting upward.

Issy?

She doesn't reply.

"My sister…" I trail off as Nolan starts flying toward the battle sounds. He pauses as we reach a rooftop, allowing me to see the scene before us.

There's a random door that seems to lead to the freezer room I was just in.

Outside of it are my three mates, as well as some other men I don't recognize.

"*Fallon*," Kaspian says, his expression one of intense relief. It's a look my two phantoms share as they rush forward.

But they pause as Ayla jumps through the threshold, her leather jacket smoldering with black flames.

Another female follows her, and the door begins to close.

"No!" I shout. "Issy—"

Ayla looks sharply up at me. "Issy finally has her voice back."

"What?" I ask, not understanding.

"The mating bond is broken," the other woman says. "Issy can *speak*."

I look between them, still confused. "Issy isn't silent because of a *mating bond*. She's... she's silent..."

"Because her voice kills," Ayla finishes for me. "So let her *kill*."

Issy? I call to her. *Talk to me, Issy!*

A little busy right now, sis, she grates out.

Nolan finally touches down on the roof and helps me to my feet, but before I can dart forward toward the door, he grabs me and wraps me up in his leather jacket.

I frown down at it, only then realizing that I've been naked this whole time.

"Er, thanks," I say to him.

He kisses my temple. "Never thank me for taking care of you, Fallon."

I glance back at him, startled by this nurturing side of him. "Yet you expected me to thank you for not killing me?"

He smiles. "Because I meant to shoot to kill, little canary." He tilts his head to the side. "But fate wouldn't let me. At least now we know why."

"Wait..." I fully face him. "You *meant* to kill me?"

"I did."

I arch a brow. "So you missed?"

"Yep."

"Meaning you didn't purposely shoot me in the shoulder, yet you've spent the last however many months insisting you weren't trying to kill me." I fold my arms and narrow my gaze. "Why?"

"Because I didn't want to give you more cause to hate me."

"Yet you're coming clean now?"

He shrugs. "Kaspian has a thing about lies. If we're all going to be in a mate circle, I have to tell the truth."

"You expect me to accept our mating after you admitted to trying to kill me?"

"Yep," he answers simply.

I gape at him. "*Seriously?*"

"Yep," he repeats.

I'm so flabbergasted that I don't know what to say to any of this. *He just... he just... And I...*

"Do you want to know why I expect that?" he asks, stepping closer to me.

Against my better judgment, I find myself nodding.

He tucks a strand of hair behind my ear, then leans down to whisper, "Because I'm the mate who will never hold back. The one you can rely on to give it to you straight, no matter how much it'll piss you off. The one who will push you even when you don't want to be pushed. The one who will ensure you're ready for everything and anything life has to throw at you."

I swallow, unsure if I like all of that. Which I suppose is his point, in a way.

"I'll also be the one to protect you with everything I am. The one willing to do whatever it takes to ensure your safety and happiness. And the one who will spend eternity trying to prove my worth to you because I fully accept the fact that I've fucked everything up between us from the moment we first met."

He wraps his palm around my nape, his multicolored eyes intense as he pulls back to meet my gaze.

"I may be entirely wrong, and you might reject me. But even if you do, I'll remain devoted to you. Because, Fallon, I've wanted you from the moment you woke up and gave me hell for shooting you." He presses his forehead to mine. "There will never be anyone else for me. Only you."

I'm so shocked by his declarations that I have no idea how to reply.

"And lastly," he murmurs, his voice barely loud enough for me to hear over the rooftop wind. "Lastly, I'll be the one to distract you when you need it most." His lips whisper across mine. "Such as right now."

He releases me before I can speak, then carefully turns me around just as my sister steps through a portal door.

"Issy!" I rush forward as she runs toward me.

My arms encircle her neck in the next breath as I cling to my sister for dear life. *You're okay. You're here. And you're okay.*

She echoes the sentiment in my head as we make up for years of not being able to hug one another.

"They're all dead," I hear Ayla say. It's probably been several minutes since I started hugging my sister. But I haven't been able to stop. "Including Daithi and a few others."

"Because of her voice?" Kaspian asks softly, his words sending a chill down my spine.

"Yes," Ayla confirms.

Oh, no… He knows.

Of course he knows, my sister replies. *He should know. He's your* mate, *Fallon.*

But he's also the Gold and Garnet King. He… he…

He what? she counters. *He's going to lock me in a basement like our father did? Kill me? What do you think he's going to do?*

I pull back to see the irritation in her expression. *Why are you being like this?*

Because you're doing that thing where you put me first instead of yourself. She arches a blonde brow. *I can take care of myself, Fallon.*

I almost point out that I found her in a freezer and had

to free her from the death plane. But her expression changes in the next second.

Thank you for freeing my soul, she says, clearly having experienced the same train of thought. *But you need to start putting yourself first. Fate just gave you four fine-ass mates to play with, and you're doubting them because of your concern for me.*

She looks pointedly over my shoulder at the men in question.

I know he's a House King. But his mating you makes you the House Queen. And if there's one important lesson to learn from all of today's events, it's to never underestimate the power of a female mate.

I turn to follow her gaze and note how all four of my mates are standing together, watching me and Issy with interest.

Not fear or disgust or even a hint of concern.

Just... interest.

Do you...? I swallow. *Do you want to meet them?*

Do I want to meet the sexy men fate has chosen for my twin? She snorts. *Stars, yes, I do.*

My lips curl a little. *You were just on a ventilator in a freezer. And now you're...*

I'm...? she prompts.

You're you, I answer simply. *Optimistic. Happy.*

Alive, she adds. *No longer tied down or mated to patriarch assholes.*

Assholes? I repeat, frowning at her. *As in plural?*

She hums, the sound one of confirmation. *Four total. And Daithi.* She shudders. *They needed my cooperation, and I... well, it took a lot of them to make it happen.*

I gape at her. *They force-mated you to* five *men?*

They did. She tilts her head a little. *But now they're all dead, and my soul is free once more.*

How can you be so... blasé about this?

She shrugs. *If I dwell on the past, I'll never be free.* She looks at me, her silver eyes glittering. *We need to focus on the future, Fallon. Embrace the gifts fate has given us. And that includes you embracing your mates.*

I have embraced them.

You've started to, but I know you, sis. You don't trust easily. However... She refocuses on my mates. *Those men have earned your trust. They're here, aren't they? Saving you?*

The Outcast Coven attacked Gold and Garnet by sending in Klas. Kaspian had to respond to that, I argue, aware of how politics work in this world.

While that may be true, he hasn't left this roof since he arrived. You're his primary concern.

I consider that for a moment. *How do you know he's been here the whole time?*

Because I know things, Fallon, she says, her gaze twinkling when she looks back at me. *I know a lot of things. Including the fact that you're currently stalling.* She folds her arms. *Now stop hiding me and introduce me to your mates. Let them prove to you how accepting they can be.*

FALLON

A FEW DAYS LATER

"FINLAND?" I repeat, my gaze darting between Ayla and Issy. "You're both moving to *Finland*?"

"King Kaspian said we could live wherever we wanted in Gold and Garnet territory." Ayla shrugs. "Then Khaos mentioned an opportunity in Lapland. Apparently, they could use someone with my tracking abilities."

They also don't seem to be all that intimidated by my abilities, Issy adds in my head. *Probably because the three brothers that govern the area have godlike heritages.*

"It'll be a good fit for us," Ayla adds. "And if it's not, then we'll just come back here."

Issy nods. *Iceland is very beautiful. So even if we stay, we'll still be back to visit. Often.*

I swallow, unsure of how I feel about this. I just finally got my family back. And now…

Now they want to move to *Finland*.

We're no longer your only family, Fallon, Issy whispers, likely aware of my thoughts.

Well, technically you are, I say. *You killed our dad...* And that was after he killed our mother. I didn't get to witness any of it, but apparently she tried to fight him after I released all the bespelled souls in the death plane.

Unfortunately, our father won the battle.

But Issy ensured he lost the war.

With just a few whispered words—ones she hasn't shared with me. And I'll never ask.

His cruelty toward me was nothing compared to the pain and misery he inflicted upon Issy. She earned the right to be his executioner.

Hell, she earned the right to kill the entire patriarchy, as far as I'm concerned.

But she did have some help from other furious witches.

The Outcast Coven is officially being overhauled now, a new matriarchy replacing the patriarchy.

Ayla wanted nothing to do with it, instead taking Kaspian up on his offer to join Gold and Garnet.

He gave Amala—the witch I didn't immediately recognize on the rooftop the other day—the same choice, but she opted to stay in New York. Apparently, she's enjoying her exile. However, she said she would be in touch if she ever changes her mind.

I doubt we'll ever hear from her again, especially with the Outcast Coven realigning their values and restructuring their inner political system.

But I appreciate Kaspian offering her the choice. Just as I appreciate him giving Ayla and my sister sanctuary.

He didn't even blink when I asked him about Issy.

"She's your family," he replied. "Of course she's welcome here. Ayla, too."

Nox, Bane, and Nolan all agreed with nods.

Then they performed a small ceremony to welcome

Issy and Ayla into the territory, giving them both a gold charm adorned with a solitary garnet gem.

It was a ritual I knew nothing about, something that surprised Kaspian when I mentioned it. But he hasn't said anything about it since.

"So, um, when do you leave?" I ask Ayla and Issy.

Ayla lifts a shoulder. "Maybe in a few days. Khaos didn't really give me a start date, just ordered up a place for us to live and said to move at our leisure."

"That was nice of him," I acknowledge.

She nods. "Pretty sure he'll be making me work for it, though. But at least I'll enjoy the job." She smiles at Issy with the words.

I might have found a way to help her track auras more effectively. Issy's silver irises gleam with pride. *You know, without being detected.*

Oh? I glance between them. *That's impressive.*

I know.

Modest as always, I see, I tease her.

She preens in response, the expression making me laugh just as Nox and Bane enter the room.

They both pause.

"Oh. Is this a bad time?" Nox asks.

"I told you to knock," Bane mutters.

"But it's sort of our room now, too," Nox replies, his words soft and clearly meant for Bane. But we can all hear him just fine.

"We'll leave you to it," Ayla says, her black eyes casting a knowing look at Issy.

Mm-hmm, my twin hums. *Have fun playing with your phantoms.*

I almost correct her and say they're not mine—a response I made a lot over the last year when she teased me about *my phantoms.*

Instead, I reply, *I will.*

She smiles, mirth flirting with her soft features. Then she winks at my phantoms and leads Ayla out of the room.

Bane and Nox both glance at each other.

"Sorry, we didn't know they were here," Nox says.

I palm his cheek. "You don't need to apologize. I know how much you enjoy barging into my room and spying on me in phantom form." It's a familiar taunt from our early days, one that has his lips curling in amusement.

"I *am* a voyeur," he replies.

"I know." I go up onto my toes to kiss him. "You're *my* voyeur."

He wraps his arm around my back, his opposite hand going to my throat. "That I am, firefly. That I am." He kisses me soundly, his tongue easily mastering mine.

It doesn't matter how young this mating is; Nox devours me with the knowledge of several lifetimes, his expert touch and embrace making it feel as though we've done this for hundreds of years.

Bane joins us by pressing his chest to my back, his lips caressing my neck.

It's a practiced move that just further proves how perfect these men are for me.

My phantoms, I marvel, lost to their embrace.

They make me forget everything and everyone. Which is how I don't realize we have company until someone clears his throat.

I look over to find Kaspian and Nolan watching us with hungry gazes.

The former I expect—Kaspian is always hungry.

But the latter surprises me. He's spent the last few days being uncharacteristically polite. Nurturing, too. It's been a bit strange to see that caring side of him. Nolan is usually all hard lines and serious looks.

"When I told you two to help prepare Fallon, I meant to brief her on the ceremony, not seduce her for the after-party," Kaspian drawls.

"Ceremony?" I repeat while Nox smirks at Kaspian.

"Yes." The Gold and Garnet King steps forward, his attire as formal as always—a three-piece suit. All black. His shoulders are straight back as well, his hands elegantly hidden behind his back.

Meanwhile, Nolan is in jeans and a leather jacket, his blond hair windswept and tousled. He has the whole badass rebel vibe going on, which is a sensual contrast to Kaspian's elegant appearance.

And they're both mine, I marvel. *Sort of, anyway.*

Nolan and I haven't yet spoken about finalizing our bond. The last thing he said to me on the topic was that he'd never reject me, but he wouldn't force me to accept him either.

"You told me the other day that you were never formally welcomed into Gold and Garnet," Kaspian murmurs. "It's something I should have realized from the first day we met—you don't wear our House colors."

My brow furrows. "Gold and Garnet?"

He nods. "You're also not tattooed—which a lot of mercenaries choose to do over wearing a symbol. But the fact of the matter is, you have neither."

"It doesn't have to be something permanent," Bane adds as he steps forward.

Then he pulls a dagger from a holster on his hip. It's the knife he let me use to eviscerate Klas last year. I frown as his thumb runs over the gold handle and the garnet gem on top.

"I wear this everywhere," he tells me. "That's how I show my House affiliation."

"And I show my affiliation by carrying around this,"

Nox says, taking a tiny vial out of his pocket. It's clear with a gold cap and appears to be filled with blood. "It's Kaspian's."

"Kaspian's…?" I trail off, trying to follow what he's saying. "His blood?"

Nox nods. "Vampire blood is powerful in the right circumstance. Especially when combined with certain toxins."

That makes sense. While I haven't seen Nox play much with chemicals, I'm aware that he's quite the wizard when it comes to the art of alchemy. Specifically, the kind that can be combined with weapons.

"I'm a little more old-fashioned." Nolan's deep voice captures my attention as he pulls a gold chain from around his neck. There's a charm on the end—*a bloody bullet.* "This used to represent my first kill as a mercenary," he tells me, his thumb brushing the charm. "But I changed it last year."

I blink at him. *He can't mean…*

"It's the bullet from when I shot you," he says, making my lips part. "A memory I'll never forget."

I… I don't know how to respond to that. Which seems to be an ongoing conundrum between us. His truths continue to leave me speechless. Because I'm realizing there's so much more to Nolan than I could ever have anticipated.

He's dark.

Broody.

And yet, there's a tenderness to him that he seems to reserve for me. But it's not a normal kind of tenderness. It's the kind of tenderness associated with keeping a bloody bullet—one that was originally meant to kill me—as a keepsake.

"Mine is also a little more old-fashioned," Kaspian tells

me, his lips twitching. "But maybe a little less… violent."
He brings one hand out from behind his back to show me
the ring on his finger. "It's a House heirloom, one meant
for the king." He shrugs one shoulder. "I also have some
Gold and Garnet weapons, ones I carry with me often."

I'm not surprised by his tokens. They're all very
Kaspian-like to me. *Although*… "I'm shocked you don't
have a Gold and Garnet three-piece suit."

He smirks. "I do, actually. But it's atrocious and you'll
never see me wear it."

"It's more of a burgundy color with a gold tie," Bane
adds. "But he's right—it's terrible."

"Now I want to see it," I say, waggling my brows.
"Maybe I'll think you're sexy in it."

Kaspian snorts. "You would find me sexy in anything I
choose to wear, Fallon."

I can't stop the laugh from escaping me. "Someone has
quite the ego."

"Someone has more than earned his ego," Kaspian
returns, stepping closer to me. "Besides, I'm all about
truths, love. And we both know I'm right—you can't resist
me." That last part is a whisper against my mouth, his
boldness and confidence making my knees go weak.

I *hate* that he can do this to me.

But I also love it.

"I could," I reply to him softly. "But why would I ever
want to?" I go onto my toes to kiss him, but he catches my
hip and holds me in place.

"You need a token, Fallon. Something you can wear
that says you're part of Gold and Garnet." His tone holds
a sternness to it that is the epitome of regal Kaspian.

"What kind of token do you want me to have?" I ask
him, unsure of what I would choose.

"This," he says, his hand—the one he's kept behind his

back since he entered the room—moves between us to reveal a tiny black box.

I frown at it. "What is it?"

"Open it and find out," he says, holding it out for me.

My throat feels a little tight as I take the item from him, my heart skipping a beat in my chest. *He brought me a token.*

It's probably similar to what he gave Issy and Ayla—a charm for them to wear on a necklace or a bracelet.

Except I quickly realize that's *not* the case as I open the box.

It's not a charm at all.

It's a ring.

My lips part at the beautiful token, my eyes zeroing in on the yellow gemstone framed by garnet accents and set in a solid gold band. "Kaspian…" I look up at him.

Only, he's no longer standing.

He's kneeling.

And he's not alone.

All four of my mates are now kneeling around me, their gazes reverent.

"The heart of Gold and Garnet revolves around our fealty pledge," Kaspian explains to me. "We're a House of mercenaries where fortune and prestige are two of our most important qualities. But it's the fealty we pledge to each other—to our House—that matters most."

I swallow, my head dipping in understanding. He mentioned some of this to Issy and Ayla.

"That said, I don't want you to pledge your fealty to Gold and Garnet, Fallon." Kaspian's words have my eyes widening. But he doesn't give me a chance to ask for clarification. "I want to pledge my fealty to *you.*"

My lips part, his words shocking me silent.

"You're our mate," Nox adds.

"Our heart," Bane murmurs.

"Our queen," Nolan says.

"Our queen," Kaspian echoes. "*We* owe you our fealty. Our love. Our devotion. Our protection. Our truths. Which is why we're kneeling for you. We pledge ourselves to you, Fallon Doyle, Queen of Gold and Garnet. And we're hoping you will accept us by wearing that ring."

I glance down at it, realizing now that there are exactly four garnet gem accents around the yellow stone. *One for each mate.*

A slight mist seems to disturb my vision, my heart beating a mile a minute in my chest.

How has this become my existence? I marvel. *Going from Klas to… to this.*

You need to start putting yourself first, Issy said to me the other day. *We need to focus on the future, Fallon. Embrace the gifts fate has given us. And that includes you embracing your mates.*

I knew then that she was right.

But seeing my four mates all kneeling for me, pledging themselves to me… *Stars,* I still can't believe this is real. That this is my life. My *fate*.

Four sexy fated mates.

And they're all mine, I marvel. *Mine to love. To accept. To spend eternity with.*

How could I ever say no to what they're offering? Why would I even consider it?

"Yes," I tell Kaspian. "Yes," I repeat, looking at each of my mates. "Yes to everything. Yes to this. Yes to… to all of you."

That last part is for Nolan more than the others. He's the only one I haven't completed the bond with, and I need him to know I accept him.

His multicolored eyes gleam in response, his gaze intent.

But it's Kaspian who takes the ring and slips it on my

finger. "We considered making it a ruby with three yellow diamonds around it, but we liked the idea of having garnet represent each of us, while the yellow diamond represents you." He kisses my hand, drawing my attention back to him. "You're our diamond, Fallon."

Nox takes my hand from him, adding a kiss of his own. "You're our firefly."

"Our burning flame," Bane says, his lips meeting my wrist.

"Our sweet canary." Nolan's words are almost as soft as his touch as he brushes his mouth against my fingertips. I reach for him as he begins to release me, needing more than that brief stroke against my skin.

He looks up at me in surprise, his irises seeming to spark with renewed color. But I don't give him a chance to react much more than that before I go to my knees in front of him and kiss him.

He's the only one I haven't properly tasted. And I need him to believe me when I say I want him.

He's mine just as much as the others are.

I want all of them. All of this. *For always.*

And I tell Nolan that with my mouth.

With my tongue.

Mine, I'm saying. *All of you are mine.* I thread my fingers through his thick hair, my teeth scraping over his bottom lip. *And that claim,* I'm telling him with my bite. *That claim includes* you.

NOLAN

MY HEART POUNDS in my chest as Fallon bites my lower lip, her fiery energy warming my skin. She seems to be trying to teach me some sort of lesson.

I'm not sure what that lesson is, but I'm enjoying it.

Which is why I don't immediately take charge of our kiss. I let her play. Bite. Kiss. *Lick*.

The moment she starts to pull away, I grab her.

"My turn," I tell her, taking a fistful of her hair and hauling her right back to me.

Her eyes widen, but she started this game.

She wanted to prove some sort of point. So I'm going to return the favor.

And my point is quite simple: *If you want to play, we'll play. But be prepared, little canary. I play to win.*

She trembles against me as my tongue slides into her mouth. I let her set the pace before because I wanted to give her a chance to explore. However, now she needs to learn my preferences. My pace. My desires.

One of which is to define her limits.

Master her pleasure.

Draw out the experience until she's bursting from the inside and *begging* me to let her come.

The others all have their kinks. But those are mine.

I *love* games of passion. I want to take Fallon to the literal stars. Make her scream for *hours*.

And I tell her all of that with my mouth. My tongue. *My teeth*.

She's not the only one who can convey messages here through touch.

By the time I'm finished with my part of the lesson, she's panting, her emerald eyes glazed with pleasure. She licks her lips, her focus going to my mouth before she glances at the others.

Kaspian is sitting on the bed, his jacket and vest gone. His dark eyes are glued to me and Fallon. I've never been into group play. He knows this. But for her... I'll oblige. Which is why I so openly fucked her mouth in front of the others.

Bane and Nox are both standing nearby, the top button on their jeans both undone.

I nearly smirk at the display of discomfort.

If they think my kissing Fallon is hot, they should see what else I can do to her.

But first, I want her worked up. Teased. *Prepared*.

"Hmm, I think your phantoms want to play, Fallon," I tell her. "As does our vampire king."

Kaspian arches a brow at me, fully aware that I don't usually do this. We've known each other for a very long time, and while there have been a few experiences between us, it's been a while since we last shared a woman.

We both vie for dominance in the bedroom.

Which can be good.

And also bad.

But for Fallon, I think we can make it *very* good.

"What do you think, Kas?" I ask, my gaze on Fallon. "Should we let the phantoms have her first? Warm her up for us?"

His midnight irises glitter with temptation. He knows what I'm offering. "Yes. But I imagine you have some requirements?"

"I do." I look at Bane and Nox. "She's not allowed to come until I say she can. Otherwise, do what you want."

Fallon's lips part. "What?"

I kiss her again, my grasp tightening in her hair. "Trust me, sweet canary. I'm going to make you sing in a way you've never experienced before." I speak the words right against her mouth, then follow it up with a nibble of my own. "Now be a good girl and let the phantoms fuck you."

She's gaping at me when I release her.

I go to sit beside Kaspian on the bed, my gaze on the phantoms as they prowl toward a still-startled Fallon. She jumps a little when Nox kisses her neck, her green eyes finding mine. It looks like she wants to say something— maybe a rebuttal about my rule—but it's silenced by Bane taking control of her mouth with his own.

I've never watched the phantoms play, but I quickly learn why Kaspian is so enamored with them. They move together as one, their hands mirroring each other as they remove Fallon's clothes, all while petting and kissing every inch of her.

"Do you like anal, Fallon?" I ask, curious if she's ever actually taken a man in that way.

I have my answer before she speaks, her widening eyes telling me that's not something she's experienced before. "I... I don't know."

"Would you like to find out?" Kaspian inquires, his English accent deepening with the words. "Because Nox is an expert in the art of fucking from behind."

The phantom grins against Fallon's neck, his chest against her back. "It's true," he says against her ear. "And I've been dying to fuck your curvy ass, firefly."

She shudders in reply, her rosy nipples beading with clear interest. Bane bends to take one into his mouth, causing her to moan loudly in approval.

These two have barely begun, and already I can see her sweet little body tightening with need.

When she comes, it'll be hard.

And I can't fucking wait to watch her explode.

"Words, little flame," Bane says against her full breast. "Tell us what you want, and we'll give it to you."

Except for an orgasm, I think. *That's not yours to give right now.*

Fortunately, she seems to know better than to ask for that. Instead, she looks from me to Kaspian and back again before saying, "I would like to try it."

"Try what?" Nox asks against her ear. "You know how we feel about specifics."

She swallows, her eyelashes fluttering a little bit. "I want to try anal."

"Mmm," Nox hums. "Just anal? Or do you want Bane and I to fuck you at the same time?"

Fallon's body convulses in response to his question, telling me our girl likes dirty talk.

Noted, I think as I adjust my jeans. They're starting to feel a little tight, thanks to the erotic display in front of me.

"I want you to fuck me at the same time," she breathes.

Damn. Those sexy words leaving her delectable mouth make me that much harder for her.

Kaspian must feel the same way because he starts to unbutton his dress shirt.

"We're going to need to make you good and wet, then," Nox informs her. "Bane?"

The other phantom grins against her breast and goes to his knees.

Fallon inhales sharply as he begins to lick her glistening folds. I pull off my leather jacket while I watch, my gaze traveling between her pussy and her breasts, watching her skin flush with heightening need.

But every time she nears the peak, Bane pulls back, pleasing me immensely.

It seems the phantoms know how to respect rules. That'll be useful in our new dynamic.

Kaspian folds his shirt and sets it on a bench at the foot of the bed. Then he takes my discarded jacket to add to the pile. I go ahead and pull my T-shirt off as well and hand it to him.

Nox follows suit, only he removes everything, not just his top, and wraps an arm around Fallon to give her some support as they both remain standing. He kisses her neck, his palm lifting to grab her breast. "How do you feel, firefly?" he asks her. "Is Bane making you feel good?"

She shivers, that flush creeping higher toward her neck. "Yes," she says, arching into Bane's face as he pulls his mouth away from her clit. A sound of protest escapes her in response, her limbs beginning to shake.

Good, I think, pleased with her growing arousal. *Keep going.*

Bane slides two fingers inside her, my vantage point from the bed allowing me to see just how wet she is as he glides in and out of her with ease. He adds a third after a few minutes, then returns his tongue to her clit, his motions teasing more than pleasing.

Fallon groans, her hand going to his head as she tries to hold him against her. He grins, amused, then slowly slips his fingers backward to her other entrance. Her eyes fly open as he inserts one digit, her pupils flaring wide as she parts her lips.

Nox catches her chin and guides her toward him for a kiss, one he uses to distract her as Bane continues his efforts below.

It's a beautiful dance, their timing exquisite.

"I see why you've been so obsessed with them," I tell Kaspian quietly.

His lips curl. "This is only the beginning. Wait until they put their mouths on you."

I glance sideways at him. "That's not my thing."

"They could easily make it *your thing*," Kaspian replies.

But I shake my head. "The only mouth I want on me is Fallon's." Because those lips of hers were made to be fucked, not just by my mouth, but by my cock as well.

She releases another delicious sound as Bane increases the pressure in her backside, preparing her to take Nox's pierced shaft.

I'm all for a little pain, but it seems the phantom prefers a different kind than I do. I'm actually rather impressed. And I'm betting that ladder pattern makes Fallon feel good.

"She's ready," Bane murmurs after another minute of preparing her, his gaze on her face.

I take in the blush painting her skin, the way her legs are almost violently shaking, and the dampness coating Bane's lips. "She is," I agree.

Kaspian stands to kick off his pants and shoes, then settles back on the bed near the headboard.

I decide to do the same, the oversized mattress leaving plenty of room for Fallon to join us with her two phantoms.

Nox leads her to the bed, his mouth occupying hers every step of the way. Bane trails along behind them while disrobing, his expression heated by the sight before him.

"Bane's going to sit in the center of the bed, and you're going to straddle him," Nox tells Fallon. "Once you're comfortable with him inside you, I'll join." He pulls her hair away from her shoulder and kisses her exposed skin. "We'll go slow, firefly. And we'll stop if it feels like it's too much. Okay?"

She swallows and nods. "Okay."

He kisses her again while Bane settles a foot away from me. Then he lifts her with ease and sets her on the bed.

She pauses when she turns toward Bane, her gaze going from the phantom to me and then to Kaspian.

It's the first time she's seeing me without clothes, and the look in her eyes tells me she very much approves of what she finds.

The feeling is very fucking mutual, beautiful, I tell her with my eyes as I admire her alluring form.

My look seems to embolden her because she shifts onto her hands and knees and begins to crawl toward Bane. Her eyes are on me while she moves, her breasts swaying as she inches forward.

It's a stunning sight.

One that almost has me demanding to take Bane's place.

However, I'm not just delaying her pleasure, but my own, too.

"Show us how well you take Bane, love," Kaspian says. "I want to see how wet you can make him."

Fallon visibly shivers, her nostrils flaring. "Yes, *my king.*"

Kaspian's lips curve upward, but he doesn't say anything in response to her sass. He merely watches with a heated gaze as she obeys his request by straddling Bane and angling his cock toward her weeping heat.

And sinking downward.

Taking him to the hilt without flinching.

"*Fuck,*" I breathe, my veins igniting with a fierce need that has my balls throbbing between my legs. I never knew watching another man fuck Fallon could be such a turn-on.

And they haven't even started yet.

"Isn't she gorgeous?" Nox asks as he joins us all on the bed. "She takes us with such natural skill, proving we were all made for each other." He kisses the back of her neck. "Isn't that right, firefly?"

"Yes," she agrees, her sweet body arching into Bane as she turns her head to kiss Nox again.

The phantom obliges her, his mouth dominating hers while he positions himself accordingly behind her. He wraps his palm around her throat to hold her in place while his opposite palm goes to his groin.

"You're going to feel some pressure," Bane warns her, seamlessly taking over Nox's previous coaching. "Try to relax for us, Fallon. Trust us to make you feel good."

She stiffens a little as Nox starts to push inside, but his movements are gradual rather than rushed, his touch reverent despite his hand's location against her throat.

He's holding her in place to protect her, to ensure he can feel her reactions, sense the way she's swallowing, inhaling, and exhaling. It's a display of great care, one that only makes me respect him more.

These men are worthy of our mate.

Now I just need to prove that I am, too.

"Fuck, you're beautiful," Kaspian breathes, his gaze on Fallon. "You look so good taking their cocks, love. So fucking good." He reaches for his dick to give it a stroke, something I long to do to my own. But I don't.

This is about Fallon.

Her pleasure.

And our mutual delayed gratification.

Soon, I tell myself. *She'll be mine soon.*

Nox pulls his mouth from hers, releasing a harsh breath. "You feel amazing, Fallon," he tells her. "So fucking amazing."

"You do," Bane echoes, his hips thrusting up into her. "I can feel Nox inside you, too. How do you feel, sweet flame?"

She digs her fingers into Bane's shoulders. "Full. I... I feel *full.*"

"That's good, firefly. We want you to feel full." He shifts his hold, his fingers threading through her hair to take control of her head. But rather than pull her back for another kiss, he guides her toward Bane.

She moans against Bane's mouth, her body vibrating between the two phantoms as they begin to move in and out of her.

Nox is gentler, his motions ensuring she's truly ready before he really begins to thrust.

But soon the three of them are fucking in earnest, their ecstasy an aphrodisiac that has my balls tightening in anticipation.

Fallon's arousal intensifies, her cheeks turning a darker pink, her full lips panting against Bane's, her chest rising and falling from the exertion.

Alas, it's not enough. I can see it in the way she's gyrating her hips, searching for that additional friction she needs. Bane could give it to her so easily just by shifting slightly. Or one of the phantoms could reach between them to stroke her needy little bud.

They don't do either of those things.

They simply continue to fuck her, their actions giving her pleasure without allowing her to reach the edge. It's absolutely perfect. Exactly what I want. And will lead to an orgasm unlike anything Fallon has ever experienced before.

She groans a little, her lips moving against Bane's as she whimpers out, "More."

He thrusts upward in response, drawing a scream from her that he swallows with his mouth while Nox increases his pace from behind.

They're not going to last much longer. Not that I can blame them. Fallon is a fucking goddess between them, taking their movements with the grace of a sensual queen.

Our queen, I muse. *Our mate.*

Nox's head falls to her shoulder, a curse leaving his mouth. "Your ass is even better than I imagined," he tells her. "Your curves... against my groin... *Fuck*, firefly, I'm going to come..."

Bane growls beneath them, the sound borderline animalistic.

Fallon visibly reacts to the primal sound as goose bumps pebble across her skin.

I note that preference as well, wondering what other feral activities she'll enjoy in the bedroom.

Her entire body seems to convulse as Nox erupts behind her, his groan causing her to arch back between them as another of those delicious whimpers leaves her lips.

So needy and wet, I marvel, admiring her slick thighs. *That'll be mine to enjoy in a few minutes.*

Or now, I correct myself as Bane follows Nox into oblivion, the two of them unloading inside Fallon while leaving her primed and not quite at the edge.

She trembles violently between them, her whimpers turning into mewls that call to my soul. I push away from the headboard to grab her nape, pulling her toward me for a kiss. "You did so good, Fallon," I tell her. "So fucking good."

Now she needs a reward. One that'll set the tone for our future. Solidify who we are together, and who I'll be for her.

NOLAN

I RELEASE Fallon long enough for Bane to slide out from beneath her. He presses a kiss to the side of her mouth. "Enjoy, sweet flame. Show Nolan just how hot you can burn."

Fallon murmurs something unintelligible in response, her mind clearly clouding over with need.

It's a need I feel throbbing through my veins in kind.

A need I want to feed just a little more, extend just a bit longer…

Fortunately, it's a need I can stoke while inside.

I settle beneath her on the bed, not caring at all that she's soaking wet from her gratification and that of her other mates. It doesn't matter. It doesn't make her any less mine.

"Are you ready for me?" I ask her, my fingers sliding into her hair to hold her in a way similar to how Nox did just moments ago. "Do you want me inside you?" It's a question with multiple meanings.

Do you want me to fuck you?

Do you want me to mate you?

Once I do this, we'll belong to each other forever.

Her pretty green eyes lock with mine, her expression fierce. "Yes." There's no sign of hesitation in her voice or her face, her answer resolute.

"Good." I thrust upward, joining our bodies and our souls and loving the way she screams my name in response.

I'm thicker than Bane. Longer, too. I most closely rival Kaspian in size.

Which is going to make this experience something truly special for her.

Something the vampire drives home as he presses his chest to her back. "Focus on Nolan for me, love," he says against her ear. "Let him make you feel good."

I translate that as, *Let Nolan distract you from what I'm about to do.*

Fallon doesn't need a distraction. She's more than ready to take us both.

But that doesn't stop me from monopolizing her attention anyway. I've wanted this woman for months. Thought about her so many times, in so many different positions.

The feel of her, however, doesn't do my fantasies justice.

Her thighs feel amazing against my legs, her pussy fucking heaven as it pulses around my cock.

And her tits… *Fuck,* I love her tits. So full. So firm. So *delicious.*

I want to take those little rosebuds between my teeth and nibble on them.

But I take her mouth instead, needing more of her tongue against mine, longing to engage in another intimate conversation.

Her teeth skim my lip, the action reminding me of how

she reacted to me barely kissing her fingertips after she accepted my fealty pledge.

I smile, translating her action as a warning. "Do you need something, Fallon?"

"You know what I need," she returns, the raspy quality of her voice exactly what I desire to hear. "*Please* let me come, Nolan."

"Mmm." I drive up into her at the same time Kaspian enters her from behind.

She freezes in response, her lips parted on a soundless noise.

"Too much?" Kaspian asks against her ear, his voice lacking true concern.

"No," I answer for her. "She can take it."

Kaspian nods. "She can." He punctuates that statement with another thrust.

Fallon gasps, but it's not a sound of pain so much as surprise. Then she flexes her hips forward and back, her body easily accommodating both of us.

It's a bold move, one that has me smiling against her mouth. "Mmm, I feel you, vixen," I tell her. "Do it again."

She clenches around me instead, then grabs my shoulders and shifts once more.

I groan, loving the way her pussy feels around my thick length. "So fucking good," I praise her.

Fate definitely made this woman for us. Because she's flawless. Absolutely breathtaking.

I kiss her, this time with a new purpose in mind. I want to worship her. Thank her. Show her how much she means to me. How grateful I am to her for accepting me, for allowing me to cherish her.

Kaspian grabs her hips, his dominance showing as he guides her into a rhythm between us. It's one that suits my needs, too, something he no doubt knows. His memory is a good one. And there are some things that never change.

But my feelings for Fallon are definitely new. No woman—or man—has ever made me feel so strongly before. Part of it may be the fate bond, but I suspect most of it is just because it's Fallon.

This woman has been under my skin since the moment I aimed a gun at her.

And now she's mine, I think, kissing her harder.

I keep my hand in her hair while I slip another between us, my thumb going to her swollen bud. She immediately jerks, her over-sensitized sex contracting around me.

The phantoms purposely riled her up, only to leave this part of her without touch while fucking her.

It kept her from reaching the edge.

But now only a few strokes have her panting.

She's exactly where I need her to be, all desperate and ready to burst. I massage her until she starts to shake, her orgasm right there, only for me to chase it away by removing my touch.

Orgasm denial is a delicate dance. It's all about finding the sweet spot. I can't push too hard, or it'll hurt. I have to make sure it's just right.

Her teeth sink into my lip when I pull my thumb away for the third time, her frustration adorable. "*Nolan*."

"Yes, Fallon?" I say against her mouth, causing Kaspian to chuckle behind her.

"Is he torturing you, love?" he asks her. "Keeping you right on the edge while we fuck you?"

"Yes," she hisses.

I take control of her mouth before she can say anything else, my tongue dueling with hers as I drive her toward the brink once more. When I pull away, she screams, telling me we've finally reached the place I need her to be in.

Kaspian must sense that as well because he lowers his mouth to her neck as her nails bite into my shoulders.

However, he doesn't bite her.

He simply presses kisses up and down the column of her throat.

I suspect it's meaningful somehow, a way to establish trust, because the action has Fallon squeezing the hell out of my dick.

Or maybe she just likes the sensation.

Either way, I play into it by turning our kiss into something hotter. More intense. And I do it by letting her feel my emotions, my tongue slowing the pace as I unleash all my secrets into her mouth.

I tell her how I worried that she wouldn't accept me. How, deep down, I don't think I deserve her. How I'll spend our existence ensuring I never let her down. How I'll forever be grateful that fate gave me such a perfect mate.

How I'll cherish her.

Always respect her.

Protect her.

Love her.

My thumb returns to her swollen flesh as I think all those words at her, vowing each one and solidifying it all with this kiss.

It's an intense experience, one that makes me a bit breathless as my hips move with her and Kaspian.

Her body tenses in response to all the sensations, all the unspoken statements, all the *friction*. I start to count down, aware of her approaching her climax.

I could stop it.

Pull my hand away.

Really make her scream.

But it would be too much.

We've arrived at her limit, and I won't push her beyond it. Not tonight. She deserves so much pleasure, so much happiness, and I love that I'm going to be the one to grant her that.

Kaspian nips her pulse, his eyes meeting mine in mutual understanding. He can feel her approaching the edge, too.

We both pick up our pace at the same time, drawing a low groan from Fallon as we ensure she feels every inch of us driving into her.

Five, I think. *Four*...

She's so close.

Three.

So fucking hot.

Two.

Right there...

One.

She freezes.

Every part of her overwhelmed by the inferno burning inside her.

And then...

She *erupts*.

Kaspian and I hold on to her, fucking her as she screams, her body bowing and trembling and rolling in waves of immense ecstasy.

So immense that she falls into a second orgasm right after the first.

Which was precisely my intention.

Someday, we'll work up to three.

But tonight, she's having two very powerful experiences.

And I'm about to join her in that fun.

Just a few more...

She clamps down around me so harshly that I find myself trapped inside her, incapable of moving. All I can feel are her tight muscles and Kaspian drilling into her from behind.

I groan, my mouth still against hers. "*Fallon.*"

She needs to let me move.

Fuck.

Her teeth sink into my lower lip, her gaze wild as she stares me down.

Then she thrusts forward, drawing me in to the hilt and forcing me to follow her into oblivion. It's so fucking erotic that I don't even try to fight it.

My canary just topped from the bottom, I muse, loving the way she demanded my pleasure.

Kaspian soon follows, his growl causing Fallon to shiver with delight between us.

Then he takes control of her mouth, kissing her while I try to regroup my thoughts, my body and soul replete. Every part of me feels *whole*. Happy. Entirely at peace.

I rest my head against Fallon's shoulder, my breaths coming in pants.

Then I smile as she lays her head against mine, her fingers sliding upward into my hair as she hugs me.

Kaspian presses a kiss to her neck on the opposite side, then pulls away, saying something about getting a towel for her.

I'm too caught up in holding her to move yet, my soul rejoicing at having found its other half.

"I guess it's a good thing you missed that day," she says softly, her fingers brushing the chain around my neck. "But you really should work on your aim."

A chuckle escapes me at her teasing words. "The only one with better aim than me is Kaspian."

"Don't let Cara or Larus hear you say that," Kaspian says as he returns. "They'll demand a shoot-out."

I lift a shoulder. "As long as Fallon isn't the target, I'll do fine."

Fallon makes a disgruntled sound that has me chuckling again.

"You're the one insulting my aim, canary," I tell her.

"Because you *shot me*."

I sigh. "You're never going to let me live that down, are you?"

"Not for at least a hundred or so years, no," she admits.

"Hmm." I pull back to study her beautiful face. "Only a hundred years?"

"Maybe a thousand."

"That sounds more accurate." I smile. "But I deserve it."

"You do," she agrees. "And you know what I deserve?"

I arch a brow. "What?"

"Another orgasm."

Kaspian laughs behind her.

But I don't. Instead, I study my mate and nod. "You do," I agree. "How do you want it?"

Her eyebrows lift in surprise. "Really?"

"Really." I brush my lips against hers. "I'll give you whatever you want, Fallon. We all will. Name it and it's yours."

"Especially orgasms," Nox says from his position on the bed. Both he and Bane took over the place I shared with Kaspian before.

"Definitely orgasms," Bane echoes.

Fallon squirms a little, her inner walls clenching around my still-hard cock. "You know, Issy was right."

My eyebrow arches. "About orgasms?"

"No. About the future."

"What about it, love?" Kaspian asks as he runs a washcloth along her backside, cleaning her up.

"She said wallowing in the past would only keep us from enjoying the future. And that the only way to really move forward was to embrace fate." She pauses for a moment, her gaze falling to the bullet around my neck. "I think there are some past events that define us. But she's right about needing to embrace fate."

Kaspian pulls the towel away and tosses it onto some of the discarded clothes. "I agree with embracing fate."

"Me, too," Nox says.

"Same," Bane agrees.

I nod. "Fate brought us all together for a reason." I palm Fallon's cheek. "To embrace *you*."

"To cherish you." Nox moves forward with the words, going to his knees beside Fallon.

"To protect you," Kaspian adds before placing a gentle kiss on her shoulder.

"To love you," Bane finishes as he settles on her opposite side, across from Nox.

Fallon glances at each of us, at the circle we've formed around her, and smiles. "I can't believe this is my life."

"It's real," Kaspian tells her, a twinkle in his gaze.

"Definitely real," I agree, my cock twitching inside her.

Fallon's smile grows. "I'm the luckiest woman in the world."

"And we're the luckiest mates in the world," Bane replies.

"I think we should show her how lucky we are," Nox suggests.

"She did ask for more orgasms," Bane murmurs.

"She did," Nox echoes. "Between the four of us, I'm certain we can accomplish that."

"Maybe make her beg us to stop?" Kaspian suggests.

"Oh, now there's a plan I like," I admit, my focus returning to Fallon. "You've been so good for us, darling canary. How about we see how long you can sing?"

"An entire night of orgasms," Nox muses. "Her pleasure only."

"Her pleasure only," Kaspian agrees. "Slide her off your lap, Nolan. I'll start by licking her clean."

I do as he asks, positioning a startled Fallon in the middle of the bed. "Consider this our true pledge of fealty, my queen…"

EPILOGUE

FALLON

A FEW WEEKS LATER

QUEEN FALLON, my sister singsongs into my thoughts, making me wince.

Don't start.

But it has such a nice ring to it, don't you think?

I roll my eyes. *The only thing I like about it is my new last name.*

Fallon Antonik, she says. *Yes. Much better than Doyle. So I guess I need to find myself a mate and change my last name, too.*

Or you could just change your last name, I offer. *I'm queen now. I can authorize that.*

She snorts. *So much for "don't start."*

There are some benefits to my new role, I admit.

Oh? Tell me more.

I consider that for a second and frown. *Actually, you know what? Not much has changed.* I glance around my room. *I mean, I live in Kaspian's quarters officially now, not in his guest suite. But... they're honestly not that much different. Just more masculine. And he has a larger bed.*

Something that has come in handy over the last few weeks.

Even Nolan usually sleeps with us.

But there are nights when he asks for me to come to him alone. I'm learning that his preference is for just me, not group time. However, he joins us more often than not.

I'm also allowed to leave the palace at will now, I add. *So I suppose that's different, too.*

Your phantoms let you leave the palace without them? Issy asks.

I frown. *Sometimes.* But definitely not very often. And even then... *Only when Nolan or Kaspian is with me. Otherwise... no.*

So that hasn't changed much, then.

Not really, no, I reply. *If anything, they're even more protective now. But I guess that comes with the territory of our bonding.*

Meaning what, exactly?

Just that they have different reasons to be protective now than they did before. I shrug. Not that she can see me. She's in Finland with Ayla, the latter of whom keeps sending me pictures of all the snow.

I don't think so, Issy replies.

You don't think what? I ask, confused.

That their reasons have changed.

I blink. *But they have. I was a prisoner before. Now I'm their mate.*

I think their reasons have always revolved around their interest in you, sis. Sure, they were trying to interrogate you before. But I think they followed you around because they wanted to, not because they had to.

I snort at that. *Pretty sure Kaspian ordered them to.*

Pretty sure they offered to guard you, Fallon, she tosses back. *No order required.*

I narrow my gaze as though she's seated across from me. *Wanna bet?*

Sure. When I win, you have to come visit for a week without the harem.

And when I win? I counter.

Name your terms, she taunts.

My lips twist to the side as I consider my options. I'm about to suggest something outlandish—just to play with my sister—when Nox materializes in the room. "You have a very strange expression on your face, firefly. What are you contemplating?"

"How long have you been watching me?"

He smiles. "A few minutes."

I shake my head. "Such a voyeur."

"Guilty." He shrugs. "But seriously, what's with the face?"

I blow out a breath and tell him what Issy just said, then add, "My sister is being a hopeless romantic, apparently."

Nox considers me for a moment. "I'd argue that she's being a realist."

My brow furrows. "What?"

"You don't think Kaspian offered us other positions in the palace?" he asks me. "Other opportunities outside of guarding you?"

I stare at him. "Did he?"

"Of course he did. But Bane and I chose you each time." He shrugs again. "We had no interest in sharing you with others, Fallon." He crawls onto the bed to sit beside me. "You've been ours since the moment we saw you."

I shiver. "Oh."

"Oh," he repeats, leaning in to brush his lips over mine.

"I feel the same way," Bane announces as he appears in the room. "In case that wasn't clear with Nox's proclamation."

"Just as there's a reason I kept you in my guest suite," Kaspian adds as he opens the door, his enhanced vampire senses obviously granting him access to our conversation without even being in the room.

Nolan follows him in. "Not sure what we're talking about, but if it's about my obsession with Fallon, I lurked outside on your balcony every night for months."

I gape at all of them, torn between shock at their admissions and having some choice comments about eavesdropping.

Fallon? Issy asks, reminding me that I left her hanging.

Uh, you win, I tell her without bothering to elaborate. *But I don't know if these guys are going to let me visit you for a week without them…*

I can almost hear Issy smiling as she replies, *I suspected as much. Just promise to visit soon.*

I will.

Love you, Issy says.

Love you, too.

Now stop talking to me and go enjoy your happily-ever-after. You deserve it.

You deserve one, too, I whisper back to her.

Issy doesn't answer, maybe because she doesn't agree.

Too bad. One day, she'll find her soul mate. Maybe even more than one. I mean, I did. And if anyone has earned happiness, it's Issy.

"There's that look again," Nox says, his gaze narrowing.

I give him a small smile. "I'm just thinking about Issy and how she deserves to be happy."

"You deserve to be happy, too," Kaspian says as he joins us on the bed. "In fact, I think you should let us all worship you as you were intended to be worshipped, *Queen Fallon*."

I shake my head. "I'm never going to get used to that."

"You will," he promises me as Bane and Nolan settle on the mattress with us. "We'll help you."

My eyebrow lifts. "Yeah? How?"

"By reminding you every day that you're *our* queen." He leans in to nuzzle my throat. "Hmm, here, I'll start." He moves his lips to my ear. "How would you like us to please you, *Your Majesty*?"

My lips twitch. "I don't know, *Your Majesty*. How would you like to please me?"

"Oh, I can answer that," Nolan says, his hands going to my thighs and prying them apart.

I'm still wearing my dress from the announcement earlier, the silky fabric covering me all the way to my ankles. Not that he minds. His palms are already creeping up beneath the skirt, his expression positively wicked.

"I believe it's my turn to make you sing," he murmurs. "So spread your thighs for me, sweet canary. And let me serve you, my queen…"

THE END

CRAVE ME

Once upon a time, a series of portals opened on Earth, allowing magic to spill into the human world.
Houses were created. Supernaturals were assigned. And a new balance was formed.
All new arrivals are required to join a House.
But this is the tale of a goddess who refused and the House King who brought her to heel.

Nyx.
Goddess of Night.
My newest obsession.

The daring female killed one of my men.
Which made it my job as the Gold and Garnet House King to make her pay.

Oh, there were so many things I wanted to do with that

disobedient little mouth of hers. But she was much stronger than she led anyone to believe.
Now I'm left with a craving I can't quite sate.
Because one bite wasn't enough.

You may be the Goddess of Night, but I'm still your king.
You will kneel.
You will beg.
And most importantly, you will bleed.

Welcome to the House of Gold and Garnet, where power defines the monarchy and blood is a preferred currency.
Proceed at your own risk.

Author's Note: *Crave Me* is a dark standalone paranormal romance set in the Immortal Vices and Virtues Universe. Every book in this shared world is a guaranteed happily-ever-after with a satisfying ending and no cliffhangers.

For fans of the Blood Alliance series, this is the story of Nyx and Vesperus, the goddess and her vampire lover that started it all...

USA Today Bestselling Author Lexi C. Foss loves to play in dark worlds, especially the ones that bite. She lives in Chapel Hill, North Carolina with her husband and their furry children. When not
writing, she's busy crossing items off her travel bucket list, or chasing eclipses around the globe. She's quirky, consumes way too much coffee, and loves to swim.

Want access to the most up-to-date information for all of Lexi's books? Sign-up for her newsletter here.

Lexi also likes to hang out with readers on Facebook in her exclusive readers group - Join Here.

Where To Find Lexi:
www.LexiCFoss.com